Painted Highway

DATE DUE		
-7 AUG 2003	3 1 JAN 2006	
1 2 SEP 2003	1 0 JAN 2007	
2 OCT 2003		
1 0 OCT 2003	2 0 JUN 2008	
2 2 OCT 2003	-3 SEP 2008	
-6 NOV 2003	2 7 APR 2009	
2 7 NOV 2003	3 SEP 2010	
1 7 DEC 2003	-5 OCT 2010	
1 2 JAN 2004	1 7 NOV 2010	
2 3 JAN 2004	2 7 JAN 2011	
-4 FEB 2004		
-9 MAR 2004		
1 3 OCT 2004		
1 9 DEC 2005		
3 1 JAN 2006		

AUDREY HOWARD

Painted Highway

Hodder & Stoughton

First published in Great Britain in 2003 by Hodder and Stoughton
A division of Hodder Headline

1 3 5 7 9 10 8 6 4 2

A CIP catalogue record for this title is available from the British Library

ISBN 0340 83039 5

Typeset in Plantin Light by Phoenix Typesetting, Burley-in-Wharfedale, West Yorkshire

Printed and bound in Australia by
Griffin Press, Netley, SA

Hodder and Stoughton
A division of Hodder Headline
338 Euston Road
London NW1 3BH

I would like to dedicate this book to Rod Serrell
who gave me the idea.

1

The tiny cabin which she had shared with her sister for most of her nineteen years was so cramped that when she tried to stretch her legs her feet jammed themselves against the wall that divided the cabin from the hold, and the bed she slept in was so narrow she almost fell out as she turned on to her back. She had become adept at fitting herself on to what was really no more than a wooden shelf with a slight curve in it to adapt to the shape of the narrowboat's prow, but sometimes, on the point of waking, when her body was totally relaxed, she nearly spilled out on to the deck.

Yawning widely, she pulled the patchwork quilt more closely about her ears, doing her best to slip back into that warm, drowsy state from which she had just awakened, but she could hear her pa talking to Magic on the towpath and knew that it was time she was moving. It would be full daylight outside, for it was June and dawn broke early at this time of the year, but just for a moment or two she allowed herself the luxury of another dip into drowsiness. Betsy, from her bed on the opposite side of the cabin, no more than eighteen inches from Ally's, murmured in her sleep and seemed to laugh and Ally wondered what she was dreaming about. Probably some chap she'd seen on a passing boat and with whom she was having a flirtation in her sleep. She lived in another world, did Betsy, a world of fantasy that had nothing to do with the life in which she and her family actually existed.

It was no good. She really would have to get a move on or

Ma would be storming across the planks that bridged the cargo wanting to know why her daughters were not out of their beds and ready to begin the day's journey. Floating on the air and teasing her nostrils was the delicious smell of bacon frying. In response her stomach growled softly and her mouth watered and with a groan she threw back the quilt and put her feet to the highly polished wooden floor of the cabin. Reaching forward, she dragged the quilt from her sister then sat back as Betsy shrieked indignantly and did her best to pull the bedcovers about her but Ma's voice rang out warningly.

"Now then, you two, it's high time yer were up. Pa's feedin' Magic and Jack's gone fer water. Come on, our Betsy" – her voice softening as did all those that addressed themselves to Betsy – "get yersenn outer bed, chuck. See, here's a nice cuppa; pass it to our Betsy, Ally," for Betsy still continued to curl up in the dark cosiness of the bed-hole.

"Don't I get one?" Ally complained, but without bitterness for after eighteen years she was well used to being considered slightly inferior, at least in her looks, and had become accustomed to the way her sister was treated not only by Ma and Pa but every awestruck person, man or woman, who clapped eyes on her. It didn't worry her unduly, her own sense of humour and tenacity of spirit allowing her to overcome what could have been hurtful, particularly in childhood. She might not be beautiful as Betsy was but she knew her own worth in other quarters.

"Course tha' does, lass. Tekk it while it's nice an' 'ot an' then get thissen dressed before Pa an' Jack come in." Not that Pa or her brother Jack would dream of entering the tiny cabin in the prow of the boat where Ally and Betsy slept. They had lived all their lives in close proximity to one another and customs, routines, a way of existing side by side despite the lack of space had been well regulated for as long as Ally could remember. They were canal boat people. Their antecedents had been canal

boat people for over a hundred years and ever since Pa's grandfather – or was it his great-grandfather? – had left his cottage
beside the canal in the early part of the century they had lived
on the narrowboat which plied her trade between Leeds and
Liverpool.

"Ma, can't I bide here another minute or two?" Betsy whined
from the depth of the bed-hole, but over this one matter
regarding her younger daughter, Edie Pearce, who was a
stickler for the proprieties, was firm. Betsy was indulged in so
many ways but certain rules must be adhered to. They were to
get under way by six. Fred and Jack had not yet eaten and the
breakfast that Edie had prepared was ready to be served. When
her family had been fed with the gargantuan feast she considered necessary to begin the punishing day, when the dishes and
frying pan were washed and stowed away and the cabin tidied,
they would set out on their journey to Liverpool. The cargo of
baled woollen goods which they had loaded at Bradford the
previous afternoon was sheeted up, and in half an hour Edie
Pearce was aware that her Fred would begin their journey, with
or without their Betsy! Not that he would leave her behind, for
he doted on her, as she herself did, but if she wasn't dressed,
out of the cabin and sitting down to her breakfast in the stern
cabin in the next thirty seconds he would not be suited.

"No, yer can't so frame yersenn, our Betsy. No, not another
word or yer'll feel the flat o' me 'and," which all three women
knew was an empty threat, for when had anyone ever raised their
hand to pretty Betsy Pearce, except perhaps her exasperated
sister when they were younger for which she'd earned herself
many a clout. Certainly neither of her doting parents. In fact
their Jack often said, in their hearing, for he was a forthright lad,
that if she'd had a bloody good hiding when she was a little lass
she might not have turned out to be such a mardy brat.

All three women, mother and her daughters, were dressed in
the traditional boatwoman's outfit when Fred Pearce entered

the stern cabin. Each wore a blouse with delicately worked pleating from the neck to the waist with long sleeves, somewhat full so that they could be rolled up to the elbow. Edie's was sprigged cotton, Ally's was white but Betsy had chosen a pale blue-green, the exact shade of her eyes, for Betsy Pearce had long ago learned the art of enhancing her own exquisite looks. Since it was summer their long, striped skirts were of cotton. Full enough to enable them to jump on and off the boat but not so full as to get in their way as they did it. Again they were decorated with tucks and rows of ribbon and over the skirt they each wore a long white apron without a bib. They had wide waistbands buttoned at the back and Betsy, knowing the enchantment of her tiny waist, which emphasised the round-ness of her high breasts, and the admiring looks it would invite from a man, wore a wide, hand-woven spiderweb-stitch belt. The belt was normally worn by a man, that or an embroidered belt and braces made in the evening by the women, but Betsy cared nothing for the custom since she was of the opinion that it flattered her own appearance and that was all that mattered to her. Their bonnets, which they had not yet put on, were the pride of their boatwoman's costumes. Made originally as a farmworker's sun bonnet, they were lined and worn like a hat, summer and winter, with the brim tipped well forward over the eyes to shade them from the sun, the crown on the top of the head and the strings tied behind the head under the hair. But the beauty of them was in the *broderie anglaise* that decorated them, the feather-stitching, the fluted pleats that fell halfway down their backs, the bows that adorned them, for it would not do to be too "plain".

Fred and Jack wore hard-wearing corduroy trousers and jackets with plain velvet collars and matching waistcoats. The jackets had brass buttons and the waistcoats were fashioned in what was known as keyhole-shaped neck openings. Today, because it was warm, they had discarded their jackets. Their shirts were collarless and made of striped cotton, the sleeves rolled up to the elbow to reveal their brawny brown arms and, as all boatmen did, they wore belts and braces, the latter to keep up their trousers and the former to act as a body strap to hold their windlass. Their belts were of leather but for "best" they wore the intricately embroidered silk belts like the one Betsy had purloined. At their throats were neckerchiefs, folded over the shirt bands. Their outfits were completed with boots and flat caps though Fred, who was proud of his independence as a boat-owner, often wore a bowler hat. Apart from the bowler and the men's caps, every stitch of clothing the family wore had been made by Edie on her Singer sewing-machine, bought on hire purchase from a firm in Liverpool several years ago and almost paid for! Before the arrival of the sewing-machine all boatwomen had almost gone blind as they fashioned their families' outfits by hand, by candlelight!

Fred and Edie's bed-hole had been closed up, the bedding had been removed and stored in a locker at the end of the cabin, and the table which had been folded out from Edie and Fred's bed-hole was laid with five bowls of creamy frumenty – Yorkshire porridge – to start with. This would be followed by plates laden with crisply fried bacon, fried tomatoes, eggs, fried bread and mushrooms, with enormous mugs of strong, sweet tea to wash it all down. Not that Betsy would eat half that her mother put out for her since she had a horror of spoiling her slender figure, but nevertheless Edie begged her to eat up as it would be hours before they tied up for the night.

"Ma, I don't know why yer keep piling me plate up like this. Yer know I can't eat it, not wi' my appetite," Betsy complained. Her brother and sister sighed, for they were aware that Betsy considered herself to be something of a lady, despite her position in life, and it was well known that ladies, real ladies, ate like sparrows, or so the daft magazines she picked up here and there told her.

"Chuck, yer know yer'll need ter keep up yer strength and eatin' a good breakfast's the only way ter do it. It's 'all up brew from 'ere'," which was Edie's Lancashire way of saying that the going would be more difficult from now on. Shipley, Bingley, Keighley, Skipton, Gargrave, winding through the valleys of the Pennine chain into Lancashire, and though neither she nor Fred expected pretty, dainty Betsy to do more than the lightest tasks she could not throw off the belief that a good breakfast set you up for the day. Both Ally and Jack ate heartily. It did her good to see them packing it away and *enjoying* it, though neither of them showed for it. Thin as rakes, both of them, with not a pick on them, but strong, cheerful and willing, a real help to Fred who, had they not been his crew, would have been forced to hire at least one man to help him.

Ally, though a good lass, didn't have the place in her mother's heart that Betsy did. Tall, she was, lean and strong as a lad with no bosom to speak of and that hair of hers, which she kept cut short with Edie's sewing scissors, was a disgrace, all over her head in a tumble of chestnut curls more like a lad than a lass. She'd got a good leathering from her pa on the day she'd first taken the scissors to it, saying she couldn't be mithered with it hanging down to her bum. Her *sore* bum had caused her to stand up for a week when her incensed pa had done with her! Mind, she'd lovely eyes, the exact colour of the whisky her Fred treated himself to now and again. They had thick brown lashes surrounding them and glowed with good health but, sadly, in Edie's opinion lads only had to get a glimpse of their Betsy and Ally became invisible. Not that she seemed to care, for her whole life, the force that drove her was centred on the canal and the narrowboats that sailed on it. She knew every craft that plied its trade between Leeds and Liverpool, narrowboats, short boats, fly boats, flats, every cargo that was carried, from where to where, tonnage, tolls, locks, and was capable, had her pa allowed it, of sailing the *Edith* single-handed.

"Try a taste, love, there's a good lass," Edie coaxed Betsy. "That there bacon's right crisp just as yer like it. Will I purrit between two pieces o' bead for yer?" But Betsy shook her dainty head, *her* hair, which fell to her buttocks in a cascade of silver-gilt curls, smoothly brushed back into a neat chignon and fastened in a net. One or two tendrils escaped, deliberately loosened, her long-suffering sister was inclined to think, wisping enchantingly about her white brow and over her delicately shaped ears and Edie felt the emotion this child of hers evoked move tenderly in her breast.

She and Fred often remarked on it in the privacy of their bedhole, the mystery of where this fairy-like child of theirs had come from. Jack and Ally were dark and, though not unattractive, were wholesome and what Edie thought of as earthy, as she and Fred were. Ally was the cleverer of the two and had learned to read and write in some miraculous way at whichever Sunday school they happened to tie up near along the route. Jack could stumble his way through a child's primer with Ally's help but Betsy, seeing no need for it, had ignored all Ally's offers of help and, though now and again she begged her sister to "say it to her" when flummoxed over the words beneath the picture of some fashionable lady in a magazine, scorned the hours Ally spent of an evening poring over the written word.

They never came to any satisfactory conclusion, deciding she must be a throwback from some ancestor, though again they couldn't have said from where. Both she, Fred and their respective families were short, sturdy, dark, come from the labouring classes who had worked the canals for over a century. Once the family had owned a cottage beside the canal near Ollerton Fold between Chorley and Blackburn. Boats were manned by men and boys then whose families lived ashore. They were land-based and enjoyed a higher standard of living than did farm labourers or factory workers. In the early part of the century this prosperity was followed by a drastic decline. Edie was not awfully sure why Fred's family had left the cottage and took to living on the boat. Fred thought it was something to do with what he called a depression after the Napoleonic Wars, whatever they were, when trade was bad and Fred's . . . would he be grandfather or great-grandfather, she couldn't work it out, had worked the canals between Liverpool and Wigan, but the wages needed for a crew apparently could not be found, Fred told her, so the women gave up their cottages and, taking their children with them, worked as crews for their husbands. Before her time, of course, and Fred's, but this way of life, the canals, the narrowboats was the only one they had ever known.

The wooden walls of the cabin in which they ate and where Edie and Fred slept were so hung about with ornaments you couldn't put a pin between them. Horse brasses, brass doorknobs, brass oil lamps, all highly polished in order to catch and reflect the light, its only source the open hatchway door. "Lace" plates threaded with ribbon with pretty painted landscapes in the centre hung wherever there was a space, and on every edge, shelves, the stove, wherever they could be tacked, were lace trims. Each item in the cabin had its own home and every member of the family knew exactly where that might be, returning it there when not in use. The muddle that would have ensued if this practice had not been strictly followed would have been, in Edie's northern idiom, a right to-do-ment!

Lustreware china and brass jugs marched in rows on shelves and every single cupboard door and hatch with a bare surface was painted with some bright picture. All the cupboards had let-down doors to act as tables or seats and the panel doors were decorated with roses or castles, come, it was said, from the cottages of the eighteenth century. The decorations themselves originated in the mists of time, copied from the great houses, filtering down through the social classes and taken up by the boat people. There were landscapes of fantastic dream-like scenes featuring a river or a stream, usually with a bridge, and so familiar were they to the family that their beauty was scarcely noticed. A canary sang its heart out in a cage and a rough dog of indeterminate breed squatted between Jack Pearce's legs, as well used to the cramped conditions and how to overcome them as the rest of them.

Ally reached for her bonnet though she would dearly have liked to leave it off. In fact she would dearly have liked to wear what their Jack wore, for there was nothing more irksome to her than the need to clamber about the boat and stride along the towpath in the long skirt women of the day were forced into. She loved the life of the boat people and had, from an early age, done the same work as Jack but without his freedom of movement. She bemoaned the fact a dozen times a day to Ma and even, if the moment seemed right, to Pa, but it made no difference. She was a lass and though she and Ma did as much, if not more than Pa and Jack, Pa could not be persuaded to allow her to wear what Jack wore.

She and Ma took turns at the tiller, at the locks, at the toll-houses, leading Magic along the towpath, even helping with the loading of a cargo, then, at the end of the day, set to in preparing a meal for the family. They scoured their living quarters, for Mam was a stickler for cleanliness, hating dirt as a believer in the Holy Bible hates sin, and it was part of Ally's working day to help Ma to remove it with what Ma called elbow grease, and if she ever resented the idle way in which Betsy spent her day, which she did, saying so energetically, it made little difference. Betsy was what Ma liked to term "delicate", for Betsy was pale and slender and – so she said – easily tired. Ma and Pa were down-to-earth, practical, sensible and not unintelligent, but where their Betsy was concerned they were as blinkered as Magic as she walked the towpath.

"I'll get started, Pa, shall I?"

"Aye, chuck." Fred lit his pipe and reached for his cap. "Magic's hitched up an' fed. Jack's fetched water so 'appen our

Betsy could clear up," casting a fond eye on his pretty daughter who was daintily sipping her tea, wiping her rosy mouth on a scrap of material she called her "napkin". Where the devil she got her fancy ideas from Fred couldn't imagine unless it was them magazines she picked up in the big towns they passed through. She loved to look at the illustrations of the great ladies in their pages which their Ally, being a good-hearted lass and clever with her reading, was often wheedled to read out to her. What was to become of her he daren't think, for she certainly wasn't cut out to be the wife of one of the rough boatmen who plied their trade on the canals. Like him!

"Oh, Pa," Betsy protested. "I'm not feelin' that well. Can I not just lie down fer a while? It's me . . . well, yer know," casting down her eyes and blushing. "Just until we gerr under way."

Fred, horribly embarrassed to be reminded of "women's things", as he called them, backed off hastily, turning towards the steps that led to the deck.

"Yer know yer ma don't like ter leave pots an' things," he mumbled.

"Oh, let 'er be, Fred. I'll see to it an' then I'll do a bit o' washin'. She can 'ang it out fer me. It's a fine day an'll dry right quick up on deck. See, our Jack, gerrup on deck an' untie lines fer yer Pa."

She turned her attention to her younger daughter, begging her to sit 'ersenn down, which was daft in Ally's opinion since Betsy had not as yet stood up, asking anxiously if she'd like another cup of tea or should she make her a bowl of "pobs", the recipe of bread and hot milk a sovereign cure for a bad stomach, for didn't it put a good lining on it? As soon as she'd tidied up she'd get out her potions, one of which, chamomile, would soon have the lass on her feet again. She had been the same before her women's monthlies had dried up, with acute cramping pains that had laid her low, but her old mam, who some said was a healer, had taught her which herbs cured what and even, on occasion, how to mend a broken bone. She knew where along the canal banks and the fields bordering it herbs grew, chamomile, rampaging anywhere, even on piles of rubble, being one of them.

Ally jumped nimbly from the prow of the boat on to the canal bank, her skirt swinging to show her neat ankles and sturdy black clogs. A man dressed like her father, steering a passing boat going towards the docks at Bradford, gave her a cheerful greeting, tipping his cap in her direction.

"Awreet, Ally?" he shouted.

"Grand, thanks, Bert," waving her hand to him. His wife and five children were clustered on deck and the sixth, a lad of ten, was leading their horse along the towpath. Most of the narrow-boat families knew one another. There was a network of communication between them offering advice on cargoes that were available and where they might be found, and bound. Work was often discovered this way, by word of mouth, and the livelihood of them all depended one upon another. That is in those who owned their own boats. "Number ones" they called themselves, the meaning of which was lost in time, but they were proud, proud of their boats, proud of their work, their heritage and, as Fred was fond of saying, wouldn't change their way of life for that of one of the grand dukes up in London.

"Got yer wool, 'ave yer?" he went on.

"Aye, thanks, Bert. If yer get goin' yer'll gerr a cargo."

"Thanks, Ally."

"Cheerio then. 'Appen we'll see yer in Liverpool."

Checking automatically that her father was ready at the tiller, having turned it into the correct working position, that Jack had untied the lines, Ally grasped Magic by her noseband and urged the animal to begin her pull. To move the loaded boat the horse had to hang forward in her collar until it broke the boat's inertia, straining until she could take another step. As the boat gathered way, with Ally murmuring encouragement in Magic's ears which were covered with ear caps crocheted by her ma to protect them from the flies, the task was easier. They would be under way for fourteen hours and Magic had to feed and drink on the move from a nose tin. Magic was well cared for, seen regularly by the farriers along the route, for on most days she walked twenty-five miles and she was re-shod every two weeks. Ma, with her gift for herbal remedies, treated her as she treated her family; one of her potions was a salve prepared from boiled-up oak bark and alum to rub on any sores her harness might cause. If there was a stable handy when they tied up Pa always made sure she was under cover despite the cost.

Once the boat was gliding smoothly on the water and Magic had found her rhythm, Ally moved to the reins at Magic's rump and, clicking her tongue, began the task of leading the animal along the towpath. Magic was an intelligent, well-trained animal and had been taught by Fred to go by herself without leading, starting or stopping to a word of command or the smart crack of the smacking whip. Not that the whip ever smacked the animal, for she was well loved by the whole family, but the smacking whips were cracked by all boatmen and women as a warning at turns in the canal. The noise they made was distinctive and could be easily heard and recognised.

The sun was hot, bringing out the fragrance of the plants that bloomed in the grass bordering the towpath. The plants were bigger, more luxuriant than those that grew further afield, due, no doubt, to the proximity of the water. There were huge docks and tall, pink-flowered willow-herb and at their feet grew the shorter wild forget-me-nots. Yellow iris lifted their heads in the water's edge and great balsam grew up to six feet in height. Leaving Magic to plod along unguided, which she did placidly, Ally gathered a great bunch into her apron and with a graceful skip and a leap boarded the slow-moving *Edith*, ready to hand the flowers to her mother. Ma was up to her elbows in soap suds. The vividly painted washtub was perched on the small deck above the rear cabin and Ma was attacking the family's washing with her usual vigour. Just coming out of the cabin, an expression of petulant resignation on her face, was Betsy who had been unwillingly persuaded to hang out the wash on the line which hung from the box mast to the luby on the topmast.

"When yer've finished hanging out the wash put them flowers in water for Ma," Ally told her sister shortly. "That's if yer've the strength."

"Don't you talk ter me like that, our Ally—" Betsy began but Edie cut her short.

"Now then, you two, non o' that there buck. See, Betsy . . ."

But Ally did not stay to hear what Ma might have to say to Betsy, leaping agilely from the deck to the towpath and taking up her position behind Magic. Moorhens swam from one clump of flotsam to another, creating a small V behind them in which their chicks followed like small fluffy balls. Ally watched them and sighed contentedly. Jack's dog, Teddy, ran after him as her brother dashed on ahead to the first of the dozens of locks that had to be passed through before they reached their destination. Ally turned her face rapturously to the sun. She was filled with a joyous happiness which she knew nothing could ever shatter.

2

The construction of the Leeds to Liverpool Canal took over forty-five years, but the journey from the warehouses on the Bradford Canal, which joined the Leeds to Liverpool, to Liverpool itself took the *Edith* five days.

Their first hurdle, if it could be called so, were the locks, five of them, at Bingley, named the Five Rise Staircase, and it was here that Alice and Jack Pearce were called upon to work as a team, one on either side of the canal. The slope of the waterway was steep and therefore the five locks were necessary to raise the boat from the lower level to the higher. Working through the locks in a staircase could raise problems. As the paddles of one lock were opened the water would usually run down to the lock below. If this was full the water would flood over the sides, but Ally and Jack had worked these locks a hundred times, making quite certain that the lower lock was emptied in readiness, which is why Jack had run on ahead. It took time, and time was money, to get through the locks system and any minute saved was a bonus. The locks were narrow and once the *Edith* was in a staircase no other boat could move in the opposite direction. Ally and Jack worked smoothly and efficiently opening and closing paddles and gates, allowing the level of water to be lowered or highered, all under the watchful eye of the lock-keeper who was ready to lend a hand if one was needed. The crew of the *Edith* had never, to his recollection, asked for or needed assistance.

When they were through and ready to journey onwards

towards Silsden the toll-keeper, whose toll office was attached
at this part of the canal to the lock-keeper's cottage, emerged
importantly. He wiped his bushy moustache with the back of
his hand, giving it an extra twirl as Betsy Pearce twinkled at him
from her comfortable place on the *Edith*'s deck where she had
plumped up a cushion, the washing flapping on the line above
her head, and settled herself in the sun. Beneath a parasol, naturally, for the idea that her face might turn the same honey tint
as her sister's filled her with horror. She gave the impression of
a lady who had inadvertently found herself in rough company
but was bravely doing her best to overcome it, as a lady would.
But whereas a lady might engage herself with a scrap of fine
embroidery, Betsy was pretending to crochet. It was called the
"poor man's lace", a description Betsy did not care for, but it
enabled the boatwomen to produce lace-like edging or fabric to
adorn themselves or the interior of their cabins, where it was
hung to shield the bed-hole among other decorations. It
was stitched to new bonnets and aprons and sometimes, in the
absence of lace, to the frill of a petticoat.

The toll-keeper carried his gauging stick with him, twirling
this along with his moustache for extra effect. Aware that Betsy
was watching him, he made a great show of weighing Fred's
cargo which was performed with his gauging stick. The *Edith*
had been weighed when new and the means of calculating the
toll depended on her displacement in water. When cargo was
loaded the boat sailed lower and it was this displacement that
the toll-keeper measured. Fred paid the toll in cash to the
collector, receiving a toll ticket which was placed with others of
the family's important documents such as Fred and Edith's
marriage certificate and the birth certificates of their children,
four of whom had died, in a special little cubby-hole next to the
hatch cover.

Betsy smiled at the toll-keeper and dimpled at any man who
happened to be looking at her, which, if Ally was truthful with

herself, and she usually was, meant every man within a hundred yards. Ma was waiting beyond the locks with Magic whom she had walked up, and after once more harnessing the horse to the towline the *Edith* moved off. This time Jack led Magic, striding out behind the animal, whistling a cheerful tune and nodding to all and sundry, especially the young women who walked the towpath or who sat on the cabin roofs of passing boats. Ally followed while Edie sprang aboard and climbed down into the cabin to brew up a pot of tea. Fred puffed his pipe with great contentment, steering expertly across the three aqueducts that lay between Bingley and Kildwick, neither he nor Edie finding anything unusual in their younger daughter lolling on the deck while Ally and Jack walked the towpath.

Ally was the same. She and Jack were so used to the favouritism showed their sister, having been told so often that their Betsy was a delicate flower who could not really be expected to bloom as they did in any old weedpatch, that she was content to tramp beside the static water of the canal. The sky was an arch of blue above her head, cloudless without a breath of wind. On her right across the canal stretched Skipton Moor and to her left Carlton Moor, both vivid glowing carpets of colour, the yellow of gorse, the purple of heather in its summer glory. There would be bilberries growing amidst them, for this was lower moorland, never more than eight or nine hundred feet where the bleakness of the upper moorland did not encroach upon the vegetation. Sheep drifted, and here and there a white farmhouse sprouted out of the very heather itself, a plume of smoke from each chimney painting a streak of white across the depth of the blue. For nineteen years, having been born on the *Edith* in the canal basin at Liverpool, Ally had walked or sailed up and down this canal. As a baby tethered to the deck, as a toddler perched on Snowdrop's broad back, Snowdrop being the horse Pa had owned then, as a youngster learning the mechanics of locks, even to the steering of the

Edith, in all weathers, fine and foul, this had been her place in life, the boat her only home. She had fished on this very spot, catching roach, dace, bream, perch and chub which Ma had cooked on the range in the cabin. She had watched, enchanted, a kingfisher flying like a bright blue flash up the canal in front of the boat, landing on a bush and then whisking away as the boat drew up to it. Wagtails wagged their tails on the towpath and the fields were black with crows looking for worms. Swallows darted for insects of a fine evening as the family sat at rest on the deck and Magic, if rain was not forecast, grazed on the towpath.

"We'll mekk it ter Skipton Pool, I reckon, our Edie," she heard Pa say to Ma as the afternoon drew to its close. The midges were beginning to bite and though the smoke from Pa's pipe kept them from him she had no such defence against their nuisance.

"Right, lad. Now then, our Betsy, stir yersenn an' gie me a 'and. There's taters need peelin' and yer'd best bring in the wash."

"Oh, Ma, do I 'ave ter? Our Ally'll—"

For once Ma was firm. "Never mind our Ally. Lass 'as bin walking that towpath all day an' so 'as our Jack an' I reckon both of 'em'd be glad ter put their feet up. There's the tunnel termorrer if we get that far an' they'll both 'ave ter 'elp yer Pa ter get boat through. That's nearly a mile, my lass an' . . ."

Ma's voice trailed behind her down the cabin steps with Betsy following, still lamenting on the state of her stomach which, despite Ma's dose of chamomile, was still paining her, she said. To listen to her you'd think she had her monthlies once a week, Ally thought.

There were no locks between Bingley and Skipton so it was comparatively easy going to edge the boat to a mooring near to a block of warehouses where there was the added advantage of stables where Magic could spend the night. Out in the country and if the weather was fine Magic could be safely tethered near the boat but here where there was the bustle of the boats loading and unloading their cargoes, where men, sometimes of a dubious character, might lurk Fred was not prepared to leave the animal where she might be either stolen or injured. There would be proven for her and a dry stable for the night. She had walked almost twenty-seven miles this day, and though he and Edith had taken their turn on the towpath, leaving Ally and Jack at the tiller, they had all been on their feet for the same length of time.

He leaped ashore, passing the tiller to Ally as she jumped the narrowing gap between dock and boat, and with Jack he hauled at the braking line and even then it took a fair drag before the two strong men brought the boat to a halt.

"Aye up, Fred, ista lookin' fer cargo?" a voice hailed them from further along the wharf. A tall, thin, harried-looking man galloped towards them and seemed ready to embrace Fred in his eagerness but Fred, who was slow, deliberate, elbowed him off since he needed to be careful that the drag of the boat did not pull Magic into the canal.

"Nay, Arthur lad," he answered at last as the man hovered round him. "I've woollen goods aboard and our Jack's sleepin' in't hold as it is. What yer got?"

"Limestone fer Liverpool," Arthur replied hopefully.

"Well, there I'd 'ave ter say no, lad."

Ally stepped forward into the light of the lamps which were beginning to be lit along the wharf. "Pa," she began," I reckon us could—"

"That'll do, our Ally," Pa cut in tartly, for it was well known in the family that Ally would almost sink the bloody boat for a bit of extra cargo. Didn't mind taking a risk if it earned them a few more bob but that was not Fred's way. Cautious, careful, thoughtful, slow-thinking and it had kept them relatively prosperous, hadn't it? A good living he made on the *Edith* and he wasn't prepared to chance her, or his trade, on the foolish whims of a lass.

Ally sighed, for she had been of the opinion that with a bit of shuffling about the bales of woollen goods could be made to squeeze up a bit and at this time of the year it wouldn't hurt their Jack to sleep on the deck. If it had been her decision she'd have taken the chance, for woollen goods did not weigh any-thing like the thirty-two tons the boat could take. Still, Pa was the master of this vessel and would stand no argument.

She was just about to descend into the cabin from where the most tantalising smell of cooking food drifted, wondering if Ma had prevailed upon their Betsy to peel the taters, when a woman's voice called out to her from the thickening gloom of the wharf.

"Did tha' say tha' were fer Liverpool, chuck?"

Ally turned to where a woman in a somewhat tattered skirt and shawl teetered on the edge of the canal basin. She clutched her shawl about her anxiously, looking round furtively as though she were afraid of being overheard.

Ally took a step towards her. She could see Jack in the light from the lamp that hung over the stable door where he had just installed Magic. He was having a gab with one of the stable lads, laughing in that infectious way he had and she knew that when they had eaten he and probably Pa would wander over to the Swan for a mug or two of ale. He was evidently arranging to meet the stable lad there.

"What can I do fer yer?" she asked the woman. "Is it a message?"

"Aye, lass, if tha' could. Me sister lives by't docks an' I want 'er ter know our Jess 'as bin brought ter bed wi' a little lad. 'Er first, an' 'appen, on tha' way back up 'ere tha' could let me know if their Albert's better. 'E 'ad a fall an' . . . well, I'd be glad of news. She'll be lookin' out fer thi', or at least some canal boat an' I'll watch out this end." Her voice ended on an anxious, apologetic note.

This was not an unusual occurrence. On a pleasant Sunday people often came down to the "cut", as the canals were called, and walked with the boats for a mile or so, gathering news, passing on their own, very often the canals being their only source of communication.

"Rightio, lass," Ally said gently, for the woman looked worried and fearful. "What's yer sister's name?"

"Aggie Wainwright. She favours me so tha'll recognise 'er. She'll be asking all the boats. She were right fond of our Jess from 'er being a bairn an' I'm mithered about 'er Albert." She tried a smile, which barely lifted the corners of her tired mouth, and Ally was tempted to ask her aboard to share the meal that Ma was making but she resisted, for she knew Ma and Pa were eager to get to their beds in readiness for the journey tomorrow. There were four locks to be got through: Holme Bridge, Gargrave which had five rises, Bank Newton which had six and Greenberfield which had three before they reached the mile-long Foulridge Tunnel which had to be legged through. A long and exhausting day and they'd be lucky to manage fifteen miles.

"Don't worry, lass, I'll look out for 'er. An' we'll be back this way in about a fortnight."

The woman smiled, a full smile, then turned and disappeared into one of the dark ginnels that divided the warehouses.

The next day was as bright and fair as the previous one. As usual Betsy complained her way out of doing any serious work, listlessly helping her mother to wash the breakfast things with water from the barrel Jack had brought from the pump on the wharf and placed on the tiny deck, which was formed by the roof of the cabin. It was brightly painted, as was every single article above and below deck, a vivid scarlet banded with yellow and white and at each end a pattern of roses like a crown of jewels. Beside it was the enamel water jug, equally vivid with paint, which was used to carry water down to the cabin, and next to that was Teddy's kennel. No dog in the world was as well or decoratively housed as Teddy, for even the simple box-like shape with its sloping roof was exquisitely adorned. The smoke stack – which could be lowered should they enter a tunnel – and the box in which was kept Magic's proven were similarly embellished. The sides of the cabin had castles painted on them, two of them, and in between was the intricately painted lettering FREDERICK PEARCE with the registration number of his barge beneath. Even the tiller and rudder and the two towing masts were similarly wreathed about with colour, the whole a glorious picture of the canal boatman's art.

Yesterday's pattern of working the boat was repeated, each one of them taking a turn at the tiller, walking the towpath behind Magic, with Jack and Ally working the locks. Even Betsy, looking quite enchanting in her frilled bonnet and turning the head of every man who glanced at her, was persuaded into leading Magic, for as the boat approached Foulridge Tunnel both Jack and Fred, who would leg it through, rested a little in preparation for the task. A timetable for entering the tunnel had been drawn up many years ago with boats allowed to enter for an hour every four hours, the times at each end being staggered by two hours. This allowed for a maximum of two hours to leg a boat through. There were men at each end who were professional leggers who would take a boat through for a few pence but both Fred and Jack scorned them, for were they not two strong and experienced leggers themselves?

Magic was freed from her harness and, nodding pleasantly to all and sundry since she knew what a charming picture she made – dainty girl leading a majestic mare – Betsy moved off to walk the length of the tunnel on the picturesque path that led to the other end.

When their turn to proceed was signalled at the entrance to the tunnel, Jack and his father lay out on planks of wood from the sides of the boat, their heads almost touching, and began the exhausting labour of "walking" upside-down along the canal, their feet thudding on the dirt-encrusted walls, their hands clutching the sides of the planks on which they lay. At the last moment, since there was nothing she could do in the inky darkness of the cabin, Ma decided she might as well walk with their Betsy. In fact it might be more prudent if she did so in view of the girl's flighty inclination to simper at every man in sight. Mind you, Edie Pearce had not yet worked out why her lovely daughter did so, for the girl had said a thousand times she wouldn't dream of marrying a boatman. Nothing but a gentleman would do for her and as Edie had said just as many times you didn't meet many of them on the towpath!

As soon as Ally's eyes became accustomed to the dark from where she was in charge of steering the boat, she could see the merest pinprick of light at the Barrowford end of the tunnel.

"You all right, Pa?" Jack panted as the light behind them began to fade. The soft glow of the candle which guided his feet gave his face a sallow, eerie look and the sweat on it stood out in great droplets.

"Course I am, yer daft gobshite," Pa answered, forgetting the presence of his daughter, for he did not like to have his strength questioned by his younger and fitter son. Their voices echoed hollowly in the close confines of the tunnel to be followed by a long silence broken only by the lapping of the water and the laboured breathing of the men. Ally, who could barely see them, concentrated on keeping the sides of the boat from the tunnel walls and not for the first time she felt the closeness, the sourness, the damp blanket of the air in the tunnel press against her face, smothering her.

Her pa's sudden cry of alarm brought her explosively from her deep attention to her task. For an instant she nearly lost control of the tiller, for her pa continued to shout in what seemed to be terror.

"Jesus . . . oh, Jesus, me foot's caught in a bloody crack . . . Jesus. Jack, it's caught . . . stop the . . ." But of course there was no way to stop the forward motion of the *Edith*, for even with the braking line it took several lengths to bring her to a halt. Ally wrestled with the tiller and Jack's scream of fear, not, it seemed, for himself but for his pa, was cut off by a splash, a bumping grind of the vessel against the tunnel walls and the crashing beat of her own heart which was being alternately squeezed with terror and horror.

"Ally . . . Ally, Pa's gone over. Oh, sweet Jesus . . ." For the worst fear of a boatman passing through a tunnel was to fall overboard and be crushed between the walls of the tunnel and the side of the boat. Jack, who had been lying down just a moment ago – she had seen him by the light of the flickering candle – suddenly hurtled past her where she clung mindlessly to the tiller and leaped over the stern into the water. A great splash and an even greater thrashing about, cries of "Pa . . . Pa, where are yer?" and still the boat continued to glide soundlessly towards the growing circle of light probably no more than four hundred yards ahead. Still the sound of splashing, of Jack's laboured gasps as he dived and dived again and then a great shout.

"I've gorrim, Ally, I've gorrim. Dear God, if yer could just stop the bloody boat."

Suddenly the mist of fear lifted from her brain and, leaving the tiller, and therefore the boat to take her own course, Ally picked up the boat-hook, which was used sometimes when they moored, and shoved the end of it with all her strength at the wall. The pressure at once began to halt the boat's passage and slowly she came to a halt. Again she pushed until she thought her heart would burst and imperceptibly the *Edith* eased herself backwards towards the struggling figure of Jack Pearce where he held his father in his arms.

"Careful, our Ally, or yer'll run over us. Good lass, that's it . . . good lass. Can yer see?" Grabbing the candle and holding it high, Ally could just make out Jack's head and resting on his shoulder that of her father, his lolling in what seemed to be an unconscious state. Between them, grunting and admonishing each other to "be careful", "take it easy", "slowly does it", they hauled the limp body of Fred Pearce aboard and at once, leaving their father lying in a wet puddle of jumbled arms and legs, knowing that there was nothing they could do, or even see here in the dark, Ally took the tiller and Jack, his young body almost at the end of its endurance but enduring even more punishment, flung himself on his back and began the almost impossible task – one man alone – of legging it towards the slowly growing circle of light that was the end of the tunnel.

Ma and Betsy were talking to the owner of the boat who was waiting his turn to enter the tunnel. Ma said something and the boatman, Charlie Jenkins, laughed and shook his head, and when Ally's scream of warning rang out everybody in the vicinity, including Ma, froze like posts to the ground. Heads turned and Ma began to moan, for their Ally was not a hysterical girl who shrieked, like Betsy, at the slightest thing.

The *Edith* glided gently out into the bright sunlight and Ally marvelled at the ordinary scene, one she had known a hundred times, that lay before her. Boats lined up awaiting their turn to travel through the tunnel, the men and women on them taking the opportunity to gossip, to exchange news of this one or that, children playing on the towpath, glad for an hour to race and skip and escape the confines of their homes on the boats. Their horses cropped peacefully at the verge of the path, dogs barked and relieved themselves and amidst it all was Ma, her hand to her mouth, beginning to move slowly towards the *Edith* as Ally steered her towards the canalside. Jack, his face gaunt with shock and exhaustion, lay back on the plank, for a moment unable even to raise himself to a sitting position and at Ally's feet lay the crumpled figure of her pa.

"Pa fell in, Ma. 'E went over . . . 'is foot caught. Jack fetched 'im out." She was weeping, herself in a state of shock, but Charlie Jenkins, regaining his senses first, leaped to the bank and then on to the *Edith*, taking over the tiller, throwing the braking line to another boatman on the towpath who had had the presence of mind to come to his aid. They were all there then, Edie bending over the quiet figure of Fred, her face white, her cheeks hollowed out, her eyes and hands doing their fearful best to assess the damage done to her husband.

"Shall us lift 'im onter't bank, lass?" Charlie asked sympathetically. "'Appen someone can run fer't doctor," looking round him as though to wonder where such a person might be found.

There was blood seeping from the wet, crumpled figure of Fred Pearce and it was not immediately obvious from which part of his body it might have come. His legs, which Edie gently straightened out, did not look right and his head seemed askew and Edie sighed with relief but only because she had ascertained that her Fred was not dead. His heart was beating to a slow rhythm and his breath seemed to bubble from between his lips but she was afraid to move him lest his very obvious injuries might be made worse. People crowded on the towpath, craning their necks to get a look at the scene on the small deck. Men had tied up the *Edith* and one had taken charge of Magic, tethering her to a gatepost which led into a field. A boatwoman had gathered Betsy, who was weeping desolately on the canal bank, to her capacious bosom and was leading her to her own cosy cabin where she would make her a nice cup of tea, she said. Ally, in a state of deep shock, wondered when anybody was going to take a look at their Jack, who was shivering uncontrollably, his back to the hatch, his arms about his knees, his head bowed. If anybody needed a bit of fussing it was Jack who had just saved his father's life and who, now that the deed was done, everyone ignored.

It seemed that nobody knew just what to do next. They could hardly carry Fred Pearce down the steep, narrow steps into his own cabin but it seemed somewhat indecent just to leave him huddled on the tiny deck. Edie, though she had been known to help in many an emergency, to set a broken limb and to administer one of her own healing potions to others, many of them, was unable to do anything for one of her own, at least not until she had recovered somewhat and pulled herself out of the senseless state into which she had fallen at the sight of her poor Fred.

There was the sound of horse's hooves on the towpath coming at some speed and when a young chap threw himself from its back and, elbowing aside the fascinated spectators, jumped aboard the *Edith*, they were all astounded when he pronounced himself to be the doctor. He had a bag of sorts with him. Within seconds he had ordered off all those who had clambered on to the cabin roof to get a better view of poor Fred Pearce and would have got rid of Ma as well if she had not hit out at him and shrieked in his ear.

" 'E's me 'usband, yer daft bugger, an' if yer try ter get rid o' me I'll box yer bloody ears."

3

They were to give thanks a dozen times a day to young Doctor Wilson and to Charlie Jenkins's eldest lad, Benjy, who had run like the wind into the village of Foulridge to fetch him. He didn't mend poor Pa but he certainly saved his life.

He was particularly gentle with Edie. It was as though the threat to box his ears, perhaps bringing back memories of his own mother in his own childhood, had revealed to him the love that was behind the words. His mother would not, of course, have used such language but he was strangely aware, he didn't know how, that it was Edith Pearce's terror that had forced them from her lips. He was a perceptive young man, which made him a wise doctor.

"Let's first get everybody off the boat who has no need or right to be on it, madam, then I can get a proper look at your husband," which Ally, who was the first to come to her senses, did at great speed. Indeed she was rude, belligerent even in her fear, not only for her pa but for Jack who seemed to have gone into a guilty world of his own as though the whole event had been his fault. Of course, Betsy was worse than useless and Ally was thankful to the kind woman whose boat, the *Firefly*, was the third in line to go through the tunnel and therefore had another couple of hours to wait. Charlie had gone, taking the over-excited Benjy with him, for he couldn't hold up the queue, he said to her apologetically.

Doctor Wilson examined the injured man with the care and precision he took to every crisis, every patient in his care, gently probing and examining the wet and inert body of Fred Pearce, barely moving him until each part of him had been inspected.

"He has broken both legs, madam," he said with his polite correctness, "and there seems to be some injury to his head and back. He is, as you see, still unconscious so while he remains in that state I intend to put splints on his legs. He must be got out of these wet clothes and into a warm, dry bed." He looked about him, summing up the small space by the tiller, then down the steps to the cabin, his face a picture of amazement, since he had never been aboard a canal boat and the lack of space was a revelation to him.

"Right, lad," Edie said, immediately fumbling with the opening to Fred's corduroy trousers but the doctor put a hand on hers. "Slowly, madam, and with great care and, may I ask, where is he to be put?"

Edie looked up at him, bewildered. "In't bed-'ole, o' course."

"Bedole?"

"Aye," indicating the steps down into the cabin. "Our Jack'll give us an 'and, won't yer, chuck?" She turned to the boy who still shook like a moth by the hatch and for the first time her mother's heart saw the state of her son. She stared about her, the accident appearing to have frozen her usual quick thought processes and her eye fell on Ally. Ally, who was her standby, her support, her rock in all things, in every emergency that had cropped up, not many, true, but Ally had always stayed calm.

"But, madam—"

"Will yer stop callin' me madam. Me name's Edie Pearce."

"Mrs Pearce, you cannot propose to put your seriously injured husband in that . . ." He had been about to say "hole" but the expression of anguish on her grey face stopped the word before it was uttered. "Perhaps there is somewhere nearby" – looking about him towards the empty canal bank – "where he might stay until he's recovered."

"Where?"

"Well, I'm not sure but . . ."

Ally stepped forward, then knelt down in the tiny space beside her mother.

"Ma, we've ter get t'cargo ter Hemingway's by Friday at latest. If we're late we'll not be trusted again nor even get another cargo, at least from them, an' they give us a lot o' business. We've never let a merchant down yet and I know Pa'd say same."

"And where is Hemingway's, miss?"

"Liverpool."

"Liverpool!" He was aghast. "You cannot intend to take a seriously injured man eighty or more miles in this vessel. He must remain perfectly still and have quiet at all times. He needs constant medical attention which, if you remain in the district, I am prepared to give him." His young face was stiff with disapproval.

"Thank you, Doctor, yer most kind but this is our livin' an it'll be no more'n two days, 'appen three. If you patch 'im up . . ."

"*Patch him up!* Miss Pearce . . . is it?"

"Aye."

"I am a doctor and I will certainly do whatever is necessary, not only to make him comfortable but to mend his injuries. First we must strip him of his wet clothes and . . . er, well, get him somehow into the cabin. Is there a bed?" His expression telling them that he was having a hard time believing that such a thing could be found on this tiny boat. "Well then, let us all work together and see what we can do for the poor chap."

Which is what they did, Edie and Jack taking their orders from Ally, for they were both still in a state of deep shock. She wondered as she carried out the doctor's crisp commands why it was she who remained calm when Ma, normally so strong, floundered from one crisis to another and Jack, who had been cool-headed when Pa was in the water, was like a puppet, doing

what he was told but standing about in everybody's way when
there was nothing further asked of him. She just thanked God,
or whoever it was that was supposed to be looking out for them,
that their Betsy was still missing on the *Firefly*. Not only would
she have been no help whatsoever, there was no doubt that the
damn doctor would have been seriously distracted by her.

Pa was still unconscious though he was beginning to move
and mutter a word or two but the doctor, who repeated time
and time again that he must be kept still for forty-eight hours,
gave him some potion which quietened him.

"Every time he shows signs of waking give him a drop or two
and then when you reach Liverpool get a doctor to look at him
at once. Tom Hartley's a good chap. We went through medical
school together in Edinburgh. I'll write his name and address
down and the minute, the very minute you dock send your
brother for him. In fact, I'll get a telegraph off to him at once
telling him to expect you. I've done the best I can with Mr
Pearce's legs and sewn up the gash in his head but his back, it
will need watching. It's bruised . . . well, you saw it, Miss
Pearce."

Again she wondered why it was he addressed every remark
to her instead of Ma, unaware that she showed a quietness, an
efficiency, a steadfastness, a feeling of being totally in control
of herself and the situation which reassured the young doctor.

He, like all men, went to pieces when Betsy was led pityingly
up the towpath by the woman who had taken her in and Ally
thanked the fates that her sister had been kept away or God
knows what the young man might have done to Pa.

"Oh, Ma," she said pathetically, throwing herself into Ma's
wide-open arms. "I've bin that frightened. I didn't know what
'ad 'appened to Pa and me 'ead's achin' that much wi' cryin'
an' though this lady give me a cup o' tea . . ."

Over her mother's shoulder she caught sight of the open-
mouthed, slack-jawed doctor and at once she dragged herself

from her mother's arms, allowing him to see the fat, crystal tears which rolled so prettily down her pale rounded cheeks. If there was one thing that Betsy could do better than anyone on earth it was cry. It was her one talent and she used it to great effect. Enormous pools of sorrow formed between her long lashes. The tears spilled over heartbreakingly, but neither her eyelids nor her nose reddened as other girls' did when they wept. Doctor Wilson was overwhelmed, on his face an expression of awe and disbelief. He was plainly enchanted and Ally sighed. Please, God, don't let the daft woman who was her sister hold them up while the doctor did and said all the foolish things Betsy seemed to awaken in men. She was so bloody perfect, fragile and dainty with the masses of her pale silk hair tumbling about her head and down her back to her waist. She had removed her bonnet and her blue-green eyes were cloudy and mysterious as though promising all kinds of delights the wide-eyed doctor could not even begin to imagine. Her soft rosy mouth was tremulous with her distress, or so she would have them believe, but so far she had not even asked after Pa! They had already lost hours and though she was aware that the others thought her hard, callous even in her determination to get on, could they not see she was doing it for Pa, and for them. Pa was safe and snug in the bed-hole, his wounds tended to, with blankets ready to be placed on the floor where Ma would sleep for the night, he was in good hands.

"This is our Betsy." Ma was proud of her exquisite daughter even in the midst of this crisis.

"M-m-miss Pearce," the doctor stammered, bending over her hand, and Betsy, who had waited for a "gentleman" since she was twelve years old, smiled and lowered her dewed eyelashes and was prepared to spend an hour or so being adored by him.

"Right, Jack, get Magic harnessed, will yer, an' you, Betsy, 'elp 'im to cast off. Ma, you look after Pa, me an' Jack an'

Betsy will get us ter Liverpool." Ally turned to the astonished, nay, outraged doctor, for surely she could not mean to work this beautiful young woman like a deck-hand, his appalled expression seemed to be saying, but Ally politely indicated that he was to leave the boat since they were about to cast off and he had no choice but to do so.

"May I know yer fee, Doctor?" she asked, and when he told her she put the money in his hand. Betsy was weeping with real distress now, for she had never been asked to work the boat before and the good doctor looked as though he were about to leap to her aid.

Ally jumped back aboard while Jack hitched up Magic to the towlines and gave the animal an encouraging "giddup" or two and, when Magic was on her steady way, having enjoyed the unexpected stop at Foulridge and the pleasure of a bit of grazing, they glided on until the next hurdle stood in their path.

The seven rises of the Barrowford locks!

Betsy's face took on an expression of cunning, for though she had seen it done a hundred times she knew quite definitely that she was not capable of helping Jack with the opening and closing of the gates. She might dirty her pretty skirt or at the very least get it wet. Besides, the lock-keeper at Barrowford always smiled at her – as they all did – and she at him and she was pretty sure if she dimpled and coaxed she could persuade him to help their Jack with the locks. She waited until they were almost at the lock-keeper's cottage, inching along the canal with Jack already at Magic's head, then leaped ashore and, picking up her skirts, ran along the path to where the lock-keeper was at his door.

"Oh, sir," she gasped, "we've 'ad an awful haccident. Pa's fallen in't water at Foulbridge. 'E was smashed up by't wall and we've no one ter 'elp wi't locks. D'yer think p'raps . . ."

The lock-keeper smiled and seemed ready to take her arm to help steady her, for the pretty little thing was all of a fluster, and but for the presence of his frowning wife might have done so.

"Course, lass, you come along wi' me and I'll see yer through. Now stop yer frettin'," as pretty little Betsy Pearce squeezed a fat tear from between her long, fluttering lashes.

Betsy jumped aboard and gave Ally, who was still at the tiller, a complacent look as though to say there was really no need for a girl to work when there were men as daft as the lock-keeper about to do it for her, but then their Ally wasn't really up to it, was she? Not with her looks, or lack of them.

Her complacency did not last long.

Ally spoke in a mild voice but there was something beneath it that was threatening.

"An' what about Magic?"

"Oh, the lock-keeper'll fetch 'er along," Betsy proclaimed airily.

"D'yer 'onestly think I'm goin' ter 'ang about at bottom o't rise waitin' fer 'im while you're lollin' about up 'ere? Now gerr off this boat and lead Magic across or you'll feel the flat o' me 'and."

"Now listen 'ere, our Ally—"

"Ger off this boat or I'll push you off. *Now!*"

Betsy did as she was told, smiling at the lock-keeper as he returned to his cottage, even managing a little stumble as though her poor, tired body were being forced far beyond its resources.

"Eeh, lass, that there 'orse is too much fer yer. Will I . . . ?"

"No, thank you, sir, I can manage, really, an' thanks wi't locks."

"I 'ope yer pa's mended soon. Yer brother's right upset."

"We all are, sir." And another tear slipped easily down her cheek.

"That poor lass," he said to his wife as he rejoined her at the door of their cottage. "It don't seem right ter work 'er like that," gazing after the dainty figure of Betsy Pearce.

"Hmmmph," his wife answered, wondering why it was men were so daft.

Ally was determined to get through the next obstacle before dark, so that when it appeared she gritted her teeth and prepared to battle with Betsy. The Gannow Tunnel was not as long as Foulridge but legging it was just as exhausting.

"We can't leave Pa on 'is own so Ma must stay wi' 'im," she announced as the tunnel came into view, "and someone 'as to walk Magic across. Betsy, you'll 'ave ter steer."

"I can't steer," Betsy began to wail but Ally was having no more nonsense. Jack was still, temporarily, she hoped, somewhere in the darkness into which Pa's accident had flung him but he was ready to do anything she ordered. Ma was crouched over Pa and didn't know, nor care at this moment where the devil they went or who was to lead them there, so it was up to her to take charge and if Betsy thought she could keep up this little-girl-lost act that she put on for Ma and Pa she was sadly mistaken.

"Yer've seen us all do it, lass, an' yer've tekken yer turn on the straight . . ." when you've felt like it, she wanted to add, which wasn't often. "Now it's your turn ter steer through't tunnel. All yer 'ave ter do is keep the boat away from t'walls. It's only just over five hundred yards. Me an' Jack'll leg it."

"Ally, I can't, 'onest. Listen, Pa's sleepin' so can't Ma come up an' steer?"

Ally lifted her arm and the slap she administered to Betsy's cheek was heard on the boat that was just passing theirs in the opposite direction. Every head on deck turned to stare at them, astounded by the shriek that emerged from Betsy's mouth, and even Jack was shocked. Their Betsy was the baby, frail and not cut out to man the *Edith* as he and Ally were, but as Ally turned menacingly towards him he dropped his gaze. He knew that Ally was right. With Pa injured and Ma tending him there were only the three of them. And who was to lead Magic across the tunnel? But Ally had spotted a young lad standing by the tunnel's opening. Most boys and young men who made a living out of the canal and the boats that sailed on it knew its routines and the boy, when asked and promised a sixpence – a great deal of money – declared stoutly that he would lead Magic and be waiting with the placid animal at the other end of the tunnel. They were ready to start.

Betsy, one cheek still pale, the other scarlet with the imprint of Ally's hand, stood desolately at the tiller, composed now but with a look in her eye that boded ill for her sister in the future. Jack, his face ashen, since he would never forget what had happened such a short while ago, and though he was terrified of that dark, menacing opening ahead of them, lay waiting on the plank. When Ally emerged from the cabin in his own best pair of trousers, her skirt discarded, both he and Betsy gasped with horror.

"Yer never goin' ter wear them, our Ally," Jack whispered hoarsely as though afraid someone would hear him and look round to witness not only Ally's shame but his own.

"I'd 've worn Pa's but they're too short fer me," Ally answered shortly.

"Ally, just stop it now," Betsy ordered. "What if someone sees yer? Me an' Ma'll never be able ter lift our 'eads again. People can see the shape o' yer legs."

"Not in't tunnel, they won't, an' if yer think I'm tossin' me legs up in air wi' me skirts round me middle yer mistaken. Now, get goin', our Jack, and you be careful wi' that tiller, Betsy Pearce, fer I swear if yer damage this boat I'll take Pa's belt to yer an' lift the skin off yer back."

For the next few hours they travelled the relatively easy waterway between Burnley and Blackburn, which was free of locks, stopping in Burnley Pool, for if they, or at least Ally, did not require rest, Magic did. They slept almost where they fell after eating the meal Ma had managed to prepare. Pa was quiet and even Ma dozed off in her nest of blankets on the cabin floor. At dawn Ally had them up, Betsy complaining bitterly and earning herself another clout from Ally who told her that if she didn't stop whingeing she'd leave her at the next town and hire a lad to take her place.

"Just you wait, Alice Pearce," Betsy hissed malevolently between her sobs. "Just you wait . . ." And though Ally turned away, unconcerned with Betsy's threats, whatever they might be, the expression on Betsy's lovely face was no longer lovely.

They reached Liverpool forty-eight hours later, going through eight sets of locks, Johnson's Hillocks with seven rises and the horrendous task at Wigan where there were *twenty-three*! Nobody helped Betsy, for there was too much commotion, too much hustle and bustle as coal was loaded into barge after barge, coal dust drifting and settling on every person in sight, including Betsy whose pretty skirt got not only wet but filthy. The look of loathing she directed at Ally twisted her features in such a way that it might have been thought that Ally had engineered the whole thing, Pa's accident and Ma's determination never to leave his side, just to get at Betsy.

Pa was beginning to mutter and heave about as though he were in pain, even when Ma dosed him. She was forcing her own mixture between his cracked lips by now, for in her opinion her herbs were of more use to him than that "stuff" the doctor had given them. She urged Ally again and again to get him to the doctor in Liverpool, her face strained and her body noticeably thinner, for in her devoted care for Fred no food passed her lips, only her numerous cups of tea.

Normally they would have turned at the new cut and gone down the five locks to Stanley Dock right on the river where their cargo would have been unloaded into the Hemingway warehouse but with Pa rambling and his condition obviously worsening Ally, who was in charge not only of the *Edith* but the family and all that concerned it, decided to continue on to the old canal basin on Leeds Street. It was closer to the city and presumably the address in Duke Street which Doctor Wilson had given them.

The boat was barely tied up when Jack leaped on to the dock and with the piece of paper Doctor Wilson had given them in his hand began to run along Old Hall Street at the end of which was the Town Hall. At his heels ran Teddy, for the young mongrel was very confused by the happenings in his home over the past few days and was not prepared to part with his young master.

Tom Hartley was just about to mount his tall, well-bred bay mare at the entrance to his house when the young man who was shambling along the pavement towards him shouted something. There was a scruffy dog at his heels. Tom couldn't quite make out what the lad said but his air of desperate agitation made him hesitate. The groom who stabled his animal at the back of the houses in Duke Street muttered something and got ready to defend himself, the mare of whom he was particularly fond, and Doctor Hartley, but the man who approached, who seemed about to drop on all fours like a dog that has run further than its capabilities will allow, leaned instead against the railings that surrounded the area in front of Tom Hartley's house. The dog huddled against his legs.

"What is it?" Doctor Hartley said, but the young man was so breathless he could barely speak.

"Rest a minute, lad," the doctor told him. "Is there someone in trouble?"

The man nodded.

"Where? What is it? Sit down on the step until you get your breath." The groom sighed, for it was well known that Doctor Tom, as they all knew him, was prepared to go anywhere and do anything to help those who had no means to help themselves.

The young man passed the scrap of paper he was clutching

to the doctor who read it, then, as light dawned on him, he helped Jack Pearce to his feet.

"Is it the chap who was hurt in the tunnel?"

Jack nodded speechlessly.

"Dick Wilson sent me a telegraph telling me to expect him. Where are you docked?"

"The canal basin, Leeds Street," Jack managed to blurt out, leaning forward, his hands on his knees, his chin on his chest.

"Right. What's your name? . . . Jack. Right, Jack, you follow me at your own pace; you're obviously tired." The poor young fellow looked as though he had had no rest for days, his face grey with fatigue.

Jack nodded and, as Doctor Tom Hartley mounted his horse and turned in the direction of Hanover Street, sank down again on the doctor's doorstep and had it not been for the groom who told him brusquely to be on his way, would have nodded off right there and then.

The first person Tom saw as he reached the canal boat was a tall, slender young man hovering beside it in what seemed to him great anxiety. There was a woman talking to him, a clean, tidy woman of the working class and the young man, though he was watching Tom's own approach, appeared to be doing his best to answer her questions.

His voice was curiously light for a male. "Yes, that's right." He pushed a distracted hand through his thick, curling hair which seemed to be coated with coal dust, then ran his hand down his trousers which were equally filthy. "I forget her name; she said she were sister to Aggie."

"That's me."

"And that I were ter tell yer . . . Jess, is it?"

"Aye, our Jess." The woman put a hand on the young man's arm.

"She's 'ad a son."

"A lad, eeeh, that's grand. Thanks, lass," she said amazingly to the young man, ready to turn away. She looked somewhat mystified, no doubt at the astonishing ambiguity of the tall figure in the trousers, as was Doctor Tom Hartley. Not a young man then, but a woman dressed as one, Tom decided as he swung himself out of his saddle. He could see the bewilderment on the face of the older woman who stood back, hesitating, ready, he decided, to eavesdrop on the conversation. The young woman in the trousers looked as if she were in the deepest trouble and though Tom was not to know it Aggie Wainwright's big heart had all the capacity in the world for those in trouble. Besides, the lass had just done her a good turn. Their Jess had suffered several miscarriages in the past couple of years and the joy of knowing that at last she had borne a son, a live and healthy son, it seemed, made the bearer of the glad news special in Aggie's estimation.

Tom Hartley stared, open-mouthed, at the tall figure of the young woman in trousers as she turned in obvious thankfulness. Her grimy features were strained, the coal dust lodging in the exhausted creases of her face, in her nostrils and ears which were only partially covered by her cropped hair.

"I'm Doctor Tom Hartley. I had a message from Dick Wilson who apparently attended an accident on . . . and then a young man caught me—"

He stopped speaking abruptly, lifting a hand to the young woman who gave the impression that she might be about to fall. She appeared to be having some sort of crisis, her mouth working strangely, her eyes wide in what he presumed to be shock. Her face twitched and her whole frame trembled.

"Are you ill, miss?" he asked her gently, this time taking her hand in his but she pulled it away, shaking her head, disturbing the coal dust that lodged in her curls.

"No . . . no. My father," pointing a shaking finger towards the boat.

"Of course. Show me the way." Then he followed the swaying figure as she turned towards the gaily painted canal boat.

Tom Hartley was not to know that Alice Pearce had looked into his kind, vividly blue eyes and without a moment's hesitation, nor wonder at how it could happen so swiftly and completely, had fallen in love with him. A love which was fixed at that moment and was to last a lifetime.

4

"He must be put in a proper bed at once, Mrs Pearce. I can't even examine him as I would like in this . . . this . . ." Tom Hartley looked about him, his curious gaze taking in the small cabin which, with himself and his patient's wife crammed into it, hardly gave him room to turn to his medical bag. It was dim and inordinately cluttered with more ornaments and lace than could be found in a lady's boudoir and it was insufferably hot, for the small stove to the left of the hatch was lit. Edie Pearce, with her instinct to feed which was her way of caring for her family, had a good stew cooking in readiness for when their Jack returned, for none of them had had a bite since they set off this morning.

"A proper bed! My Fred's never slept anywhere but in bed-'ole since 'e were born. Besides, where am I ter find one o' them?"

"Perhaps . . . lodgings? Until your husband is fit to travel again." Which by the look of the poor tormented man in the *hole* would not be for a long time.

"Lodgings!" Edie was aghast. Of course she knew what they were but the idea of her and her family staying in such a place was anathema to her. What was wrong with her own little home which, though it needed a good "bottoming" at the moment, for she had sadly neglected her housewifely duties during the past few days, she would attend to as soon as the doctor had seen to Fred.

"There must be many a place hereabouts, madam."

"Dear God, will yer stop callin' me madam. T'other 'un were't same. Edie Pearce is me name."

"I'm sorry. Do forgive me, Mrs Pearce." His manners were lovely, just like the other one, Edie thought distractedly as he pulled back the quilt which she herself had embroidered.

Despite the lack of space Tom managed to examine Fred's injuries, changing the bandages on his head and legs and staring worriedly at the enormous bruise on his back, repeating that he really must be got to a full-length bed, a cool, comfortable room, preferably with a fireplace in case it should turn cold and where he himself could call on him each day. He should recover consciousness soon and when he did Mrs Pearce was to try and feed her husband with broth, eggs whipped in milk if they were to be had, anything light and nourishing, and to send that lad of hers to find suitable lodgings.

"I shall call tomorrow, Mrs Pearce, and hope to find you in better circumstances."

"There's nowt wrong wi' these, lad," Edie bristled.

Tom laid his gentle hand on her arm and with that gift he had for putting patients' worries to rest and soothing their anxious relatives told her that she was right but for the moment it was in Fred's best interests to be moved.

"He will do better, Mrs Pearce, I promise you." And Edie was somehow comforted as he had meant her to be.

He almost fell back into the cabin as he climbed the couple of steps to the deck, for standing at the top was quite the most exquisite young woman he had ever seen. She was smiling at him and, mesmerised, he smiled back. She wore a crisp white bodice of fine lawn, a pretty frilled skirt in a shade of buttercup yellow sprigged with daisies and a frilled muslin apron. Her hair was tied back with a yellow ribbon, curls escaping about her face. Her smile revealed white, even teeth and two dimples in her rose-tinted cheeks. He was not to know that from the very moment he climbed down from his horse, Betsy Pearce had been busy with a bucket of water, soap and her hairbrush in the tiny confines of the cabin she shared with Ally. She knew a gentleman when she saw one and by the look of his fine horse, his clothing and the handsome leather bag he carried, a wealthy one. And he was not going to get his first sight of her in the filth that had accumulated about her on their journey from Foulridge. She looked a picture, if not exactly of elegance, for her outfit was a boatwoman's and not of a lady from society, but it was perhaps this very simplicity that charmed Tom Hartley. Standing beside her was the tall and gawky young woman who was still dressed in a man's shirt and trousers. She had evidently washed her face while he was in the cabin and brushed her soft mop of copper-brown curls but the difference between her and the other one could not have been more marked.

"How is he?" she asked baldly while the lovely one continued to smile in a delightfully bashful way. His heart was bounding in his chest and he let out a long-drawn sigh, for the sight of such perfection was not often to be found.

He managed to tear his gaze away from the beautiful one, looking into what seemed to be tortured anxiety in the eyes of the plain one. For the first time he noticed that though she might be thin, awkward, indeed downright comical in her get-up, her eyes were the most unusual colour and shape. He was reminded of almonds, the outside corners slanted upwards, and the colour as clear as amber. Long, thick lashes, dark and curling, surrounded them and for a strange moment the lovely one ceased to exist.

"You are?" he questioned, slightly bemused by the intensity of her steady gaze.

"His daughter, Alice Pearce."

"And I'm Elizabeth," Betsy told him, giving herself her full name. He turned back to her. He couldn't help himself. She was like a child, wide-eyed, innocent, modestly lowering her lashes when he gazed in admiration at the wonder of her, but the plain one cleared her throat.

"Shurrup, our Betsy. 'Ow's me pa, Doctor?"

Tom Hartley pulled his scattered wits about him and became professional again. "He is . . ." He hesitated.

"Tell me't truth. I must know't truth."

"He is gravely ill, Miss Pearce, and he cannot stay in that small cabin any longer. He must be put in a warm bed, clean—"

" 'Tis not dirty."

"I know that but he needs to sleep properly. He needs careful nursing, good food and even then . . ."

"The truth, Doctor Hartley."

"He may never walk again."

"Oh, Jesus . . ."

Despite Alice Pearce's obvious distress he could not keep himself from turning to the one who had called herself Elizabeth, who continued to smile at him. He knew he should concentrate on Alice Pearce who was genuinely upset by the news he had just given her. Not that Elizabeth was unfeeling, he was sure of that, but she was still a child, unaware of the seriousness of the situation. His eyes drifted of their own volition to the sweet swell of her breast which belied his last thought, for her figure was womanly, rounded. He hastily tore his eyes away from her, missing the small triumphant smirk that flitted across her face, turning once more to Alice.

"Miss Pearce, as I was saying," he began when a slight commotion on the wharf caught his attention. He had flung the reins of his horse to a barefoot young boy, one of those who were always hanging about in Liverpool in the hopes of making a few pence, but beside him a woman, matronly and respectable, called out, indicating that she would like to speak to someone.

Alice turned as he did but she was pale beneath her grime and her face was blank with what appeared to be shock.

"Can I 'ave a word, queen?" the woman asked.

"What?" Alice quavered.

"I think she wants to speak to you, Miss Pearce," Tom told her, taking her elbow and, with the manners bred in him as a boy, was ready to help her off the boat and on to the wharf. There was a great deal of activity. Dozens of canal boats were moored, discharging their cargoes, which were carted away by dockers to their designated warehouses. Men whistled and others sang. Enormous shire horses clanged their great hooves on the wet cobbles and nodded their great heads, waiting to be off, and the men of the canal boats leaped from boat to wharf and back again. Their wives watched what to them seemed to be some emergency on the *Edith*, most of them with some work in their hands, either crocheting or weaving the rope decorations for which they were famous. And not only were the ropes for decorations. Rope fenders were fashioned to protect the side of the boat when it docked, plaited crowns to place around the top of the rudder post, another for the tiller and the actual ropes for mooring. Others were knitting the guernsey jumpers – ganseys – with the oiled wool which made them waterproof and which their men wore in cold, wet weather.

In a daze Ally allowed the doctor to hand her from the boat, his very touch an exquisite pain to her. Her heart wrenched, for she had seen the way he looked at Betsy, as *all* men looked at Betsy, and for the first time in her life she *minded*. Half an hour ago her sister's looks and the magnet they were to all males, whatever their age, had made her smile, but on the whole they had been an indifference to her. But not this time, dear God, not this time. Tom Hartley . . . oh, Lord, Tom Hartley had lit something in her with one look and she knew that that light would never go out, never. She couldn't seem to concentrate on what was in hand, for two events of enormous importance had happened within the space of thirty minutes. She had met

a man and instantly loved him and she had been told that her
father might never walk again. Somehow she must pull herself
together, get herself in motion again, become that steady,
worthwhile person she knew herself to be and make the arrangements that would protect her family. She knew perfectly well
that she was the only one to do it. Pa was injured, Ma weakened
by it and concerned only with caring for him; Jack, though big
and strong, was still a boy who needed constant direction, and
Betsy a careless, useless, self-centred child. Lord help her. If
there had been a church on the wharf she would have run
screaming to it, flinging herself to her knees and asking God, if
he existed, to get her through this. Instead she took a step
forward, ready to collapse into the arms of the motherly little
woman who stood on the wharf.

"Wharris it, lass?" Aggie Wainwright asked her, her round
face creased with concern.

"What?"

"I can see summat's up an' what wi' you bein' so kind,
fetchin' that message from our lass . . . what's ter do?"

Doctor Tom took over, for it seemed Ally Pearce was, for the
moment at least, incapable of speech.

"Miss Pearce's father has had an accident."

"Eeh, God love 'im."

"Indeed. I wondered if you live nearby?"

"Aye, I do, in Blackstock Street. Five minutes away just off
Vauxhall Road." Aggie looked mystified, for what was where
she lived to do with this well-set-up young doctor. Oh, aye, she
could tell he was a doctor by the cut of his clothes, his fine horse
and the bag he carried.

"Do you happen to know if there are lodging houses around
here? Miss Pearce's father and mother need somewhere to stay
while Mr Pearce recovers. He cannot remain on the canal boat
and I was—"

Aggie's face lit up and she stamped her foot in triumph. It

was a habit she had when she was pleased and one which Ally was to know intimately.

"Well, would yer credit it. It must be fate or summat. Or 'appen someone's lookin' out fer yer, lass. I've rooms ter let. Me gentleman got married last week an' a right good do it were an' all. I were just waitin' fer't right one ter come along cos I'm partickler but though I can't say I like what yer gorron" – casting a disapproving look up and down Ally's figure – "that little miss on deck looks a treat. Clean an' decent, like."

Tom Hartley turned to look at Betsy who had draped herself gracefully by the steps of the cabin, for Tom's benefit, of course, and it was evident from his expression that he agreed whole-heartedly with Aggie Wainwright.

It took all Tom's determination and comforting prophecies to get Edie Pearce's permission to move her husband from the cabin where they had spent their married life, all twenty-five years of it, into Mrs Wainwright's achingly clean house in Blackstock Street. While Ally sat with Pa, Ma walked round to Aggie Wainwright's house, for she made it clear she wasn't taking her Fred to any old dump, nearly causing Aggie to cancel the whole thing. Doctor Tom was patient, kind, soothing both women's pride. His low voice, quiet but not hesitant, kept everybody on an even keel, as Fred, with Edie anxiously supervising his every movement, was transferred from the cabin on to a hand cart, well padded and wrapped about and walked round to Aggie's house where he was installed in Aggie's front bedroom, approved for its immaculate condition by Edie. When Fred was comfortable she sat in the rocking-chair by the bed and made it plain to all concerned that this was where she would stay until her lad was recovered.

Betsy went with her, walking beside the tall figure of Tom Hartley who led his bay, ready to take his arm in a proprietary fashion but not quite daring to just yet. She had plans for Tom Hartley and she didn't want to spoil them by being too forward. Not for an instant were her emotions involved, but Tom was a gentleman and Betsy had always wanted a gentleman. Pa's accident was a blessing in disguise, she told herself as she was shown to the room next to Ma and Pa's which was to be hers. It was plain, clean and its former occupant, Aggie's son Albert, didn't seem to mind moving up into the attic, for though only twelve years old he had fallen under Betsy's spell and would have slept in the yard shed if it meant she was comfortable.

The house was tall, narrow and attached on both sides to another just like it. From the street you stepped into the long narrow hall off which was a "best" parlour which was to be put at the disposal of the Pearce family, a kitchen, warm and cosy from the heat thrown out by the blackleaded range against one wall and a scullery which led into a tiny back yard. There were three bedrooms and two attic rooms and Mrs Pearce was to have the use of the kitchen to cook her family's meals, Aggie said. All very satisfactory, Doctor Tom agreed, after checking that his patient had survived the journey comfortably and with no damage.

"I'll be over in the morning, Mrs Pearce, but if you should need me I'm sure Mrs Wainwright's son can fetch me from Duke Street."

"Is that where yer live, Doctor?" Betsy asked artlessly. She was made up with the arrangements. She had never cared for life on the canal and the knowledge that she would not only have the company of this thoroughly suitable gentleman – she meant to make sure of that – but would also have the run of the shops and all the lively entertainment that this dynamic city promised, thrilled her to the core of her shallow heart.

"It is, Miss Pearce," Tom answered with great good humour.

"Is it far?" She smiled up at him, the colour of her eyes a combination of jade and lapis lazuli. They reminded him of an

exquisite brooch his mother wore at her neck, a family heir-
loom, he had been told, passed down from bride to bride, which
would one day adorn the person of his own wife. For a moment
the picture of this beautiful creature misted in the virginal white
of a bride took his breath away but Betsy, knowing the ways of
all men, saw something move in his face and felt the jubilant
victory of success in her two small, greedy hands.

As the slow procession had moved off, the cart with Pa in it,
Ma walking by his side, Betsy smirking up into the doctor's face,
all making for the entrance to the canal basin and thence to
Blackstock Street, Ally turned away and moved wearily down
into the cabin. Jack had returned. He sat on the side opposite
the stove, Teddy on his lap, his face set in lines of despondency,
for he had not the slightest idea what he and Ally were to do
next. The cabin seemed huge and empty without the bustle of
his ma and the smell of Pa's pipe, the silly chatter of their Betsy.
He was so tired he could have dropped off sitting bolt upright,
as he had nearly done outside the doctor's house, but the smell
of Ma's stew which was still in the oven reminded him that he
hadn't eaten for hours.

"Shall us 'ave a bite, Ally? S'no good lettin' Ma's stew go ter
waste."

Ally, who had sat down next to him, lifted her head and stared
at some distant thing only she could see. She didn't like the look
of it, whatever it was, her expression said, but what was to be
done, *must* be done and there was only her and Jack to get on
with it. It was no good sitting about here wallowing in the misery
Pa's accident, not to mention Tom Hartley and their Becky, had
pitched her into. There was a cargo to be delivered before
anything else could be considered and she and Jack could
manage that on their own. Back along the canal, down the locks
to Stanley Dock, unload bales of woollen goods into
Hemingway's warehouse and then, and only then could she and

Jack eat Ma's good stew. Then they could rest and tomorrow
. . . well, tomorrow was another day which she would face when
it came.

She washed herself all over, put on her Sunday outfit of white,
long-sleeved blouse, tucked with a dozen narrow rows horizon-
tally across her breast, and her blue and white striped cotton
skirt. Over the skirt she wore the traditional white cotton apron,
embroidered with flowers and birds, white on white, and inset
with narrow panels of crochet so fine it looked just like lace. She
had washed her hair and at the last moment decided against the
boatwoman's flattering bonnet, leaving her riot of copper-
brown curls to stand about her head like a chrysanthemum. She
had slept the sleep of the dead in Ma and Pa's bed-hole and had
awakened refreshed and able to think more clearly, and for some
reason the image of Aggie Wainwright had popped into her
head. She would go and discuss this situation with the woman
who had taken in her family and though Mrs Wainwright wasn't
a boatwoman and presumably had never been on a canal, it
seemed to Ally she might be of practical help to them all.

Jack was still asleep, crammed into the bow cabin and she
left him to it. He'd worked himself to a standstill yesterday
unloading the boat, opening and closing the locks to allow them
to get down to the dock, then back up to the canal basin, and
after eating his meal like a zombie had moved to the bow cabin,
Teddy with him and there he still was. He would wonder where
she was when he woke but he wasn't a lad who worried over-
much; he would wait patiently, probably in the public house
behind the canal where all the boatmen drank, until her return.

She found Blackstock Street without much trouble, causing
the heads of a few men to turn as she strode out, for she was
worth looking at in her fresh, attractive outfit. The sun shone,
putting copper glints in her long, golden eyes and she walked
with the easy, graceful stride she had learned on the towpath.

She was very thin but she was supple, long-limbed, the pale weariness gone from her face which was tinted the colour of honey with a touch of carnation at each cheek.

Aggie opened the door to her confident knock, greeting her with such warmth Ally was quite taken aback.

"Come in, lass, get yersenn inter't kitchen. Don't yer look a treat. Better'n yesterday I must say. I've just brewed up. Now, yer pa's come to . . . oh aye" – looking as pleased as punch as if it was only to be expected after his transfer to her excellent establishment – "an' 'e's askin' for yer. No, now no; afore yer go up I want ter talk ter yer. Another minnit's not gonner make any difference. Yer ma's with 'im but" – she sniffed with great significance – "yer sister's gone out." It was plain their Betsy had sunk way down in Aggie Wainwright's estimation. "No, don't ask me where cos I don't know. I can tell yer doctor's bin an' she followed 'im out, but you an' me need a birrof a chat."

The pain had returned to Ally's chest at Aggie's revelation regarding Betsy, but what else did she expect? It struck just below where she supposed her heart to be, a sinking pain that was not physical but hurt pretty badly all the same. She sipped the tea Mrs Wainwright put in her hand, staring into the flickering coals of the small fire in the range and Aggie watched her compassionately. This lass, for she was no more than that, had the whole bloody burden of her family on her shoulders and what's more she knew it and that flibbertigibbet of a sister of hers was chasing after the man she fancied. Aggie, who had known great sadness in her own life, had seen it right off but she said nothing. At least about that.

"Now, lass, dost want ter talk about owt? If yer do I'm a good listener burrif it's not asked for I don't give advice. Yer ma and pa are safe 'ere wi' me and I've tekken a great likin' ter that there doctor. 'E'll keep an eye on yer pa. Now I know your Betsy'll not be interested in comin' wi' yer burrif you an' yer brother – aye, yer ma told me about Jack an' wharra good lad 'e is – if yer thinkin' on keepin' up yer canal work then gerron wi' it. There's lads on the docks'd be glad of a job so . . . 'Ear, will yer listen to me, arrangin' yer life an' me what's just said I don't 'and out advice. It's just I only want yer ter know that . . . well, I'll shurrup."

Ally began to weep silently but not as prettily as Betsy, the tears washing across her cheeks and falling into her tea, her eyes reddening and her nose running and she had time to be glad that Tom Hartley had been and gone.

" 'Ere, none o' that, yer daft queen. There's nowt ter skrike about. I know yer pa's badly but that doctor's a gradely lad. I've asked about an' they say no matter what time o' day or night 'e'll come out. 'E goes all over, down them ginnels ter terrible places, tenements, folk 'oo mekk no effort ter pay 'im an' 'e works at th' infirmary fer nowt. Private money 'e's got. Now, lass, give over. Dry yer eyes an' go up an' see yer pa. An' just let me say, that there Betsy o' yourn don't stand a chance wi' a sensible chap like Doctor Tom, so there's no need ter . . ."

Ally lifted her head and glared at Aggie Wainwright, drying her tears, tears of worry and the anxiety of the last few days, she would have Aggie believe.

"What's it ter do wi' me what Doctor 'Artley does? 'E's nowt ter me an' if 'e's fool enough ter be tekken in by a featherbrain like our Betsy, then 'e deserves 'er."

"Good lass. Now go an' see yer pa an' think on about what I said."

She and Aggie were about to go up the slip of a staircase when there was a knock at the front door.

" 'Old on, chuck, I'll just see 'oo it is. Next door, I shouldn't wonder, wantin' ter borrow a cup o' sugar."

The sunlight which managed to infiltrate the narrow street fell on the bared head of Doctor Tom Hartley, burnishing his dark hair to almost the same copper shade as Ally's. He looked somewhat distracted, for beside him was Betsy. She didn't look distracted, she looked annoyed, one might say peevish, an expression which Ally knew meant she had failed to get her own way and the cause of it was Doctor Tom Hartley. She pushed her way past him and flounced into the parlour without a word.

"I'm just bringing Miss Pearce home," he told Aggie. "I'm about to visit a . . . well, a patient in a part of the town where it would not be appropriate for her to go. She's . . ."

What he was about to say, if he had not been such a gentleman, might have been that Betsy was hard to get rid of, dried up suddenly as he caught sight of Ally standing behind Mrs Wainwright.

"Miss . . . Miss Pearce?" he asked hesitantly.

She smiled, a smile as jubilant as Betsy's, for, woman-like, she had been mortified that he had seen her – but not *seen* her – in the muck and muddle of the journey's end in the canal basin. Now she knew she looked well, and his eyes said the same. Hers narrowed like those of a cat and she smiled, not one of the sickly sweet smiles Betsy doled out but one of warmth and genuine humour, clear and whole-hearted and Tom wondered why he had never seen it before. Why he had never seen *her* before. He stood for a moment, dithering, Aggie thought, quite bowled over by the young woman at her back and she felt the satisfaction go through her. She hadn't taken to Betsy but she already had a great respect for Ally.

"Well, I'd best get on. Good-day to you, Mrs Wainwright, and to you, Miss Pearce."

"Ally."

"I beg your pardon?"

"Me name's Ally, or Alice."

"Mine's Tom, or Thomas."

They grinned at one another, then, turning, he strode towards where he had tethered his bay.

★

She and Jack and a broad-shouldered young lad named Davey, who happened to be Aggie's niece's lad, took on a cargo of mine machinery for Wigan, roadstone for Burnley where a great deal of building was taking place, raw cotton for Nelson and lime which was used as fertiliser for the soil of the Lancashire farm-land. They also carried a message to Aggie's sister regarding the condition of her Albert's leg, which was mending nicely. He'd fallen out of a tree, as daft boys will, Aggie told Ally, and she only wished she'd known about Doctor Tom then, for she was sure Albert would not have the limp the fall had left him with.

At the last moment, just a week after their arrival in Liverpool, Aggie dragged Ally into her arms and begged her not to worry, she'd keep an eye on them all, including that little madam who was her sister and she'd tell Doctor Tom, when he came to see her pa, that she'd be back soon.

5

Thomas Edward Hartley was twenty-six years old, the eldest son of Edward Hartley, who owned the export and import firm of Hartley Shipping in Bath Street overlooking Princes Dock. From his comfortable first-floor office Edward could sit in his leather chair and look out of the window to watch the graceful flight of the sailing ships and the less attractive ploughing of the steam ships on the great commercial highway which had made his family their fortune. Four generations of them. Their vision and drive and keen brains had made the name of Hartley respected in the world of commerce, of shipping and all that that entailed and they had become one of the foremost Liverpool families, up there with the Hemingways, the Osbornes and the Latimers. Across the broad stretch of Princes Dock where were berthed small, full-bodied merchant ships, brigantines, four-masted barques, schooners and the elegant lines of the fast clipper ships which sailed to the ends of the earth, he could study the sliding pewter waters which brought his wool from Australia and South Africa, his beef from Argentina, his wheat from Canada, Mediterranean fruits, Indian tea and rice and timber from many parts of the globe. He watched the loading of the ships which carried his cotton piece goods, his engineering goods, machinery, chemicals, railway equipment, salt, coal and pottery to the four corners of the earth, adding up in his shrewd head the profit he made each day from importing and exporting these commodities and knew he could call himself one of the richest men in the city and was filled with a satisfaction that never lessened.

The only disappointment to mar his life had been his eldest son's absolute refusal to come into the business when he was of an age to do so.

"I want to be a doctor, Father. I feel I am not cut out for a commercial life," he had said stubbornly again and again. "And with four more sons to carry on after you I hardly feel that my participation will be missed."

"That's not for you to decide, boy. You'll do as I say and that's an end to it. The eldest son has always become the head of the firm and that is what you are to do. I'll brook no more arguments, do you hear? John and Teddy will no doubt follow you and James and Arthur, though they are still very young—"

"So you see you really don't need me at all, Father."

"Don't you interrupt me, sir. I will say what is needed in my own family and I do not need a son of mine to become a doctor. I never heard of such a thing. A doctor . . ."

"What's wrong with being a doctor, Father? It's an honourable profession. When I leave school I want to go to Edinburgh where I believe—"

"Not another word," Edward Hartley thundered. "You are making your mother ill."

"Then if I were to become a doctor, sir, I could cure her."

"Go to your room, you impudent young devil and stay there until I give you permission to leave and if I hear another word . . ."

"I *will* go, sir. If I have to leave home and—"

"Get out of my sight before I take a strap to you."

And so it had gone on for months and months but Tom Hartley, who had been known for his resolution at school in defence of younger boys, since he had always hated the cruel bullying that was part of a public school education, having suffered it himself, finally wore down his father and reconciled his mother. He had left the comfort and luxury of his home, spending six years of his life learning to become a member of the medical profession. He had worked in a very junior position in a great London hospital and had a brief spell abroad. He was a quiet man, gentle and patient with the frightened men and women who knocked on his door, often in the dead of night, his intellectual curiosity arousing in him certain radical ideas which would have infuriated his father had he known, but which led him to serve, not those with money in their pocket to pay his fees, but those who had not.

But Tom was by now settled in Duke Street, his own man and though he visited his family home, Rosemont House east of West Derby, for his mother's sake, attending the dinner parties she regularly arranged in her attempt to get him married to some suitable young lady of her choice, he lived his own life as he pleased.

It would not have been difficult for his mother to find him an agreeable, socially acceptable, well-brought-up and well-trained young girl to be his wife, for not only was he the wealthy son of an eminent Liverpool family but he was an extremely attractive young man. He was not handsome in the accepted sense of the fairy-tale prince variety but he was completely male, even slightly earthy, which was a throwback to the ancestor who had come, generations ago, from some dark, possibly Celtic race to make his way in the growing port of Liverpool. He was tall, long-boned, hard-muscled and his shoulders had broadened ever since he had been persuaded, against his mother's will, to take up boxing at school. He had a narrow waist and strong thighs, with long, shapely legs which were in exact proportion to his body. His azure-blue eyes glowed with health and humour and his strong, uncompromising young mouth had an endearing curl at each corner as though it would, at the slightest provocation, break into a wide grin. His skin was a warm amber, always freshly shaved and his dark hair curled crisply into the nape of his neck. He walked with the grace of an athlete which was not surprising, for he still spent time when he could at the Mechanics Institution in Mount Street where a gymnasium had been recently opened.

It was almost dark when he reached Duke Street, walking his bay, named Abigail but shortened to Abby, round the back of the houses to the stables where Jem, the stable lad, was waiting for him.

"Long day, Doctor?" Jem remarked laconically, clenching his pipe between his teeth. He and his missis lived above the stables with the little girl whose life Doctor Tom had saved when she was desperately ill with the morbid sore throat, or as it was correctly called, diphtheria. Sat up with her for two nights had Doctor Tom, for it was known that the disease could lead to heart failure. His little lass was only three and if there was anything Jem and his Sal could do, anything in this world, they'd do it for Doctor Tom. Jem didn't care what time of the night the doctor came home, he was always there to rub Abby down, to feed her and put her to bed, so to speak, and now, with another on the way, it was comforting to Jem and Sal to know that Doctor Tom would be there to give a hand if it was needed at the birth.

"Much as usual, Jem."

"Sleep well then."

"Thanks and goodnight, Jem."

"Night, Doctor."

Tom walked slowly round the building to his own front door, stopping for a moment to watch the changing colours in the sky. The sun had sunk below the roof-line of the houses opposite but the sky itself was turning to the palest lemon streaked with green. Outlining the houses on the other side of the small garden in the square, it was fast turning to beige and orange and as he watched it spread an arch of pure rose pink beyond the roof of the Custom House at the end of Duke Street. He stood on his doorstep and was mesmerised by the beauty of it, a beauty one did not expect to see in the smoke and grime, the pall from the thousands of chimneys that hung above the city of Liverpool. The sky over the river became violet, then turned slowly to the purple of a plum and as he watched the twilight glow a shooting star pricked its brilliance in a sweep beyond the river. There was a fragrance clinging to the air, that of the honeysuckle which had mysteriously attached itself about the trunk of an enormous horse chestnut tree in the garden. The tree must have been there when Liverpool was no more than a fishing village, he thought idly, since it would have taken hundreds of years for it to have grown to the size it was now.

He craned his neck to look directly above him to a strip of almost aquamarine that lay over his own roof and into his mind's eye drifted the soft beauty, the silken hair, the perfect figure of the amazingly lovely girl who had, to Aggie Wainwright's indignation, for this was *her* house, opened the front door to him this morning. Smiling, innocent – look at the way she had followed him from the house the other morning, unaware of the dangers she might encounter with an unknown male – innocent, yes, and yet mysteriously sensual, Betsy Pearce was the epitome of all male dreams. She had the power to make his heart beat faster and cause his trousers to tighten at his crotch and feel uncomfortably indecent, but though she came from working stock she was a good girl, a *decent* girl and must not be dallied with as he might dally with a willing girl from the lower orders.

He had just come from the house in Blackstock Street. He sighed deeply, for he knew he would soon have to tell the Pearce family that Fred Pearce was never going to recover from the injuries he had sustained in his fall from his boat. He had been legging it through the Foulridge Tunnel, Miss Pearce – Ally – had told him, before she went away, which meant walking the boat where the horse, Magic she said her name was, could no longer tow it. What an interesting life the boat people lived, he reflected and had it not been for the round he must make he would have liked to stay and talk to them. But with scores of overcrowded courts to visit, courts which were meant to house hundreds . . . he could not spare the time.

The older sister, the plain one was bright, intelligent, humorous and though she was obviously uneducated it seemed she read a newspaper whenever she could get hold of one and was surprisingly knowledgeable about national affairs, it seemed. She had read of the marriage of the Prince of Wales and Princess Alexandra of Denmark and was interested in the progress of the American War though she had to admit, she said, that she didn't understand it and could he explain to her the cause of the riots in Ireland. He would dearly have liked to sit and talk to this extraordinary young uneducated woman but her sister, looking quite the most sublime picture of woman-hood he had ever seen, would keep interrupting with childish remarks, with foolish chatter, which, he thought indulgently, she didn't know were foolish. With questions about his own family and position in what she liked to call "society". Did he live in a big house and how she would dearly love to live in a big house. Did he have brothers and sisters, or perhaps, widening her already enormous blue eyes, was he married? When he told her he wasn't she smiled that enchanting smile and lowered her extravagantly long lashes. She was what might be called ingenu-ous and had she been of his own class would have delighted his mother. It didn't seem to occur to her that he found what her sister said of interest. He drank the tea Mrs Wainwright put in his hand, as black as tar and probably just as lethal, and had pondered on the difference in the two sisters, one so plain, like a crystal-clear drink of water but bright, intelligent, wanting to learn, it seemed, the other the most glorious creature he had ever met with nothing in her young head but the frivolously enchanting, a sparkling and effervescent flute of champagne!

Ally, as she told him to call her, was to be away for several days, depending on what cargoes she and Jack could pick up, but when she returned he must find the courage to tell her – for who else could he talk to? – that though his injuries were healing nicely now her father was being properly nursed not only by his wife but by Mrs Wainwright, his mind seemed to be clouded. He could not say whether it would be permanent but even if it were not, he would never again be able to leap on and off a canal boat as he once had done.

He remained for several more minutes on the doorstep, knowing he must soon go inside, for Mrs Hodges, his cook and housekeeper, would have a meal waiting for him, but somehow the recollection of Ally and Betsy Pearce had unsettled him and he continued to idle about watching the trees and the sky darken. The lamps were lit in the windows of the houses opposite and in his own sitting-room window and, as though sensing him on the doorstep, his young retriever set up a hullabaloo on the other side of the door.

"What's ter do, daft dog?" he heard Mrs Hodges complain. She never called the dog by anything other than "daft dog" though his name was Blaze and when she opened the door, railing at him for "hanging about like some big, soft lad", he moved inside, warding off the rapturous welcome of the retriever who threatened not only to knock him down but carry him across the pavement on to the cobbled street.

"Any messages, Mrs Hodges?" he asked automatically as he handed her his hat and bag.

"When is there not, lad, but there's no need fer yer ter bother. Have yer meal. They can wait," she told him. "Never a minute's peace do they give yer, night and day, day and night, an' if yer ask me it's time yer told 'em so."

"Who is it, Mrs Hodges?" he asked patiently, for if she had her way she'd tie him to his chair until he ate the good food she cooked him.

"Never you mind. Summat an' nowt, I'll be bound."

"Who is it, Mrs Hodges?"

"Well, that lad from one o' them courts off Prussian Street. His lass 'as started and's havin' a difficult time of it, 'e ses, but yer know 'ow they exaggerate. Get yer meal inside yer an' then . . ."

But it did no good. "What time was this?"

"Eeh, I dunno, an 'our, 'appen, but, lad, another few minutes won't mekk any difference."

"Put it in the oven for me, there's a dear." And snatching his bag, which she still held in her hand, he was off, banging the door behind him.

"Eeh, I dunno," she said to the dog. "They'll kill the lad between 'em, and then what am I ter tell his mama. When did 'e last get a decent night's sleep, tell me that. No, yer can't, can yer." And the pair of them moved slowly and disconsolately up the hallway to the kitchen where Tom Hartley's dinner was spoiling.

Ally took to wearing Jack's shirt and trousers and an old wide-awake hat with a low crown and a wide brim that had once belonged to Aggie Wainwright's dead husband. Aggie's husband had worked in the office at the top of the locks that led down to Stanley Docks, an important job involving the receipts the canal boatmen handed in, those that told the canal owners to whom the tolls went, that their tolls had been paid and to add up their profits which were considerable. A good job which enabled him and Aggie to rent the decent house in Blackstock Street. They had neither of them been young when they married nor when their Albert, their only child, was born. Albert, who was now twelve, had been nine years old when Percy Wainwright had taken some fever from one of the thousands of sailors that flooded into Liverpool, come from some God-forsaken spot on the globe where such illnesses were common. "Sailor's town" Liverpool was called because of its huge population of seamen in transit so was it any wonder one of these nasty diseases crept ashore to smite her Percy, Aggie had grieved, but she was not a woman to go under, which was why she so admired young Ally, and with a child to see to she set about earning a living for them both and they had survived.

She did odd jobs here and there, a bit of cleaning in one of the big houses on the outskirts of town, once, when things were at rock bottom, in the laundry in Banastre Street, but it was her gift for making a home, a "home away from home" as she liked to call it, that had finally put her and Albert on their feet. Lodgers, seafarers, decent men who, though they liked a pint, never came home drunk or tried to introduce women of a certain sort into her rooms. Three to a bedroom at first, clean beds, one each, good, nourishing, plain food, and the feeling that they were at home with their own mothers who had scolded them and cherished them as she did. Not soft though, oh no, far from soft, for let one of them put a foot wrong and he was out so fast his feet didn't touch the ground.

She had a bit put by for a rainy day, as she called it, and when the Pearce family arrived on her doorstep she took them to her heart. There were three of them, for Ally and the lad slept on the canal boat when they were in Liverpool, so she was not out of pocket and her rent was paid without fail by Mrs Pearce into whose hand the lass, as Aggie always thought of her, put the money she and Jack had earned on their last trip. If only she could take to the other little madam, she often sighed, because she had come to enjoy having a woman in the house after the endless succession of seamen to whom she had given shelter over the last three years, but then you couldn't have everything, could you. But if Edie, as she had been told to call her, didn't watch out there was bound to be trouble with that there little minx. Talk about airs and graces. Why, only this morning she'd had the damn nerve to tell her, Aggie Wainwright, to put the kettle on while she sat on her bum in the parlour. And did she ever attempt to make her own bed? No, never, leaving her poor mam to do it for her and what's more, Edie let her get away with it. Ruined, she was and the way she made eyes at that young doctor was a disgrace and her mam should tell her so. Mind, the poor woman was out of her mind with worry over that husband of hers and could you blame her? Him all knocked about and mazed in his head not knowing where he was or, if she was any judge and Aggie Wainwright usually was, even who he was, poor sod. No, that lass in her trousers – oh, aye, Aggie was disapprovingly aware that Ally Pearce still wore the indecent garments – had her work cut out to keep their . . . well, she supposed it was called a business going.

But what else was she to do? Someone had to pay the rent and put food on the table and though she, Aggie, was sorry about it, she couldn't afford charity. She had Albert, a growing lad, to think of. She meant to make something of Albert, did Aggie. A decent job like her Percy once had and to do that he must have some schooling and every day he trotted off to the Mechanics Institute to learn English, writing, mathematics and, for an extra charge, chemistry and French. Pity about that lass though.

Ally worked the *Edith* up and down the Leeds and Liverpool all that summer, still wearing the trousers and shirt she had taken to when Pa had his accident. She and Jack and Davey, who had turned out to be a real find and worth every penny of the wage she paid him, though he had never set foot on a canal boat in his life, worked the boat like a well-rehearsed team. They carried sugar and turpentine, rice and olive oil, bales of cotton and heads of tobacco, dried fruit, boxes of oranges, wheat and oats, clean commodities, to Wigan and Blackburn, Accrington and Burnley: all the industrial towns of Lancashire and across the Pennines to Skipton, Keighley and Bradford and Leeds. On the return journey they carried the products of the textile trade, wool bales from Yorkshire, raw cotton from Lancashire, as well as finished goods.

She found, to her surprise, that not being as fussy as Ma on the domestic side – the boys were glad of anything to eat as long as it was hot and plentiful – she could spend more time as a man would, looking and bargaining for cargoes, also finding to her surprise that she was good at it, and since they were all three young and fit, worked longer hours. Well into the dark evenings sometimes, pushing on towards Leeds or Liverpool when, at dusk, other boats had tied up for the night. It was a risk, for the canal was without lights apart from the odd row of cottages that lined the route. They couldn't negotiate the locks in the dark, of course, but despite this they cut a great deal of precious time off the journey and Ally began to realise what a slow, pipe-smoking, plodding man her father had been. She had not the faintest idea what Pa had earned in the thirty-odd years he had been a canal boatman or where the profits had gone but she meant to find out. If it had been half as much as *she* made it was more than enough to feed and clothe his family, his horse and maintain his boat. He had always been generous with her and Jack and Betsy – especially Betsy who had demanded pretty gee-gaws at every market they could get to – but surely every penny he had made had not been spent. Pa was an old man at over fifty – she was not sure of his exact age – and had been content to sail placidly along knowing that when he was past it he had a son and at least one daughter to carry on his business, but Ally Pearce was not. How many times had she been ready to argue with her pa over taking some small risk, which she believed must be done in business, but he had always shut her up.

She would lie awake in the bed-hole that once Ma and Pa had shared, the boys screwed up somehow in the tiny slit of a cabin that had once been alive with Betsy's whining voice, and her head would be in a whirl of activity, darting from one possibility to another. Where was Pa's money, if he had any? How could she exploit this challenge she had been given to make more? Could she expand? The possibilities were endless and all these thoughts were kept alive by her need to shut out the vivid blue eyes that smiled at her in the dark. The eyes that smiled at her but which always moved on, coming to rest on the girlish love-liness of her sister. He had never really seen her, she knew that, for his eyes were full of Betsy but he had awakened some emotion in her that she had never before experienced. What was it that moved so strongly inside her whenever she thought of him, that made her want to spit and scratch at Betsy's smirking face and shout, "Look at me, look at me"? As thoughts like these invaded her head and prevented her from sleeping the sleep she so desperately needed, she welcomed her vague ideas for the expansion of her father's business.

Before she left the boat in the canal basin in Leeds Street and walked round the corner to Blackstock Street, she always changed from her trousers, waistcoat, shirt and jacket into the skirt and blouse, the bonnet and, as autumn and winter began to creep on them, the gansey her ma had knitted for her as she rocked peacefully at Pa's bedside.

It was November before she saw Tom Hartley again.

6

Betsy Pearce had never been so content with life and though she felt sorry for pa, naturally, who lay all day in bed, and for ma who was tied to him and his requirements twenty-four hours a day, she herself was as free as a bird. For the first time in her life she did exactly as she liked without check nor hindrance, for though Ma asked her where she was off to every time she left the house she barely listened to Betsy's answer. Well, don't be long, she would say, frowning with anxiety as she spooned something or other into Pa's mouth, which opened obediently like that of a child. Betsy had to turn away when Pa was fed, for the sight sickened her. He often dribbled, again as a child would, which offended Betsy's delicate stomach and she was glad to get away from him and from that Aggie Wainwright who looked at her as though she were something the cat had dragged in. Betsy wasn't used to being judged and she resented it from someone she thought of as beneath her in the order of things.

It had been touch and go at first. Betsy was the only one in the Pearce family who was not proud of being one of the boat people. She knew she looked very fetching in her boatwoman's bonnet, her pretty ruched and frilled blouse, her skirt and delicately embroidered white apron, but the outfit classed her as a *working* woman and more than anything she wanted to look like one of the elegant ladies who peopled Tom Hartley's world.

It was over her clothes that she crossed swords with Ma and for the first time in her life almost lost the battle. If Pa had not had a slight relapse during the night, that's what Doctor Tom called it, which necessitated calling him out, she knew she would never have won. Ma had been worried out of her mind, distracted, hanging over Pa, watching his every move lest he have another of the strange turns he had suffered and at first had scarcely seemed to hear Betsy's request from the open bedroom doorway.

"Ma, I need some money," she announced baldly and though Ma didn't look at her, Aggie, who was helping Edie turn Fred as the doctor had directed, did, her sharp eyes turning suspicious.

"What for?" she asked and at once Betsy took umbrage and went on the offensive.

"I weren't talkin' ter you," she snapped. "You're not me ma."

"No, an' if I was I'd fetch yer a clout that'd 'ave yer on yer knees. Can't yer see yer ma's busy?"

Betsy deliberately ignored her, crossing the room to touch her mother's arm, keeping her eyes averted from Pa's slack face.

"Ma, did yer 'ear me? I need some money ter buy some material from't market. Ally's back at th'end o't week an' Jack can fetch sewin'-machine an' I thought yer could run me up a couple o' frocks. I've got picshers in me bedroom. I'll run an' fetch 'em—"

"Can't yer see yer ma's gor enough on 'er plate," Aggie interrupted unwisely and though it could not be said that the vindictive expression Betsy turned on her alarmed her, for it took a great deal to alarm Aggie Wainwright and certainly not this narrow-eyed, sharp-mouthed little madam, she began to realise that to make an enemy of Betsy Pearce might be hazardous.

"Will yer keep out o' this, yer interferin' old busybody," Betsy began venomously and it was perhaps these last words that alerted Edie's frantic mind to the tense argument that was taking place beside her Fred. Fred needed peace and quiet and the devoted care she and Aggie, without whose support she could not manage since Betsy was far too delicate to help, provided or he would not survive. She had been aware for the past few moments of their Betsy pleading for something but her mind was on Fred. He'd been like this for weeks now, like a young baby not yet quite in control of itself, head lolling, arms and legs flopping, its movements jerky, and his poor bum sore on account of him filling the napkins she and Aggie put on him every few hours. Washing! She or Aggie were constantly at the dolly tub and the mangle and he depended on her for every morsel of food she put in his mouth. Her Fred! Her well-set-up, handsome Fred, or at least she had thought so, reduced to this and if it hadn't been for Aggie she'd have gone under. Apart from Fred's condition, which was bad enough, her whole way of life had been shattered into a thousand confused pieces. Even to sleep without the slapping of water and the gentle movement of the boat under her was an impossibility. To stop in *one* place, week in, week out was like being in a cage, tethered like some beast and only her own willpower, her love for Fred and her growing friendship with Aggie kept her sane.

But what was their Betsy babbling on about and, more to the point, what was Aggie answering?

"What?" she murmured, running her hand dementedly across her grey hair, then cupping it tenderly round her Fred's cheek. He seemed to look at her, she swore he did, and even tried to smile but Betsy pulled at her arm and she turned on her sharply.

"Wharris it, our Betsy?"

"Ma, I were askin' yer fer a few bob fer material ter mekk a new frock when Mrs Wainwright stuck 'er nose in where it don't belong an'—"

"Yer what?" Edie was incensed at the way Betsy spoke about Aggie who had been so good to them.

"Well, it's nowt ter do wi' 'er, is it? I mean what our family does. I'm not askin' 'er, am I? I'm not askin' 'er ter put 'er 'and in 'er pocket, am I? But honestly, Ma, I can't be expected ter go about like this, can I?" holding out her arms to indicate what a fright she looked in what she had on. How could she be expected to entice Tom Hartley to take her about, to the Music Hall outside whose doors she had lingered; to the park where fashionable ladies paraded and, most importantly, along Bold Street where the best shops were. And, a delicious thrill setting her veins on fire, to *Rosemont House* to meet the Hartley family. "I mean, what do I look like?"

"What d'yer look like? *What d'yer look like?* Yer look like a boatwoman, my girl, which is what yer are an' why yer should 'ave a face on yer like a thundercloud is beyond me. Anyroad, what yer talkin' about?"

"I want ter dress like ladies dress, Ma. I feel like a guy in this get-up. It's not much ter ask, is it? I promise when we get back ter't canal I'll wear proper clothes but until then I don't want folk starin' at me."

A shrewd move this, for no one knew better than Edie Pearce that they would never be boat people again. Not her and Fred and certainly not their Betsy.

"Oh, please, Ma, let me 'ave a few quid."

"It were a few bob a minute since." Aggie's voice was caustic.

Betsy whirled on her. "You keep outer this. It's between me an' Ma."

"Yer ma's gorr enough on 'er plate wi'out you mitherin' 'er, my lass."

But just at that moment, as though through the fog of his injuries Fred had heard the pleading in his little girl's voice, he made a harsh sound in his throat and Betsy, ever the opportunist, leaped on it, taking advantage of Ma's weakness.

"See, Pa wants me ter 'ave it, don't yer, Pa?" And overcoming her aversion she took Fred's hand in hers and lifted it to her rosy lips. "Look, Ma, Pa's smiling."

Because a moment ago she had thought the same thing herself, Ma sighed then smiled lovingly, not at Betsy but at Fred. "Pass me't box then."

Though they had known of its existence no one but Edie and Fred had ever seen the contents of the box. It had been carefully concealed in a secret locker on the *Edith*, brought out when Fred and Edie were alone. Now it was hidden under Fred's clean nightshirts in the top drawer of the tallboy in the bedroom allocated to them by Aggie Wainwright. It was here that Edie and Fred's documents, transferred from the ticket locker on the boat, were kept under lock and key.

Betsy put the box in her mother's hands, watching with avaricious eyes as Edie turned her back on both her and Aggie. The box was locked with a key which had hung round Fred's neck but was now hidden beneath the blouse Edie wore. The box had clinked mysteriously as it was passed from hand to hand, like the sound coins make when they are rattled, Betsy decided. She knew that when Ally came back to Liverpool cash was passed from her to Ma, all except the rent money which was given to Mrs Wainwright. Ma never went out but she was aware that Mrs Wainwright bought the food that Ma cooked on the kitchen range. In fact the two families, the Wainwrights and the Pearces, were slowly merging into one, for it seemed that both Ma and Mrs Wainwright agreed that to cook separately and eat separately was a waste of time and money. Pa came downstairs when Jack and Ally were in Liverpool, carried by Jack and Davey, sitting, or rather sprawling in front of the parlour fire. Giving him a change of scenery, Ma called it, as if he noticed in his daft state, Betsy thought, but what did she care. Her life lay elsewhere and when she'd got her new frocks and perhaps a bonnet or two she'd have Doctor Tom Hartley wrapped round her little finger.

"'Ow much d'yer reckon, Fred?" Edie asked automatically, for Fred was still the head of the family, then, realising, shook her head sadly. "Eeh, will yer listen ter me," she said vaguely.

"'Appen a guinea, Edie," Aggie answered for Fred. "That should buy some grand roll ends on St John's Market."

"A guinea! I told yer ter mind yer own business—" Betsy began furiously but her mother remonstrated feebly.

"That's enough, our Betsy." Edie could tell that Fred was becoming restless with all this chattering going on so, to Aggie's amazement and Betsy's delight, five golden guineas were thrust into Betsy's greedy hands, the key turned in the lock, the box returned to its hiding-place beneath Fred's nightshirts and Fred was gathered into Edie's loving arms.

It was an era of bold contrasting colours, magenta being named the "queen of colours". The cage crinolines had been replaced by a revival of the bustle which moved the bulk of the skirt to the back. There was also the introduction of the hitched-up "walking dress" enabling women to take active outdoor exercise. Not that Betsy was in the least concerned with that but she did like the idea of putting on view her slender ankles and dainty feet, showing off the coloured stockings that had become fashionable.

For days, with her five guineas sewn safely into the waistband of her skirt – she had abandoned her apron since she did not wish to be confused with a kitchen-maid – and with her pretty blue and cream shawl clutched tightly about her, she haunted the shops in Bold Street and its smart arcades, in Regent Street and Church Street, studying their Parisian – whatever that was – flowers and feathers, their blond lace, nets and ribbons, their parasols, their straw Leghorn bonnets, their gloves and fans, and the glowing folds of the fabrics artistically and discreetly displayed in the bow-fronted windows of the dress shops and milliners through the doors of which great ladies passed to and fro, stepping down from their carriages like queens. Which one day she would do! She was sensible enough to realise that as yet establishments such as the ones they entered were not for her, but give her time and in the meanwhile she had five guineas to spend.

Betsy, whose fragile loveliness, even with the woollen shawl about her silver-gilt hair, attracted attention wherever she went, knew instinctively what suited her and it was not the emerald green, purple, vivid blues and pinks, nor scarlet and orange which other ladies wore. She was not naturally shy, nor modest, lacking neither confidence nor the bold belief that she was as good as anyone. Her beauty had imbued in her from an early age the belief that given the proper clothes in which to go about, she could "go about" wherever she chose, and on the arm of Tom Hartley. But she had to start somewhere so, haughtily ignoring the amazed stares of the other shoppers who were, in the main, young housewives who made their own clothes, and knowing exactly what she wanted, she entered a rather smart haberdasher's in the Upper Arcade on the corner of Colquitt Street and Bold Street, demanding imperiously to be shown patterns for a "walking dress". Though she didn't say so to the assistant, she didn't need any indoor dresses, for who of importance would see her there? Even Tom Hartley thought her charming in her boatwoman's costume. It was the world *outside* Blackstock Street that she meant to impress, to dazzle, to shine in, to star in, to *conquer*.

Watched still by open-mouthed shoppers, by the almost speechless shop assistant and by the manageress who had been hurriedly brought from the back reaches of the shop, she carefully chose two patterns, aware that she had caused a minor sensation, for *shawled* women, *working-class* women, of whom they thought she was one, did not frequent an establishment such as this. But she was perfectly polite – did she not mean to be a lady? – and had money, a whole golden guinea to pay for her purchases, telling them she would be back to buy one or two other little things; besides which her smile was enchanting, her loveliness unique and they, as most were, even of the female sex, were stunned to silence.

Her next stop was St John's Market where, as Aggie had told her, there was a stall that sold fabrics of all descriptions from ends of rolls, some come from great dressmaking establishments such as Madam Lovell's of the House of Lovell in West Derby Road and the Misses Hawkins who "dressed" the fashionable wives of the wealthiest men in Liverpool.

The stall-holder, an elderly woman who catered to the sort of women Betsy had encountered in the haberdasher's, was patient at first as her radiantly beautiful young customer inspected every scrap of dress material on her stall, bowled over and therefore willing to show forbearance over the lass's minute scrutiny of her stock. To be honest she was afraid to take her eyes off her lest she turn out to be one of the dozens of thieves who haunted the market, slipping many an article under a shawl or into a deep pocket.

Women who had paused at her stall moved on, tired of waiting, and the stall-holder became irritable but Betsy would not be hurried. Twice more she went through the entire stock before she made her choice and the stall-holder watched her go, wondering who the devil she was and hoping to God she never saw her again since, through her, she had lost several sales in the past hour.

Still, she'd been a bonny lass and the material she had chosen had been of the very best. Delicate shades which would suit her delicate beauty, wondering on her own fancifulness before turning to a cheerful, stout, florid-faced country woman who wanted several yards of red and white checked gingham for a new dress. The contrast between her and her choice and that of her previous customer could not have been more startling!

After she, Jack and Davey had unloaded the bales of cloth from Blackburn and Darwen which were intended for the Indian market they had brought the *Edith* back up the locks from Stanley Dock and moored her where she was to remain until the following day when they were to return to pick up barrels of nails, tons of oak bark, eighty-two bales of flax, some fir timber and a dozen boxes of Irish glass.

The boys had gone off laughing and pummelling one another on the back over a job well done, as young men do, making for the pub. Fetching buckets of water from the barrel on the deck, she had closed the hatch door, stripped herself naked and scrubbed away every memory of the hard, sometimes dirty labour she had performed over the past fortnight. Even her hair was washed and brushed until it gleamed and in her best boat-woman's outfit, ironed with the box iron she heated on the small iron shelf that was attached to the front of the stove, she set off to walk to Blackstock Street. Not for a minute would she admit to herself that the extra care and attention she had lavished on her appearance had anything to do with a tall, lean man with piercing eyes of sapphire blue, but her pulses were racing faster than her own eager feet as she turned the corner of Vauxhall Road into Blackstock Street.

The house had been empty of all but Ma and Pa, glad to see her, at least Ma was, and they settled down in front of the kitchen fire, her eyes going constantly to the door that led into the narrow hallway.

When it finally opened, for the space of several moments she did not recognise the radiantly elegant young lady who entered Aggie's kitchen. Whoever she was she must have wandered by mistake not only into the wrong house but the wrong street, indeed the wrong district, for ladies did not step out of their world in the big houses on the outskirts of the city into the mean streets about dockland, but this one had.

Behind her was Tom Hartley.

" 'Ello, our Ally," the vision said casually, visibly pleased with the impression she had made. "When did yer get back?" She glided across the kitchen and sank down gracefully into Aggie's chair, peeling off her gloves which exactly matched the rich biscuit colour of the fine woollen dress she wore, then threw back some sort of short cloak which Ally later was to learn was called a "pelisse-mantle", this in a soft shade of cinnamon. She had on a bonnet, a wisp of cream straw, its brim edged in the same cinnamon as the cloak. It was known as a Leghorn, though naturally at the time, since Betsy had not yet boasted of it, Ally was ignorant of the fact, as she was of all the details of the clothes her sister wore, only that she looked quite glorious, her eyes gleaming beneath the bonnet's brim, which was tipped saucily over her eyebrows.

"Is there any tea in't pot, cos I'm fair clemmed. It don't 'alf give yer a thirst, walkin' on that there parade. In't that right, Tom?" She turned to Tom and smiled archly, and in Ally's heart, which had lurched at the sight of the tall figure at Betsy's back, something sweet and precious died. She barely had the faintest inkling what it was, only that it had taken root there on the day she had looked on the face of the tall figure of the man who had climbed down from his horse on the dock of the canal basin in June. She could feel the devastation of what seemed to be loss chill her blood, slowing her pulses to the sad beat of a funeral march and she was dragged down with a pain she did not understand.

She turned to stare at Ma who sat opposite her placidly sipping her tea. She had been up to see Pa who was asleep, and taking advantage of Pa's quietness Ma had come down with her.

"We'll 'ave us a brew while Aggie's out," she told Ally, just as though Aggie Wainwright begrudged them a cup of tea and they had to take advantage of her absence.

They had talked quietly, discussing Pa's progress, or lack of it; Jack who, thinking himself a man now, had gone to the pub for a pint without asking before coming to see his ma and pa;

the cargo Ally, Jack and Davey, who was proving a Godsend in his willingness to do the work of two men though but a lad himself, were to load on the *Edith* tomorrow. Ma had been astounded at the amount of money Ally had put into her hand, slipping upstairs to secrete it away in the box after counting out Aggie's rent which was placed beside the clock on the shelf above the range.

"Yer done well, our lass," Edie said to her daughter, "an' yer pa'd be proud of yer, an' our Jack. Yer work 'ard, I can see that an' . . . well, 'appen I shouldn't say it" – casting a sad glance at the ceiling to the room above where Fred slept – "yer mekkin' more money than yer pa did. 'E were a 'ard worker but 'e 'adn't the . . . the *need* in 'im that you 'ave an' so 'e liked ter tekk 'is time over things. We never went short, yer know that, but where money were concerned yer pa . . ."

Ally sat forward and took Ma's hand in hers. "That's what I wanted ter talk ter yer about, Ma."

Ma looked surprised. "What, money?"

"Aye, yer see I want ter . . . well, did Pa 'ave a few bob put away anywhere? Anything over, like, that 'e saved."

Edie Pearce drew back suspiciously, her mouth hardening; surely this one wasn't going the same way as the other, then her expression softened, for never had two sisters been less alike. The last six months had shown her that, if she had not been aware of it before. She loved that beautiful lass of hers and was filled with a great pride that she was hers but she hadn't the good heart this one had. Her mind went to the box into which, only half an hour ago, she had counted the money Ally had given her from the last trip, the box in which their Betsy took a great deal of interest. But that box was her – what would she call it? – her protection against a rainy day which surely had arrived. A bloody deluge, more like, that could drown the lot of them if she wasn't careful. Her security for the old age that was fast catching up with her and Fred. Ally and Jack were keeping the *Edith* afloat and doing nicely too, so they'd be all right and if they were careful, working in the way Fred had done, they'd not go under. Now here was their Ally, plain, hard-labouring, steadfast Ally asking about money.

It was at that moment that Betsy had entered the kitchen, mincing in the manner of some great lady, all done up like a fashion plate in the outfit Edie herself had sat up night after night making for her.

"Go on, our Ally, pour us a cup o' tea will yer? I'm done in an' I'm sure Tom wouldn't say no, would yer, Tom?"

Ally sprang to her feet, the colour flooding her face then draining away leaving it gaunt.

"Dear God in 'eaven, never mind damn tea, where did yer get that lot yer got on?" she cried, turning to stare accusingly at Tom Hartley, since he was the most likely person to have rigged their Betsy out like the grand lady she evidently thought herself to be.

Tom's face hardened, stabbing Ally to the core, for though he himself had wondered where Betsy had found the cash for the elegant outfit she wore when he took her walking on the Marine Parade, as she had begged him to do, it was evident from Ally's expression she believed he had supplied it. And if that was the case, what had pretty, artless Betsy given him in return?

He pushed himself away from the wall where he had been leaning, his face cold, his blue eyes, usually warm as the summer skies, turning to the icy hue of winter, hard and brilliant.

"I won't stay for tea if you don't mind, thank you, Betsy. I'll go and look at Mr Pearce" – which was the real reason for him being here in the first place – "then I must be on my way."

His eyes had softened again as they looked at Betsy, in them that longing that affected all men whenever they gazed at her exquisite and delicately breakable loveliness. He bowed his head courteously in the direction of Edie, then Ally.

"Mrs Pearce, Miss Pearce. No, don't get up, Betsy."

But Betsy had risen graciously, playing her part to the hilt as though, instead of a dock labourer's cottage kitchen, she were in the drawing-room of the great house in West Derby. Where, there was no doubt in her mind, one day she would be. Her, what she liked to call, in her own mind at least, "courtship" of Tom Hartley, though slower than she would have liked, was proceeding nicely. He had, so far, taken her walking on the Parade and on the paths between the flowerbeds of Princes Park; over the water on the ferry to New Brighton and to the Art Gallery where there had been an exhibition of some artist's work he admired. Don't ask her who, for she didn't care enough to remember. In fact she was bored to tears though she had kept it well hidden. She hadn't yet managed to get him to kiss her, which was her first goal, but then he was a gentleman, wasn't he? All he seemed to want to do at the moment was *look* at her and, apart from the arm he offered her as they walked side by side, had not yet touched her. But she had her plans!

After seeing him out she sauntered back into the kitchen, on her face a self-satisfied expression, like a cat deciding when to lap at the saucer of cream placed before her. She smiled smugly at her sister and did not even flinch as Ally hissed through clenched teeth.

"Would someone mind tellin' me what the devil's goin' on 'ere?"

7

"Are yer tellin' me that Ma give yer five guineas ter spend on dress material, then broke 'er back over 'er sewin'-machine ter mekk that flamin' get-up yer gorron. I can't believe it. 'Asn't she enough ter do seein' ter Pa wi'out spendin' all 'ours God sends trickin' you out like some damn—"

"An' why shouldn't she? Just because you don't mind goin' about like some kitchen-maid wi' yer apron an' yer cap, don't mean ter say I do. This gown, that's what they call it, norra *frock*" – preening herself like a member of the royal family who was about to take her place at court – "cost no more'n a guinea an' me other one—"

Ally was aghast, leaping to her feet in fury. "Yer mean yer've more'n one?"

She turned to Edie who was wringing her hands by the door that led into the passage, ready to escape upstairs to her Fred who was at least quiet and where peace of a kind might be found. She had never seen Ally in such a temper. Normally she was cheerful, good-humoured, content with her lot, happy to help her family, which included Betsy, loyal and trustworthy. Now she was incensed as though the money Edie had given Betsy had been thrown away on frivolities, which she supposed it had. But would you look at their Betsy! See her walk down that smart street in town she was always on about – Edie couldn't remember its name only that it impressed their Betsy – and you'd take her for a lady. A real lady. That there doctor evidently thought so, for he was never off the doorstep and Edie couldn't think of anything more suitable, more *safe*, than their Betsy married to a respectable man like him. She knew nothing about his family, since he never talked about them, imagining some decent folk in a . . . well, to be honest she hadn't the faintest idea what sort of a house folks lived in, of any sort, since she had never been inside one, only Aggie's. But Doctor Tom seemed a well-set-up sort of a chap and would look after her little girl, since there was nothing more certain than that her little girl couldn't look after herself. Not like their Ally.

"Ma, what were yer thinkin' about? Givin' this . . . this scatterbrain fool five guineas. She's nowt but a child wi'out the brains she were born with. D'yer know what we could 'a bought wi' that five guineas? Fodder fer Magic fer a whole—"

"That's all yer think about, our Ally. If it's not ter do wi' damn boat it don't exist. Well, let me tell yer I mean ter be more than some drudge sailin' up an' down't cut fer't rest o' me life. Me an' Tom . . ."

Betsy's voice, though it was loud, piercing, challenging, faded away to a bird twittering that drifted about Ally's head in some sort of mist which thankfully allowed her, for the space of a minute or so, to escape it. She was still nailed into place by that furiously contemptuous look Tom Hartley had directed at her when it must have seemed to him that she was accusing him of wrong-doing with Betsy. Now that she knew where Betsy had got the money she was ashamed of herself for believing that an honest, upright *gentleman* such as Tom Hartley would interfere with a virtuous girl like Betsy. The look he had thrown her, his polite bow, his use of her surname had knifed her already wounded heart, and the sadness she realised she would always know, no matter what the future brought, settled about her. Her love, she admitted it now, would never die and not only that, she was to live with him in her life as the husband of her sister, if what Betsy was implying was true. She had wanted to scream, hit out at something, preferably Betsy, who was to have the only man who had ever awakened the smallest feeling in Ally Pearce's heart and she couldn't stand it, but she must. She must dismiss him, she told herself, get on with her life, her dreams, the plans that spun round in her head the moment it hit the pillow. But would she ever get over it, accept it, or would she be afflicted with this injury to her heart and mind for the rest of her life? The answer to all the questions must be "yes".

She had known in her mind, which was sensible, practical, *realistic*, what was in Tom Hartley's when he looked at Betsy. He couldn't hide it, didn't try to hide it, and could you blame him? Could you blame any man, who didn't know her true character, self-centred, self-willed, vain and cunning, for being pole-axed by Betsy's sweet comeliness? A joy to look at, sending the senses of all men reeling, inducing in them a feeling of wonder. Frail, submissive – to the outward eye – and yet as hard as concrete in her heart. Strong she was, greedy and manipulative: look at the way she had had Ma and Pa in her thrall since her birth and if she had set her sights on Tom Hartley, which it seemed she had, Tom, poor fool, never stood a chance. No matter what she herself did, making the most of what God had given her, he wouldn't look at Ally Pearce. She was a woman in the true sense of the word. She would have worked her fingers to the bone to advance Tom Hartley, for like her mother she had no idea of his family's background. She would have made a good doctor's wife – dear God, would you listen to her – for, unlike Betsy, she *cared* about people. There was only one person Betsy cared about and that was Betsy. And Betsy was to have him.

Her heart was breaking and she knew if she turned to Betsy her devastation would have shown in her face for Betsy to see, to gloat over, to laugh about. Hastily she picked up the brass poker and gave the fire a vicious poke, allowing herself another moment to bury her emotions in the hidden depth of her shattered heart. Ma still dithered at the kitchen door, turning with relief when the street door opened and Aggie came in, her shopping basket on her arm, her deep black bonnet shadowing her cheerfully smiling face.

"Oh, Aggie," Edie moaned. Edie Pearce, once as strong and cheerful as Aggie, had been weakened disastrously by Fred's accident and the woman who had once lovingly controlled her husband and children and the activities on board the narrow-boat couldn't seem to cope with what was going on in the kitchen, never mind in her life.

"What's up, lass?" Aggie hurried along the passage, then stopped abruptly at the sight of "madam" as she privately called Betsy, smirking and posturing in *her* kitchen like a bloody duchess, treating her poor demented ma to all sorts of tantrums, and now it appeared she and Ally were facing each other like two cats in an alley.

"Well, lass, if yer've spent five guineas on new clothes," Ally was hissing, "yer can damn well earn it. Yer comin' wi' me an' Jack termorrer an' until I reckon yer've paid Ma back that money yer wheedled out of 'er, that's where yer'll stay. An'—"

"Is that so? Well, yer can go ter 'ell, Ally Pearce," Betsy sneered. Ally had moved menacingly forward as Aggie entered the room and she and Betsy were face to face, no more than six inches separating them. "I'm goin' nowhere, see, until I marry Tom Hartley."

"Tom Hartley! Tom Hartley'd no more marry you than 'e'd marry Aggie 'ere," wishing she believed it. "No disrespect to Aggie but Tom Hartley's a gentleman an' yer've only ter open yer mouth, our Betsy, to realise yer no lady. Oh, I dare say yer look the part done up in that outfit yer've gorron but no one'd be tekken in by 'em an' let's be quite clear, them's the last. There's ter be no more. It seems Ma an' Pa 'ave gorra bit put by. They must 'ave ter fork out five bloody guineas an' if they 'ave then I've some ideas of me own on 'ow it's ter be spent. D'yer understand?"

"'Ave yer, oh, 'ave yer? Let me guess. Yer gonner spend it on that soddin' boat."

"Betsy, lass," her mother wailed.

"I'll not 'ave language in my 'ouse," Aggie began but the two incensed sisters didn't hear either Aggie or their mother, or if they did, chose to ignore them.

"As it 'appens, fer once yer right. There's money ter be made on't canals which Pa didn't take advantage of. But I mean to. The Leeds and Liverpool passes through one o't most 'eavily populated areas in't land where manufacturin' tekks place an' it's not tied to any one particular trade nor traffic neither. There's coal, wool, cotton, limestone, grain, general cargo—"

"What do I care about that?"

"No, burr I do. Though the railways 'ave tekken over in some ways the canal companies 'ave come out on top, beatin' off the railways' rivalry by bein' more competitive, more efficient and quicker on some routes. An' while it lasts I'm gonner get my share. I've bin readin' . . ."

Betsy yawned and turned to look at Aggie as if to say had she ever heard such nonsense, but Aggie was looking at her sister with growing interest and respect.

"Anyone wi' foresight will get ahead. And expansion's the key but it needs money, capital, and let me tell yer that yer gerrin no more from Ma, Betsy Pearce, d'yer 'ear? I do t' work in this family an' what I earn, I spend so—"

"Ma'll decide that, not you." Betsy had no idea what "foresight" meant and besides, they had lived, at least in her opinion, a hard, poor life on the boat and the idea that Ally could make more money than Pa was laughable. She had no idea what was in Ma's box but with Ally off up the canal and Ma easily handled she meant to find out and treat herself, who had never known treats before, to her heart's content. "She's in charge o't box—"

Instantly Ally's eyes narrowed and Betsy knew she had made

a mistake. In the doorway the two women watched, Edie with anguished apprehension, Aggie with growing triumph.

"What box?" Ally asked quietly, though of course she knew of its existence.

"It's nowt ter do wi' you," Betsy shrieked but Aggie stepped forward, putting her hand on her arm. Betsy was so amazed she fell silent for a moment. Aggie put her basket on the table, removed first the hatpins that held her bonnet in place, then the bonnet with great deliberation, pushing the hatpins into the crown. She placed it next to her basket on the table and they all waited for her to speak.

She smiled at Ally. "Yer ma's gorra box in a drawer, in't that right, Edie?" turning to Edie who nodded. "Now I know it's none o' my business—"

"Yer right there, yer daft old woman," Betsy began to shrill, but Aggie's smile only deepened with what seemed to be great satisfaction.

"But since you an' your Jack are't breadwinners now," she went on, "it seems ter me yer should be . . . well, be in't charge o't funds. Yer mam 'as enough ter do lookin' after yer pa an' would right gladly 'ave the responsibility o't . . . management tekken over by you. In't that right, Edie?" Aggie again turned to Edie and with a compassion, a sweetness which spoke of how highly she regarded this new friend she had made, took her hands in hers. "You an' Fred 'ave a few bob purr away, 'aven't yer, queen?"

Edie nodded again and Betsy began to fill the kitchen with her wailing.

"Well, yer know your Ally'd allus look after yer, don't yer?"
Edie nodded for the third time.

"Yer trust 'er?"

Edie began to smile and she relaxed. "Oh aye, I would that."

"Well then, fetch that box an' give it to your Ally then we'll 'ave a brew."

Betsy sprang forward. "No, I won't 'ave it, Ma. Why should our Ally tekk it all? She'll only chuck it inter't cut."

Aggie moved Edie gently into the passage and led her to the foot of the stairs. "You go an' sit wi' your Fred, lass, an' I'll fetch yer both a drink o' tea. Build up fire cos it's turned real cold out. Now, off yer go an' me an' Ally'll be up in a minnit. We've a few things ter clear up." One of them being the shrieking vixen who was ready to tear her hair out at the awful possibility that Ally and not herself was to benefit from whatever Ma and Pa had in the box.

Ally watched her, her face expressionless, but inside where no one could see or hear was the wonder of the simple elegance of the dress Betsy wore. She could hardly believe that Ma had made it. Naturally she was used to the outfits her mother had "run up", as she called it, for the three of them as boatwomen. The skirts and blouses, pintucked and frilled, the exquisitely embroidered aprons they had taken for granted, the intricate bonnets and the spiderweb belts, not to mention the more mundane shirts, trousers and waistcoats she had fashioned for Pa and Jack. But Betsy's new dress was a miracle of crafts-manship and though Ally knew nothing of the prevailing fashion she was sure the dress was as stylish and up to date as any in Liverpool. Betsy would have made sure of that. Several times when Ally had been back in Blackstock Street she had seen Betsy poring over a magazine in which the latest fashions were illustrated, beside her Aggie's son Albert, her willing slave, reading the words to her, thrilled to be so close to his idol.

The bodice and skirt was cut in one without a seam at the waist, fitting flawlessly and in Betsy's case needing no corset to keep it at eighteen inches. It had a square neckline which revealed the top swell of Betsy's white breasts edged with a creamy lace frill which was repeated at the wrist in what was known as a peg-top sleeve, gathered at the shoulders but tight below the elbow. The front of the skirt was flat, ungathered, the material drawn back to a small bustle down which a waterfall of cream lace frills cascaded. It was a marvel of graceful, tasteful elegance and how Ma had contrived it was a miracle. To match the warm biscuit colour Betsy had on cream kid boots with high heels, bought from a market stall and far too small for her but that was a small price to pay as she tripped about town on Tom Hartley's arm.

"Now then, settle down, me lass, unless yer wanner feel the flat o' me 'and about that pretty face o' thine," Aggie said conversationally to Betsy. "I'm not right pleased ter see yer ma upset like this so yer'd best—"

"Sod off, yer interferin' old busybody. It's nowt ter do wi' you what we do in our family and when Ma comes down I'm gonner—"

The slap which rocked Betsy's head on her neck made Ally wince but she found she really could not care one way or the other. The small success she had made on the narrowboat had fired her with the enthusiasm to expand, for the truth was on her last journey she could have picked up and carried more cargo than the *Edith* could manage. With another boat, one of the new "compartment" boats to carry coal which she had heard some clever engineer was proposing, even passenger boats, the possibilities were endless, and what about *steam* power! Fly boats towing two or three "dumb" boats. And then there was boat-building! Why should not a woman be as involved with commerce as men were? She had come across some tricky situations over the last six months since she and Jack had taken her father's place on the *Edith*. The men with whom she dealt had looked askance at the sight of a woman trying to do business with them, and not only a woman but one who was indecently dressed.

"Gerron wi' thi'," they had bellowed, "an' fetch tha' pa. Ah know 'im an' I'm prepared to let 'im carry me woollen goods ter Liverpool but I'm damned if I'll do business wi' a lass. Gerron back ter yer boat an' tell yer pa . . ."

"Me pa's 'ad an accident," she tried to explain but the manager of the mill was not to be pacified.

"Well, I'm sorry to 'ear that but I'm not dealin' with a woman."

And so, wearing her hat pulled down to the tops of her ears and with the brim resting on her eyebrows, her short curls tucked well up inside, she had been forced to let Jack do the bargaining for a cargo. It had often turned into a comical three-sided affair, for Jack had no head for figures, for getting the best out of a deal and the man with whom they were trying to make terms was often baffled by Jack's constant need to turn to his "brother" for instructions. Even so they had managed to strike a lucrative bargain and perhaps for the first time in her life she had been glad of her own lack of curves beneath the over-large gansey she wore. They had sailed up and down the Leeds and Liverpool Canal picking up what cargoes they could, the biggest being coal, for everyone, everywhere, wanted it. It was used to burn limestone, evaporate brine, brew beer, fire pottery, for domestic purposes and if a certain cargo was not available, there was never a shortage of demand for coal-carrying. It was a dirty cargo, mostly carried by coal boats which dealt with nothing else but Ally was prepared to carry anything that paid a return. It would take a full day for three men, one of them herself, to unload a boat with sixty tons of coal aboard, two shovelling and one wheeling and tipping, but the *Edith* could hold no more than thirty-two tons, and managed it in half a day, which was one of the reasons Ally was gripped by the idea that with an extra boat, perhaps just a longboat carrying coal from Wigan to Liverpool, she could expand into calling herself a "carrying company".

Aggie and Betsy were still bickering, if you could call Aggie's firm admonishments and Betsy's shrill complaints by that name. Ally stood up, stretching her back and squaring her shoulders, glancing idly about her as though she had never seen the inside of Aggie's kitchen before. It was November, the winter afternoon drawing to its close and the room was dim but for the flickering light of the good fire Aggie always kept.

On the wall a likeness of Percy Wainwright looked down sternly, his chin propped on a stiff collar, his bowler hat clasped in one hand across his chest. He wore fierce side whiskers and a moustache but the photographer had somehow caught the kindness in his small eyes. On each side of him was an incongruous picture of puppies and kittens, bought by Aggie from the market, for she had thought them quite charming though she herself would not have used such a word. On the dresser opposite the range was stacked Aggie's collection of best English stoneware, serviceable and, in Aggie's opinion, as pretty as the puppies and kittens: dinner plates, tea cups and saucers, side plates, vegetable tureens and a gravy boat. And on the wall beside the range set on shelves were her frying pan, baking dishes, roasting tin, saucepans of every size and all the equipment necessary to "knock up" what Aggie considered a decent meal. Above the range was a shelf and from it hung six inches of frilled pelmet dangling small chenille pom-poms. On the shelf sat a slow-ticking clock of bronze with a hand-painted porcelain dial given to Percy by his employers on the occasion of his marriage to Aggie. He had been well thought of, had Percy.

The round table in the centre of the room surrounded by six ladderback chairs, two of them occupied by Aggie and Betsy, was covered with a red chenille tablecloth to match the pelmet above the range. Everywhere something bright and highly polished twinkled; candlestick holders, a tea caddy, tongs and a poker next to the hearth, a fender and a handsome coal scuttle. Looking out into the back yard was a window across which at night thick red woollen curtains were drawn. The flagstones on the floor were a mix of what had once been buff, beige, dark red, blue and grey but scrubbed until their colours had almost gone. In front of the range was a hooked rug and what Aggie called her "tuffet" on which, at the end of the day, she rested her tired feet.

Watched by Aggie and Betsy, Ally moved slowly to the scullery window, staring out into the gloom to where Albert was briskly shovelling coal into a bucket. Good to his mam, was Albert. There was an outhouse of sorts where the coal was kept and a barred gate which led into a back alley. The gate was kept locked, for not all the inhabitants of the area were as honest as Aggie and the coal was a great temptation to those not as well set up as the Wainwrights.

There was a noise at the door that led from the kitchen to the passage and all three women turned to watch as Edie Pearce slipped into the room. Under her arm was a wooden box and Betsy was seen to sit up eagerly. Ally watched as her ma took a key from a bit of string that was hung round her neck and, looking directly at Ally, she put the key in the lock and turned it.

With great deliberation, still looking at Ally as though this concerned her and no one else, she tipped the box upside down and from it the savings of thirty years fell on to the red cloth in a golden, tinkling shower of coins.

Tom Hartley rode his mare towards Duke Street through the stream of traffic which did its best to hinder his progress along Dale Street, everybody, it seemed, bent on some important errand of their own which brooked interference from no one. Though it was late afternoon postmen wearing the smart livery of cut-away coats and waistcoats were on their last delivery. An assortment of street musicians filled the already cacophonous air with their penny whistles, their accordions, drums and mouth organs and along the street vehicles of every description vied with one another for what they considered to be their rightful place. Coachmen swore at barefoot urchins who darted on street corners in the pursuit of their trade which was sweeping the street of the accumulated detritus of horse droppings. There were carriages from the aristocratic splendour demanded by ladies in which to visit their dressmaker, their milliner, to the simple gigs brought in from the country by the wives of tradesmen, drays hauled by massive, patient shire horses and loaded with goods going to or coming from the docks, smart barouches driven at reckless speed by men about town, and men on horseback like himself who were in danger of their lives and injury to their animals among the mad mêlée.

Tom scarcely noticed. He was accustomed to it, for did not he deliver himself into its bustle every day of the week, but as he guided Abby expertly along Dale Street and into Castle Street his mind was not on where he was going but on where he had just come from. Tom Hartley was in a quandary. Tom Hartley was in love though as yet he could not quite bring himself to admit it, for he did not wish to be in love, at least not with Betsy Pearce. He was a doctor and his need was for a sensible wife who would support him in his chosen career, accept the fact that his and her time would not be their own. He was fetched out to what he called his "work people" day and night, for illness, a difficult birth, the needs of a feverish child did not happen neatly between the hours of nine o'clock in the morning and five o'clock in the afternoon. Sometimes his bed was not slept in for several nights in a row, Mrs Hodges finding him some mornings in an exhausted state, sprawled in an armchair having been too tired to climb the stairs to his bed. He needed a wife who would accept his work, his hours, his patients. He needed a wife who would be concerned with the dangerous state of the houses thousands lived in, the safety of the water they drank and the quantity provided, which was not enough in the back streets, the courts and tenements where they were crammed. He, and men like him, abhorred the overflowing swill tubs in places like Naylors Yard and Maguire Street where disease was rife, where there were rotting garbage heaps and the drinking of contaminated water was common; the woman he married must share his concerns. A sensible woman then, and a woman of whom his family would approve which, he thought ruefully, would not be the case if he took the daughter of a canal boatman home, no matter how beautiful she was.

He had been as shocked as her sister when he saw her in the tastefully elegant outfit she had worn for the first time last week, made, unbelievably, by her own mother. He was aware that should she be invited to one of his mother's soirées the guests, ladies all of them, would have been enchanted with her sweet modesty, her submissively downcast eyes, her artless attempts at conversation, which would be quite acceptable to them for their own daughters knew nothing of the world and were expected to be interested in embroidery, a little painting in watercolours and playing a sweet tune on the piano. Her ignorance would have been thought delightful, her manners charming, a perfect young lady of their own class . . . until she opened her mouth to speak! He himself thought her broad-vowelled northern pronunciation of the spoken word quaint and the humorous idioms she used amused him. He had heard Mrs Wainwright mutter something about "peas above sticks" which meant that Betsy had ideas above her station, but what was wrong with trying to better oneself? he asked himself.

God, he wanted her! When she looked up at him with her clouded blue-green eyes, her face as sweet and delicate as rare porcelain, her silver-spun curls tied with a knot of ribbon to match her new gown, it took all his control not to sweep her into his arms and kiss her pouting, rosy lips until she allowed him the ardent liberties he longed to take. How innocent she was, unaware of how she affected him when she arched her back and her lovely rounded breasts peaked against the fine wool of her bodice. She had no idea of what she was doing to him as she peeped admiringly up at him from beneath her long, fine lashes, her small, gloved hand clinging in the crook of his arm, her breath sweet on his cheek. He felt like a god and yet that wasn't true, for he wanted her as a man wants a woman. Was her skin as fine and white beneath her clothing, he wondered, were her breasts as smooth and full, the nipples pink and hard, as he imagined them when he lay sleepless and restless in his bed at night? She affected him deeply, like no other woman had before. She was slender, graceful, but he knew that she would be womanly in her nakedness which he ached to uncover . . . Dear sweet God, how did he know, he only guessed and if he didn't find out soon he would go mad. He must have her. He *must* have her but though she was from what his mother would call the lower orders, she came from a decent family and only marriage would do for them.

He sighed, bowing his head in the thin slick of rain that began to fall as he turned into Duke Street.

8

"Yer'd best get yer pa to 'ave a look at 'er, Miss Pearce. He knows a good deal when 'e sees it"

"An' so do I, Mr Bridges. Besides, Pa's ill."

"Aye, I 'eard he 'ad an accident leggin' it through Foulbridge but I'd no idea he were still poorly. I'm right sorry."

Oh yes, all these men with whom she tried to do business, were all sorry about Pa, but their sympathy did not extend to being of service to his daughter. Time and time again during the last nine months she had had to fight tooth and nail to wrest a cargo from a manufacturer or merchant and if she had not had Jack to stand in for her the family in Liverpool would have been in dire straits. It was funny really, though she didn't laugh at the time, for they all knew, the managers of the woollen mills, the cotton mills, the collieries, the brickworks, that she was number one on the *Edith*, that Jack and Davey took their orders from her, but as long as she recognised her place, which was that of a woman, a boatwoman, true, but a woman nevertheless, and did not try to bargain with them, they were happy to do business with her, through Jack. She was aware that Pa's reputation as a reliable, conscientious honest boatman with over thirty years' experience of the Leeds and Liverpool, the trade and his connections with manufacturers and merchants at one end and the shippers at the other, followed him and so far since his accident his "lad", for she didn't count, had never let them down.

And she had done well, adding to the money which was

mounting in what was called Ma's box. Sometimes she wished she knew what to do with it until the time came for her to buy the new boat or at least a decent second-hand one. She knew nothing of banking, or investments which she had read about in the newspapers she picked up along the way but which were a mystery to her, for it struck her that the money in Ma's box could be put to a better use than nestling in a drawer in Aggie's room. She had been reluctant to take such an amount with her on the canal and to leave it where Betsy could get her hands on it was tantamount to chucking it in the cut. If only she and Tom Hartley were on better terms. She was sure he would have advised her on the best place to put it, but ever since that day last November when he had taken offence over her unspoken accusation that he had supplied Betsy with her new outfits and had been rewarded for it in the only way a woman can reward a man, they had been no more than coolly polite with one another. His eyes followed Betsy about the room, and Ally was well aware that she moved from here to there and back again with the sole purpose of having him look at her swaying, slender figure, the thrust of her high breasts, which naturally he did. He still kept up the pretence that he had called to keep an eye on Pa, but they all knew, sadly, that Pa would never recover and that Tom's calls, as a doctor, were no longer needed. Pa was fed, washed, even *talked* to by Aggie, Edie and Albert, who read to him from his own story books, but it was obvious that daily Pa was slipping away. The front parlour had been abandoned and each day, Ma, Aggie and Albert carried him down to the kitchen, propping him in a chair by the fire, much to Betsy's disgust which she managed to keep hidden, for it was hardly the place for Tom and her to do their "courting" as she liked to describe it, not with Pa dribbling in his nest of blankets by the hearth. Each time Ally came back to Liverpool she half expected Tom to have declared himself but so far he had not done so. Ally was not aware of the struggle Tom Hartley was having between his own consciousness of his class and that of the Pearces, and his escalating desire for the body of Betsy Pearce.

Ally was dressed in the full glory of her boatwoman's outfit, her riot of curls which she'd kept cut short hidden beneath her pretty bonnet. If she had been in his company for any other purpose than to do business with him, Arnold Bridges would have been charmed with her. He had seen her on the *Edith* a time or two, staying modestly beside her mother and sister while Fred Pearce consulted him about a minor repair to his canal boat, and now here was the little madam addressing him, as bold as you please and looking around his yard as though she were any other customer. A male customer!

The boatyard was busy. Bridges of Burnley was a small yard but it had a reputation for a good standard of work and honest dealing. It took two to three months to build a boat, employing two craftsmen, two labourers and an apprentice full-time but should some urgent repair work come in all other work at the yard would stop for a few days and all available men would help. Bridges was not the only boatyard on the canal, some of them so small they varied their work as carpenters and blacksmiths to the local community, others big companies which built and repaired only their own boats.

A boat had been pulled out sideways on to a slipway and two men were involved in caulking her joints. There could be half a mile of joints on one boat alone requiring many strands of oakum to make it properly watertight. But not much work was being done on it at the moment, nor on any of the jobs on hand as the men employed glanced at her from beneath the peaks of their caps, nudging one another and grinning widely. It was a male-dominated, male-operated business and from the first, as she stepped from the deck of the *Edith* on to the towpath which ran along the length of Mr Bridges' boatyard, she had been conscious of the men's amazement, with their adzes, drawknives, caulking irons and augers suddenly stilled in their hands. Some watched her curiously, others with undue familiarity, for surely a lass who came into their domain could not be respectable. Like the gentry, they kept their women apart from the rough and tumble of the workplace where other men might eye them with the insolence they themselves were directing at the boatwoman. One even moved forward, ready to direct her away from the yard, thinking she had wandered in by mistake, but she had smiled and asked for Mr Bridges. They were all sturdy North Country men, wearing cloth caps, shirt sleeves rolled up, cord trousers and heavy hobnailed boots, but their disapproving expressions said they did not care to have a woman in their workplace.

"I'm lookin' fer a boat, Mr Bridges," she told him casually, just as she might ask for a pound of best butter.

"A boat, Miss Pearce?"

"Aye, a boat. You 'ave such a thing, don't you?" Smiling at him as a mother might smile at a puzzled child whom she was doing her best to enlighten.

"But yer pa already 'as a boat." He turned his head to stare in consternation to where the *Edith* was moored.

"True, but there's no law ses 'e can't 'ave another, is there, Mr Bridges?"

"Yer mean yer pa wants ter sell the *Edith*?"

"Oh no, we're just . . . expanding."

"Yer what!" Mr Bridges' face assumed a truculent expression, for he hadn't time to waste on some daft girl. He looked about him, moving his head as though troubled by a cloud of midges, glaring at the men within earshot who had all downed tools and stood listening, their expressions as bewildered as his.

"Yes, I want another boat, new or second-'and depending on t' price. I'm not sure whether you—"

"Now look 'ere, young woman, I've 'ad enough o' this nonsense. You comin' in 'ere asking for a boat as though it were a bloody bonnet." Mr Bridges didn't approve of swearing in front of a female but this one was enough to try the patience of a saint. Every man was standing about and watching as though it were a damn peepshow and not one doing a hand's turn and her as calm as you please, looking about her as though choosing a boat among those being built on the wharf next to the canal was a tricky decision.

"'Ow much fer a new boat, Mr Bridges?" she suddenly asked, walking slowly towards two men who were caulking a boat on the slipway, one evidently almost ready to be launched. He had no option but to follow her, though his inclination was to pick her up and dump her in the bloody canal. The men who had picked up their caulking irons, thinking the fun was over, stepped back hastily as she ran her hand across the new wood.

"Clinker construction," she murmured absently and the men, including Arnold Bridges, exchanged wondering glances. "A fine boat," she went on. "Is she for sale?"

Mr Bridges had had enough. "No, she bloody well isn't," he bellowed, so incensed he would not have let this cheeky madam have the boat if she *had* been on offer, which she wasn't! "The Leeds and . . . Sweet Jesus, what the 'ell am I bletherin' on about?"

"I don't know, Mr Bridges. But if yer too busy ter build me one like 'er, I'll tekk me business ter Bank Hall in Liverpool. Mr Banks 'ad one, some chap gone bankrupt so order were cancelled. Two hundred pounds 'e wanted fer 'er an' I were tempted but your reputation . . ."

"If yer pa wants a boat built ask 'im ter come an' see me. Ter send a lass to do man's job just isn't right. Tell him I can build him a boat, or 'e could 'ave a look at that one there," nodding in the direction of the narrowboat that was having some repairs done to her hull by a couple of men. They were hammering oakum made by the inmates of Burnley Gaol from old rope or sacking teased out into yarn and moistened with oil. The men had already hammered the oakum into place with a caulking mallet and iron. When they had finished the seams had been sealed with pitch to hold the oakum in place and the hull would be painted with tar.

Ally, unconcerned by Mr Bridges' fury, wandered across the littered yard to watch the men who began to apply the tar. They were both embarrassed, not at all sure whether to stop and touch their caps to her, or carry on. Their employer had a face on him like a ripe plum and they could see he longed to order the lass off his premises as he would any trespasser, but she was a female and he could hardly lay hands on her, could he?

"I'm interested in this 'un, Mr Bridges. How much are you askin' fer 'er?" she asked pleasantly.

"Miss Pearce, 'ow many times 'ave I ter tell yer," he began through gritted teeth. 'I don't do business wi'—"

"I know, a woman, not even if she's t' cash in 'er 'and so ter speak. Let me an' me brother go over 'er, an' if she suits yer'll 'ave money in yer pocket within the 'our."

"*If she suits!* Let me tell yer that's a fine boat. Belonged ter Wigan Coal and Iron Company. They're goin' in fer steam so they're getting rid o' 'er."

"That's what I mean ter do, Mr Bridges, when time's right. Steam, but in't meanwhile I'm interested in this 'un. So name yer price."

It was probably Jack's presence that finally brought about the change in Arnold Bridges' attitude. It could not be said he became genial but at least he was prepared to listen to Ally's offer, through Jack of course, and after a certain amount of bargaining the *Harmony* as Ally named her, was registered in the name of the company.

"What company?" Mr Bridges asked suspiciously.

"Me family's company."

"Oh aye, and what might that be?"

"Pearce and Company, of Liverpool."

"So, is yer Pa ter 'av 'is name on 'er?"

"No. Alice Pearce. I am the owner with my brother as partner. Jack has the amount asked for. Give it to Mr Bridges, Jack." And Jack did as he was told, for it was obvious to Ally that even if it meant losing the sale of the second-hand boat Mr Bridges would not take the asking price from a woman's hand. There was a company belonging to a woman on the Liverpool and Leeds Canal with a fleet of boats which travelled from the cotton mills of Lancashire to the River Mersey, but Mr Bridges never dealt with her and had this lass not had her brother with her, despite the lad being a bit slow, he would never have had any dealings with *her*. And if Ally had not been so hungry to start her own fleet she would not have suffered the long and tortuous transaction which Arnold Bridges insisted upon. She spoke the words to Jack who repeated them to Mr Bridges, who answered Jack, who then repeated what he had said to Ally. Talk about long-winded! Even the papers regarding the purchase of the *Harmony* had to be put in Jack's ignorant hand. They were passed to Ally who counted out the money on to Jack's palm and he put the coins into Mr Bridges' grasp, where again they were counted.

At the end Mr Bridges shook Jack's hand. "A pleasure doin' business wi' yer, Mr Pearce," he said cordially. "Now when will yer pick up boat?"

Jack looked enquiringly at Ally.

"Well, we've a horse ter find, an' crew, so next time we're this way I'll drop off an' let yer know."

Jack repeated this to Arnold Bridges who nodded and shook the bewildered Jack's hand again before showing him politely off the premises.

Betsy Pearce was at that precise moment alighting from a horse-drawn cab at the handsome wrought-iron gates of a house on Smithdown Lane in West Derby. But for the fact that the gates were firmly closed she would have instructed the cab driver to take her up the immaculately raked gravel drive to the front door of the house which could not be seen from the road. Perhaps if he had even she, who had an overbearing confidence in her own ability to tackle any hurdle or pitfall life might place before her, would have quailed at the prospect of knocking on its door. The name on the pillars at the gate proclaimed it to be Rosemont House.

It was March, and spring was burgeoning throughout the country in all its delicate loveliness but nowhere as pleasing to the eye as in the acres of ground that surrounded the house where Tom Hartley had grown up. There were trees coming into leaf standing thickly side by side right up to the high wall that surrounded the property, which is probably why Betsy had no sight of the house from the winding driveway. Yew, thick and lumpy, jostled with the tall grey-barked aspen, beech, and the narrow shape of English elm. Oak, sturdy and ancient, protected the small shape of whitebeam and beneath them starring the sprouting shoots of new grass was a rich yellow carpet of wild daffodils. Overhead the sky was a silvery blue, pale and lacking the depth of colour that summer brings. There was a patch of what was called a "mackerel" sky high above the city, waves and ripples that looked like fish scales, stripes of blue and white ethereally lovely on this Sunday when the factory chimneys were idle.

As Betsy moved up the driveway she glanced about her, giving the impression of someone who might consider buying the place should the price suit. She was not a discerning woman, being interested only in what, from any situation, might benefit her, but inwardly she was impressed by what she saw. To the front and side of the house as it came into view were wide lawns, rolling from the terrace surrounding it into a gentle slope down to the lake where swans and ducks glided and willow trees hung over its edge. There were gravel paths as smoothly raked as the drive, lined with flowerbeds, at this time of the year alive with red, white and yellow tulips, winter aconites, with hyacinth, crocus and scilla, edged with dog's-tooth violets.

But it was the house that held her attention, for, if she had anything to do with it, she meant to be its mistress. She knew Tom was the eldest son and in their world, meaning *his*, he was heir to all this. She had almost brought him to a declaration of his feelings for her on several occasions but each time he had drawn back. She was realistic enough to be aware that it was her body he lusted after, though she supposed he thought himself to be in love with her since he was that kind of man. He called regularly at Blackstock Street telling Ma and Mrs Wainwright, who welcomed him with great respect and even affection, that he was keeping an eye on Pa. He left potions of some sort which she supposed were to ease any pain Pa might feel but it gave her, Betsy, no opportunities to get him alone. To show him what she had to offer! Slowly and surely to draw him in like a fish on a line until he promised what she was after: marriage. To be Mrs Tom Hartley. To live in this splendid house. To have a carriage like the ladies on Bold Street. To have made for her the expensive and fashionable gowns *they* wore. To have servants. To go to balls and parties as she was sure they did, but after nine long months of flirting and posturing, enrapturing and bedazzling, in tantalising and trying every trick, of which somehow, she knew a great many – she didn't know how she knew, and didn't try to analyse it – she was no nearer hooking him than she had been on the first day they met. Some deep primeval female instinct told her exactly what was needed to set a man on fire and of course she had the added advantage of having the face and figure that few women could boast but it made no difference. She saw the longing not only in Tom Hartley's eyes but in those of every male whose path she crossed, even young Albert who wasn't exactly sure what his boy's body yearned for.

So far with Tom, at least, she had had little success. So she had taken a few bob from Ma's purse while she and Mrs Wainwright were upstairs seeing to Pa and had engaged a cab from outside Lime Street Station and here she was about to present herself to Tom's family, as *he* should have presented her, she told herself.

Recently she had taken a walk from St John's Market where she had often poked and prodded among the second-hand clothing stalls looking for some decent garment, or a bonnet, that Ma could convert into something Betsy might condescend to put on, bitterly bemoaning the fact that she had no money for anything else. She had sauntered in the pale spring sunshine along Hanover Street, turning left into Duke Street, intent on looking over the house where Tom had told her he lived. A decent-looking house, tall and elegantly simple, of the Regency period, though Betsy was not aware of this naturally. A terraced house set in a quiet and respectable crescent with a small park dividing the street from the houses opposite. The park was shaded by trees just coming into leaf, with benches on which a nursemaid or two sat chatting while keeping their eyes on their charges. The area was pleasant, for some families still occupied the houses though most had now been split into apartments, one to a floor. There was even a well-polished brass plate beside the newly painted door, which had his name on it, "Doctor Thomas Hartley, MD" and Betsy had preened with pleasure. She had been tempted to ring the bell and enquire if Doctor Hartley was in but something, some female instinct had stopped her.

She had stepped back, admiring the bright polished windows, the brass doorknocker, the scrubbed steps, the window boxes vivid with spring flowers, and had sighed with satisfaction. Yes, this would do until the day she and Tom moved into the house he talked of up West Derby way. But first she must make herself known to his family, force his hand so to speak, show him that she was . . . well, capable of holding her own with anyone. She always had, hadn't she? Everywhere she went men and women had been charmed by her, bewitched by her beauty, bowled over by her innocence, her shy modesty, which she could turn on with a blink of her long lashes, and Tom's family would be the same.

But Betsy Pearce knew nothing of what was called "polite society", of the rigorous conventions that ruled their lives, their careful choice of acquaintances who must, naturally, be of their own class. Friendships were not easily formed, not until the character, the position, the wealth, the background, the pedigree of a man or woman was thoroughly checked. There were strict lines drawn regarding the receiving and making of calls, calling cards, the behaviour of newcomers to the district, the giving or accepting of invitations for dinner and, more than anything, the careful choice of a husband or wife for one's children. Betsy knew nothing of etiquette, of the strict code of conduct that ordered their lives from birth to death, from when they left their beds in the morning until they fell into them at the end of the day.

Smiling complacently, she climbed the steps to the imposing front door and rang the bell.

9

The door opened and framed against a hallway of such vast proportions even Betsy was slightly overwhelmed was a lordly being, so lordly in fact Betsy at first decided he was the master of the house. He was dressed as she imagined a gentleman would dress in a black frock coat with trousers of grey and black stripes. His waistcoat was black and his high cravat a spotless immaculately ironed white. He wore white gloves which she thought strange and though for a moment only, as he looked over her shoulder, his face creased into what might have been bewilderment, at once it froze into an expression that really *had* no expression at all. Totally blank, grim, bleak, his eyes a frosty grey.

He raised his eyebrows, keeping his hand on the knob of the door. "Yes?"

Just that one word but Betsy Pearce, vain, self-seeking, arrogant, avaricious, shallow Betsy Pearce was not easily put off, since she believed totally in her own capacity to charm the birds from the trees, should such a thing be necessary, and wasn't this chap a mere member of the opposite sex who were more easily tempted than bloody birds. "Good morning." She smiled, dimpled really. "Is Tom in?"

"Tom?"

"Aye, Tom Hartley. His family does live 'ere, don't it? This is the Hartley residence in'nit?" She was particularly pleased with the word "residence" which Albert had told her meant house, or home in higher circles.

"Master Tom is not at home, miss," the lordly being intoned and would have shut the door in her face, for Sinclair, butler to the Hartley family for over fifteen years now, and before that employed as footman to a landed earl, knew as soon as the woman on the step spoke her first words she was not the sort of caller Mrs Hartley would allow over the threshold unless it was the one in the kitchen. Elegant she looked in a gown of silvery blue-grey with a straw hat, under the brim of which were silk flowers of the same shade and a frill of lace. Her hair, quite glorious, the man buried deep beneath the butler, had time to think, was a pale silver gilt arranged in charming clusters of curls beneath the hat's brim and she had the most exquisitely beautiful face he had ever seen on any woman, and in his working life in great houses, he had seen many. Her parasol was of muslin, pale grey-blue, her gloves were grey, as were her boots and all purchased from the market and "done up" by Betsy and her ma.

Had she not spoken, and had there been a carriage with a coachman standing by, Sinclair would have had no hesitation in asking her in even though it was not the hour at which his mistress received callers, but before the door was completely closed she had slipped in, being slender, young and agile, and to his astonishment began to wander along the hall. She gazed about her and even picked up one of Mrs Hartley's fragile porcelain ornamental vases. Sèvres they were, with hand-painted panels and elaborate gilding and only Clara, the head parlour-maid, was allowed to dust them.

"I beg your pardon, young woman," Sinclair thundered, so enraged he quite forgot to keep his voice to the well-modulated tone that was expected of him. The young woman in question was totally unconcerned, continuing to pick up this and that, to gaze at the pictures on the walls, to wander about and study objects as though she were in the Walker Art Gallery and had every right to poke about as had all members of the public.

"May I ask what is going on here, Sinclair?" a well-bred voice asked from a doorway leading off the hallway. "Who is this young woman? And what is she doing in my house?"

But before the mortified Sinclair could answer or indeed take the visitor by the elbow and show her the door as he longed to do, Betsy spun on her heel and glided towards the woman who had spoken.

"Mornin', Mrs Hartley," she uttered, smiling that winning smile of hers which had always, *always* brought an answering smile from whoever it was aimed at. But Betsy Pearce had never been in the company of the gentry, what was called "good society" and Mary Hartley, who could claim kinship with aristocracy, was of that number. The young woman who approached her so confidently and who had apparently got the better of Sinclair by the look of gall and wormwood on his face was not. She was a beautiful young woman, elegantly dressed, tastefully dressed, with none of the vulgarity that gave away the lower classes, but she had nonetheless come from common stock. Mary Hartley knew that at once even before the woman trilled a greeting.

"Who is this person, Sinclair?" Tom Hartley's mother icily asked her butler, totally ignoring Betsy who came to a floundering stop a foot away from her.

"Madam, I do apologise. When I opened the door she just . . . walked in," which of course gave away her social status at once to both himself and his mistress. No one of the Hartley's acquaintance would do such a thing. A lady would sit in her carriage and send her coachman to hand in her card and enquire if the mistress was "at home", and naturally she would call at the correct time of the day, and certainly not fifteen minutes before lunch was to be served.

"Mrs Hartley . . ." Betsy lifted her head, her bonnet and her nose a further couple of inches and straightened her already straight back. She was a friend and hopefully more of this

woman's son and could see no reason why she shouldn't call
to see his ma. She was as fashionably dressed as Mrs Hartley,
indeed more so, for the woman had on an old pair of gloves
and an apron with pockets from which protruded what looked
like gardening tools. Not that Betsy had ever looked too closely
at soil or plants or the tools with which a person might
approach either. Perhaps she wasn't Mrs Hartley. Perhaps she
was the . . . the gardener's wife or something, for surely no
lady, a lady who was Tom Hartley's mother anyroad, would
wear such an outfit. But then what was she doing in the
doorway to what looked like a quite glorious room and talking
like that to this high mucky-muck who had opened the front
door?

"I've come ter see Mrs Hartley," Betsy said imperiously.
" 'Appen yer could tell 'er Miss Betsy Pearce 'as called, a friend
o' Tom's," she added.

She might not have spoken for all the notice the woman took
of her. Betsy perceived that she had a smear of dirt on her cheek
and wondered, quite thunderstruck, what they were doing
letting a woman like her into this beautiful house.

"Show this . . . this person out, Sinclair, if you please," the
woman said haughtily, beginning to turn away, "and ask Miss
Angelina and Miss Catherine to come down and then serve
lunch. I'll wash . . ."

" 'Ere," Betsy stuttered, the withering temper with which her
family were so familiar surging to the surface, "I'll 'ave you
know I'm a friend o' your Tom's an' 'e'll be none too pleased
when 'e 'ears 'ow you've spoke to me. I were—"

"Perhaps you might care to call Hill or Dwyer if she proves
. . . intractable, Sinclair."

But by this time Sinclair had regained that majestic command
which he had honed to perfection in his service of the best
families in the land. "I don't think that will be necessary,
madam." He moved forward purposefully but he had not reck-

oned on the equally purposeful nature of the red-faced Betsy
Pearce.

She had come here to call on Tom's mother, to make herself
known to the family of which, when she had brought Tom to
declaring his intentions, she would be a member. She was
mystified by the fact he had not done so already and was rapidly
coming to the conclusion that drastic measures would have to
be taken. By which she meant *seducing* him. She had hoped that
as things, meaning their courtship, were going she might have
persuaded him to proceed in the customary fashion, courtship,
engagement, marriage, in the proper way of things, but though
it was obvious to anyone who looked at him when he was
looking at *her* that he was badly smitten, he had done no more
than hold her hand and kiss her with a great groan as though he
couldn't help himself. He seemed to think, which was what she
wanted him to think, that she was shy, modest, innocent, a
young girl who might be badly startled if he made advances to
her, but after nine months, nine long bloody months, she had
decided she must force his hand. First she would make herself
known to his family then, when they had met her and recognised her as a suitable wife for their son – they would be able to
tell that by her beauty, her taste in gowns, her charming
manners – she would hurry things along a bit by getting Tom
alone and showing him what was underneath it all. But first she
must make the acquaintance of Mrs Hartley, who, amazingly,
appeared to be this woman.

Throwing off the butler's restraining hand she hurried across
the hall and followed Mrs Hartley into her drawing-room,
though Betsy, never having seen the inside of one, was not
aware that that was what it was called. It was here that the lady
of the house would receive her carriage callers, where they took
tea and chatted about the inconsequential things in which ladies
of their ilk were interested. There were spindly-legged gilt and
velvet-upholstered chairs the like of which Betsy had never

before seen, dainty rosewood tables which had been polished by generations of housemaids to a mirror-like shine. There were silk walls, deep curtains and carpets of a pale biscuit shade, lovely ornaments like the ones in the hall, mirrors and pictures and lamps and in the white marble fireplace an enormous fire burned, putting an apricot glow on every wall. Clocks ticked and flowers, bowls of them, exuded a heady fragrance and Betsy was mesmerised by it all.

Mrs Hartley, who was just about to go through a wide doorway on the far side of the room which seemed to lead into an enclosed garden by the masses of flowers that filled it, stopped and turned autocratically to face Betsy, but Betsy for once was speechless, the sight of so much luxury, comfort, loveliness taking her voice and halting her in the doorway. Dear God, this was it, she was thinking, this is for me, this is what I was meant for. This is what I want and will have and this frozen-faced madam can do or say what she wants. I'm having it. Through Tom. But first she'd have a try at making friends, which had always been easy for her, especially with men and surely she could sweet-talk this woman, bring her round, charm her and, through her, have the fairy-tale romance and wedding, with Tom of course, that she felt were her due.

She smiled, while at her back Sinclair hovered menacingly, his hand reaching out to her arm though he felt it was somewhat beneath him to lay hands on a woman physically, drag her to the front door, probably kicking and screaming, for from the look of her she was the sort that would not go peaceably. Forced her way in, she had, and now would you look at her, advancing on his mistress who drew herself up warningly.

"Young woman, I have no idea who you are but if you do not remove yourself at once from my drawing-room and my house I shall be forced to ring for my footman to do it for you. Sinclair, ring the bell and—"

"Look, Mrs Hartley . . . It is Mrs Hartley, i'nt it? I only came ter introduce meself, like. Tom an' me are good friends."

"What my son does and with whom is his own concern since he is a grown man and I suppose men must have their . . . their little diversions." Her patrician nose wrinkled distastefully, as though the mere idea of her son and this person doing what young unmarried and *married* gentlemen did was anathema to her. She was well aware of men's appetites and someone had to see to them, taking the odious task from their wives, and providing they were discreet, she and her friends had no objection to the practice. Her Edward had left her alone after Arthur's birth ten years ago but the very idea that this . . . this low person who had pushed past Sinclair was demanding entrance to *her* home, was outrageous.

Betsy wasn't awfully sure what a "diversion" might be but she could guess and the implication that she, who was a good girl, and Tom, who was a proper gentleman, were up to no good – even though she meant to lead him on to that point – incensed her. The deep blue-green of her eyes narrowed to chips of ice and she drew herself up, as imperious in her way as this woman in whose house she stood.

"Now you listen 'ere," Betsy hissed, her smile gone, her best party manners gone, the pseudo gentility gone, "I come ter see yer, ter call on yer in good faith an' I'll not be treated like trash."

"Then do not behave like trash. No lady of good family would dream of—"

"My family's as good as yours. Tom thinks so, else me an' 'im wouldn't be walkin' out—"

"Walking out! You and my son? I think you are mistaken, young woman. We don't 'walk out' as you so quaintly call it, not in our circle. My son is a gentleman. He is the son of a gentleman and will one day marry a lady and that is all there is to be said. What he does with a woman of your sort is entirely his own affair."

" 'E does nowt wi' me, I'm a decent woman an' 'e knows it an' when 'e fetches me 'ere—"

"He will *never* bring you here, girl, never. I would not allow it and he is well aware of it. As I have said, one day he will choose and marry a young lady of his own class. Now I must ask you to leave. My family and I are about to sit down to lunch. Sinclair will see you out."

"No 'e bloody well won't. I'll not be chucked out like some beggar what's lookin' fer a 'andout. Just wait until Tom 'ears about this. You'll soon see wharra I mean to 'im."

But Mrs Hartley, who was annoyed with herself for even crossing swords with this . . . this trollop, had turned away, taking a pair of small pruning shears from her apron pocket and moving into her conservatory where she had been working before Sinclair's outraged voice had brought her into the hall. From behind her, Sinclair had both Betsy's arms in his firm grip and was beginning to drag her backwards, a difficult task, for although Betsy Pearce had an air of delicate fragility about her she was as strong as old Magic who towed the canal boat. She was shouting for Tom as though he might be hidden somewhere in this lovely and luxurious house. She had dug her heels into the carpet. In fact she had let herself go limp and it was not until Hill and Dwyer, footmen to the Hartley household, burst through the door that led into the kitchen, both of them astounded, then excited at the thought of handling the pretty girl struggling with Sinclair, that the three of them managed to get her, not only through the front door but down the steps, along the winding driveway and out beyond the fine gates into the road. The gates were closed behind her and Hill, who had got a good feel of her rounded, bobbing breasts, leered out at her. He winked, but Betsy Pearce glared at him malevolently.

Her lovely gown was disarranged, her hair was trailing down her back but she was not beaten, the glare told him, *and* those who had spurned her.

Betsy had noticed on the journey to Rosemont House that there was a taxi rank in Holland Place just outside St Mary's Church in West Derby and after trudging the length of Chatsworth Street and along Wavertree Road she climbed into the first one to come along. She had rearranged her bonnet but her bodice buttons, two of which had been torn off in her struggle, were open to reveal the fine white skin of her upper breasts. Her skirt had mud on the hem since Hill had dragged her across a flowerbed and had a tear in it. She was not hurt, apart from her dignity, but into her shrewd brain had come, fully developed in every detail, a plan to achieve what she had always wanted. A plan that should not only fulfil her dreams but wreak revenge on that cow up at Rosemont. She looked like some bedraggled kitten that had been caught in an alley by a tom-cat, which suited her purpose magnificently. She made no attempt to tidy herself. In fact when she was on her way, she deliberately scratched her own cheek with her fingernails which made her cry, for Betsy Pearce could not bear pain. The tears dried on her cheeks and with the smear of blood enhanced the picture she wanted to create.

"What's ter do?" the cabby had cried as she dragged herself into his cab. "Lass, who's . . ."

"Nowt, just drive me ter Duke Street."

Mrs Hodges exclaimed loudly when she opened the door. She would have shrieked but Mrs Hodges wasn't a shrieking sort of woman, besides which she had seen more than a few sorry sights at Doctor Tom's door. But still she was quite horrified at the sight of the poor knocked-about young lady who leaned against the basement railings, supported by a concerned cabby, and in his surgery where he had just seen out the last patient from the back door into the yard, Tom Hartley, alarmed, stood up and hurried to the door into the hall.

He was just in time to see his housekeeper almost carry the weeping figure of Betsy Pearce across his threshold. Out on the step a cabby hovered, his hand out for his fare, his face, which had been filled with sympathy for the poor lass, turning to truculence when he was ignored.

"Betsy . . . sweetheart. Who's done this to you?" Tom was saying, taking her from Mrs Hodges' arms into his own, holding her shaking, trembling body against the length of his which immediately responded. He had wanted this for months and despite the circumstances, being male, which was known for its unthinking waywardness, caring for nothing but what nature made it for, it surged against Betsy Pearce.

Betsy, her face buried against Tom's chest, felt it and smiled triumphantly. It was going to be so easy. "Oh, Tom," she sobbed.

" 'Ere, wharrabout me fare?" the cabby railed.

"What's up, then, lass?" Mrs Hodges pleaded, while about their feet Blaze barked dementedly.

"Close the door, Mrs Hodges," Tom begged, but the cabby had his foot against it.

"Listen, I come from West Derby wi' this lass an' that'll be two an' six, if yer please."

Tom turned to stare at him, the mention of the area where his family lived taking him temporarily from the delight of having Betsy Pearce clinging to him.

"West Derby . . . ?"

"Aye, an' tha'll be two an' a tanner."

"Pay him, Mrs Hodges, please. Now then, Betsy tell me what's happened to you. Who did this? Dear God, I'll kill him. What were you doing in West Derby?" He lifted her up into his arms and carried her into his surgery, laying her tenderly on the leather couch where, when they were at the end of their tether, he often placed his patients, perhaps a woman moaning in labour, or a man with a badly injured arm. There were many accidents in the often dangerous, careless work about the docks where the safety of the workers was of little importance.

Mrs Hodges, who had paid the cabby, reminding herself to ask Doctor Tom for the two and six she had taken out of her purse, for *she* couldn't afford such a sum out of her wages, if he could, hovered at his back, as she had noticed the great deal of satin-white flesh which peeped from the young lady's bodice and surely a chaperone of sorts was needed here.

"A brandy, I think, Mrs Hodges, if you please. Miss Pearce is in shock and cannot tell us what's happened in her present state." And when Mrs Hodges continued to dither at his shoulder, turned to her impatiently. "Did you hear me, Mrs Hodges, a glass of brandy from my decanter in the sitting-room."

Betsy continued to sob and hiccup, needing, it seemed, Tom's arm about her shoulder and his free hand to hold the glass of brandy to her lips, but she wished the old woman would sling her hook, for she could do nothing with her hanging about, could she, and it was becoming increasingly difficult to keep up the shuddering, the tears and the moans.

"Can you tell us what happened, Betsy?"

Tom's anxious face was inches from her own, and his eyes, which reminded Betsy of their Jack's dog Teddy when he had misbehaved and was trying to get back in Jack's favour, gazed into hers. They were blue, gentle, a dark blue as worry deepened their colour, but Betsy Pearce saw nothing of the kindness, the gentleness, only the opportunity at last to manoeuvre Tom Hartley into the state she had connived at for months. To trap him into a declaration of his feelings followed by a proposal of marriage. That stuck-up old woman at Rosemont would be sorry she had ever crossed Betsy Pearce, but first things first.

"Thank you, Tom," she whispered, "that – what was it? – brandy is . . . were very soothin'. Could I 'ave another sip?"

Mrs Hodges, frowning disapprovingly, was sent for another, which Betsy sipped, a lovely flush of rose creeping into her cheek. Her bonnet had fallen off when Tom picked her up and her hair had come tumbling about her shoulders and back in a silver, silken riot of curls and though Mrs Hodges thought it somewhat immodest she couldn't help but admire it. A bonny lass who, though Doctor Tom needed to question her about how she had got into such a state, was now inclined to drop off to sleep. Not used to brandy, Mrs Hodges thought, and happen a rest would do her good.

"I'll get back to me kitchen then, sir," she whispered, studying the young woman who in her opinion looked like a sleeping child, all flushed, lovely and innocent. They'd find out soon enough when she had got over her shock what had been done to her. She wasn't sure she quite liked the way Doctor Tom hung over her but then wasn't he always concerned with anyone, man, woman or child, who came with trouble to his door.

Betsy waited for a few minutes, conscious that Tom was still kneeling beside the couch. She could smell whatever it was he put on his face after shaving and she supposed it must be the soap he used. Lemon, she thought. She could feel his breath fan her cheek. When she opened her eyes, blinking a little as though with surprise, it was the most natural thing in the world to lift her lips to his. But this time it was no shy hesitant kiss but a passionate, urgent, *deep* kiss, not just on his part but hers.

"Oh, Tom," she murmured, "I do feel queer," making sure she had an excuse for her behaviour when it was all over. Well, she couldn't be blamed if Tom had got her drunk, could she?

"Oh, Tom. I do love you." And with a thrust of her breast she managed to burst the remainder of the buttons on her bodice – which she had worked loose in the cab – so when her white, rosy-tipped breasts erupted Tom's hands were there ready to receive them.

He hurt her a bit when he put his . . . his "thingy" in her, for after all she was a virgin, but who the hell cared about that. It was a small price to pay for becoming engaged to Doctor Tom Hartley!

10

It was almost four weeks to the day since the *Edith* had left the canal basin in Liverpool and Ally was anxious to get to Blackstock Street to see how Pa was. She had never stayed away so long but the purchase of the *Harmony*, the search for a decent horse to tow her was not something to be rushed and Ally and Jack, who had an eye for a decent animal, were careful. A good horse might cost as much as thirty or forty guineas and every guinea in Ma's box must be made to count. The animal must be of a medium size, as Magic was, but strong and healthy, one that had been well looked after, that had not been worn out by a company and was biddable as Magic was. From Burnley, where they had been forced to leave the *Harmony*, since Magic could not tow two boats, they had moved back along the canal towards Liverpool carrying various cargoes, as Ally could not afford an empty boat. Through Accrington and Blackburn, until they reached Burscough, not far from Liverpool. Ally had been tempted to go to see Ma and Pa but the *Harmony* had to be collected and a horse found to tow her and so with a cargo of timber for Mr Bridges, which he had asked them to carry, she and Jack inspected the horses for sale.

Burscough was known as a wonderful place for horses. Canal horses were kept on a farm belonging to one of the big companies, those that plied their trade on the Leeds and Liverpool. It was where Pa had always bought his provender for Magic, a mixture of hay, bran, corn, beans, peas and oats, and it was here that Ally and Jack, leaving Davey in charge of Magic and the

Edith, studied every horse in the field that was for sale. There had never been a true boat horse strain. The scows on the Forth and Clyde were pulled naturally by Clydesdales, Welsh narrow-boats by cobs with short legs. On the Grand Junction shires were used but every type of horse was put to use on the inland waterways from cart-horses to old carriage horses. Most were mares or geldings and when Ally saw the placidly cropping, gentle-eyed grey mare, already broken to boat haulage, she was told, she knew she had found the animal to tow the *Harmony,* the second canal boat in her fleet. Her fleet. How grand that sounded. *Harmony* and . . . and . . . what should be her name? Jack had looked at her teeth, her eyes, her hooves, run his gentle hand down her legs and along her back, searching carefully for signs of sore shoulders caused by collars that were in poor condition or badly fitted. She stood patiently under his hands.

"She's a gentle lass," Jack ventured, standing back to watch the mare move slowly away from them.

"Aye, she is that," the man who was in charge said, "but right willin'."

He, like the others on the canal, totally ignored Ally who stood back submissively, for in this Jack knew more than she did.

"What d' yer want fer 'er?" Jack asked casually and Ally held her breath.

"Well" – the man took off his cap and scratched his grizzled hair – "she's one o' me best."

" 'Ow much?"

"Well . . ."

"If yer don't know I reckon I'd best go elsewhere." Jack began to turn away and it was all Ally could do to prevent herself from grabbing his arm and telling him not to be such a damn fool.

"Mekk me an offer," the chap said.

"Well, bearing in mind she's not young, I'll say fifteen guineas."

Both the chap and Ally gasped.

"Give over, lad. Fifteen bloody guineas, she's worth twice that."

"Right then, I'll bid yer good-day. Come on, our Ally," turning to the speechless Ally and winking.

"'Old on, lad, 'old on, 'ow about twenty-five?"

"Nay . . ." But after a great deal of haggling, head scratching and a bit of swearing on the seller's part, for which he apologised to the gape-jawed Ally, they led the mare to the stables, where all the paraphernalia of harness, browband, noseband, bit, blinkers and the like might be purchased.

"Gentle," Ally said as they approached the *Edith* which was moored to the side of the canal and where Davey sprang to his feet from the upside-down bucket on which he had been waiting and watching for them. Even Magic lifted her head from grazing the fresh new shoots of juicy grass on the towpath where she was tethered.

"Yer what?" Jack turned to stare at her.

"We'll call 'er Gentle."

"Gentle!"

"Aye, Gentle by name and Gentle by nature."

And so she proved. She was harnessed at once to the *Edith* as they moved back in the direction of Wigan and its twenty-one locks, moving across three aqueducts and one embankment and Gentle proved strong, willing, obedient and patient. Magic must have thought she'd died and gone to horse heaven, Davey remarked, for she did nothing but plod along beside the boat, stopping when they did, cropping at the grass verge and settling down each night beside her new workmate.

"Well, Jack, what d' yer reckon?" Ally, cramped with two big lads in the small cabin where Ma and Pa used to sleep, placed a heaped plate of meat and potato pie, mashed potatoes and cabbage in front of her brother, then did the same for Davey.

"Wharrabout, our Ally?" Jack answered through a mouthful of pie. It was hot and delicious, just purchased from the inn beside which the canal boat was moored. Ally just didn't have time to cook the meals as Ma had once done, for it needed the three of them to look after the boat and two horses. When they went back to pick up the *Harmony* at Burnley, they would have to look for two, at the very least one man to get them back to Liverpool, for the *Harmony* must have a crew. She meant to take back the two boats jammed in every available space with manufactured cotton goods, even in the cabins, for nearly everything in Ma's box was gone in the purchase of Gentle and *Harmony*. She and the lads would just have to wrap up warm and sleep on the deck and hope the weather stayed fine. It was nearly April and mild so with a bit of luck and a smile from the gods, who had looked kindly on Ally Pearce so far – at least in business – they would reap a decent profit from this trip.

"About all this," she continued, sitting down by Jack and picking up her knife and fork.

"All what?"

"Fer God's sake, Jack. We own a *fleet* now. More 'n one boat's a bloody fleet. So what d' yer mekk of it?"

"This meat 'n' tater pie's good, Ally, almost as good as Ma's."

Ally sighed. For an hour this afternoon she'd had the sudden, shining hope that Jack was to be a real partner, for he'd worked a miracle over the horse, but she realised now that it was only among animals that Jack showed signs of a bit of sense. He worked hard, he was willing to take orders from her, glad to have the responsibility his father had once borne put squarely on Ally's shoulders. He offered no opinions on cargoes or their destinations, leaving all decisions to her, glad to do so, a boy really in a man's body and she supposed it was just as well or she and him would be arguing all the live long day. There could only be one number one on a canal boat but still it would have been grand to have someone to talk to. Someone who would understand how she felt about her sudden elevation; no, not sudden, for it had taken her nine long months to reach the dizzying heights of a "fleet owner". If it hadn't been for Ma and Pa's frugality, their thrift and careful hoarding of their hard-earned cash it could not have been done, for every business, if it is to get under way, needs capital. But her ambition, her energy, her tenacity in defying the merchants from whom she sought cargoes, her sheer bloody-minded determination to succeed, to make her way in this male-dominated world which did not want her in it, had been the real source of her steady advance. But what satisfaction she would get if she had someone, she hated to use the word, but someone intelligent, someone with a grasp of the commercial world, to discuss it with. To gloat over it, to boast a little, to rejoice on her progress. To tell her how clever she was. Jack and Davey were boys with nothing much in their heads but larking about, hardworking, true and steady but with no conception of how to run a business, just as she had been before Pa's accident. Then they had all mucked in on the canal boat, loading and unloading cargoes, steering, walking Magic, legging it through tunnels, knowing hard times and good times, but they had left the decisions to Pa who was their leader, so to speak. Now it was up to her and so far she had done wonderfully well even if she said it herself. In a few short months she had acquired another canal boat and a horse to tow her. She had more than doubled the cargoes they carried and would show a handsome profit when they reached Liverpool. A big hole had been made in Ma's box but – what was the expression she had heard or read somewhere? – you had to speculate to accumulate, and though risks must be taken, risks which had her head spinning and made her heart thud painfully in her chest as she lay in her bed at night, the gamble must be taken.

As she lay in her bed at night! Ah yes, and whose face

imprinted itself behind her eyelids when they closed in an effort
to sleep? She might be totally exhausted, indeed she was, but
that face, that face which she had studied when he wasn't
looking at her, fierce and stubborn: over what? she had
wondered. Perhaps the determination to fight disease, illness,
desperate injuries such as Pa's, even death itself. And she had
seen it kind in his sympathy for Pa's suffering. He was fierce
and yet amiable, challenging and yet compassionate, his eyes a
blue flint sometimes when he was irritated and then just as
suddenly as soft and lovely as the bluebells that grew in spring
beneath the trees that lined the canal. A man impossible to
describe, not handsome but a face that drew glances, admiring
glances from women, and she supposed respectful ones from
men, since it was strong and humorous and they recognised a
true man when they saw him. He had a wide mouth, a gentle
mouth which quirked at the corners, ready it seemed to laugh
at life, at anything that struck him as ridiculous. A sense of fun
that would be wasted on their Betsy, who had no humour in her
at all and was often bewildered when something that struck the
rest of them as a laugh passed her by like a drifting mist.

He was with her then, in her head and her heart, the man who
loved her sister, and she agonised on how she would manage to
control her emotions when he declared himself. The pain that
would not leave her alone as her imagination ran wild at the
thoughts of him and Betsy together. Why could she not stamp
it out, kill it? Why did it not die for lack of nourishment? she
asked herself as she buried her face beneath the blanket she was
wrapped in. She was plain, practical, level-headed and since
womanhood no man had ever earned a second glance from her,
which was just as well since she earned none from them, not
with Betsy beside her. But now one man had called to something in her, not intending to, of course, and that something
which was buried beneath the exterior of sensible, plain Ally
Pearce had answered and it was devastating her.

Thank God she had this passion in her, this ambition, this need to build Pa's small business into something that would equal if not overtake the big companies like Pickfords or the Wigan Coal and Iron Company which had a fleet of more than seventy boats, and many others. She longed to talk of her aspirations, her plans for further expansion and to discuss with someone who might understand and, what is more, advise her on how to manage the profits she intended to have. And who else in their small circle but Tom Hartley, who surely had investments in . . . in all the many ventures like . . . well, she had read about railways and mining and . . . and other concerns that could make a man an honest return, but Ally Pearce had no idea how to go about such a thing. She felt a great need to slip Ma's box out of Aggie's drawer and take what was left in it to a . . . well, a bank, she supposed, where it would be safe from Betsy's greedy fingers, but she was a woman, a boatwoman with no idea of how to go about such a thing. After her purchase she had brought the box containing the money back to Liverpool, deciding that it was not safe on the boat, for who knew what ruffian might not come aboard while she or Jack or Davey were busy on the docks at which they moored. But surely Tom would know. She had gathered from his conversation, not directed at Betsy whose head was filled only with the latest fashions but all the occupants of the kitchen in general, again wondering why, for who among them understood, that his pa was in business about the docks and shipping, so surely Tom would have some idea how she was to begin. Dear Lord, how sweet to be somewhere with him in private and open her heart – about business only of course – to him, ask him to explain to her about investments, savings, accounts, rates of interest, which bank among the many in Liverpool he favoured. Where in fact her money, the profit she was to make on this trip alone was to be put. Two canal boats to be maintained and two horses to be fed and cared for. The wages for three men, or four if she counted Jack, who surely should be paid for the work he did, the upkeep of Ma and Pa and Betsy, and here it all was spinning round in her head which before Pa's accident had fallen into deep sleep the moment it hit the pillow.

It didn't do that now. If she wasn't tossing and turning in the small space she had allotted herself in the prow of the *Edith* going over figures, adding and subtracting one from, or to, another, considering cargoes, where to cram them on the boats, the tolls that would be gauged at each tollhouse, the time it would take her to get from one to the next, where she was to find the crew for the *Harmony*, she was brooding about Tom Hartley and her interest in him. Interest! That was a bland word to describe what was hidden inside her for the man who loved her sister. She lay on her back in a drifting dream in which Tom Hartley's face came to smile at her. He was a good man and deserved better than their Betsy she thought drowsily, soothed now by the motion of the boat and the warmth of Teddy who had crossed the tarpaulin from the stern and came to snuggle in her back. Betsy was not a fit partner for Tom Hartley, and he was a fool not to know it, but then most men seemed to be fools when it came to choosing a woman. Not her ma and pa, for they suited one another in every way and always had done, coming from the same world, the same class, plain, no-nonsense sort of folk and where in hell Betsy had come from was a mystery to them all.

She turned over on to her stomach and cradled her head on her arms. Jack and Davey were at the stern of the boat and the night was so still she could hear the pair of them snoring. They had spent an hour in the Green Man by the side of the canal where half a dozen other craft were moored, not exactly drunk when they returned but merry as trivets, laughing and pushing one another as young men do and falling instantly asleep among the bales of manufactured cotton goods they had picked up in Nelson. She had been told of a cargo of coal, in containers, for many cargoes were come across by word of mouth and which, when Gentle was harnessed to the *Harmony*, Ally would pick up at Wigan and carry on to Liverpool. They would travel one behind the other, providing they could find a crew; if not then the three of them would have to work two boats. It would be hard work but they would manage, she told herself. They would have to!

Tomorrow they were to pick up the *Harmony* in Burnley. Two boats, one packed with cotton goods, the other with coal and though the toll-keeper would extract a heavy due when he used his gauging stick to measure the cargo, it would be worth it.

She and her small fleet entered the first lock, which with four others led down to Stanley Dock. Since picking up the *Harmony* in Burnley they had legged it through two tunnels and worked their way through forty-five locks with only the three of them to manage it. Ally felt as though a rough word might break her into a thousand splintered pieces she was so tired, so fragile, as were Jack and Davey, and even yet she was not finished, for their cargo of coal which was containered on the *Harmony* and the cotton goods on the *Edith*, had to be unloaded, checked and delivered into the hands of the merchants who were to purchase them. There were the toll tickets to be scrutinised by the toll-master at the top of the locks to tell him that her tolls had been paid, and altogether by the time she and Davey and Jack had moored their boats, settled Magic and Gentle in their stables, seen to their feeding and general welfare, the three of them were almost swaying on their feet in their complete exhaustion. They had managed it, three people, one of them a woman, bringing back two canal boats and their cargoes, but Ally knew she would have to find at least one more man, an experienced man, a strong man to work one of the boats with Davey. They could hardly go up and down the canal in harness, so to speak, for the cargoes were to be found in different places along the length of it from Liverpool to Leeds, but that could wait until tomorrow. Now all she wanted was to get back to Blackstock Street, perhaps have a bath in the tin tub Aggie kept hanging on a hook on the door of the washhouse and fall into bed. Any bed, even the one she would probably have to share with Betsy.

They climbed the steep slope of Dublin Street, not speaking, for the effort was too great. She had walked virtually the whole length of the canal from Burnley to Liverpool, for she had taken on the task of leading the two horses round the locks and beside the tunnels, while the lads had performed miracles, opening and shutting lock gates, legging it through tunnels, and she had made up her mind to give both of them some sort of bonus.

Hardly had they got through the door of number 10, opened by Albert who still held the book in his hand he had been reading to Fred Pearce, than Betsy was flaunting herself in the doorway of the kitchen. It had turned colder and Ally was thanking the gods they were home and not forced to sleep on deck, and the kitchen was a haven of warmth, but Betsy's first words turned not only the kitchen but Ally's whole world to ice. She even had the distinct feeling she was shivering as a body does when intense cold hits it.

Betsy crowed triumphantly, "Me an' Tom's engaged. Innit excitin'? I'm plannin' a June weddin' an' o' course you'll be one o' me bridesmaids, our Ally. 'Appen I'll 'ave three cos Tom's got two sisters. Oh, aye, Angelina an' Catherine, so they'll want ter be in on it an' all."

She might have stood there for ever, frozen to Aggie's bit of coconut matting, her face haggard with exhaustion and blanched of all colour in her shock, had Jack not pushed his way along the passage with Davey in tow past Albert, past herself and Betsy who was waiting for their joyful congratulations as was her due, thumping into the kitchen, for they were famished, he was saying.

"Well, Jack Pearce, if all you can think about is yer belly at a time like this, I'll think seriously about askin' yer ter't wedding," Betsy said petulantly.

"What weddin'? An' wheer's me dinner. Me belly thinks me throat's cut an' I could lay down on't flags an' sleep fer a week."

"Well, if that's not the giddy limit. 'Ere's me ter be't wife o' one o' Liverpool's richest men—"

"What are yer babblin' on about, our Betsy? Can we not gerrinside t' kitchen an' tekk our boots off afore yer go on 'alf-cocked about some daft scheme yer've gorrin yer 'ead about Tom Hartley."

"It's norra daft scheme, our Jack," Betsy shrieked. "Me an' Tom's engaged. I've bin in 'is 'ouse an' met his ma and—"

"Give over, yer daft besom, you an' Tom Hartley? Now shurrup." He turned to Davey. "Come on, Davey, put yer bum down an' tuck in. Eh, Ma," as Edith Pearce rose from her chair and held her arms out to her son. "'Ow are yer, Ma, an' 'ow's Pa?" turning, one arm round his mother to look pityingly at Pa. It was four weeks since he and Ally had left Liverpool and it was evident that in that short time Fred Pearce had deteriorated further, his face slack and grey, his eyes blank, his mouth curiously lopsided, a track of saliva dribbling from the corner. No one, not even Doctor Tom knew exactly what was wrong with Pa. His injuries had healed but something in his head, in his brain, Tom Hartley suspected was not right, but who could see into a man's head and if it was possible, how could it be healed?

There was a great deal of swirling about, chairs being pulled out from the table to accommodate Jack and Davey who, after a perfunctory enquiry of Fred Pearce as to how he was, to which they received no reply, fell to on the heaped plates of scouse Aggie placed before them. It was only minutes, less really, but it gave Ally time to unglue her feet from the floor of the passage and move stiffly into the kitchen. Ma, with something in her eyes that Ally did not understand, exchanged a look with Aggie, then opened her arms and enfolded her elder daughter within them.

"Lass," she said softly. " 'Ow are yer then? Yer look done in."

Ally found her voice reaching inside herself for something she was not even aware she had but which gave her the strength to keep herself upright, helped by Ma's arms.

"Aye, Ma . . . I'm a bit tired."

"Sit yer down then, love an' get summat inside yer."

"Pa . . . ?"

"As yer see, no better. But 'ave a bite then yer can tell us all about yer trip."

"Aye, sit down, queen," Aggie added, her kindly face troubled, sad even, for this young woman who worked so hard for her family had become very dear to her. Not like the other one, the flibbertigibbet who could jabber about nothing but what she would do when she married Tom Hartley, God help him. Her expectations of her life at Rosemont House, the balls she would give, and attend, the glory of what she had seen in the company of Tom's ma, the butler who wore white gloves, the loveliness of the house and gardens and they could only believe her, amazing as it seemed, since it, meaning the life the Hartleys led – including the butler with white gloves – would be impossible to describe unless Betsy had actually seen it. Mind you, the little madam was very evasive about how, and with whom, the visit had taken place. Doctor Tom, "my affianced" Betsy called him, had sat in her kitchen frozen-faced, Aggie was inclined to think, and did not argue with her, or contradict what she prattled on about so it must be true. Look at her now queening it over Ally who sat obediently at the table and spooned Aggie's nourishing scouse into her mouth. She had regained a bit of colour in her cheeks but her eyes still retained that wounded look of an animal close to death, and naturally, since they were not daft or blind, both Aggie and Edie knew why.

"D'yer know, our Ally, I reckon yer jealous o' me," Betsy pronounced with deep satisfaction, pacing smugly from the kitchen door to the fire, twitching her skirt as she imagined great ladies did. "You've said nowt about me an' Tom an' I ask meself why an' the answer is yer jealous. Jealous cos 'e fell in love wi' me."

"Be quiet, girl," Aggie thundered, so ferociously even Fred jumped. "Can yer not shurrup about you an' Doctor Tom an' let yer sister get summat down 'er. Look at 'er" – which they all did except Fred – "ready ter drop an' there's you babblin' bloody nonsense. Give 'er a chance ter get 'erself pulled together, 'ave a bath, 'appen, an' a rest."

"Don't you speak ter me like that, Aggie Wainwright," Betsy began, but Aggie, who knew Edie was weakened by her husband's illness and therefore not up to giving this lass of hers a clout round her ear'ole as she deserved, was not to be so easily subdued.

"I'll speak as I like in me own 'ouse, madam, an' if yer don't like it tekk yerself off ter that grand place yer'll have the orderin' of when yer wed Tom Hartley. If yer ever do."

"If I ever do. What the 'ell d' yer mean by that, yer old—"

"Betsy." Ally's voice cut through her sister's tirade like a hot knife through butter and in the silence that followed, but for the bright crackling of the fire and the deep slurps of enjoyment coming from Jack and Davey, her voice was slurred with what she hoped would be mistaken for weariness.

"I'd like ter get ter bed if . . ."

Aggie bustled over to her at once, almost lifting her from her chair.

"O' course, lass, an' yer shall 'ave our Albert's bed. Yer don't mind do yer, Albert? Yer can sleep on't sofa fer a night or two.

I'll light fire. Run an' fetch tub from t' wash'ouse, Albert, see. Edie, put water on ter heat. Gerrout o' me way, girl" – to Betsy – "or do summat useful. What? I don't know, but summat ter earn yer keep fer a change. Now, lass," she said tenderly to Ally, "you come along o' me," leading Ally Pearce, who was sorely wounded, Aggie knew, from the kitchen.

"Well!" said Betsy to no one in particular.

11

She was down in the Stanley Dock basin by seven o'clock the next morning, telling Aggie, who begged her to stop in bed, that she had things she had to attend to, but in reality she was desperate to be out of the house before Doctor Tom, as they still called him despite his engagement to Betsy, came on his daily visit to Pa.

" 'Ave a birra breakfast, chuck. See, let me fry yer a slice o' bacon an' 'appen an egg."

"No, Aggie, I must be away!"

" 'E won't be 'ere while ten, lass."

" 'Oo? 'Oo won't be 'ere?"

"Nay, chuck, yer ma an' I know." Aggie's face crumpled in distress but Ally drew herself up imperiously, ready to berate Aggie for her presumption, then her own face dissolved for a moment in misery as she allowed, for that moment only, the warm comfort of Aggie's arms about her, then she flung them off savagely.

"I don't know what yer mean, Aggie. What's Tom Hartley ter do wi' me? – I've things ter see ter at docks. Two cargoes ter find, a man ter crew an' them lads" – who had gone back to the *Edith* to sleep since there wasn't a bed to spare in Aggie's small house – "will still be i 't bed-'ole if I don't root 'em out."

Davey, who was Aggie's niece's son, though his mam lived close by in a court off Naylor Street, was, as Aggie put it, "made up" with his position as crew on the Pearces' boat and had taken to it like the proverbial duck to water. He thought it grand to be mates with Jack who was a couple of years older than himself. Though he was still a boy in many ways he was a man like Jack in others. Stocky, well muscled, strong as a young ox with the firm belief that as a crewman on the *Edith*, or the *Harmony*, he didn't mind which, he was perfectly entitled to have a pint of ale at the pub down at the bottom end of Dublin Street, where many of the sailors from the ships docked in Liverpool did the same. He and Jack, after the gargantuan meal Aggie had begged them to "get that lot down yer, lads!", would have stopped off at the Black Swan, the result of which would be a great reluctance, indeed an impossibility to raise their heads from their pillows this morning. Two good-natured lads with a few bob in their pocket which Ally had slipped them, since it was her belief they deserved it, their weariness, being young and healthy, forgotten.

"Right, queen," Aggie said gently. "You gerroff, but let me tell yer, yer not crossin' that doorstep wi' nowt inside yer. There's bacon ready an' even if yer 'ave ter eat it in't street, seeing as 'ow yer 'aven't a minute ter spare, I'm makin' yer a bacon butty. Yer ma's seeing ter yer pa." This was a long and arduous task since Edie Pearce, the Edie Pearce who could not abide muck of any sort, would not allow her poor husband to be carried downstairs to be examined by Doctor Tom until he was washed and put in a clean nightshirt. The clean bedding and nightshirts, which were needed every day, meant a lot of washing for the two women. Five people, five beds to change, not every day, of course, like Fred's, and that there little madam, who spent the day God only knew where, never lifted a hand to help her ma. Lazy little slut she was and how she'd got Doctor Tom to propose to her was a bloody mystery. Mind, there was no arguing with the fact that she was the bonniest lass Aggie had ever seen, even her own twelve-year-old Albert ready to worship the very ground she walked on.

"Aggie, really, I'm not 'ungry."

"Whether yer are or whether yer not, yer can't go out wi'out summat inside yer. D' yer want ter mekk yersenn poorly? Yer t' breadwinner, my lass, an' yer ma an' pa rely on yer. I suppose yer'll be off up that canal again soon."

"I've ter find a man, Aggie."

"Aye, well, best yer get yer bonnet on then an' tekk this butty." All the while Aggie had been talking she had been busy with the bacon and the bread, shoving it into Ally's reluctant hand and smiling encouragingly like a mother trying to persuade a fractious child to eat before school. "An' don't get bacon fat on that frock neither."

"Oh, Aggie, I never thanked you." For while Ally had been sleeping, a deep dreamless sleep which had restored her indomitable spirit, Aggie had washed and ironed her skirt and blouse. Ally had gone to Albert's narrow bed clean and glowing, even her short crop of washed curls springing in a shining mass about her drawn face, and now in her immaculate boatwoman's outfit she was ready to step out before Tom Hartley called, weakening her again, and find herself two cargoes and a crew for the *Harmony*.

It was a glorious spring day, one of those that seemed determined to announce that summer would be here shortly. The sky stretched like blue silk across the river, not yet marred by the smoke that would soon pour from hundreds of thousands of chimneys, house and factory. There was not a cloud to be seen from horizon to horizon and though on the short walk from Blackstock Street to Stanley Dock there wasn't a flower or a tree that had taken root, Ally had the strange feeling that she could smell the fragrance of spring, of marsh marigolds and wood sorrel, of sweet violets and wild daffodils, all the wild flowers that lined the banks of the canal. Ridiculous, she knew, for here where the world's shipping came and went only *their* smells filled the air. Tar and coffee beans, timber and spices, all the cargoes come from the four corners of the globe. Though it was not yet seven the streets leading to the docks, the docks themselves were teeming with workers on their way to the blue-silvered ribbon of life, which led to the wide estuary. In contrast to the day the vast docks and quays cut in the grey granite blocks of Lancashire were bleak and colourless. There was scarcely any breeze but what there was sang a merry song through the denuded rigging of the sailing ships, winches creaked as goods swung from hold to shore and overhead the graceful wheeling of gulls accompanied the sound with harsh cries of their own.

The two canal boats were moored prow to stern against the looming warehouse where, yesterday, they had unloaded the manufactured cotton goods which would, it was said, fetch up in some far foreign country on the other side of the world. The foreman, who had overseen the unloading, speaking of course to Jack, had told them of a cargo of bales of raw cotton which was becoming more plentiful now that the American Civil War was over. It was to go to the cotton mills of Lancashire where for the past few years great hardship had been suffered through lack of raw cotton to spin and weave. She had come . . . or rather *Jack* had come, he said, at an opportune moment, though the foreman had not used that expression, for the sailing ship *Caroline* of Boston had just discharged her cargo of cotton at Princes Dock for the firm of Cropper, Benson & Co. If they looked lively they might pick up enough to fill to capacity both their canal boats.

Jack had been exultant at the time, but Jack and Davey were both still "driving the pigs to market" as Ma in better days had called it when Pa had imbibed too freely the night before, tossing fretfully from her hand when she tried to wake them. Only Teddy, curled between them, lifted his head and yawned, following her back up on deck to the water bucket, the contents of which Ally meant to fling into the bed-hole. He leaped adroitly on to the canal bank and relieved himself on the wall of the warehouse before jumping back on board. He sat down and, cocking his head, looked up at her as though to say, "Where's me breakfast?"

There was an elderly man squatting on his haunches beside the *Harmony*, a clay pipe between his teeth. He drew on the pipe, blew smoke into the cold air, then pointed with it at the *Harmony*.

"This 'ere your family's craft?" he asked with an air of total indifference as though he were merely making conversation. He wore what could be called a boatman's outfit, broad cap, waistcoat, collarless shirt and neckerchief with patched corduroy trousers. His jacket was buttoned, hiding what might have been a spiderweb belt that would have proclaimed him to be a true boatman, otherwise he might have been any labouring man.

"Yes," she answered shortly, lifting the bucket of water.

"Fred Pearce?" He was frugal with words.

"Is my father." So was she.

"I 'eard 'e were lookin' fer a crew."

"Did you?"

"Aye, is 'e?"

"No, he's not. I am."

For a second or two his brown, weathered face, which looked as though it had spent its whole life in the open air, registered surprise, then shock, then contempt.

"I'm workin' fer no woman." Then curiosity, which he did his best to conceal, got the better of him. "Anyroad, what's yer pa doin' lettin' a lass like you—"

"Sir," she said pointedly, though the "sir" was out of place when applied to this old chap, but perhaps it pleased him for he stood, as a man should in the presence of a woman, "am I ter understand yer lookin' for work?"

"I might."

"Either yer are or yer not."

"Now look here, my girl."

"I'm not your girl. I'm the owner – number one – of this boat, both these boats. I need crew: a strong man who knows his way along t' cut an' you don't seem ter fit the bill."

If she had not been so ferociously wretched she might have laughed at the comical expression that crossed the old fellow's face. On it was disbelief, amazement and fury. He stamped his feet in what would have been called a tantrum in a child, and his pipe almost fell out of his mouth. He could have been anywhere between fifty and ninety, she thought, dried up as a prune and yet he seemed spry enough the way he hopped about in his indignation. Even Teddy stood up and eyed him warily, ready to bark. But the man seemed to get over his momentary high dudgeon, looking her up and down with the rheumy eye of a man long past the nonsense men fell into.

"I can sail owt what floats on water," he told her. His lip curled, quite amused by her female intrusion into the male world, his world. "I mekk it me business ter know what's goin' on round these docks an' I 'appen to 'ave 'eard a man's needed on this 'ere boat."

"In the ale-'ouse, I suppose. Me brother's a right chatter-box."

"Aye, I noticed. Yer'd best purr a clamp on 'im an' that boy with 'im unless yer want all Liverpool ter know yer business. Only thing 'e didn't mention were you, or I wouldn't 'a bothered."

"Well, yer best look elsewhere then . . . er . . ."

"Me name's Pat, Pat Maloney, an' I reckon you an' me'd gerron well, wi' a birrof give an' take," intimating that she'd be the "giver" and he the "taker". "Neither lad's got sense they had at their mam's breast. So wi' you an' lad on *Edith*, me an' yer brother on *Harmony* travellin' together until we're satis-fied," meaning until he was satisfied. "A good split that. We can't put them lads on't same boat or we'd get nowt done. Three chaps ter do hard work, leggin' it an' such, you wit' hanimals an' cookin'. A few bob a week an' me grub an' . . ."

She began to laugh and for some reason was rewarded with what might have been a twinkle in the pale blue eyes of Pat Maloney.

"Yer seem to 'ave it all worked out, at least to yer own satisfaction, Mr Maloney."

"Pat."

"I've not said I agree yet."

"Lass, there's not many chaps 'd work fer a woman. It strikes me we're both comin' at this from a 'ard place. A disadvantage, if yer tekk me meaning. I'm knockin' on a bit, an' you're a woman. Mebbe we can 'elp each other, like."

Suddenly he grinned, showing a mouthful of broken teeth. He was clean, though, tidy, beside him a bundle in which she suspected was everything he owned. The dog at her side began to wag his tail and for some ridiculous reason this made up her mind for her. Or perhaps it was that with Pat Maloney to help her – which meant she had no need to search out and interview a crew – she would get on her way from Liverpool all the quicker with no need to meet Tom Hartley, at least on this trip, and with a few weeks to get used to the idea that he was to be her brother-in-law she would cope with it more easily.

She was wrong. Pat, to the boys' disgruntled astonishment, had them out of their beds and on their unsteady feet within the next five minutes. Just give him time to sling his "duds", as he called the bundle, into his cabin, the one of his choice being in the stern of the *Harmony*, expecting no argument, and getting none, telling her to get kettle on an' a bacon butty 'd be welcome, he had Jack and Davey, speechless and shivering, on the stern deck beside the tiller.

"Aye up, 'oo d' yer think," Jack began, ready to argue with this old chap who was chucking orders about as though he owned the bloody boat, and again Ally was forced to smother a smile. Pat Maloney, about whom she knew absolutely nothing but whom she was inclined to trust, made it quite clear he'd stand no nonsense from the likes of these two little squirts, even though they were both twice his size. He allowed them the cup of tea and bacon butties Ally put in their hands, his included, then he herded them like two bewildered sheep towards the stables. He made a fuss of Magic and Gentle, the "hanimals", as he was always to call them. Under his stern eye, the two lads had them groomed – oh yes, he liked a well-groomed hanimal – watered, fed and harnessed to the boats in readiness for the cargo. He organised the loading from the Cropper, Benson wagons to the *Edith* and the *Harmony*, which Ally had arranged with Mr Cropper and by noon they were ready for their journey to the cotton mill in Nelson.

"We should be at the top o' t' locks in an hour," Ally began shouting across from the *Edith*, which she and Davey were to crew, to the *Harmony* where Pat was definitely in charge of the tiller, and Jack. "I'll have ter 'ave a word wi' me ma then."

"Off yer go, lass," Pat shouted, "me an' t' lads can manage. Meet yer at top. We should be in Burscough by dark."

"But . . ."

"Why will a woman allus argue?" he asked a bemused Jack who shook his head which was still thumping. He and Davey had been invited to try a tot of rum the night before by some drunken sailors and not only was his head ready to split but his stomach, despite the bacon sandwich or perhaps because of it, was heaving like the waters of the Mersey in a storm. He decided no answer was needed to this chap's question.

"But, Mr Maloney—" Ally began.

"Pat, missus."

"I really think—"

"Gerron. Go an' say ta-ra ter yer mam and us'll see yer on't canal at top."

She knew the moment she turned the corner into Blackstock Street that Tom Hartley was still at number 10. His tall bay mare was tethered to the boot scraper beside Aggie's front door and for a second or two, as her heart began to flutter in her chest then moved into her throat, she was tempted to turn and run back to the canal, but how could she? Ma would wonder where she was and even if she sent a message by one of the numerous small boys who hung about the docks and were willing to do anything or go anywhere for a penny, or even less, Ma would be bewildered and anxious. Did Ally want to burden her mother with any more tribulations than she already had?

As she entered the room he rose courteously from the chair at the table where he had been holding Ma's hands. Ma was doing her best hurriedly to wipe away her tears and Aggie was patting her shoulder with a gentle touch, wanting to comfort, or so it appeared, but not intrude. There was no sign of Pa. Betsy, dressed as though she were off to take tea at one of the fine houses on the outskirts of Liverpool, was elegant in her silk gown. She immediately moved to put a possessive hand on Tom's arm.

"Miss Pearce," Tom said, standing quietly, not exactly shaking off Betsy's hand, but looking embarrassed by her behaviour and Ally wondered how her sister had persuaded this man, this good sensible, *intelligent* man to propose marriage to her. What tricks had she used, what sly underhand stratagem had persuaded, or perhaps forced Tom Hartley to this desperate measure? It had been evident from the first that he had been overwhelmed by her delicate loveliness, as all males were, even Albert. Betsy had assumed that shy modesty and artlessness, that look of pure and virginal innocence that clouded a man's brain, took his breath away and persuaded him to fall in love with her at the first glance. As Tom had done. And yet he did not look happy – he looked trapped. That was the word. Trapped by his own masculine desire to own the exquisite creature who clung to his arm.

It took all her strength, all her resolve, all the teeth-gritting, jaw-clenching determination she could gather to hide her sorrow, the weight on her spirit as she gazed calmly into Tom's clouded blue eyes. She loved this man who was to marry her sister. There was no way she could hide it from herself but, by God, she'd make sure neither he nor Betsy knew how she felt about him. She had her work, thank the good Lord, though the sadness of how it had come about was a load she would have to carry for ever, but at least it got her away from this house, from Liverpool where, presumably, Tom and Betsy would settle to married life, bear children – oh, dear Lord, please keep her upright – and where she need only spend enough time to pick up and deposit a cargo. She supposed he and Betsy, when they were married, would go to live at that great mansion Betsy had gloated over and of which one day she meant to be mistress, but until then she, Ally, would spend as little time as possible at number 10 Blackstock Street.

"Doctor Hartley," she murmured, her expression serene, no sign of the tumult of emotion that raged inside her. "I'm just off. I came ter say goodbye ter Ma an' Pa an' tell 'em I'll be . . ."

"Ally . . . lass," her mother moaned. "Oh, Ally." Again her heart surged in her chest and she sprang forward, crossing the room in a stride. She knelt at her mother's knee and took between her own the rough, hardworking hands which moments before Tom had been holding.

"What? What's 'appened, Ma? Pa . . ." She turned to look in Tom's direction, meeting his quiet gaze, that sensitive expression of looking directly into her soul and knowing exactly what was needed to lighten it. His manner seemed to bestow a blessing on her, calming her turmoil and she realised why it was all the hard-pressed multitude who were crammed into the crumbling courts and alleyways off the dockland area trusted him so implicitly.

"He will not last much longer, Miss Pearce," he said, treating her as he would any sensible woman, with the calm, the quiet assurance that could not be denied. She was an adult and was accorded the truth and respect an adult should have. Betsy had begun to weep noisily, for was it not expected of her, but strangely it was not to her he turned but to Edie Pearce. He hunkered down, as Ally was doing at her feet, and smiled up into her face, a smile of singular sweetness and had Ally not already loved him, she would have done so then.

"Mrs Pearce, you would not want your Fred to linger on as he is now, would you? He is in no pain since I have kept him free of it but he is weakening daily. I have a feeling, though why I can't tell you, since we know so little of the human brain, that he is aware on some level and would not thank us for holding on to him. Your care, yours and Mrs Wainwright's have kept him comfortable but I believe he has given up. It's for the best, Mrs Pearce."

He stroked her hands, his shoulder against Ally's and from it she felt the warmth, the comfort, the quietness flow, giving her peace, as she could see it giving her mother.

"Well . . ." Betsy wailed. "Wharrabout *my* grief at Pa's—"

"Be quiet, Betsy," Tom said, without looking away from Edie Pearce. "Your mother is in . . . is suffering a great sorrow."

"I like that! It's my pa you're—"

"Be quiet, Betsy," he repeated and amazingly she was.

With one last thoughtful smile at her mother, Tom rose to his feet, holding out his hand to help Ally up. His hand was warm, slender but strong, and as hers rested in it for a moment, no more, some curious pulse quivered between them, startling them both so that for a second or two their flesh clung, then they both stepped away.

Ally, flustered, ashamed that she should have such a feeling when she had just been told that her father had not long to live, swung round to stare from the window, not caring to watch the way Tom had turned to Betsy, who was nestling against his chest.

"How long?" she asked, addressing Aggie's snow-white nets.

"A few weeks, perhaps . . . not long." His mouth was in Betsy's tumbled silver-gilt curls and Ally felt her heart tear harshly as she turned back to him.

"I'm . . . Jack an' I . . . we've a cargo for Nelson. I'm not sure whether . . ." Dear sweet Christ, it was hard and again she felt the guilt wash over her. To be agonising over her own pain at the sight of Tom's arms about Betsy when her ma, who was to lose her lifetime partner, was in such deep suffering over it.

"Miss Pearce, let me assure you," Tom was saying, his arms still about Betsy. One hand stroked her hair and it struck her then that he gave the appearance of a man soothing a fretful child. "Your father will still be here; please deliver your cargo." He smiled, the smile that broke her heart over and over again, though she continued to fight her bloody wounding battle to hide it from him. "I heard from Mrs Wainwright here how well you had done. Congratulations." Then Betsy pulled petulantly at him, crystal tears wetting his ruffled shirt front.

"Thank you," Ally said.

"Will you manage, the three of you with two boats?" He was genuinely interested, she could see that, but Betsy was sobbing, looking quite stunning as she knew so well how to do, and he was forced to look down into her face, his attention dragged from Ally.

Ally felt hollow and sick. She loved her pa and he was dying but the hollowness, the nausea were not, sadly she admitted it, for Pa. They were for Ally Pearce who had to watch the man she loved love another woman. But not just another woman! Her own sister who she knew was worthless and would make Tom Hartley as miserable as she herself was. But it would not do. *It would not do!* She must find within herself the courage, the control, the power to remain dignified in the face of so much heartache.

"We've found a man," she answered shortly, wondering why

she was bothering, for it seemed they all had their own concerns. Aggie was busy with Ma who at least was genuinely suffering. Tom was smoothing Betsy's back, his hand lingering in some way that Ally recognised, though she knew nothing about it personally, as sensual and really could she bear it? She knew herself to be a loving woman who would give a man the whole of herself, her love, spiritual and earthy, her friendship, her laughter, her decency, since she knew herself to be decent, the very essence of Alice Pearce. Tom Hartley's happiness was important to her but could she honestly say, and believe it, that her sister would supply what he needed? Was she being presumptuous in thinking she was the woman who could? It pierced her sick heart and she knew she must get away. Get away from Tom Hartley and Betsy.

"I'll go and see Pa, then I must be off. I'll be back soon as I can. They're waiting for me at top o' t' locks."

She ran up Blackstock Street, her head filled with the pictures she would take with her for ever. Pa already like a corpse, grey, emaciated, eyes staring unfocused at the ceiling. Ma weeping in Aggie's arms, and Tom Hartley cradling Betsy to his chest, but worst of all, Betsy's eyes drowning in tears but glinting just the same in malicious triumph.

12

Tom Hartley smiled politely at the young lady who sat to his right at his mother's dinner table. He was doing his duty, as the eldest son of the house was meant to, as indeed were his brothers – apart from James and Arthur who were too young – John and Teddy, and his sisters, Angelina and Catherine.

It was a large party, one of those his mother gave every month or so, an equal number of ladies and gentlemen, the former friends of his mother, the latter his father's business acquaintances. Four older couples with their children to make up the numbers to twenty, which Mary Hartley believed to be a perfect arrangement for what she called an informal party.

The dining-room looked magnificent. The candles his mother favoured were lit, forming dozens of golden stars soft and caressing, flattering the faces of the people about the table. The conversation ebbed and flowed, heads turned, nodding, smiling, all perfectly at ease with one another, since this was where they belonged, this privileged class of society. There was the chink of glass and cutlery, the unobtrusive movements of the servants, the colours of the ladies' evening gowns, the stark contrast of the gentlemen's dinner suits, the crackle of the flames in the white marble fireplace, the scent of the flowers, many bowls of them, all from his mother's conservatory.

The young lady's name was Emily, Emily Maynard, seventeen years old, sweetly vivacious, agreeable, pretty, well brought up, healthy, first-rate marriage and child-bearing material and was his and Emily's mother's hope for the future joining of their two families.

He had to admit that his mother was superb at what she did, which was to be the mistress of Rosemont House. Her entertaining skills were extensive. She had learned this from her mother who had been trained by *hers*. She had a book listing the name of every guest, many of them business associates of her husband from abroad, and their wives. Against the names were their likes and dislikes, not that they were likely to voice them, but Mary Hartley took note and acted upon it the next time they were guests. Perhaps Mrs Hungerford preferred goat's milk to cow's, or Monsieur D'Acre was partial to a particular cheese not available in his own country, the favourite wine of a certain American gentleman with whom Edward did business. She had domestic routines that ensured her house ran smoothly, lists of menus so that no dish was ever served more than once in any month. She knew the names of all their wives and even their children. Everything in her home that should be polished was polished thoroughly by her excellently trained servants, every item of linen requiring starch was starched to perfection, every inch of upholstery and carpet meticulously brushed. Her larders would be full, her drawers and cupboards scented with lavender, her staff respectful, respectable and efficient and they, in turn, were well looked after, for it was her belief that a contented servant was a *good* servant. Her house was the epitome of order and competence.

Tom, automatically doing what was expected of a gentleman when seated next to a lady, had helped Emily with her napkin, the disposal of her gloves and fan, then began the task of engaging her in the kind of conversation that was considered suitable for a young lady of her age and station in life. It consisted of discussions on her preference for art, for music, her favourite flowers, the gentle mare her father had given her for her last birthday and which she called Ariel, all the correct social formulas which his mother insisted upon, but he noticed she was watching him with careful attention and knew she had not forgotten the incident of Betsy Pearce!

And neither had he. How could he ever erase from his memory that outpouring of woe, of innocent bewilderment that at first he could not understand, a sobbing hysteria that seemed to imply that she had been set upon by a gang of would-be rapists and murderers who had handled her indecently and all because she had paid a friendly call on his mother.

Tom, sleepless in the night, wondered how in hell's name he had ever got himself into such a pickle.

"Sweetheart . . . sweetheart, begin at the beginning," he had implored her. "I can't make head nor tail . . ."

"I were only tryin' ter be . . . sociable," she had hiccuped in that northern accent somewhere between Lancashire and Yorkshire and which he thought so quaint.

"But who did this to you?" he asked, trying to lead her towards the surgery and the antiseptic he meant to apply to her scratched cheek, when as she seemed in imminent danger of collapsing, he had swung her into his arms and carried her.

Which was where it had happened. He had lost his head, he had known that the minute her rounded breasts had fallen obligingly into his hands but though his cool brain, which made life-and-death decisions every day, was screaming *madness* his hot male body took over. All it was concerned with was the soft, coral-tipped breasts, the white silken thighs, the moist cleft surrounded by crisp silver-gilt curls – the same colour as those on her head, his inflamed mind noticed – and the desperate need of his body to invade it. It was over in five minutes, less, he supposed as he watched Betsy pat herself into orderliness, swiftly doing up buttons, arranging her skirts, smoothing her hair, then smiling with that enchanting innocence which, unlike herself, seemed quite unaffected.

"I suppose this means you an' me 's engaged ter be wed then,

Tom?" she said, shy, artless, *untouched*. He remembered as he
sat beside Miss Emily Maynard at his mother's dinner table that
his mind had skittered about like a mouse cornered by a cat,
looking for escape but he was still in that state of foolishness
which a man's . . . well, he might as well be honest – the state a
man's cock gets him into and he could only squat at her feet in
the very position where he had eagerly flung himself five
minutes ago. He had heard the words, and he supposed there
was some searching for the truth in them but how trite they
were.

"My heart sank . . . my heart stopped," even "my heart
broke." He was a doctor and knew none of these things was
physically possible but nevertheless his heart did just that, at
least the first two.

"Betsy . . ." he stammered. He knew she had been a virgin,
the blood on her thighs told him that. She was a decent girl, not
of *his* people, of course, but come from a decent family. She
had bewitched him the moment he set eyes on her, but that was
no excuse and now, having had her virginity taken, she
expected him to marry her.

He had thought he was already shattered, dazed, at the mercy
of the recent event when the next words threw him into deeper
mire.

"An' yer'll tell that ma o' yours that I'll not be treated like
some muck what she's picked up on 'er shoe." She was all pink
and white, blue and silver, eyes ready to fill up with her crystal
tears and for a moment he was fascinated by her ability to
change from – well, what had *she* done five minutes ago besides
allow it? – to this exquisite delicacy, this fragile, endearing
creature who had professed to feeling "queer" and who had told
him she loved him. Now she was all briskness, ready to be about
the next step in whatever plan she had.

"What?" He knew he sounded half-witted but that's how he
felt, as though half his wits had been taken from him.

"Yer ma, an' that Sinclair an' all. I'd sack 'im if it were up ter me, Tom. 'Im an' that other chap. 'E purris 'ands on me . . . well . . ." She dimpled and blushed, for hadn't Tom himself just done the same.

"Sinclair?"

"Aye, 'igh an' mighty . . ."

"Sinclair? The butler at . . ."

"That's 'im. 'E an' that other one chucked me out, Tom, an' all I did were call ter see yer ma." She began to cry in earnest, the memory of her humiliation, her fury, her disbelief at being treated as she had been, causing her rosy mouth to quiver and her body to tremble. She looked appealingly at Tom, waiting for his arms to rise comfortingly about her but he merely sat back on his heels and stared at her in bewilderment.

"You've been to my family's home?"

At once, recognising what was in his voice, she reared back, her face flushed. "An' what's wrong wi' that? Me an' you 'ave bin friends fer a long time now." And still would be just that if I hadn't pushed things on a bit, she thought, though naturally she didn't say it.

"But, my mother . . . she wouldn't understand."

"Understand what? There's nowt wrong wi' bein' friendly."

"No, I suppose not but you see my mother would . . . they . . . my mother's friends do things differently. They leave cards."

"Cards? What sorter cards?" Betsy knew she was ready to frown, to fly off the handle as her ma called it, to give Tom "what for" as she would anyone else who upset her but she knew she mustn't. Not yet, not until she was more sure of him, so instead she hung her head and sighed prettily, though it cost her all her self-control which was not a lot at the best of times.

"It's just a silly custom . . . but enough of that, sweetheart," his heart constricting – there he went again about his damned heart – at the sweet expression on Betsy's face. His little love, his beautiful girl; yes, *his*, for he had made her so only minutes before.

Tom Hartley's good strong heart, which amused him at times, his compassion, his sympathy for his fellow man, for any living thing hurt or distressed, whether it be animal or human, and which had always got the better of him, did so now. The great Reform Bill of 1832 devised by Lord Derby, which had improved the lives of so many oppressed men and women though he had been but a small boy at the time, had, as he grew into a youth and then a man, been his guiding star. Universal suffrage was the only way, that and education and . . . oh, he could go on and on. There was to be a demonstration near Hyde Park soon, the Reform League of London proclaimed, demanding the immediate extension of the suffrage. He would dearly love to march with them, but the hard-pressed inhabitants of Naylors Yard, Raymond Street, Pope Row and the teeming, tottering tenements that surrounded them, needed him more.

"Tell me what happened, Betsy, when you visited my mother."

Her face crumpled as she did so, dwelling on his ma's coldness, her absolute refusal to talk to her – "never even offered me a drink o' tea" – and then the dreadful attack by the two servants, *men* mind you, who had not only handled her indecently but had thrown her into the road tearing her new gown, grazing her cheek. She had feared for her life, or at least her honour, she told him, though not in those words, for Betsy Pearce was an ignorant, illiterate young woman and unless they were read to her, by Ally or the adoring Albert, they were not in her vocabulary.

"Yer'll 'ave ter 'ave a word wi' yer ma now, won't yer, Tom," she finished, wiping away her tears, disconsolate as a child unjustly punished. "I mean if you an' me's ter be wed an' we're ter live at Rosemont House she'll 'ave ter, ter . . ." She almost said "to be made to toe the line" meaning, as her daughter-in-law, Betsy had the rights and privileges that went with it. She would be Mrs Tom Hartley and that old cow would have to accept her. Instead she sighed deeply again, peeping up prettily between her long silken eyelashes. "She'll be all right when yer tell 'er 'oo I am, Tom, she didn't know before or she'd not 'ave thrown me out. It was 'orrible, Tom, ter be treated like that. She'd no right an' yer must tell 'er so."

Tom could feel something in his chest move painfully. There was a drop, an emptiness as though his body had hollowed out. There was nothing more sure in his world than the absolute certainty that his mother, his father, his family and the circle of friends of whom they were a part would never accept Betsy Pearce, no matter how beautiful, no matter how fashionable, no matter how *he* felt about her, and even that was ambivalent!

And Betsy believed he had only to speak to his mother, to chide her for the way in which she had treated her, Betsy, and all would be set right. What was he to say to Betsy herself? She had no conception of the rules that governed the society from which he had come, of which he was still a part. His mother would be kinder to her own scullery-maid who knew her place than she would to pretty, uneducated Betsy, who did not! If he should go along with Betsy in the belief that she and he were engaged, she would expect to be invited into his family home, to be petted and pampered, made much of as the heir's future wife. But it would not happen. They would not allow her over the doorstep, even the one at the back of the house, which led into the kitchen. She was of an inferior class to his own, of the lower orders, come from common stock and not a fit wife for the eldest son of the house. He would be forced to accept it or he would be cast out, disowned, be considered dead in his family's eyes. His generous allowance from his father would be stopped, and he would be forced to exist on the small inheritance his grandmother had left to each of her grandchildren if he was to continue to care for the unwashed, miserably housed, *non-paying*, neglected mass of humanity in Naylors Yard and its environs. How would he support not only himself, but her who expected so much? Even a smart practice, a *paying* practice, would be out of the question, for patients of that sort would, like his family, not accept a wife who came from the labouring classes.

So here he was with his family and their guests and so far neither he nor his mother had mentioned his mother's unwelcome guest. They must do, of course, when the guests had gone. This was the first time he had been home since Betsy's visit, and though his mother would not be unduly worried about her son having a liaison with a woman of the lower classes since that was what all young, virile gentlemen did, she would not be pleased that one of the creatures had had the audacity to invade her home. She and his father would take him to task about it and it was then that he must face the appalling dilemma of what he should do.

". . . you like to ride, Mr . . . I beg your pardon, Doctor Hartley?" the light girlish voice beside him asked. He dragged himself back from that day to this evening. He knew his mother was watching him intently. Immediately he turned to smile at the young face beside him and for the rest of the meal his manners were faultless. He divided his time between Emily on one side and Mrs Johnson on the other.

The ladies left the room, the gentlemen relaxed at one end of the table with their port and cigars. His father, an older edition of himself, tall and still upright, shot a fierce glance at him and as they moved to rejoin the ladies in his mother's drawing-room he grasped Tom's arm, murmuring in his ear that his mother and himself would like a word with him after their guests had gone. Tom knew that the moment had come.

He and his father sipped a brandy. Tom stood by the fireplace in the drawing-room, one arm resting on the mantelpiece, looking about the room which was so familiar to him and where on many occasions he and his brothers and sisters had known, if not the open demonstrations of parental love others might know, at least a comforting security. But the atmosphere tonight was cool, frosty even.

His father cleared his throat and both Tom and his mother turned to look at him expectantly.

"Your mother was extremely distressed the other day when some young woman, claiming to be a friend of yours, gained admittance to our home. Apparently she pushed past Sinclair before he had time to stop her" – dear God, Betsy . . . Oh, Betsy – "and demanded to see your mother. She was obviously not a lady, indeed had the manners and the vocabulary of a gutter-snipe. Now we are aware that young men must" – he turned politely to his wife – "I beg your pardon, my dear, but this must be said" – turning back to his son – "must sow their wild oats."

Edward Hartley had allowed this personable, *soft-hearted*, as he thought it, son of his to go his own way. Perhaps it was as well, he had thought, for would a man with his son's tender feelings, his lack of the toughness needed, have done well in the cut and thrust of the commercial world?

"I have no idea who this . . . this person is and what you might have said to her which led her to believe she would be welcome in . . . in our world but I must insist—"

Perhaps it was the word *guttersnipe* that did it. Betsy was *not* a lady in the way his family defined a lady, but she came from a decent, hardworking family and was not the low woman men paid for favours, as his father believed.

He held up his hand and his good-humoured face hardened. "Before you go any further, or say anything else which might worsen the situation, let me tell you that Miss Pearce and I are to be married. She is an enchanting young woman and I . . . I admire her. Now I know she is . . . is not from our world and therefore is ignorant of our . . . your customs. She imagined she had only to call on you and extend the hand of friendship and you would welcome her. She was wrong but she will learn and—"

"Not in my home, she will not," his mother hissed, her face as cold and white and hard as the marble fireplace. Even her lips, normally rather full and pink, for she was a pretty woman, lost all colour, thinning until they were no more than a slash on her face. "I don't know how this . . . this outrage came about, probably through your contact with the dreadful people you minister to but it is to finish at once, do you hear? You are the son, the eldest son of one of the most illustrious families in Lancashire. You have the pick of any girl, even one with a title if you choose, and this nasty association must stop. Oh, use her as young men of good family use these low women—"

"Mary," her husband gasped, shocked beyond measure that his well-bred wife, who herself had a title or two in her background, should speak, even *know* of such things.

Mary Hartley raised her hand imperiously, then stood up as though to lend weight to her words. "I am willing to forget the incident since none of our friends knows of it and the servants can be trusted not to speak of it. Indeed I have already had a word with Sinclair, so if you will give me your word that this dashing, but quite insane desire that you have to make an *honest*" – her lip curled – "woman of her will be put aside we will say no more on the subject."

There was a long silence and Mary Hartley sat down again though she kept her eyes on her son. Her first-born and, if she was honest, the dearest of the ten children she had borne. Three had died of one of the strange fevers that carry off infants in the first months of their lives. Of the remaining seven all had survived, thrived and been a satisfaction to her and Edward. This one was a fine son, a son to be proud of, the only disappointment his obsessive need to enter the medical profession. He was young yet, idealistic, but when he got over this absurd folly he had to treat the ills of the lower classes, would settle into a fine practice among his own people. With the right wife he would do well and so this foolishness, this madness, this incredible tomfoolery must be nipped in the bud. Dear sweet heaven, had he lost his senses, his loyalty to his family, his own class, over this infatuation with a woman who would bring only disaster to him, to his family and to his future?

Tom spoke at last. "I'm afraid I can't do that, Mother. I have given my promise. I am very . . . fond of Miss Pearce."

"You do not speak of love, Thomas," his mother said harshly, not that she knew the meaning of the word, for she had been married at seventeen to the man her father chose for her. She had not been unhappy. She had made a good life. She was respected. She was the wife of a wealthy, prominent and successful gentleman fifteen years older than herself and had become known as one of the great hostesses of Liverpool. She had never been in love though, which was why it was curious that she should mention it to her son.

"Surely if I am to marry Miss Pearce it follows that I must be." Why could he not use the word, a small corner of his mind was asking, the part that was standing outside of himself looking on, so to speak. Why could he never say, "I love Betsy Pearce," and that same honest corner, though he did not listen to it replied, "Because you don't. Because what you feel is need, desire, bewitchment, tenderness, fascination." He was in thrall to her. The part of him that was his heritage, his logical *rational* self argued that his mother was right. He could never, *never* bring Betsy here, even had his mother agreed, for she would simply be overwhelmed by it, by the life, the people, their standards which never faltered. But he had taken her virginity and she had assumed in her innocence that meant he would marry her. So be it. To have constant access to that beautiful slender body, parts of which he had already glimpsed, would be no hardship. His rooms in Duke Street were comfortable and his grandmother's legacy would keep them from starving. She loved him and she would be content.

Tom knew nothing of the *real* Betsy Pearce: the woman who loved no one but herself; who was obsessed with Rosemont House; who hungered to be mistress there; who craved the life Tom Hartley's wife would have, not as a doctor's wife, but as the wife of the eldest son and heir to a vast fortune. She had not been born a lady but by any method at her disposal she meant to become one.

Edward put out his hand imploringly, his face anguished. "Son, don't do this thing. I didn't meet the woman but the description your mother gave of her was . . . she is not one of us. I would not allow her to associate with your sisters; even the way she spoke, your mother said, was appalling. I cannot say I approve but could you . . . if you must have her, could you not set her up in some small house somewhere? I would be prepared to make you . . . her . . . and any children an allowance, but, dear God, don't ruin your life for—"

"I have promised to marry her, Father." Tom's voice was flat and toneless.

"So you said but a woman like that—"

"She is the daughter of a man as honourable as you. Would you have me shame him and her family?"

"Don't talk such bloody rubbish." Edward Hartley was becoming so infuriated he disregarded his status as a gentleman and swore in the presence of a lady. The lady in question looked as though she herself would like to swear.

"Let me bring her to meet you. She is quick, clever, she would soon learn our ways."

"Don't be ridiculous, Tom." His mother's voice was flat, dismissive.

"Why is it ridiculous?"

"Stop it, boy." His father turned from him and strode to the window, staring at his own reflection in the glass. "You either give up this woman or set her up where she can harm no one or . . ."

"Yes, Father?"

Edward turned and Mary Hartley put her hand to her mouth, for even now she could not believe that her son would cast off his family for the common creature who had, against all the rules of her own society, invaded her home.

"Or leave your home, and your family for good, marry her if you will. I cannot stop you, but when you do you will cease to be my son. I shall disown you. Your name will not be mentioned—"

"Edward . . ." Mary Hartley whispered.

Edward silenced her with a lifted hand. "Which is it to be, Thomas?"

Although he had expected it Tom felt the constriction in his throat and it ached in an effort not to choke on words of pleading. Though he had gone against his father's wishes in the matter of his career and had not lived at home since he was a boy, apart from school holidays, he had a great love for this gracious house in which he had been born and which had been in his family for generations. His father had bowed to his wish to be a doctor but it had always been accepted that one day Rosemont House would come to him. Primogeniture had been created in order to avoid the splitting up of great estates but its existence applied to small ones like this. John and Teddy, James and Arthur when they married would have the wherewithal to purchase their own splendid mansions, as his father's brother had, but now if he was disowned John would inherit, would become the heir, and though the money, the business did not concern him, to lose this lovely house was almost more than he could bear.

"Well?"

"Tom, dearest . . ." His mother had never called him dearest before.

"I cannot . . . desert her."

"She is with child?" His father fastened eagerly on the small hope that this was the reason for his son's obstinacy, his madness, the arbitrariness in him that was beyond belief. Perhaps there was some hope, money, something to induce the slut to loose her hold on his son.

Tom straightened up, his body stiff and rigid, his shoulders surprisingly painful. He had not realised he had been holding himself so tensely.

Was Betsy pregnant? How did he know? She certainly could be, which would make his determination to marry her all the more necessary. He didn't quite know what to do next. His mother and father were looking at him, their faces bearing exactly the same expression, though what it was he couldn't have said. He stepped carefully across his mother's deep-pile carpet towards the door that led into the hallway. With that sixth sense all good butlers seem to have, Sinclair was at the front door, Tom's evening cape and top hat in his hands.

Tom turned to look back, hoping, he supposed, for his parents to break down the barrier they had built against Betsy Pearce, but they were both frozen-faced, staring at nothing.

"Goodnight, sir," Sinclair said as he draped Tom's cape about his shoulders and handed him his hat.

"Goodnight, Sinclair," he answered as he stepped into the carriage, his mother's carriage, which was to carry him for the last time from his home.

13

Jack, Davey and Pat were loading a cargo of bricks on to the *Harmony* when a voice hailed Ally. They were at Church, close to Accrington, the boats moored alongside the warehouse beside which were the stables where Magic and Gentle had spent the night. She was leading the two mares along the towpath which was busy with men on the same business as herself, loading bricks, and unloading the sand and other materials that went into their manufacture, harnessing horses, swearing at dogs and children who got under their feet. They, like her, were eager to be away from the tall grimy warehouses, the dangling cranes, the smoke and fumes, the acrid smell of industry, which was a constant menace to the lungs. There was the penetrating stink of the chemicals from the canalside works, built to supply the textile printers, and from the coke ovens, and Ally was doing her best not to breathe too deeply.

Beside the factories there were many cotton mills in Lancashire. Her small fleet had in fact just come from Burnley which was a cotton-weaving town, and the *Edith*, fully laden with woven cotton goods, was moored behind the *Harmony* waiting for Ally and Jack to get her under way. The three men had been needed, first to let the two boats through the Gannow Tunnel between Burnley and Church, and then to load the containers of bricks. Both cargoes were headed for Liverpool.

It was August, high summer, the sky above her yellow with the slow penetration of sunlight through the pall of factory smoke. The humidity was oppressive and already so early in the morning her clean blouse was dark beneath her armpits and across her back with sweat.

She turned as her name was called, looking out across the floating mass of canal boats and the sluggish canal water from where the voice seemed to come. There was a boatwoman waving frantically as the boat on whose deck she stood moved northwards towards Clayton-le-Moors. Her bonnet bobbed and Ally's heart bobbed with it, for she recognised her as Jenny Worsborough, wife of a number one. They were evidently come from Liverpool, for their boat was low in the water and covered from the cratch in the stern to the boxmast in the prow with weatherproof sheeting. Probably bales of raw wool, Ally had time to think before Jenny's voice floated out over the busy scene, only just heard above the hubbub. On the deck beside her was a toddler tethered by reins to a hook beside the hatch. On the back of the horse towing the boat sat two more children, for wherever a boatman and woman went so did their family.

"Yer pa . . . I'm sorry, chuck . . . back as soon as yer can," Jenny was shouting, her hands cupped round her mouth. ". . . funeral . . . woman said . . . yer ma's . . ." It was evident that George Worsborough, Jenny's husband, who was at the tiller, his mind concentrating on the delivery of his cargo, had no intention of stopping the slow plod of his horse. But Ally, the reins of her own two horses slackening in her hands, had received the message that her pa was dead.

It was over three months since Tom Hartley had told them that Pa was not long for this world but miraculously – though she was not sure Pa would agree it was a miracle – he had lasted until now. It was thanks to Tom, of course, whose constant attention, sometimes twice in one day, his careful adminis- tration of potions to dull Pa's pain and help him to sleep, his willingness to sit beside Pa, hold his hand, talk to him, smile at him, make him feel worth while, had held Pa in this world. He had made Pa comfortable, content even to spend a little more time with the woman he had loved for so many years.

The horses, unattended, had found a bit of grass growing between the cobbles on the canalside and were chewing peaceably until one burly labourer with a wheelbarrow of coal he had just shovelled from a boat cursed loudly and plunged his broad shoulder into Magic's stomach, making her squeal and rear into Gentle. Both horses panicked, shying away, causing some chaos among the men who were working at the canalside.

"Yer wanner watch them bloody 'orses, girl," the man snarled, aiming a kick at Magic's fetlock. "There's men 'ere tryin' ter work an' us could do wi'out a lass gerrin' in us way. If yer've nowt ter do but . . ."

Ally, her heart dragging in pain at the news of the loss of Pa and her need to get the boats loaded and on their way to Liverpool, was in no state to consider the consequences of her action. She picked up a long-handled shovel and brandished it in the man's face. He grinned, then, obviously amused by her action, turned to wink at the other men who were busy with their wheelbarrows. Ally, incensed, did not notice that they all gave him a wide berth. He was a particularly brutish-looking man, six feet or more tall, with big muscled shoulders, legs like tree-trunks and hands the size of the business end of a shovel. His hair, greasy with sweat and coal dust, was shaved close to his head, his face was that of a boxer, or a wrestler, red and lumpy and knocked about, and his wet lips when he smiled revealed stumps of decayed teeth.

"You touch my 'orses again an' I'll knock yer teeth down yer throat," she hissed. The man's grin deepened. He was delighted by this diversion, the grin said. He wouldn't hurt her of course, though he could have killed her with one swipe of his meaty fist, but he would certainly enjoy having her struggling female body in his arms. She was not much to his taste, for she was too skinny with a face on her like a corpse but a bit of fun might be had nevertheless.

He lowered the handles of his wheelbarrow and strolled over to where another chap stood with the captured horses. Again he winked at the frozen figures of his workmates, then, raising his fist, punched Gentle between her frightened rolling eyes. Not a hard punch, not the punch with which he could knock a man senseless but it was enough to make the animal squeal and buck. But he made the mistake of turning his back on Ally Pearce and the horrified spectators gasped in unison as she raised the shovel and hit the brute a blow to the back of his head which, big as he was, had him off his feet. He fell like a pole-axed ox, lying at the feet of the man holding the horses and in grave danger of being trampled on by their stamping hooves.

"By gum, lass, I think yer've done him in," the man said.

"Give over," Ally replied contemptuously, throwing down the shovel. "A man like 'im's too thick-'eaded to be damaged from a blow wi' a shovel."

" 'Appen yer right, burrif I was you I'd gerrof quick sharp afore he wakes. 'Whipper' Ogden's not one ter turn t' other cheek."

"Filthy scum."

"Aye, lass, yer right but I'd get the 'orses 'itched up an' be on me way, just same."

The two boats were halfway to Blackburn before she told Jack that Pa was dead.

The hearse was outside the door of number 10 Blackstock Street when she and Jack turned the corner. It was a magnificent affair and, ashamed of the thought, Ally wondered how much of the money she had hidden in Ma's box beneath Aggie's immaculate underwear, for it would not take much to persuade Ma to squander it on the sort of funeral Betsy would think appropriate, still remained. The glass hearse shone in the dim narrow street, all a-glitter with silver trimmings and pulled by

four black horses with nodding black plumes. Just coming from
the house was the splendid coffin, carried shoulder-high by
Tom Hartley, Albert Wainwright who was as tall as the doctor
and two strangers, all decently clothed in the black of mourning.
On the coffin was a wreath of white lilies. Behind, also respectably done up in black bonnets, gowns and knee-length veils
were Ma and Betsy, and Ally knew without a shadow of a doubt
that all this was Betsy's doing.

The street was lined with open-mouthed spectators, every
door open, every curtain drawn in respect, the men holding
their caps to their breasts, the women, most of them Irish and
Catholic, crossing themselves reverently, though not one of
them knew the dead man. Betsy had a scrap of black-edged
fabric to her eyes but Ma stared straight ahead, her eyes dry and
blank.

"Bloody 'ell," Jack breathed, then, still in the dishevelled,
grubby state in which he and Ally had travelled day and night
to get to Liverpool for Pa's funeral, he began to run along the
cobbled street, his stout clogs making a great clatter. Every head
turned in amazement as the hush was broken, for surely it was
not right to make such a commotion on this solemn occasion.
They were even further bewildered when the young man
shoved aside one of the coffin bearers and took his place at the
front. It was somehow comical, though naturally they did not
laugh, for the chap was shorter than the others and the coffin
was now lopsided. But that was not the end of their entertainment as a young woman they remembered seeing now and then
at number 10 took her place – and her without even a decent
black bonnet which surely any woman could manage – on the
other side of the widow.

" 'Ere, our Ally," they heard the dead man's beautiful
daughter say, "yer can't go ter Pa's funeral dressed like that. Yer
look dreadful. It's not respectable. Tell 'er, Ma. She'd best stop
at 'ome. An' our Jack's no better. Look at 'im in 'is clogs."

"Be quiet, Betsy," a quiet voice behind her said. "Yer upsettin' yer ma."

"*I'm* upsettin' Ma. Wharrabout 'er? She looks like a rag-picker's clerk. If she 'asn't the decency ter come to 'er own pa's funeral in a suitable gown an' a bonnet . . ." As I have done, her prim expression said, but, to the chagrin of the inhabitants of Blackstock Street, the coffin being safely stowed away, and led by a black top-hatted undertaker, the cortège set off, the mourners falling in behind, despite the lovely one's protests.

They were a strange sight. Two women in the deepest black, all very proper, the tall chap, who was said to be the family doctor, dressed the same. Aggie Wainwright was in her dark grey everyday coat, her plum-coloured wide-brimmed bonnet tied beneath her chin in the fashion of a decade ago, and then the young woman and the lad who had galloped up the street just as the whole thing was about to start. They were in the strange outfits of the boat people who travelled the canals, but the pair of them were so unwashed, so untidy they looked as though they'd been to bed in what they had on, and hadn't seen a drop of water for days. Which was how it had been for Alice and Jack Pearce as they raced to Liverpool, on the go night and day in time to see their pa buried.

All along the route, as was the custom, beshawled women with baskets on their arms, and men who held their caps and bowed their heads, stopped and stood soberly at the side of the road as the cortège made its slow way along Lime Kiln Lane, to St Martin-in-the-Field Church on Tatlock Street and the cemetery beyond where Fred Pearce would be laid to rest. Ally clung to Ma's arm and on Ma's other side, Jack did the same. Jack cried silently as the coffin was lowered into the ground, for though he was on the whole a merry-hearted lad, he had loved his pa.

Across the grave, as Ally turned her face towards the river, to the canal, the canal basin and the locks that had been Pa's life, she was surprised to see the seamed expressionless face of Pat Maloney and beside him young Davey. Neither of them had known Pa and she was aware that Davey, left to himself, would not have given a thought to Fred Pearce, but Pat had, and she knew it was because of her and the strong bond of affection and respect that had formed between them during the last five months. Pat would not have admitted it, not for a gold clock, but he had made her life easier in so many ways on their journeys up and down the cut and here he was, because of *her*, at her pa's funeral.

The only real impression that seemed to worm its puzzled way into Ally's grieving mind was the strange fact that Tom and Betsy were not yet married. March it had been when Betsy, crowing her triumph, had announced that she and Tom were engaged, implying that it would not be long before she would be moving up to West Derby where Tom's family lived. There she was to have the kind of life that Betsy Pearce, with her beauty, her charm, her elegance, deserved and yet here it was August and the wedding had not yet taken place. Why not? There seemed to be nothing to stand in the way of an early marriage. Tom was well able to support a wife, wasn't he? So why was Betsy still at number 10? Each time Ally travelled down the locks to Stanley Dock she prepared herself for the news that at the weekend, next week, or even the following day the wedding was to take place. Of course the sort of wedding Betsy would certainly expect would take weeks of preparation, not to mention a great deal of money which presumably Tom would supply. The wedding gown, the trousseau, which Betsy explained to her meant lots of new dresses and bonnets and even a fur or two, the wedding cake, pictures of which Betsy pored over, young Albert beside her to "say it to her". Where would it take place and where would the celebrations – was it called the wedding breakfast? – be held? At Tom's family home in the presence of Tom's family and if so how would she and

Ma, Jack and Aggie, for Ma would go nowhere without Aggie, fit into Tom's genteel background?

These thoughts flew round in her head like a flock of swallows, seeming to take for ever but in fact covering no more than a minute or two. She felt ashamed that her mind, which should have been on Pa, was absorbed with such things at a time like this. She heard the parson's voice intoning the words and felt her ma sway as she threw the soil, which had been put in her hand, on to Pa's coffin. Betsy wept softly, prettily, leaning heavily on Tom's shoulder, playing her part to perfection as she always did, gaining the sympathy of the onlookers, none of whom Ally knew but who always seemed to gather on occasions like this.

Then it was over and she found herself helped gently into a hansom cab, which was waiting at the church gate. Tom's hand on her elbow, and placed beside Ma and Aggie. There was a second cab behind in which it seemed Tom and Betsy were to travel. Jack elected to walk with Pat and Davey and would see them back at the house, he said, glad to absent himself even for a few minutes from the trappings of death. It was quiet apart from the noisy chorus of a flock of swifts, which were chasing one another about the roof of the church. The parson, his duty done, was already hurrying away towards the parsonage on the far side of the cemetery, and Betsy's words could clearly be heard.

" 'Onestly, Tom, yer'd think at a time like this yer ma'd have lent yer t' carriage."

"Sweetheart, how many times must I explain . . ." His words were lost as he turned to Betsy.

"Well, I think it's about time yer . . ." Then the cab in which she, Ma and Aggie were to be driven to Blackstock Street moved on. Ally, her hand still holding Ma's, stared blindly out of the window, her mind, which really was so exhausted it wanted nothing more than to sink into an unconscious state, wearily circling the meaning of Betsy's words but unable to make sense of them.

They sat about the parlour where a fire had been lit despite the warmth of the day. Jack, Tom, Pat, Davey and Albert leaned against the wall, while Aggie served tea so hot, black and sweet it was like drinking treacle, the sort Aggie considered a good heartener on a day like this. She had made a rich fruit cake and some scones, a couple of raised meat pies, a dozen fruit turnovers and a lemon cheesecake, all of which Pat, Davey and Jack tackled enthusiastically, since they had lived on nothing but Ally's stews and pub food for the past three weeks.

Tom had a look about him that she had not noticed before, but she could not have said what it was: strained perhaps, or tired? He was all in black, what was known as a frock coat, the waist low, the "skirt" to his knee. Beneath it was a black waistcoat, his trousers, also black, were tight-fitting, emphasising the shape of his long, slender legs, his black necktie in a small bow.

His look of fine breeding was highlighted by the three working men who lounged next to him, but he did his best to engage them in quiet conversation, listening with great interest to Jack and Davey's description of their last journey. Pat said nothing much, despite being Irish, a race known for their garrulity, but nobody seemed to think it strange that Pat, a comparative stranger, should be among them.

Tom caught her looking at him and smiled warmly, holding her glance, ready to come and squat at her knee and talk to her, she thought, commiserate with her on her loss, then Betsy made a great clatter with her cup and saucer and the moment passed. Ally thought he did not look happy, wondering why.

He drank his tea and accepted a slice of fruit cake from Aggie then apologetically said he must be going. Betsy seemed to be in a huff about something, speaking to no one. She sat aloofly like a member of another class forced to mix with the hoi polloi, not getting up to see Tom out and totally ignoring the other men. Davey and Jack thanked Aggie and cleared off. Pat touched Ally's shoulder when he was sure no one was looking, directed a private nod at the widow and followed them.

"I'm that tired," Betsy said fretfully as the four of them sat on, their knees to the fire as though it were winter, Edie and Ally side by side on the red plush sofa, Aggie and Betsy on the matching chairs.

"I'd best ger these pots washed," Aggie remarked but made no effort to move.

"I'll give yer a 'and." This from Edie. "I can't sit about doin' nowt." Now that her Fred was gone what *would* she do?

"I might 'ave a bath." Ally looked down at herself with some distaste. "I'll put water on ter boil."

"Albert'll do it, won't yer, chuck," his mother said fondly, smiling at him where he leaned against the wall. "Fetch bath in, there's a good lad."

"I'm ever so tired," Betsy repeated since no one had taken any notice the first time.

Aggie's voice was tart." 'Appen yer'd best ger yerself ter bed then." It was evident, because of the day, she was doing her best to keep her tongue still, much as she would have liked to lash Betsy with it.

"Aye, lass, you go up," Edie added. "Ger yer 'ead down fer an 'our. Our Ally can . . . can sleep wi' me ternight. Me an' Aggie'll do 't pots."

Ally felt the tension, the tumult of emotion that emanated from Aggie Wainwright which Ma, who was ensconced in her own sad world where Pa no longer existed, did not seem to notice.

Edie and Betsy had disappeared up the stairs, presumably to get Betsy settled comfortably and Albert, after having humped in the enamel bath, disappeared on business of his own. Aggie was fussing with pans of water on the fire. She still wore her bonnet, and her plump-cheeked face was flushed, whether from the fire or her recent indignation over Betsy, though Ally was pretty sure it was the latter. What a good friend she had been to the Pearce family. What would they have done without her, Ally mused, and what chance had led them to Aggie's sister on the canalside at Skipton?

"What's up, Aggie?"

"Nowt."

"Don't tell me nowt. Summat's up. I don't mean Pa dyin' an' the funeral, though that's bad enough an' Ma'll be—"

"Don't you worry about yer ma, chuck, she'll be all right wi' me. Right good friends we be an' I'll tell yer this, yer ma's right clever wi' 'er fingers on that there sewin'-machine an' if madam 'd leave 'er alone—"

"Madam?"

Aggie banged a pan down so violently on the fire that water slopped over the rim, hissing on the coals.

"Aye, that little madam yer ma pampers an' pets an' wears 'erself to a bloody shadder waitin' on, mekkin 'er this an' that, dippin' into that box of 'ers ter provide what madam calls a 'trousseau', wharrever tharris when it's at 'ome. Sooner Doctor Tom tekks 'er away the better an' why 'e 'asn't done I don't know. As far as I can see there's nowt ter stop 'em gerrin wed, but 'ere it is August an' nuthin' said, never mind planned. As far as I know, an' believe me she'd be broadcastin' it from rooftops if she 'ad, she's not met Tom's folks. She reckons she's bin in 'is 'ouse up West Derby, talkin' about butlers an' that, an' t' gardens, but that were in't spring an' she's never mentioned it since. There's summat goin' on she's not tellin' us. She couldn't wait ter ger 'er claws into 'im. Now, that's if yer dare mention it, she more or less . . . if she weren't such a lady" – smiling ironically – "tells me ter mind me own bloody business."

Ally digested this amazing piece of information, agonising on its meaning. Betsy had indeed been full of the glory of the house

where she and Tom were to live and the wonderful life she was
to have, but each time Ally returned to Liverpool Betsy was still
here. Tom was quiet, so kind to Pa and Ma but his eyes fixed
on Betsy's stunning beauty, and, she realised suddenly, that that
was how he was. *Stunned*, speechless sometimes. Betsy was a
peach, ready for plucking, so why didn't he damn well pluck
her and get it over and done with? Get her out of Aggie's house
and away from them all so that they could pick up the pieces of
their lives without Pa. It was apparent Betsy had been in Ma's
box again, probably when Aggie was out of the house, for the
clothes, the bonnets, the veils which she and Ma had worn
today had not been cheap, at least *Betsy's* weren't. Why the hell
didn't Tom take her away before she drained the family of all
they – she, Ally – had worked for? She wanted another boat.
She wanted to put the money she had earned into some safe
place, invest it, but with Betsy hanging round her neck, working
on Ma who was so vulnerable just now, whenever she, Ally,
took a step forward, Betsy dragged her two steps back.

But what had Aggie said? She seemed to imply that Ma might
take up dressmaking and when Ally remembered the lovely
fashionable gowns Ma had made for Betsy, she supposed it was
possible. Not that the wives of the working men in this area
would aspire to what Betsy wore, but surely, with material from
the market and the sewing-machine in Ma's bedroom and if
Betsy and Tom . . .

She bowed her head and sighed and Aggie watched her
compassionately, then, jumping up, began to empty the pans
of hot water into the tub.

"Come on, chuck, ger them duds off yer so I can wash 'em
and gerrin't bath." And when Ally looked dumbfounded, Aggie
smiled and smoothed a hand over Ally's tangled curls. "Nay, I'll
lock both doors, front an' back, an' you 'ave a good soak in front
o' t' fire while I change our Albert's bed. Now, no arguments.
Albert's a good lad an' won't mind sleepin' on't sofa."

She fell asleep in the bath, guarded fiercely by Aggie who had washed her as though she were a small child, even her hair. She barely remembered Aggie helping her from the bath, rubbing her down with a coarse but clean towel, even brushing her damp hair, then pulling her into her arms.

"Oh, Aggie . . ." was all she could manage to moan but Aggie knew exactly what was wrong with her and this time Ally did not pull away.

"I know, chuck, I know . . ."

"What am I ter do?"

"Nowt, my lass. She's gorrim where she wants 'im, an' 'im, poor sod, don't know which way's up. There's summat wrong, summat that's stoppin' them gerrin wed burr I can't fer the life o' me guess wharrit is. Now gerrup them dancers. Yer'll feel a different woman when yer've 'ad a good sleep."

Ally smiled tremulously, accepting Aggie's smacking kiss on her cheek, and even being tucked into Albert's narrow bed. She fell asleep at once, while down at Stanley Dock Pat supervised the unloading of the *Harmony* and *Edith* and the stabling of Magic and Gentle. The two young men grumbled but did not dare argue and only when Pat was satisfied that all had been done that could be done did he allow them to fall, still in their clothes, into the bed-hole they shared.

He lit his pipe. At his age he didn't need much sleep so, strolling in the close night air, ignoring the whores who offered to give him a good time, he found himself crossing Regent Road, skirting Trafalgar Dock and moving along the Marine Parade in the direction of the Observatory.

There was a tall man dressed totally in black leaning on a bollard, staring with what seemed to Pat to be utter despair into the dark moving waters of the Mersey. Pat recognised him at once but made no move to speak to him, passing behind him. He was a great believer in minding his own business, was Pat.

14

"I don't think it's . . . it's right fer us ter be married wi'out yer ma an' pa an' t' rest o' t' family bein' there, Tom. Yer their son, the eldest, an' it beats me why yer can't persuade 'em."

"Sweetheart, how many times must we go over this? I have told you they don't approve."

"Of me, is tharrit?"

"Of me marrying at my age," Tom lied, knowing his tone of voice sounded artificial. He was lying, as he had been lying for months now to the glorious creature sitting opposite him. The child really, who, like a child, could not understand why it was deprived of the particular treat it craved. He often wondered why it was he could not simply walk away from her, go back to the calm, satisfying life he had known before he had first seen her on the canal dock. He had not made love to her again after that one time in his surgery. He wanted to. His male body was roused to a torment of desire whenever she allowed him a chaste kiss on her pursed, rosy lips, but when she drew back, acting out the part she had made for herself he was relieved, if he was honest. That one time had not impregnated her and he had been unprepared to take the risk again if she had been willing, which she was not. She was respectable. She was to be married. She wore the amethyst ring he had bought for her on her finger which told the world that they were engaged. It was not the enormous diamond she had set her heart on, showy, catching fire in the sunlight, but Tom, for once, had been adamant, saying that he could not afford it. Perhaps later when he was more . . . affluent. He did not say when that might be or how, since he was well aware that he would never become rich, or even make enough to live on with the pittance he earned in Naylors Yard or Pope Row.

"But we can still be married, Betsy." His quiet voice could scarcely be heard above the genteel hubbub of the magnificent drawing-room of the Adelphi Hotel. Though he himself did not care for the place, being where the elegant and wealthy society of Liverpool gathered to take afternoon tea, it was for that very reason that Betsy pleaded with him to bring her here. She loved it, for was it not the most exclusive and magnificent hotel in the city, where one might see, and presumably be seen by travellers of the highest order. It was a favourite "stopping place" of the royal family when visiting or passing through Liverpool. Princes of foreign royal houses had honoured it with their presence. Ambassadors from Washington had made it their home when going to or returning from their missions and indeed there were few visitors of importance to the country by way of the River Mersey, and from Liverpool itself who did not at one time or another stay or dine at the Adelphi. She loved its opulence, its luxury, its crimson-coated porters, its deferential waiters, the swirl of well-dressed men and women in and out of the palatial front entrance. She loved the sweet cakes she ate in great quantity and the fragile, almost transparent rose-decorated tea cups from which she drank innumerable cups of tea, convinced that everyone about the room was watching her which they probably were, for her beauty was quite breathtaking.

Today, for the first time, she wore a gown of rose-coloured surah, unadorned and simple with a well-fitted bodice, so well fitted it revealed the bobs of her nipples, a fact noted by every man in the lounge, including the waiters! It was fastened from neck to waist with tiny buttons covered in the same material over which her mother had strained her eyes hour after hour. Her bonnet matched her dress, and beneath its brim was fastened a tiny bunch of white silk rosebuds. She had abandoned her mourning black as soon as Ma had completed the gown and though Aggie had raged at the extravagance, saying that Ally didn't do the work of two men on that canal so that Betsy could squander what she earned on new frocks, Betsy had tossed her head and told her to mind her own business, wheedling Ma into allowing her a few bob. After all, she was the fiancée of a gentleman from a well-known and respected Liverpool family and could not be seen about with him in the same couple of gowns, could she? She always called frocks "gowns" which infuriated Aggie to such a degree that she came close to strangling Betsy Pearce. Indeed the ways in which Betsy aggravated her were legion!

Betsy's eyes ran greedily over the three-tiered silver cake stand set with lace doilies, and bearing a dozen cakes and pastries, most of them stuffed with cream, meringues being Betsy's favourite. She chose one and with great delicacy transferred it to her plate, then attacked it with her silver cake fork. She was like a child in her pleasure and Tom felt his heart soften.

"Did you hear me, Betsy? I don't have to have my parents' permission to marry, you know that. I have a small income left me by my grandmother and as I've explained a dozen times, it's enough to live on. Even with two of us, if we're careful. I have a home to offer you in Duke Street and I promise you'll want for nothing."

If we're careful. Those were the words that filtered out of all the others into Betsy Pearce's mercenary mind. If we're careful! She didn't want to marry Tom Hartley to live the life of a poor family doctor. She didn't want to live in rooms in Duke Street, watching every penny, making one do the work of two like Aggie Wainwright. She didn't want to shop in St John's Market, a basket on her arm like the housewives she had seen when she went there seeking the materials and decorations for her clothes.

She didn't want to be forced to search out the bargains on the food stalls, the cheapest cuts of meat, which stall sold reduced farm produce, the most inexpensive fish and all the other little economies like the wives of the working classes. She didn't want children who she herself would be expected to look after. She didn't want children at all but if she had them, since she knew of no way to avoid them, there must be some woman to bring them up.

In other words she wanted, needed, was desperate for the world that Tom's mother, his sisters, the future wives of his yet unmarried brothers, and friends peopled. Servants, a life of leisure, of doing and being exactly what *she* had always dreamed of in that splendid house in West Derby, and unless Tom could be persuaded to become reconciled with his mother and father it would be denied her.

She licked her fingers, her little pink tongue emerging from between her soft lips, moistening them, looking up playfully from beneath her long lashes, kittenish, enchanting, bewitching Tom Hartley, so for that moment he knew absolutely why it was he could not walk away from her.

"I know that, Tom" – becoming serious, for this was a serious matter she would have him believe – "burr I can't bear to be 't one ter separate yer from yer ma an' pa. Yer say they don't want yer ter be wed but truth is, go on, admit it, they don't want yer ter wed *me*. I medd a bad mistake goin' ter Rosemont 'Ouse." Oh, how she loved saying those two words, Rosemont House! We live at Rosemont House, she would say when she and Tom were married. My husband has a place in West Derby called Rosemont House. That was where she meant to be and Tom must be made to persuade, to do everything he had to, to make it up with Mr and Mrs Hartley. She just wouldn't believe it was not possible, but she must walk a very fine and tricky tightrope in the meanwhile. He was telling her they could be married at once and that suited her down to the ground, for she was fed up of living at Aggie Wainwright's on Blackstock Street, where she had been for over a year now. She didn't want to lose Tom, for he was the kind of man she had always wanted but, and it was a big but, she wanted Rosemont House as well. And until she was sure of the house and all that went with it she didn't want to antagonise Tom.

"I shouldn't 've gone bargin' in like that," she continued, "but can yer not explain ter yer ma that I didn't know it were wrong. We all mekk mistakes, Tom, an' if yer ma was ter meet me, wi' you beside me she'd see we was well suited. I'm a quick learner an' I'd not show yer up."

She had no idea, not the slightest conception, of what was expected of Tom Hartley, of his brothers and sisters, indeed of any generation of his class. Of the points of etiquette, the conventions and customs, the appearances that must be kept up, the absolute importance of marrying one's own kind, the behavioural patterns to which Tom must conform, nor that in declaring he had chosen a woman *out* of it he was committing social suicide. In their minds his family had no choice but to cast him out.

Tom leaned forward and put his hand on hers where it rested on the damask tablecloth. Those about them who speculated on the family background of the exquisite creature who accompanied Edward Hartley's son, for there were several who knew his family, watched avidly. At the table nearest to them the lady and gentleman seated there could hear a word or two, and were quite appalled, for it was apparent from her speech that the woman was not of their sort. Of course young gentlemen were allowed their dalliances but this particular one spoke with the accent of the slums, and surely Edward Hartley's boy should have known better than to bring her here.

"Sweetheart, I cannot, really I cannot. My people, my friends would not accept our marriage. They would ostracise you . . . us."

"What does that mean?" Betsy withdrew her hand, her expression suspicious, and Tom's heart sank, as it was wont to do these days, for not only did Betsy lack the well-bred speech of his class, but the understanding of the words he uttered.

"It means they wouldn't have anything to do with you," he said bluntly.

"D'yer think I care?" Her tone was scathing, for she had never had a friend in her life, admired and loved only by her ma and pa. Anyway if she was living at Rosemont House she was pretty sure all these folk Tom talked about would be only too glad to make a friend of Betsy Pearce, Betsy Hartley as she would be then.

"It wouldn't do, sweetheart."

"What d'yer mean it wouldn't do?" Her voice was becoming shrill and Tom could feel the disapproving stares of those about them. The eagle eye of the headwaiter lifted over the heads of those taking tea and with that gesture which those born to it instinctively use, Tom summoned the waiter and asked for his bill. That was another thing, he thought distractedly as he glanced at it, then sprang to his feet to pull Betsy's chair out. He could no longer afford to bring Betsy to places like this, not since the allowance his father had given him had stopped abruptly. He could only just manage on the small inheritance from his maternal grandmother.

"Let's go for a walk down to the river," he said encouragingly as they passed into Ranelagh Street and the autumn sunshine. There was the chill of approaching winter in the air and Tom helped Betsy adjust her pretty patterned shawl more cosily about her shoulders. That was another grievance Betsy harboured! All the other ladies in the Adelphi drawing-room had had fur capes draped on the backs of their chairs. Betsy had coveted them and sighed dramatically as she flung her shawl, pretty as it was, carelessly about her shoulders.

He held out his arm and she took it grudgingly as they sauntered along the crowded pavement of Ranelagh Street, passing the Lyceum and into Hanover Street. At the end of Duke Street, which ran into Hanover Street, he was tempted to coax her back to his rooms, which he knew would be a disastrous move. His body ached with desire. It had been denied hers for months and though he knew it was by his own choice it made it no easier. He glanced down at the delicate and gamine shape of her white neck which could be seen beneath her bonnet and imagined his hand caressing it before removing the pins of her silver-gilt hair and letting it fall in a drifting cloak down her back, of undoing all those tiny buttons and taking her gown from her, pushing it down to her feet, then, one by one removing her undergarments until she was naked. He had for a brief moment seen and held her high breasts, taken the peaked bobs of her nipples in his mouth and marvelled at the pale triangle of dense hair at the base of her stomach. Then he had been eager to enter her, to plunge his body into hers so that his sense of sight had not been totally satisfied. And that was what he wanted now. To have her stand before him without a stitch of clothing. To dream over her slender body, to touch and taste and smell her before laying her down and piercing her with his fierce male need. He could feel the crotch of his trousers become uncomfortably tight and was appalled at his own inability to control his erection and, not only that, to walk naturally! Beside him Betsy was silent, sulking, he knew, because she had failed in her persuasions and it was not until they had reached the end of Water Street, turning right towards St Michael's Church, that the sullen spell was broken.

"Tom, Tom Hartley," a cultured masculine voice called out from behind them. "Hold on, old chap." And when they both turned they saw the tall, loosely put together figure of an extremely well-dressed young gentleman hurrying to catch them up.

"Tom, you old devil," the young gentleman was saying, his right hand, which was encased in a beautifully made grey kid glove, held out in greeting to Tom. He grasped Tom's hand, his face beaming in what seemed to be enormous delight, showing his perfectly even white teeth. His silver-blue eyes, long-lashed and wide apart, narrowed smilingly with great good humour. His hair, revealed when he whipped off his hat, was fair, a silver blond that was similar to Betsy's and he was incredibly handsome with a certain arrogance that is the stamp of those of privilege and pedigree. He was obviously of the same class, custom and culture as Tom, well bred, well polished, but boyish with a long, elegant mouth, a straight patrician nose, his hair falling like pale gold feathers across a wide forehead. He had a light lounging charm that bewitched Betsy Pearce, who at once fell hopelessly in love with him.

Tom was more restrained. He took the beautiful young man's hand politely but there was none of the unguarded delight that the newcomer conveyed.

"Robin, good to see you." His voice was non-committal.

"And you, old chap and after so long. When was it? Now don't tell me . . . Yes, I believe it was Amanda and James's wedding day when all the young gentlemen got so disgracefully drunk the servants were called to put us to bed. Now then, how have you been? Well, I trust."

"Indeed, very well."

"Good, good."

Robin, as he seemed to be called, though he addressed his greetings to Tom, could not prevent his fascinated gaze turning again and again to Betsy, who was gazing at him with equal fascination, which didn't surprise him since he was used to the admiration of young ladies. He was a man who had from early youth known of his own attraction to the opposite sex.

"But are you not going to introduce me to the lovely lady on your arm?" His smile deepened and he bowed his head slightly in Betsy's direction. The gleam of sunshine, which at that moment strayed from behind a drift of cloud, lit his hair to a

gleaming gold and placed a chip of blue fire in his fine eyes. He
was so god-like in his appearance that Betsy could do no more
than, well, the only word was gawp at him, her eyes wide and
excited, her lips parted in wonder.

"I beg your pardon, Robin, may I present my fiancée, Miss
Betsy Pearce. Betsy, my . . . What is it, Robin, second cousin
twice removed? Sir Robin Lovell."

Sir! She was actually in the presence of a sir! A man with a
title. Betsy clung frantically to Tom's arm, lest she fall in adora-
tion at the god's feet. She held fast to the man who, until a few
minutes ago, had been the peak, the absolute pinnacle of all her
dreams. Not dreams of love, of course, which was the goal of
all young girls, but of a rich husband, a husband from a higher
class than the one into which she had been born. To *be*
someone. To live in a grand house with servants to wait on her.
Tom would, if she was patient, give her that, but in one elec-
trifying moment, with one curling smile from *Sir* Robin Lovell's
well-shaped lips, one clear blue and penetrating glance from
him to her, and her sights, and not only her sights, but her heart
were aimed in another direction. Not only could this man make
her into a lady, a real honest-to-God lady, but she had in a blink
of an eye fallen in love with him. She could feel her body, which
had been unmoved by Tom's, grow hot and weak under her
clothing. It pleaded for something her mind could not even
imagine, yearned towards this stranger as though *it* knew
exactly what it required from him. This confusion of her mind
and her body was something she had never before experienced,
the physical sensations, the banging of her heart, the tingling of
her breasts and the hot moistness between her legs, the flushing
of her cheeks, the latter very apparent to the experienced Robin
Lovell.

"Miss Pearce." He somehow had hold of her gloved hand
and was bowing over it, his lips a bare inch away from her
knuckles. "You're a lucky dog, Tom. And cagey too, keeping

this enchanting creature to yourself. When is the wedding to be, may I ask?"

"As soon as I can persuade her to name a date." Tom's answer was stilted. Not only was the recent argument with Betsy still fresh in his mind but his natural male instinct to protect what was his was surging through his veins. Robin Lovell was well known from as far back as their schooldays together for his predatory designs on the female sex, and not only that but his success at it. Bets used to be laid in the dormitory on how long it would take him to get inside the drawers of certain girls, the daughters of tradesmen, farmers, landlords of public houses, maidservants, even the wives of respectable men. It had been a source of great amusement and even admiration to his chums, one of whom had been Tom Hartley, and when he was eventually expelled for a particularly scandalous incident involving the wife of a teacher, their lives had been the duller for it.

"Now then, Miss Pearce, may one ask why you are holding back on this splendid fellow here? I'm sure he's longing to" – he almost said "get you into his clutches" but one did not make such remarks to a lady – "to make you his wife." He smiled encouragingly.

At their backs was the grey, silent hulk of St Nicholas Church. They were standing at the head of the steps that led down to the Marine Parade, causing something of an obstruction. Those going down were tutting with annoyance as they were forced to stand to one side to allow those coming up to get to the top, but the lady and the two gentlemen seemed oblivious. That was typical of the gentry, thought those who were on dock business and could not afford to stand about and chat as they were. A ship had just discharged a cargo of gaunt, ragged Irish immigrants and they milled about jauntily or stood in confused family groups according to their nature, waiting for someone in authority to tell them where to go. The ferry from

Woodside chugged its way to its mooring, flinging down its moving walkway with a crash, delivering its passengers from "over the water". Men in cloth caps and aprons of sacking shifted barrels from decks to docks, shouting cheerfully to one another, others whistling the tunes of the day. Men with huge hammers struck at objects Betsy could not even guess at, and besides, her whole being was totally concentrated on the man before her. Great horses pulled wagons, laden with immense blocks of wood, barrels and bales. There were women saunter-ing along the docks with a bucket on their head, dogs barking and threatening disaster as they got under folk's feet, and bare-foot urchins, ragged and dirty, looking for any chance to make a farthing. Tools lay about, tangled with chains and pulleys and along the waterside were a forest of masts flying the pennants of countries from around the world. As far as the eye could see, north and south, were the granite hulks of the warehouses, from which poured coal, salt, glass, iron bars, nails, hoops, manu-factured goods, pottery, copper, and into which came raw wool and cotton, fruit, sugar, tea, tobacco, wine and timber.

Betsy spoke for the first time. She had an air about her of a child standing with her nose pressed to a window, beyond the glass of which was the most magnificent display of sweetmeats. Or before a Christmas tree, one of those introduced by the Queen's husband, decorated with presents exciting enough to delight the heart of the most demanding child.

She dimpled, as only she knew how.

"Well, we're not right sure yet, are we, Tom? Me pa's not bin dead long an' me ma needs me at 'ome," she lied. "Anyroad there's all sorts o' things ter be . . . well, we need ter bide a bit. 'Appen in spring, aye, Tom?"

She turned a bright, almost glassy stare on Tom, for the last thing she wanted to discuss with this superior being was her pending marriage, and so missed the thunderstruck expression on Robin Lovell's face. His mouth opened and closed in a way that was unlike him, and he turned to look at Tom who glared back at him as though daring him to say the wrong word.

His charming smile returned. Understanding, or so he thought, he turned back to Betsy, but not before he presented Tom with a knowing wink.

"In spring you say. Well, there's no better time for a wedding, or so I've been told."

"Yer not wed then, Mr . . . er, Sir . . ."

"Oh, please, Miss Pearce. Call me Robin and, if I may, and if I have your . . . fiancé's permission" – winking again at Tom and raising his eyebrows suggestively – "I shall call you Betsy. You don't mind, do you, old chap. I know we have only just met but I feel I know you already and no, I'm not married. I have yet to meet the lady who could tempt me on such a course." His eyes looked warmly into hers, deliberately giving her the impression that perhaps he now had. "Now, if Tom doesn't mind, Robin and Betsy it shall be."

Betsy was enchanted.

"O' course 'e don't, do yer, Tom?" emphasising even more to Tom the dreadful division between her world and his – and Lovell's – where no gentleman would presume to call a *lady* by her Christian name on such short acquaintance.

"Indeed," he answered stiffly. He felt churlish and out of place, as though he were the odd one out in this threesome, but he knew exactly what was in Robin Lovell's mind and was offended by it. He knew himself to be infatuated with Betsy. He had promised to marry her, against his own better judgement, but although it infuriated him at times, he was a man, who, once a promise was made, felt compelled to keep it. He supposed Lovell was right in a way. If he could have had Betsy Pearce without marriage, if he could have had further access to her body after that first time, this captivation he felt would have worn itself out, but Betsy was shrewd, knowing, clever without being intellectual, an animal cleverness that kept him painfully yearning after her. So was it any wonder, having heard her speak, that Robin Lovell thought that Tom was merely playing the game that all gentlemen played with girls of a lower class than their own. He would know, since his parents would be the same, that Tom's mother and father would rather he was cast out of the family home than admit a girl like Betsy.

"And where are you off to on this lovely autumn day?" Robin was saying, his whole admiring male attention focused on Betsy. He was playing a part, pretending Betsy was worthy of it, polite, gallant, his charm overdone, his tongue in his cheek, as his speculative eyes ran over her, and Betsy was taken in by it.

"We was only goin' ter look at ships in't river. Why don't yer come wi' us?" She didn't even glance at Tom.

"How very kind of you and again if Tom's agreeable, I shall avail myself of your offer."

Betsy was in seventh heaven, walking on clouds of pure swansdown, as Robin offered her his arm. She strolled between them, conscious of the splendid picture they made, a beautiful lady such as herself with her arms through those of *two* gentlemen, of the curious and admiring glances that came their way; of the joy she would have later relating the events of the afternoon to those at home, and of what a dull dog Tom was when compared to the wit, the charm, the deference and the beauty of Sir Robin Lovell. Naturally, since she was not daft, she was sweet to Tom despite her passion for Robin, since a bird in the hand was worth two in the bush, as her ma had been known to say. She was not so gormless as to think she could snare Sir Robin Lovell as easily as she had Tom Hartley, so best be nice to him but, by God, she'd rather be Lady Lovell than Mrs Tom Hartley any day of the week.

15

The hand on her shoulder startled Ally and she was even more surprised when she looked up into the humorously smiling face of Tom Hartley.

"What are you doing idling your time away on a bench in the gardens? I thought your business was hurtling along at such a speed you barely had time to turn round, let alone brood by yourself in the park. And on such a cold day, too. You must be frozen."

He sat down beside her, his shoulder comfortably but surprisingly close to hers.

"I didn't know I were broodin'."

"Oh yes. I've been watching you as I walked along the path and you were in a world of your own, your thoughts far away and they didn't seem happy ones."

"No, not really un'appy, just . . ." She hesitated. "A bit worried."

"Worried? Tell me what you're worried about. Perhaps I can help. You know what they say?"

"No. What?"

"Two heads are better than one. Or is it a trouble shared is a trouble halved?" Tom bent his head and peered under the brim of her bonnet, which shadowed her face as she looked down at her clenched hands. His expression was gentle, kind, quizzical and Ally felt her insides move with that familiar warmth of love that he had evoked in her from the first. Over a year ago since she had first looked on his beloved face and her love for him had come to rest in her heart, where she knew irrevocably it would remain for ever.

"You look very smart," he said somewhat abruptly, as though the compliment had been wrenched from him against his will.

"Thank you," she managed to answer, doing her best to keep the breathlessness from her voice.

"I haven't seen you before without your boatwoman's costume. Not that that wasn't very becoming," he added hastily, "but . . . well, what you're wearing suits you. The colour matches your eyes. Autumn colours . . ." He stopped as though confused, then added, "Tawny, perhaps amber . . ."

"I thought I'd better look . . . like other women when I'm not on t' canal. Me ma made it."

"She's very clever."

"Aye, she is that."

Her dress was simple, plain, but the colour, which Tom was right in describing as "tawny", did suit her. The bodice fitted smoothly to her slight figure and the full skirt gave her a look of elegance. Her bonnet of cream straw was neat, close-fitting, the brim edged with a ribbon of the same colour as the dress. Her shawl, which was draped carelessly about her shoulders, was patterned in autumnal colours, cream, gold, bronze, russet, and she wore cream kid gloves. The only inharmonious note was her sturdy black boots.

Ally felt a certain peace, a tranquility fall about her like a warm cloak on a cold day. It seemed so natural to be sitting here beside Tom shoulder to shoulder, quiet, at ease, in harmony somehow with one another, though she didn't understand why. She loved him. He loved Betsy, but nevertheless in this soft-hued moment in time it didn't seem to matter.

There were squirrels scampering across the oval of grass in front of them, which was densely carpeted with fallen beech leaves, flaming orange, russet and gold and on to which more drifted as the season separated them from their branches. The squirrels darted in search of beech nuts, becoming abruptly still as they sensed some danger, then were off again and up the trunks of the trees to store their hoard for the winter. There was a sudden angry roar from the menagerie and again the remaining squirrels froze.

"Now may I ask what brings you so far from Blackstock Street?" Tom asked, having, it seemed, nothing more to say on the subject of her appearance.

"Oh, I needed a bit o' peace an' quiet ter think a few things through, so I thought I'd 'ave a walk and ended up 'ere. Aggie 'ad spoke of it. She said she used ter bring Albert ter see the animals when 'e were a little lad. It must be lovely in summer." Her voice trailed away vaguely then she seemed to collect herself. "I've a problem, yer see, which 'as bin botherin' me fer some time; well, ever since I bought the second boat really. I know nowt about business. Oh, I can get cargoes an' deal with all that side o' things but . . . we're doin' well, me an' Jack, Pat and Davey but what with . . . Nay, I shouldn't be mitherin' you, not when you an' . . . It's not your problem, burrif I don't do summat she'll . . . Whereever I 'ide it . . . Ma's too soft wi 'er, always 'as bin, 'er bein' so . . . so lovely. Well, *you* know . . ."

Tom had turned towards her in astonishment, perching himself on the edge of the bench in order to look more closely into her face. He took her hand in both of his, bringing the rambling discourse to a halt.

"Ally, Ally, please stop. You're making no proper sense. Start from the beginning and tell me what it is that's troubling you. I might be able to help."

"It's nor up ter me ter speak about . . . well, you an' 'er are ter be wed, but I *must*."

"You're speaking of Betsy?" His voice was so quiet it could

barely be heard, and a strange expression crossed his face. His blue eyes, a lovely hyacinth blue a moment ago, darkened and his brows dipped in a frown. His mouth tightened as though in pain, then relaxed into the warm smile they all at Blackstock Street had come to know so well.

"What's she been up to now?" Just as though the woman he was to marry had committed some childish prank.

Ally sighed deeply and though she didn't want to she gently withdrew her hand from his.

"Tom, you and Betsy are ter be wed an' why yer've not done so already is a mystery to us all. It's nowt ter do wi' us, o' course but my worry is . . . where ter put the brass we earn on t' cut."

"Brass?"

"Aye. Cash. Money. When I get paid fer t' cargoes I carry . . . well, I reckon, no, I'm absolutely certain it should be put in a bank, so that norr only will it – what is it? – earn *interest*, but be safe from—" She stopped abruptly, biting off the rest of her sentence.

"From?" Tom questioned.

A man sauntered past them with a young spaniel on a lead. The dog veered towards them, doing its best to place its nose on Tom's knee. Tom put out a hand and laid it on the animal's domed head, momentarily distracted, and its short tail moved frantically.

"I beg your pardon," the dog's owner said, raising his hat in their direction.

"No, not at all," Tom answered. "We have one just like it at home." And again that strange sad expression dulled his eyes.

Ally noticed it at once, wondering, despite her own anxieties, what it was that made the man beside her look so sad. This time it was her turn to put *her* hand on his.

"Is . . . really, it's nowt ter do wi' me, bur is everything all right?"

"All right?" He kept his face averted and Ally sighed.

"Look, lad, let's be honest wi' each other. I'll tell you what's up wi' me an' you tell me what's botherin' you." She could have added that the way she felt about him had given her the ability to sense his every mood. Not that she saw him often now that Pa had gone but when she did she seemed to divine whether he was at peace – with Betsy, of course – or in a state of dejection, again determined by Betsy. These days Betsy was rarely at home, going off either to " 'ave a look what's in t' shops", "to meet Tom" or simply for a walk. Ma was worried about her, she knew, but Aggie kept her mouth shut with the attitude of "least said soonest mended". Betsy had bought some more material while Ally was away, a lovely shot silk in a shade of buttercup yellow and, so Aggie grumbled, had had Ma bent over the sewing-machine half the night, and Ally knew that if she, Ally, didn't do something soon, every penny she earned would be found and frittered away between Betsy's greedy fingers.

It was Tom's turn to sigh, a sigh that turned into a short laugh. He leaned back on the bench, stretching out his long legs, crossing them at the ankle.

"You're very forthright, Ally."

"Am I?"

"Oh, indeed, but as we're friends . . . we are friends, aren't we?"

"I hope so."

"Very well. You go first. You spoke of money and seemed to imply that Betsy had something to do with it, so it appears your sister is at the heart of both our troubles."

Ally turned her head sharply but he was watching a couple of well-wrapped-up children running through the leaves on the grass, kicking at them, then picking them up and throwing handfuls at one another. A well-starched nanny, who was pushing a perambulator on the path, called out to them but their delight in their pastime persuaded them to ignore her. Putting the brake on the perambulator she stormed across the grass and took them, one to each hand, giving them a shake before dragging them back to the perambulator.

"You're 'avin' trouble wi' Betsy?" Ally sounded shocked.

"I said you first."

For a moment Ally was silent, then she began to speak.

"We've made money since I took over, Tom. I suppose, bein' younger an' more ambitious, me an' Jack've done well wit' two boats." She paused and Tom, who had turned to watch her face as she talked, was inclined to think it was not Jack Pearce who had "done well", who had the gumption to increase business, but the woman who spoke.

"Go on."

"I've fetched brass 'ome an' done me best ter pur it some-where safe but I 'ad ter tell Ma in case she needed summat, but . . . she's soft with our Betsy an' Betsy gets it out of 'er. I need financial advice, Tom, a bank, an account to purrit in. Cash, I mean, where our Betsy can't get 'er 'ands on it. I've never 'ad 'owt ter do wi' t' money side. I reckon Pa just purrit in t' box an' saved it up an' that's 'ow I come to 'ave the cash ter buy the *Harmony*. But now, wi' the added profit I can't just go on doin' that. It needs . . . investin'. Is that the word?"

"That's the word."

"But I've never bin in a bank in me life. I were tryin' ter get up courage ter . . . well, just go inter t' first one I come to but I walked right on an' fetched up 'ere. If I want ter keep our Betsy's 'ands off it, I'll 'ave ter pur it in a bank or tekk it wi' me on't boat tomorrer. But there's some bad devils on't canal . . ." Remembering Whipper Ogden whom she'd seen a time or two since the incident on the canalside at Church but who, thank-fully, had not noticed the *Edith* going by.

Tom sat up and turned to her with a laugh. "Ally, my dearest Ally, it really is the easiest thing in the world to go into a bank and open an account. All you need—"

Ally, offended and not a little confused at being called "his dearest" – which she knew well she wasn't – sat up straight and moved away from him. She stared at him, her face scarlet with indignation.

"Not fer some, it's not, Tom Hartley. You might 'av bin brought up ter think such things commonplace but I weren't. Me pa'd turn in 'is grave if 'e knew what I were to do, but what else . . ."

"Ally, I'm sorry." He reached for her hand again and they were both a little surprised at how many times their hands had touched this afternoon and how they had both enjoyed it. Tom was a peaceable fellow who rarely raised his voice in anger and hated to see people in pain or distress, and it appeared that he had distressed this girl beside him. He had a distinct urge to put an arm about her, comfort her, tell her not to give it another thought, for the answer *was* simple. After all, she was to be his sister-in-law. But that was the trouble. He was involved – what an odd way of putting it, he remembered thinking – with Betsy Pearce, this young woman's sister, and should not be concerned with thoughts of consoling her.

He stood up, holding out his hand to her, taking hers and helping her to her feet. Surprised, she let him.

"We'll go at once to my bank. The Royal Union Bank in Castle Street. The manager is Mr Moore, who, let us say, looks after my family's money."

"And yours?" she asked warily as though any man who was good enough to look after *Tom's* money was certainly good enough to look after hers.

His face closed up, his smile replaced by a grim expression.

"Well, what there is of it." He looked away across the wide expanse of the gardens. To their left was the deer house and park where the gentle deer grazed behind their wire fence. To their right was the menagerie that contained the pacing, padding tigers, the chattering, grinning monkeys and other equally sad animals. There was a concert room where the élite of Liverpool gathered to listen to classical music. Most of them were bored and restless but were prepared to suffer for the sake of being seen to be cultured in the arts. The buildings were set among lawns and flowerbeds threaded by wide pathways along which promenaders strolled in the tag end of the autumnal sunshine, making the most of what remained before winter closed its teeth upon the land.

He seemed to have gone somewhere else, his mind winging away to whatever was troubling him, but when she touched his arm he swung round to face her again.

"Shall we have tea?" he asked her with an attempt at cheerfulness. "There's a tea room beyond the deer house."

"What's troubling yer, Tom? Yer promised we'd share our problems. I confessed ter you an' yer've offered a solution. 'Appen if yer was ter tell me I could do t' same fer you."

He looked deeply into her eyes, his own narrowed speculatively as though to see her better, wondering why he had not noticed before the honesty, the concern, the wide loveliness of them. They were dark and yet a clear brown, the colour of polished chestnuts, the pupils as black as sable, surrounded by lashes so long and thick they threw shadows on her pale cheeks. Before, when they had first met, he had likened them to amber, but now they had changed colour, as his had done if he had but known it. Their glance clung and a surprised and powerful empathy suddenly found expression between them. Each was bewildered by it so that they stood like two statues facing one another. They were so still a passing couple, arm-in-arm, stared at them in consternation, but Tom and Ally did not see them go by. Their eyes were fixed on one another, and they were rooted to the spot by the strangeness of it.

Tom was the one to break the spell. His grin was wobbly but he took her arm and led her across the soggy autumn leaves on the grass towards the pathway that led to the tea rooms. When he had seated her at the table, he managed a smile for the trim waitress, ordering tea and lots of cakes, his pretence of normality slowly bringing Ally from her trance-like state.

They sipped their tea and both took cakes which neither ate. They smiled and made some attempts at ordinary conversation: the beauty of the multicoloured autumn trees, the approach of winter, Ally's forthcoming journey when she was to travel the length of the canal to Leeds, which would keep her away for several weeks, until finally, in the silence that eventually fell, Ally's voice quietly repeated her question.

"Why aren't you an' our Betsy wed by now, Tom? It's bin months an' yer seemed ter be tellin' me . . . yer said, about money, 'What there is of it.' 'As Betsy . . .'"

He placed his cup carefully in his saucer, his face showing increasing strain, then he shook his head, sighing deeply. "I can't get her to name a day, Ally. For the wedding, I mean. She was enthusiastic in the beginning, making plans."

"Aye, I know. Ma was pleased. She's right fond o' you; but whar 'appened? Summat did. She keeps fobbin' us off wi' one excuse after another."

"Me too. She says she . . . well, I suppose I might as well tell you." He picked up a cake fork, fiddling with it, his eyes concentrated on it as though it fascinated him. "My family . . . Dear God, it is hard saying this to you, her sister, but they won't accept her. They have disowned me – Jesus, it sounds like something out of a cheap melodrama – and . . . and stopped my allowance. I've told Betsy I can still support her, I have decent rooms and if we were careful we'd manage, but she says . . . She won't believe I can't persuade my family to take me back, and *her*. She doesn't want to be the one to keep us apart, she says. I made a promise to marry her, Ally, and, as a gentleman my honour demands that I keep that promise but I can't force her. She says wait. My mother and father will relent, she says, but I know they won't. They are . . ."

"Gentry." Ally's voice was soft with sympathy. "And Betsy is not."

"She's a beautiful young woman, Ally," he said passionately. "I . . . I love her and I thought she loved me but whenever I call she's out, no one seems to know where . . ." His voice petered out and again she felt the need to take that restless hand, the one that fumbled with the cake fork and hold it lovingly in her own. There was a pleasant hum of conversation in the tea room, the clink of cutlery on china, a child's voice begging someone for another cake and Ally's heart broke again and again on the waves of pain that crashed against it, not only her own but Tom's. She knew her sister well enough to realise that Betsy and Tom would have married months ago if Tom's family had agreed to it, if Betsy could have had the smart wedding her calculating heart was set on. With Tom's family and well-bred friends to see it all, she would have settled herself in that splendid mansion she had described, and queened it over Mrs Hartley herself. That was what she craved. Not Tom Hartley, but only what he could give her, and with that gone, though she was keeping Tom tied to her by his own integrity, and, Ally supposed, his love for her, she would wait until he got her dream back for her. Until that day she would hang on to him for, after all, he was a gentleman, and better than nothing. Her inflexible mind would not conceive that for once, something she had set her heart on was not to be hers.

But she could not say this to the man who loved her, could she? His misery was palpable, and his confusion. They said that love was blind and Tom Hartley's eyes saw nothing but Betsy's extraordinary beauty, the modesty and innocence she pretended, the artless fluttering of her long, silken eyelashes, her rosy pouting mouth, the faultlessness of her perfect figure. Her affected airs and graces, her pretence at refinement were to him an indication of her suitability as his wife, but surely he understood that the way Betsy spoke, her rough northern accent, which Ally herself had, her lack of education, would never be acceptable to the class from which he came.

She stood up and moved towards the tea room door while he paid the bill. He opened it, then followed her outside.

"Shall we go to the bank now?" he asked courteously.

She hesitated, then began to walk along the path to the gate that led out on to Boundary Road. He fell in beside her, matching his stride to hers.

"I'd 'ave ter go ter Blackstock Street fer t' box, Tom an' . . . our Betsy might be there. 'Appen it'd be best ter . . ."

"Tomorrow then, I could meet you somewhere."

"I've ter be off at first light, wi t' days gerrin shorter."

"Of course. Well, shall we say when you return I'll make arrangements to see Mr Moore at the bank."

"That'd be best, an' thanks, Tom. I 'ope you an' our Betsy'll . . . Well, you know what I mean."

"Thank you." His voice was grave, then became brisk. "Now I'll give you my address and when you return from Leeds I want you to send a message by young Albert to let me know and I'll come with you, as I said, and we'll open an account for you."

"Tom, yer don't know 'ow much that 'elps me."

"I do. Good luck, Ally Pearce, and safe journey." Unexpectedly he took her hand and raised it to his lips, then turned and strode off into the gathering dusk. It was only as he went that she wondered what he had been doing in the Zoological Gardens in the first place.

Ma was in a state when she arrived home. It had become full dark as Ally walked the length of William Henry Street, crossing Scotland Road and turning left into Blackstock Street.

The streets were busy with last-minute shoppers, beshawled

women coming from St John's Market where, at this time of day, perishables were going cheap. Scotland Road, where these women lived, was notorious for its poverty and Tom Hartley was well known by its inhabitants. Neatly dressed shopgirls hurried home after a long, wearying day on their feet, expertly dodging the hansom cabs and carriages, the ponderous wagons that moved between the crowded pavements. A fog was coming down and on the river the long mournful hoot of a foghorn drifted on the chilly air.

She knew as soon as she opened the front door that some drama was taking place. Albert was sitting dejectedly on the bottom step of the staircase with Teddy on his knee, his face buried in the dog's fur.

"What's up, Albert?" she asked as she shut the door quietly behind her.

He shrugged a boy's shrug that told the world that if he lived to be a hundred he would never understand the goings-on of the adult world.

Ma swung round in her chair as Ally entered the kitchen, an expression of great relief on her face which quickly turned to worry when she saw who it was in the doorway.

"Oh, Ally, 'ave yer seen our Betsy on yer travels?" she wailed. "It's dark out an' she's not bin seen since she went out this morning."

In the part of her brain that was not concerned with financial problems, with the expansion of her business, with her sadness and love for Tom Hartley, Ally had time to ponder on why it was that Ma was so tearfully anxious about their Betsy when she, Ally, had also been missing nearly all day, and had not returned until nightfall? She knew Ma trusted her to be sensible, careful, with no inclination to be led astray by the many distractions that so attracted her younger daughter. In fact it would just not occur to her that Ally could ever get into trouble. Plain, practical Ally Pearce could come to no harm since temptations were not directed at her, but pretty, artless Betsy was considered to be in mortal danger should she be out after dark.

"Now, lass," Aggie was saying, putting a cup of tea in Edie Pearce's trembling hand, "get that down yer an' stop yer frettin'. Your Betsy'll be 'ome directly. It's only just gone six."

"But where *is* she, Aggie?" Edie turned frantically to Aggie. "Our Ally's not seen 'er 'ave yer, chuck, so where's she got to?"

" 'Appen she's called in ter visit Tom."

Edie was shocked. "Eeh never! She'd not go to 'is rooms on 'er own." For in her mother's eyes Betsy was the soul of propriety, a good girl, a well-brought-up girl, one who was to marry a gentleman.

"She'll be in soon, Ma," Ally said soothingly and at that moment the front door opened with a clatter. Teddy began to bark excitedly as Albert stood up, his young face beaming with pleasure.

"See, 'ere she is."

"Oh, thank 'eaven," Edie said with such feeling one might have been mistaken in believing that her beautiful young daughter had just fought her way through a horde of savages, all with designs on Betsy's person.

"Lass, where've yer bin?" she cried, standing up to fold Betsy in her arms but Betsy shrugged her away irritably.

"Give over, Ma. Anyone'd think I'd bin ter China an' back."

"Bur I've bin right worried—"

"An' yer've no call ter speak ter yer ma like that," Aggie unwisely interrupted.

Betsy turned on her, her face a bright pink, her eyes with a kind of cat-like satisfaction in them, her mouth swollen in some strange way and if Ally had not herself been with Tom for the better part of two hours, she might have been led to believe her sister had just been thoroughly kissed.

"You mind yer own business, Aggie Wainwright. Where I go's nowt ter do wi' you."

"But it's ter do wi' yer ma—"

"Oh, sod off."

They all gasped, even Albert who stepped aside hastily as Betsy pushed past him and made her way upstairs where they heard her bedroom door slam.

16

Betsy Pearce's naked body heaved beneath that of the man who groaned and shuddered on top of her. Her eyes were closed, the lids fluttering and her mouth was stretched in a soundless scream. Her nails raked his bare back, drawing blood which trickled among the raw trails with which it was already marked and he arched backwards, whether in pain or passion was not clear. He reached for her breasts which were as bruised as his back, pulling at her nipples cruelly. He drove himself even more savagely, more deeply inside her, pounding against her, but despite the pain her hips rose to meet him. They were like two rutting animals, grunting and grappling, copulating on the floor of the bedroom among the discarded remnants of their clothing. Betsy began to scream out loud now, writhing with frustration as she strove to reach her climax, swearing at her partner, biting his shoulder, drawing blood until at last, in a fierce explosion of sound and movement, they came together, their bodies arched, but fused.

After several long moments Robin Lovell fell heavily across her in a state of what seemed a living death, his breath harsh and rasping in his throat and chest.

"Bloody hell, Betsy, that's the best fuck I've ever had." At once Betsy reverted to the quasi-refinement she adopted whenever she was in his company. She might be what he said *now* but she was determined he would recognise that she would be a lady worthy of his consideration as a wife.

"That's norra nice word, Robin," she scolded.

"Bugger that. Now how about a little post-fucking teaser?"

"Oh, Robin," she began, pretending to be offended but complying just the same. He sat up and moved to one side, wincing at the scratches and bruises on his body.

"Lie back."

She did so. Her spectacular mass of silver-gilt hair was tangled about her head, fanning out on the carpet. She stretched her arms wide as though she were nailed to a cross, her breasts peaked and full, then opened her long slender legs, bending them at the knee and Robin began his ritual which pleased not only him but her, first with his hand at the wet core of her womanhood which lay in its thick mat of blonde hair and then, bending his head, with his tongue.

Only when Betsy, moaning in ecstasy, climaxed again and again, did he collapse, his face on her belly.

"Jesus Christ, I've never had such a good—"

"I know, Robin, but don't keep sayin' that word. It's not nice."

He shouted with laughter. "After what you've just done you're quibbling about the word that describes it. I've never met a girl like you, my pet, never. You look like an angel with your clothes on but the minute they come off you're like an animal, begging for it."

"Robin, 'ow could yer? An animal indeed." Betsy sat up, aware of the lovely high shape of her breasts as they fell forward. He bit at her peaked almond-shaped nipples, his body beginning to respond at once, for Robin Lovell was a highly sexed animal himself. She aimed a cuff at his head but lay back willingly and for the next half-hour fought and bit and scratched until he impaled her and this time it seemed, for the moment at least, they were both satisfied.

Betsy Pearce had been besotted with Sir Robin Lovell since the day Tom had introduced her to him on the Marine Parade. They had strolled in the September sunshine among all those

enjoying the last days of summer and when Tom had excused
himself for a moment to speak to a man with a bandaged hand
who sat on a bench, Betsy was not surprised when Sir Robin
had whispered urgently that he must, absolutely must see her
again. By the time Tom rejoined them, explaining that the man,
a common, low fellow in Betsy's opinion, was a patient of his,
Betsy had arranged to meet Sir Robin the next day.

"You know I've fallen in love with you, don't you?" were the
first words he said to her as he took her hand, drew off her glove,
and there, on the corner of Shaws Brow and Whitechapel by
the entrance to St John's Church, kissed it with the practised
art of the seducer he was. He cared naught for the amazed stares
of those who passed by. He cared naught for Betsy's reputation,
indeed was not aware that a woman of her class could have any,
and as for his own, his arrogance, his pedigree, his family and
their connections gave him the belief that what he did was
nobody's business but his own, and if it caused hurt to anyone
that was their concern not his.

Robin Lovell's father had died when Robin was twenty and
with his death he had inherited the title and the family seat in
Cheshire. A vast tract of thousands of acres, which included
moorland, forest, farmland with a dozen farms whose rents
gave him a small income, but little else. The Lovell men were
known for their profligacy and love of gambling and only a
wealthy young wife could save the present baronet's inheritance. But until one came along, a task his mama was working
on at the present moment, he was enjoying his freedom from
the responsibilities he would soon have to face. He hadn't the
faintest notion or concern for the young woman his mama had
her eye on, but would, when summoned, do his duty, no matter
who she might be. As long as she was young, healthy, capable
of producing an heir and very rich, that was all that mattered,
and Emma Goodson was all three. Her father, a third generation of commercial gentlemen concerned in railways, mining,

ship building, and any industry that brought him a handsome dividend, was well able to buy his daughter a title, a vast estate and an ancient country seat to go with it.

In the meanwhile here was this enchanting creature whom Tom Hartley claimed was his fiancée, which Robin found hard to believe, for Tom was almost as well bred as himself. So what better way to amuse himself until he heard from his mama.

That first day he took her at once to his suite at the Adelphi. The fact that he had no money did not in any way deter Robin Lovell from staying in the best, the most luxurious hotel in town, nor from occupying one of their most opulent suites. He was Sir Robin Lovell whose address was Lovell Hall, Cheshire. Just that. An old, well-known, highly respected family who, though as poor as church mice at the moment, had great expectations. Expectations which those in business, even the hotel business, found it advantageous to know about.

Within an hour from their meeting at the church gate he had her and himself stripped naked, ignoring her protests that she was a decent girl, and, flinging her on her back, brought to a shuddering climax, the first of many that day. He was an expert lover of fourteen years' standing, having had his first experience at the age of twelve between the plump thighs of his mother's dairy-maid.

Betsy, from that first moment, was in a constant state of nervous excitement, of quivering panic, of nerve-jumping alarm, of ecstatic joy, of hopeless despondency as Robin led her from one new thrill to another.

Though she was scatterbrained, frivolous, self-centred and devious, she was also cunning. Since meeting him she had had hopes and dreams that her relationship with Sir Robin Lovell would bring her the life she had so long desired, but she was sensible enough to realise that if this didn't come about, she must have Tom Hartley to fall back on. At the present moment the situation with Tom and his family was in a high state of disturbance, and until it improved, despite him being of the class she longed to be part of, she was keeping him at a distance. She didn't want to lose him so he and her family must be kept in ignorance of her "friendship" with Robin and it was this that had her in such a dither.

Robin took her to the races at Aintree, moving among the gentry of the vicinity, the sporting gentlemen, many of them guests at the Adelphi. Robin was recognised by those of his own class, though those who bowed to him, why they could not have said, were somewhat uneasy about the glorious creature on his arm as though instinctively they were aware she was not one of them. He made no attempt to mingle with them, nor to introduce her to them. They sailed over the water on the ferry *Queen* to Woodside, taking lunch at the Woodside Hotel, then sauntering northwards to Bidstow Hill where there was a fine view from the top of the lighthouse over the water to Liverpool, westwards to the Welsh mountains and south to Cheshire where Robin's family seat lay, he told her lazily. They were tourists, Robin insisted, so she must sign her name in the visitors' book but when she declined, since Betsy could neither read nor write – which she did not tell him, of course – he merely laughed in that arrogant way he had and told her she was quite right. It was ill-bred to follow the herd and though she didn't know why, or even understand really, she agreed with him.

The difficulty was that he expected her to accompany him day *and* night to whatever took his fancy, which was proving enormously difficult. The first time he had asked her, or rather told her that he was taking her to the Music Hall in Bold Street that evening, she thought she had lost him.

"D'you mean to say you are refusing to come with me?" They were in his bed at the Adelphi where they spent so much of their time. His voice was icy and Betsy drew back apprehensively. It was the first time she had seen the vicious temper his family knew so well and which they and their servants did their best to avoid. Springing from the tangle of bedclothes in which he and she had been lolling, he strode naked and taut with anger across the deep pile of carpet to the fireplace where a blazing coal fire roared up the chimney, throwing out a splendid warmth. Everything in the bedroom was splendid, for only the best was good enough for Robin Lovell and the Adelphi Hotel provided it: the restrained opulence, the elegance of the Georgian period from which it had been copied, the silk wallpaper of pale duck-egg blue, the high sculptured ceiling, the crystal chandelier, the magnificent bed with its bedframe of pleated duck-egg blue muslin, the Axminster carpet in a design of roses and birds, the wardrobe, dressing-table and tallboy of glowing satinwood, the full-length cheval-glass, the low velvet chairs over which hung Robin's hastily discarded trousers. Empty champagne bottles and crystal wineglasses, overturned during an orgy of sensual ferocity, had spilled their contents on to the polished perfection of slim-legged rosewood tables. On one wall there was a door leading into a bathroom which contained a large enamel bath where he and Betsy had spent many exciting hours, and another opposite which led into an equally sumptuous sitting-room. Robin Lovell had been a guest at the hotel for almost two months and had not yet paid a bill!

He reached savagely for the cigar box on the mantel over the fire, flung it open, snatched out a cigar and lit it with a taper from the fire. He drew in the smoke then blew it slowly at the ceiling. He looked quite magnificent, his male body flaunting its beauty, strong, straight, perfectly proportioned, hard. A body that would take on weight as the excesses of his dissipation took hold but which was now wide at the shoulder, narrow in the hip, his stomach taut and flat. She adored him. She would do anything for him – hadn't she already proved that in the perverse and exotic pleasures she performed for him? – but she was walking a tightrope between him, Tom and her family and if she fell off God only knew where she would finish up. She couldn't just announce to Ma that she was off after tea. In the dark of a November night! The consternation, the questions as to where she was going and who with would cause such a commotion, she couldn't imagine how she could overcome it. How could she produce an answer that would satisfy her mam, and that would keep Aggie, who was an interfering old busybody, off her back? An answer that would placate them both, soothe them into believing that . . . that she was not up to something, that Tom wouldn't mind, that she would be safe and . . . dear God, it would be impossible. Ma would rather lock her in her room than allow her over the doorstep after dark fell. It was difficult enough as it was, balancing her life. He must be made to understand, to accept, but in God's name, how?

"Robin, luv, I can't just . . ."

"So you don't care to come with me to the Music Hall." He glared at her, then softened somewhat, for she did look most mouth-wateringly tantalising crouched in the bed among the tangled sheets. Her hair tumbled about her head in a dishevelled mass of silver falling across her shoulders and over her breasts, a cloak through which rosy, engorged nipples peeped out. Her eyes were a wide brilliant blue, ready to spill with childish tears and his manhood rose and twitched eagerly. He had never known a woman in all the years since he had fumbled his way between the thighs of the dairy-maid who had satisfied him as this woman did. A woman as aggressive as he was himself in bed, who was eager to partner him in the inventive and often coarse practices that titillated his male senses. But he needed obedience, instant compliance to whatever activity took his fancy. Instant servicing of his needs and she must learn it.

"Very well, my pet. If I can't tempt you, I'm positive I can find some other woman to entertain me. I'm sure you must have noticed the number of pretty females in the lobby of the hotel."

"Robin, yer wouldn't," she began to wail.

"Wouldn't I?"

"I couldn't bear it. I luv yer, yer know that."

"Do I? I'm not so sure." He strolled out of sight into the bathroom, his voice floating back to her where she cringed like a small, wild, terrified animal on the bed. "It seems to me if you can't make the effort, or perhaps have no interest in enjoying an evening with me at the Music Hall, your love is somewhat fickle."

Unlike Tom who, kind-hearted and loving, aware of her illiteracy, did not use words or phrases he thought she might not understand, Robin's remarks were often beyond her, but at the centre of Betsy Pearce was a core of steel, a furnace of heat which made her flare up to defend herself when under attack.

She jumped off the bed and marched for her clothes, which were scattered in half a dozen resting places, wherever Robin had flung them as he tore them from her. Petticoats, all frills and ribbons, her drawers, chemise, stockings, her lovely gown of buttercup silk and her dainty shoes, one of which she couldn't find. Bugger it! If she had to she'd hop through the lobby of the hotel minus a shoe and sod the lot of them, including him, she muttered, her face scarlet with fury, as she did her best to pull on her drawers. Her breasts jiggled, her hair fell about her like that of a madwoman just escaped from the insane asylum in Myrtle Street, and from where he leaned against the doorframe Robin Lovell chuckled, good humour restored.

"And where do you think you're off to?" he enquired pleasantly, the cigar held between his teeth, his mouth curving round it in a smile.

"Where d'yer think? If I'm not 'ome soon Ma'll 'ave perlice out lookin' fer me. I'm not one o' yer ladies o' t' night what can wander about wi' nobody givin' a damn where they are, or 'oo with. We're decent folk an' if she knew . . ."

"Betsy, darling, you're safe with me. You know that."

"Me ma don't."

"And you must know how much I adore you."

"No, I bloody don't."

"Really, your language, my pet. No lady would speak—"

"So I'm no lady. Yer knew that when I met yer, an' 'appen that's why yer don't talk o' marriage. After all I've done fer yer an' all."

Her bare breasts were heaving and Robin felt the explosion of need surge through him, the thrust of his manhood growing even harder. Her reference to marriage was something not even worthy of a reply.

"And what might that be, my love, that any other female could not provide?" He grinned insolently round his cigar. He took a step towards her, his purpose very evident, but reaching behind her, her hand found a heavy marble clock, a handsome thing with gilt engraving. Picking it up, she drew her arm back and, considering its weight, threw it at him with considerable force. Had it found its mark it would have brained him. The cigar dropped from between his lips, the lit end landing on his foot, and for several moments he hopped about swearing obscenely. His eyes narrowed and his lips curled back in a livid snarl.

"You little bitch," he hissed, moving towards her, his hands held out in the evident intention of throttling her.

"You bastard . . ."

"You'll pay for that, you little whore. First I'm going to punch you until you scream the bloody place down, then I think I'd enjoy giving you the hiding of your life. Afterwards I intend dragging you downstairs and asking the porters to throw you out into the street where you belong. I'm sure you'll find dozens of likely gentlemen willing to pay a good price for your undoubted talents."

He was knocked off balance by the swiftness and severity of her attack as she launched herself across the room. They both fell on the floor, kicking, biting, scratching, screaming, spitting and shouting, and she only fell still when a vicious swing with the back of his hand across her cheek knocked her senses spinning away into a dark place.

When she came to he was sprawled on his back on the carpet beside her, his breath rasping in his throat, his chest rising and falling so rapidly she thought he might pass out.

"By all that's holy," he wheezed, "we'll have to do it like that again. To have you unconscious . . . was most diverting, my sweet. Now then, get up, get dressed and let's away to the Music Hall. Jesus, I'm hungry, I think we'll have something to eat in the buffet first and perhaps I'd better send for some ice. That face of yours is a bit of a mess. I'm sorry, precious, I was a bit rough with you." He indicated with his hand the blood between her thighs where he had been "a bit rough" with her.

She began to weep. She was bruised, bloody, dishevelled, her mouth swollen, her breasts sore, her eye slowly closing, but when he put his arms on her shoulders, kissing her in what seemed a passion of love she clung to him.

"Robin, I do luv yer, I do. Don't mekk me go. I couldn't live wi'out yer now. I luv yer so . . . I luv yer."

"I know, sweetheart, I know."

"But yer do luv me, don't yer?"

"Of course I do, but really, we must get up."

"Promise yer'll not leave me."

"Betsy, my pet, I wish I could promise you that, I really do, but I must go home soon."

"Why, why must yer? Aren't yer 'appy 'ere wi' me?"

He was inclined to be patient with her. His satiated body was at peace and so was his mind. When she sat up he gently smoothed his hand through the tangle of her hair, pushing it off her face, grimacing somewhat when he saw the state of her face. Not that he was unduly concerned about it, nor about what folk might think, about her or him, when they saw it, and it would soon mend. They spent most of their time up here anyway.

He sighed. "My pet, I'm stony broke. I cannot even pay my hotel bill. I've managed to win a guinea or two at the Royale."

"What's that?"

"It's a sporting club where gambling takes place, but I've lost more than I've won, so at the end of the week I intend to leave Liverpool."

"*Leave Liverpool!*" Her voice rose to the high pitch of hysteria and she sprang up and away from him, crashing into the bed, falling across it, jumping up again and stumbling about as though she had lost her mind, or her sight. This man was her life now. She had blithely told herself that if, or when it was over she still had Tom to make her dreams come true but that wasn't possible now. She couldn't live without the rapacious and insatiable need Robin awoke in her. He was cruel, coarse, obscene, rampant in his own desires, yet there was something in him that called to something in her and she had no choice but to answer it.

She whirled about, her hair flying out like a banner, her eyes burning a brilliant blue. Despite the wreckage of her face, and the blood and bruises on her body she looked quite magnificent, like some warrior queen who had just done battle.

"Tekk me wi' yer, I'll go anywhere, do owt."

"My sweet, I have to go home. I have responsibilities."

"Yer need money?"

He was beginning to lose patience. "I do, and unless—"

"I know where there's money." Her face was as hard as the marble clock that she had thrown at him, her rosy mouth thinned to a white line of resolution. "I can get yer money bur yer've ter promise ter tekk me wi' yer."

Ally moved slowly up Dublin Street, the many-windowed side of Clarence Warehouse towering on her right. The lowering sun was on her back throwing her shadow, long and thin and wavering, before her. Behind her Jack and Davey larked about and she wondered tiredly where they got their energy after the long, exhausting trip they had just endured. Jack was only two years younger than she was but he acted like a boy just out of school. He had had no schooling of course like their Betsy and it was perhaps his ignorance of the world that allowed him cheerfully to let her, Ally, shoulder all the responsibility and the management of the two boats. To judge where they were to go, what they were to carry and make all the decisions that had once been Pa's. The men she did business with along the canal and at the warehouses were slowly becoming used to dealing with her instead of always turning to Jack and that pleased her. But then that was partly due to Pat Maloney who, despite being elderly and wizened, seemed to emanate some element of menace, she couldn't put a name to it, which made them think twice about crossing her. Not that they attempted to "twist" her but one or two, trying to overlook her, since they did not approve of a woman doing business with them, had backed off when Pat had stumped up to stand at her side. He was good on the canal boat, spry as a man half his age, which she didn't know, and as untiring as Jack and Davey at legging it through the tunnels. She had left him on the *Edith*, the *Harmony* moored behind her, the horses stabled and fed, Pat informing her that he was off up to George's Baths on the parade.

"Time I 'ad messen a good wash," he said, sniffing under his own armpits. "It's bin a while." And though she said nothing she agreed with him. Mind, she'd grown used to the smell of male sweat and strong tobacco that hung about him, finding it strangely comforting.

The coins in the bag fastened at her waist under her skirt clinked pleasingly and she smiled, bending to pat Teddy's head as he pattered at her side. Teddy knew where he was going after all these months at Blackstock Street and though he wouldn't desert Jack, or the canal for the world, he did enjoy the few days they spent at Aggie's place. The good food, the comfort of the rug in front of the fire, especially at this time of the year, was a treat he looked forward to.

Davey left them at the corner of Blackstock Street, going on to his mam's place, but he would see Jack later, he shouted, winking comically. Ally smiled, for she knew the two lads would be off to the pub on the corner that they had just passed.

Albert let them in, his usually round and smiling face set in solemn lines though he did hunker down to make a fuss of Teddy.

"What's up, mate?" Jack asked him casually as Ally moved into the warm, fire-lit kitchen, but Albert merely nodded his head in its direction, shrugging unhappily. Not a great one for words, was Albert.

As Ally and Jack entered, both Ma and Aggie sprang up from their chairs, the inevitable cup of tea in their hand, putting them down on the table to sweep first Ally then Jack, somewhat embarrassed, into their embrace. Betsy crouched in the third chair, her face averted, and it was not until Edie began to cry broken-heartedly, that Betsy turned truculently towards them.

They both gasped, even Jack shocked into silence for several moments, and Ally put her hand to her mouth in appalled horror.

"Jesus, our Betsy, 'oo did that ter yer?" Jack said, ready, it seemed, to rush out into the street and find the bastard who had ruined his lovely sister's face. He and Betsy had fought like two cats tied in a sack but secretly he had always been proud of her beauty.

"Oh, Jack," Ma quavered, hovering by her younger daughter, longing to pick her up and fold her in loving arms but Betsy shook her off irritably.

"Don't fuss, Ma, it'll fade."

"But what 'appened?" Ally faltered.

"Some chap attacked 'er in t' street," Aggie told them curtly, and for some reason Ally got the distinct impression that Aggie was not quite satisfied with this explanation for Betsy's battered face.

"Dear God in 'eaven, did yer send fer t' police—" Ally began, but Betsy stood up abruptly.

"There were no need fer that. Tom came an' put summat on it."

"But 'ooever it were needs lockin' up."

"Or a bloody good 'iding."

Aggie sat down wearily, giving the impression that they had gone over this again and again to no good purpose. She reached for her tea. "Lass didn't want it so that were that. She weren't . . . yer know . . ." nodding delicately at Jack, then eyeing Betsy, telling them both that the worst had not happened.

There seemed nothing more to be said. Betsy ignored them all, picking up a magazine and flicking through it, looking at the pictures, and when Ally nodded at Ma and they left the room together she seemed to be ensconced in the world of fashion contained within its pages.

Aggie watched her impassively, sipping her tea.

17

Whipper Ogden watched the flurry of activity as the two boats, *Edith* and *Harmony*, were expertly moored one behind the other on the canalside at Church. The two lads, agile as monkeys, leaped from the boats to the towpath, busy with the mooring lines, the unharnessing of the two horses, while the dried-up old chap who was part of the crew watched, his teeth clenched on his pipe which he removed only to issue orders. Of the woman there was no sign.

The lads led the horses round the side of the warehouse to which they were delivering a cargo of mine machinery, heading towards the stables, their young voices lost in the babble of noise. The level of sound and movement was normal as the frantic business of loading and unloading the canal boats took place. The boatmen, many of them number ones who owned their own boats, had no time to waste, going about their affairs with as much speed as possible, for time was money and money was hardily earned.

It was a stirring scene and a colourful one. Each boat seemed to radiate a rainbow hue that dazzled – and pleased – the eye but those who were at the canalside and threading their way through the constant two-way stream of traffic on the canal were too busy, and too accustomed to the sight, to take any notice.

It could not be said that Whipper Ogden was concerned with the aesthetics of what lay before him. He'd seen it all before a hundred times a day, for he'd laboured on the canal and in the warehouses that stood along its length for as long as he could remember. A vigorous, swaggering lad he'd been when he was hired as a labourer. He didn't know how old he was, or barely where he had come from, he only knew that he'd lived by his fists, a bully – though he didn't use that word – ready to take a crust or a farthing from anyone, male or female, weaker than himself, and that was everyone he had ever known. He had no friends. He was too volatile for friendship; the men with whom he worked, and drank, kept an uneasy distance between him and them and the pint pot he held in his enormous fist, for he was just as likely to brain you with it if a word was uttered he took exception to. And as for the women, wives of the labourers, or the boatmen, the barmaids in the public houses in Church and its environs, they kept a healthy distance between themselves and Whipper. Those who had been unfortunate enough to be cornered by him had learned, to their cost, that he was as brutal a man in his handling of them as he was with those who worked beside him or with animals and children, crushing their vulnerable female bodies against a wall, lifting their petticoats and taking what he wanted. A threat of terrifying menace kept them quiet about it; nevertheless his senseless savagery was whispered about and men kept their womenfolk out of his way. Sometimes he was forced to resort to the whores who hung about the public houses but even they darted into a convenient dark doorway at his approach. Whipper did a bit of prize fighting and wrestling now and again which earned him a purse or two, his great strength and recourse to merciless trickery making him triumphant in the ring so that even here men, as big and brutal as himself, avoided a bout with him.

But though Whipper Ogden was illiterate, uneducated, ignorant and uncivilised, he was cunning, with a sharp brain and a long memory and he had not forgotten the girl who had not only given him "cheek" before his workmates but had knocked him senseless with a shovel. Three months he had watched out for her, had even seen her at the tiller of one of her boats going up towards Clayton-le-Moors, or down to Blackburn, but this was the first time she had moored on the canalside at Church. He had been astonished to hear, when he had come to from the blow she had given him, that she *owned* the bloody boats, that she was a number one, but that cut no ice with him. He'd have her, and he meant *really* have her, if it was the last thing he ever did. By God, he'd get her behind the warehouses, strip her, beat her black and blue, then poke her in every "orifice" – though he did not use that word since it was not one in his vocabulary – in her female body. Treat her like an animal and when he'd done with her and made every male in the vicinity aware of what he'd done to her, she'd never be able to look another man in the face again and no man would care to look at *her*. He'd teach her to take a shovel to Whipper Ogden!

His lewd thoughts brought about the inevitable result. He could feel the swelling in his sagging crotch strain and pulse with bursting energy as his imagination took hold. With a practised hand, practised because it was a while since he'd had a woman to thrust it into, he hurriedly undid his buttons, took out his enormous "thingy" as he called it, and relieved the throbbing ache, wiping his hand down his already filthy trousers.

It was mid-afternoon but at this time of the year it was already getting dark. The two daft lads were coming back from the stables, pushing and shoving, acting the goat, their usual way of communicating with one another, and the old geezer on the *Edith* spoke tartly to them which brought them up sharply.

"Give over acting daft," Whipper heard him say. "Pair o' daft young buggers. There's this machinery ter be unloaded before us gets to our beds. Early start termorrer wi' them bricks."

"Sorry, Pat," one of them mumbled, still grinning.

"An' yer can wipe that gormless look off yer face an' all. Yer sister's gerrin us meal ready but yer'll get none until both boats 're unloaded."

"Aw, Pat," one of them was unwise enough to say, but just at that moment a dog, a stray mongrel, was foolish enough to take exception to Whipper's hulking form in the dark at the corner of the warehouse, and began to bark, its ears back, its hackles up. Whipper, quick as a striking cobra, lifted his boot and drove it into the animal's side. The barks became an agonised yelp as the dog was lifted into the air, landing several feet away. Whipper, incensed, picked up a brick, one dropped from a crate, and with no more thought than he would have given to stepping on a spider, smashed the dog's head in, grunting with satisfaction as it was silenced.

He returned to his hiding-place, patient and impassive. He watched the two lads and the old chap unload the machinery, helped by a couple of labourers who were lifting it on to a wagon, then, when it was completed, the three men disappeared into the cabin on the *Edith*. He settled down to wait.

Ally had made an enormous meat pie in the oven, which was tucked neatly at the bottom of the steps, just inside the door to the cabin. On the top of the oven, blackleaded and shining as she knew her ma would like it kept, was a pan of boiling potatoes and another of carrots and turnips, all of which would be mashed and heaped on to the men's plates. The table set in the wall had been released and set with one of Ma's snowy table-cloths on which four places were laid out. The kettle spluttered in its turn on the oven top and the teapot was ready, containing four heaped teaspoonfuls of tea. There was milk and sugar and a big tin still half full of Aggie's biscuits, coconut macaroons, of which Jack was inordinately fond, for "afters", and the four of them squashed shoulder to shoulder, tucking in. There was the sound of hungry men hugely enjoying a hearty, tasty, well-cooked meal. Even Teddy had a plateful of what they had, wolfing it down so quickly it was gone in a minute, at which point he began to edge up to the others, sitting down, his eyes moving from one face to another in the hope of a titbit.

"Well, our Ally, that were bloody good," Jack sighed, reaching for the mug of tea before him, then somewhat self-consciously bringing from his pocket the clay pipe he had taken to smoking in imitation of Pat. He filled it with tobacco, tamped it down, lit it and drew on it as he had seen Pat do. Davey watched admiringly and Ally did her best to hide her smile. She knew what was coming next. He turned to Davey.

" 'Ow about 'alf a pint at pub, lad?" Just as though there were many years between them instead of two, Davey the boy and Jack the man.

"Well, we've an early start termorrer, our Jack. Them bricks 'll need some shiftin.'"

Pat looked at one young, hopeful face to the other. They were boys really, doing men's work and they did it well and willingly. They played around, like puppies sometimes, but they deserved a treat and " 'alf a pint" wasn't too much to ask, was it?

"Well, I fancy a drink messen, so I reckon it won't 'urt. Only one each, mind, 'an then it's back ter t' boats. Orlright, lass?" turning to Ally.

"Oh, gerron, the lot o' yer, but only one or yer'll get sack."

Whipper watched them go, the two lads behaving themselves in the presence of Pat, disappearing up the towpath and into the night.

Whipper, in common with many big men, could move as silently as a shadow. His enormous weight as he stepped on to the *Edith*'s tiny deck tipped the boat an inch or two into the water but Ally was engrossed with the notebook in front of her on the table and though she felt it she took no notice. Teddy did though. He lifted his head and pricked his ears, looking towards the cabin door at the head of the stairs. He stood up, stiff-legged, and began to growl softly.

"What's up, lad?" Ally asked absently, her mind occupied with what was written in the notebook. She kept a record, a rough record, which she did not recognise as her first attempt at bookkeeping, of every penny she and her boats had earned; every penny she had spent: on the boats' maintenance, the tolls, the upkeep of the animals, wages, and the day-to-day living of herself, her crew, and her family and what she saw sbalanced at the end of her calculations pleased her. Tomorrow when their cargo of bricks had been loaded and delivered to Clayton-le-Moors, she meant to travel on to Burnley and into what was known as the Weavers Triangle where there were many cotton mills and factories and where a cargo might be found. There she would tie up at Slaters Terrace, a canal warehouse that had living accommodation on the top floor to house the workers in Slaters Mill. There would likely be a cargo waiting for her of bales of woven cloth to transport to the docks of Liverpool. She hoped so, for the quicker she returned to Blackstock Street the better. She was not at all happy about the situation there. She knew Aggie and her ma did their best with Betsy but neither of them had any control over her, Aggie because it was not really her business to keep a rein on Betsy, and Ma because she was still vulnerable after Pa's death. Aggie had told her Betsy was out of the house for the better part of every day, and not with Tom either, who had his patients to attend. They didn't know where she went, for she was evasive, even angry when questioned and Betsy in a temper was to be avoided.

And Ally was eager to see to the opening of the account with which Tom had promised to help her. She and the two boats had had to leave early the next morning after the disclosure of Betsy's attack and she had been unable to meet Tom and visit the manager at the Royal Union Bank in Castle Street. Pat had come thundering up from the docks with a message that there was an urgent cargo for Church and she had no option but to leave at once, much to Ma's distress. Cargoes were not in such plentiful supply that she could afford to turn one down!

When the cabin doors were silently opened outwards, though Ally might have felt surprise that her crew were so quiet, she didn't even glance up and it was not until Teddy began to bark furiously, his barks interspersed by savage growls, that she turned, looking up at the enormous hulk of a man she did not at first recognise. The last time she had seen him she had just learned of Pa's death and her mind, though incensed at the cruelty directed at both Magic and Gentle, had been preoccupied by her need to get back to Liverpool as soon as possible. She recalled his size, though, the snarl of outrage in his voice at being impeded by the horses, the flicker of gratification in his eyes when she stood up to him, marginal images, but his face as a whole was a blur to her. The memory of the shovel that had come to her hand, her own livid fury, the words a man spoke to her warning her to take flight for he – she couldn't recall his name – was a man to be wary of, these were vivid flashes in her stunned, not yet frightened, but confused brain.

And here he was, the very man whom she had faced three months ago and it was very evident that he had not forgotten and what was now on his mind. He didn't speak, just grinned evilly as he did his best to force his massive proportions through the small doorway and down the steps to the cabin where she sat frozen to the bench. The tiny cabin was no more than four feet in height and six feet across. The breadth of his shoulders jammed themselves against each of the doorposts and he grunted angrily as he did his best to force himself, like an over-large cork into a small bottle, into the cabin and it was this that gave Ally a moment's grace. Whipper Ogden, in his greedy, lustful need to get at the girl who had shamed him in front of the men he called mates – though none of *them* claimed the honour – had forgotten the lack of space on a canal boat, and the agile contortions needed to insert oneself into the cabin.

Though he wriggled and grunted and shoved and heaved, he was stuck fast, captured by his wide girth.

His eyes, small, black, deep-set and completely expression-less, narrowed to slits of frustrated rage. The malevolent cruelty of the man showed in the contortions of his face and his manner and the way he struggled, barely able to get his arms or even his ham-like hands beyond the cabin door. Teddy's frantic, high-pitched barking was inciting him to even greater effort and fury since the noise the dog made was bound to attract attention, but try as he might he could not get his broad, muscled shoulders through the door.

"I'll 'ave you, yer bitch," he roared, forcing his cropped head through the narrow opening. He was so incensed that his inflamed mind could not grasp that all he had to do was turn sideways and bend his knees to gain entrance to the cabin and the open-mouthed, white-faced woman who was backed as far as she could go, which wasn't far, against the table, and though it would still be a tight fit, it could be done. "No one tangles wi' Whipper," he thundered, "d'yer 'ear, not an' gets away wi' it. Man or bloody woman. I've not forgot what yer did ter me last back-end an' by Christ, yer'll pay fer it."

He was spraying spittle across the cabin, maddened not only by memory but by his inability to get at the girl, so near and yet so far from his tortured grasp.

Ally, her shock turning to terror, began to scream. The sound of her voice, and Teddy's echoed round and round the cabin and though it seemed obvious the man, the brute, the night-mare that was trying to get in to her, was having a great deal of trouble in doing so her hands scrabbled about on the table behind her in search of some weapon to defend herself and Teddy, who, brave as a lion, was snapping his teeth at the man's worn and filthy trousers. A knife, perhaps a fork, anything that might act as a weapon.

She was still screaming. A hesitant group of men had begun

to form on the towpath, but recognising the man whose voice was splintering the night air with his howls of rage so that even the horses in the stables were rearing in fright, none of them had the nerve to tackle him, not yet, not until there were a few more of them. A lass was making a great deal of noise and folk on other canal boats were popping their heads out of their hatches but Whipper Ogden's reputation was such that none was game to make the first move.

Ally's hands suddenly found the windlass that an hour or so since she had removed from her belt, the iron windlass that was used to fasten and unfasten lock gates. It was heavy and solid and she felt a moment's thankfulness that, instead of hanging it on to its usual hook she had carelessly left it on the table. She had been in a hurry to get the pie in the oven, she remembered, so that Jack, Davey and Pat would have a hot meal waiting for them. Now she picked it up. She was as awkward as the ferocious, slavering, stinking man who was trying to get in to her, for she had no headroom to lift the windlass and brandish it but she did her best.

Keeping out of range of his clutching hands which, in the small space, were hardly a foot from her face, she struck at him with the windlass.

"Ger outer my cabin," she shrieked, though he could not be said to be *in* it, aiming another wild blow at him.

"Sod off, yer bitch, I'm coming in an' when I do . . ."

"I'm warning yer. Yer'll get this in yer filthy face if yer don't gerrof my boat."

"Don't you threaten me," he howled, but this time her aim found its mark. The windlass struck him full in the face and she heard the crunch as his nose broke.

His scream was as loud as hers and this time he fell back, crashing against the ram's head which, when the boat was on the move, held the tiller. Blood streamed from his nose and into his open mouth and Ally felt the nausea rise in her stomach.

Teddy had followed the man up the steps and as he reached
the small deck he went for him in a place that, had he been
human, he could not have chosen better. Teddy's teeth sank
viciously into Whipper Ogden's crotch and the man's shriek
rent the air in agony. He drew himself up but the dog clung on,
his paws leaving the deck so that he hung, still snarling his
defiance, from the front of Whipper's trousers. As Whipper
swung away, so did Teddy. As Whipper scrambled to get off
the boat, he carried Teddy with him and it was not until Jack
and Davey, having heard of the commotion, had come running
with Pat not far behind, hauled him off, his teeth still reaching
for the man who had invaded Teddy's territory, that he became
calmer. Even then he snarled at the retreating back of the
intruder who, having pushed to the ground two men who had
bravely tried to stop him, vanished into the blackness behind
the warehouse.

They were all round her then, the men who felt somewhat
ashamed that they had not leaped to her aid and the women
shuddering at the terrible price this lass would have paid had
she, and her dog, not beaten him off.

But again they begged her to leave as soon as possible.

"I've a cargo ter pick up," she told them where they crowded
on the towpath vicariously excited, as even decent people are
at the troubles of another, and on the boat's small deck. Several
women, two of whom she didn't know, fussed about her in the
cabin. Her teeth chattered against the brim of the mug of tea
one of them pressed into her trembling hand. Shock had set in
and she wanted to weep, to have her ma's safe strong arms
about her, or, failing that, those of Tom Hartley, which was
hardly likely, was it? Teddy's part in it was much praised, for it
was partly his bravery that had helped to save her from Whipper
Ogden's depraved attentions. Jack and Davey were all for
getting up a search party to look for Whipper but they met a
shamefaced reluctance on the part of other men and when Pat,

his voice flat, but one to which the lads always listened, said no, that was that.

"E'll be far gone now. 'Oled up somewhere."

"Police should be fetched."

"They'll do nowt. Ally's not been touched—"

"'E threatened 'er, Pat," Jack interrupted hotly. "An' look what 'e did to Magic an' Gentle that time. Man's bloody mad an' wants lockin' up."

"Aye, but we've ter be off termorrer ter Clayton, so best get to our beds. I'll sleep 'ere on t' deck—"

Ally knew, of course, that there would be no sleep for Pat Maloney. He'd settle himself down with his back to the hatch door, perhaps with Teddy, who had proved himself this day, between his knees, both of them defending her.

"Nay, Pat, me an' Davey'll . . ." Jack interrupted hotly, the blood of youth surging through his veins.

"Do as yer told, lad," Pat said calmly, and he did, he and Davey clambering obediently to their cabin in the prow.

They were loading up the containers of bricks the next morning, starting with the *Harmony*, which was just as well as it turned out, when a voice could be heard shouting above the babble of noise on the canalside. Did anyone know where the *Edith* was moored? it was asking.

They had spent a quiet night with no sign of Whipper Ogden, though Ally had only dozed, brought to terrifying alertness at every sound. When the voice, that of a boatman, was carried across the hubbub to the four of them, even Teddy stood up and turned his head, while Ally's heart rose into her throat, banging and surging in panic. A labourer was pointing in their direction to a man whose eyes followed his finger and they stood waiting, as though something inside all of them, even Teddy, knew he brought bad news. The tradition, which was part of life on the canal, of carrying messages from one boatman to another, or from family to family had once before struck dread in Ally's heart and she stood like stone as the man approached.

"Alice Pearce?" he asked.

"That's me."

"I were in Stanley Dock t' other day an' this woman, Aggie Wainwright she said she were, asked me where I were off to. When I said Burnley she said would I look out fer yer on the *Edith*."

"What is it?" Ally's face, already palely gaunt from her experience the day before, and her lack of sleep, whitened even further. She leaped over the side of the boat on to the towpath, grabbing the surprised man by the arm and shaking him. "What is it?" Please God, not her ma, she couldn't bear it if her ma was poorly, which must be the case if Aggie had sent this chap with a message. Frantically she dragged at the man's arm again, and affronted, for he was only doing her a good turn, the man began to pull away.

A quiet presence beside her loosened her ferocious grip on the man's arm and, amazingly, Pat's own arm rested comfortingly about her shoulders.

"Steady, lass, let the chap 'ave 'is say."

"I'm sorry . . . what . . ."

The man relented, for the young woman was obviously under a lot of strain, he didn't know why and didn't want to. He was off to Burnley and he was losing time hanging about on the canalside at Church, but the ways of the boat people must be recognised.

"Yer ter go 'ome, at once, woman said. There's—"

"Why, what's 'appened?" Again Ally was ready to grab at the stranger, to shake it out of him in her frantic terror of what might be taking place at Blackstock Street, and again Pat held her firm, while on the *Harmony* Jack and Davey watched intently.

"Nay, I don't know, lass, she weren't about ter tell me 'er

business, but she looked fair demented. The wife said we'd watch out for yer and that's all I know. Get back ter Liverpool, woman said."

He waited a moment, perhaps expecting a word of thanks, while all about him men whistled and shouted, cranes dangled over canal boats lowering cargoes on to their planks between the stretchers where crew members were arranging the goods prior to covering them with sidecloths. A frantically busy scene which had been interrupted on the *Harmony* with the arrival of the canal boatman. When nothing was said to him he left, grumbling later to his wife that that was the last time *he'd* go out of his way to take a message to anyone about owt.

It was Pat who took over, leading Ally back on to the *Edith* where he expertly made her a cup of almost black, sweet tea, put it in her hand and ordered her sternly to sit herself down and wait until he returned. Drink that tea, he told her and do as you're told, when she showed signs of disobeying him.

"I must get—"

"Yer must do nowt till your Jack comes back with Magic then you an' 'im'll sail ter Liverpool."

"But the bricks?"

"Me an' Davey'll tekk *Harmony* up ter Clayton, 'appen gerrus a cargo, then go on ter Burnley. You an' your Jack—"

"Pat . . . Pat . . . what . . ."

"Give over, lass, it's no good mitherin' over what's 'appenin' in Liverpool. Drink yer tea while Jack fetches Magic, then geroff back ter yer ma, the pair o' you. Me an' Davey'll do t' rest."

"Pat, I bless the day I found yer . . . 'onest."

"Don't talk bloody daft, girl. Bugger off to Liverpool an' we'll catch up in a few days."

It took them two days to reach the canal basin on Leeds Street, mooring there since it was quicker than going down the four locks to Stanley Dock. Besides, they had no cargo to discharge.

Leaving Jack to stable Magic, Ally ran like the wind despite her exhausted state up Leeds Street, along Vauxhall Road, whirling round the corner into Blackstock Street. Tom's bay mare was fastened outside number 10, which did nothing to allay her fears. Rather it increased them and as her fist thundered on the door it was no louder or more savage than the thunder of her heart.

Aggie seemed to have lost weight, her normally plump and florid face sagging in pale folds as she opened the door. She shook her head and bit her lip, standing back to allow Ally to fly past her into the kitchen.

Tom was there, as haggard as Aggie, and Ma, thank God, in her chair by the fire. The kitchen was as it always was when Ally returned, warm, welcoming, teapot keeping warm by the fire, cups of tea being drunk, even by Tom who stood up as she entered.

Ma began to weep and Ally wondered idly how many times in the last eighteen months she had seen her mother in tears. Her strong, steadfast mother who in all the years since Ally was a child had never been anything but cheerful and smiling.

"Ally . . . Oh, Ally, what are we ter do?" she moaned.

"What's ter do, Ma? What's 'appened?"

"Lass, it's our Betsy."

For several relieved moments Ally wanted to smile, to ask, "Now what's she done?" but Tom put a hand on her mother's shoulder. A hand of comfort and support and Ally was made aware that this was something more serious than one of Betsy's childish escapades.

"What?"

"Betsy's gone, Ally," he said quietly.

"Gone? Gone where?"

"We don't know. The police . . ."

"I don't understand, where can she 'ave gone? She don't know anyone."

A strange expression crossed Tom's face then was gone.

"We don't know," he repeated. "She disappeared three days ago."

"Three days, but . . ."

"Oh, Ally. Ally, me little girl's gone an' . . . Oh, Ally . . ."

"What is it, Ma?" Though of course she knew.

"She's tekken yer money."

18

Betsy had never been on a train before and the excitement of being about to do so was so intense she thought she might faint. She clung to Robin's arm as he strode, with the arrogance of his class, along the station platform, expecting those who were also waiting for the train to make way for him which, naturally, they did, the crowds parting before him like a field of corn in a wind. The air in the high, vaulted building was acrid with smoke, noisy with the hiss of steam and the shriek of engine whistles, each one making Betsy jump. There was a great clattering and squealing of unoiled wheels as porters scuttled here and there trundling trolleys, one of which was piled high with Robin's expensive luggage.

"Keep up, fellow," Robin told the porter, his voice imperious as they made their way to the first-class compartments, and the sweating red-faced fellow accelerated his pace, to the physical danger of several travellers in his path. Excited voices rang in Betsy's ears as swarms of would-be passengers and an equal number of those arriving at the great railway station in Lime Street teemed about her. Where were they all going, she wondered dazedly as she hurried to keep up with Robin's long, impatient stride, and where had those alighting come from? The platforms were alive with people and at each platform other trains stood, their doors flung wide. There were uniformed guards, resplendent with the badge of their important office; top-hatted gentlemen arm-in-arm with elegant ladies in furs, for the day was bitterly cold; men in cloth caps making for the third-class compartments and be-shawled flower sellers holding out wilting bunches of violets, their pinched faces hopeful, their thin faces huddled into even thinner shawls.

A stray beam of sunlight, which had managed to creep through the high, smoke-blackened roof windows of the station, touched a strand of Betsy's curling hair where it had escaped from her bonnet and at once it was lit like spun silver. The intense joy of leaving Liverpool in the company of Sir Robin Lovell with the conviction that soon they would be married had intensified her beauty so that men, catching sight of her, bumped into one another in their open-mouthed awe. Her flawless face was pale but at her cheekbones was a hint of carnation. Her eyes were luminous, a blue-green scattered with diamonds, and her mouth, full and a soft coral pink, was parted moistly. She held her head gracefully, her back straight, and her breasts were pert and taut above her tiny waist. But for her shawl, which was pretty enough, she would have looked as expensive as the other ladies who were being handed into the first-class compartments by their companions, for her gown of blue-green cassenette was beautifully made and was the exact shade of her eyes. Her boots were of pale grey kid with a square toe and had peg-top heels, the tops one and a half inches high, reaching above her ankle. They had blue satin rosettes on the insteps. Her tiny hat was called a puff bonnet, perched at the front of her shining hair, and was decorated on its crown with silk lily of the valley. Her appearance drew admiring glances from men and women alike, even from Sir Robin Lovell who was used to her loveliness and for the fraction of a second, but no more, he felt a surprising pang at what he was about to do to her.

He remembered the moment three days ago now, when with the triumphant delight of a child she had put into his eager hands a tin box, its lid decorated with a picture of their young

Queen and her husband, a box produced in its hundreds of thousands on the occasion of Their Majesties' marriage.

"Open it, Robin," she told him, ready to clap her hands with glee, again like a small child and he remembered wondering how a woman who was as shameless, as amoral in their bed as she had proved, could be so childlike out of it.

He opened the lid and looked inside, not knowing what to expect, but what he saw was not totally unexpected, for how could a young woman whose people were, or so she had told him, *boat people* who worked on the Leeds and Liverpool Canal accumulate the sort of money he needed?

He had begun to laugh, throwing back his handsome head while she stared at him in amazement, an amazement that quickly turned to narrow-eyed effrontery. Betsy Pearce had gone to a great deal of trouble searching for and finally finding the money Ally had added to what was already in the box after her last trip. It had taken all her patience, which was not much at the best of times, to wait until that last amount had been added, and a great deal of ingenuity to get it, to hide the carpet bag filched from Aggie's room, for she did not intend to leave her lovely gowns behind, creep out of the house in the dead of night and into a cab to the Adelphi.

The young gentleman receptionist had stared in astonishment, along with several porters who hung about the desk, for it was barely dawn and the lobby was empty. She had snapped imperious fingers as she had seen Robin do, and since she had been seen in the company of Sir Robin Lovell many times, the porter took her and her bag up to his room. She did not know that, warned by a chambermaid sent up hurriedly by the receptionist who was eager to avoid a scandalous scene, Sir Robin had just time enough to get rid of the young and pretty actress he had met that night at the Theatre Royal, and who had shared his bed. He was still in it when Betsy arrived.

"What's so bloody funny?" Betsy enquired tartly, as he

emptied the contents of the box on to the bed. He was completely naked, sitting cross-legged on the bed, somewhat
languid, for he and the actress had been very energetic for the
past four hours, but Betsy, never observant, appeared not to
notice. The coins showered between his thighs and he continued to laugh, completely abandoning himself to whatever it
was that amused him. He slapped his naked legs, shrieking with
mirth while Betsy became more and more incensed, ready to
slap not only his legs but his face as well. She had often seen
and heard others laugh with huge enjoyment though she herself
could find nothing funny, wondering why it was, and now she
was the same, staring, hands on hips, at Robin's convulsions.

"Well," she spluttered at last, "if what's in that box mekks
yer laugh I'll not bother yer wi' it. It'll buy me a few new
gowns."

"That's just it, my pet. That's *all* it will buy. Dear sweet
Christ . . ."

"Right then, give it 'ere."

His face hardened and as she reached for the pile of coins,
which nestled against his flaccid manhood, he struck her hands
away.

"No you don't, my beauty, never mind new gowns. This will
at least pay my account here at the hotel and buy a first-class
ticket to London."

She squealed in joy, again ready to clap her hands and hop
up and down like a child promised a treat.

"London! Oh, Robin, I've always wanted ter go ter London."
She had been greatly disappointed by his reaction to what she
saw as a treasure-trove, which would keep them in the lap of
luxury for a long time but the word "London" drove everything
from her mind.

"Well, I didn't—" he began, then bit off the words like
scissors through thread. He stared at her speculatively, his eyes
narrowing as they ran across her laughing face, the tossed fall

of her silver-gilt hair, her exquisite figure, and he began to smile, a warm smile of good humour, though his eyes, so like hers in colour, remained cool.

"London it is, then, my pet. I see you've brought your . . . luggage," eyeing Aggie Wainwright's battered carpet bag with the contempt it deserved. He leaped up, opened the wardrobe and began to throw the contents on the bed.

"Here, help me to pack. Your things can go in with mine then I'll run down and settle the bill. But first I must just drop a line to my mama telling her that . . . well, it's family stuff, then I'll find out what time the London train leaves and order a cab." He beamed good-naturedly. "I wonder what they'll make of this lot" – indicating the scattered coins on the bed – "down at the desk? I'd like to bet none of their guests has paid with pennies and halfpennies, and even farthings before."

Betsy, hastily stuffing her gowns into Robin's fine leather trunk, had no idea what he meant and didn't really care. She had an idea what he was writing to his "mama" about, of course, she thought jubilantly. She didn't know why they were going to London first; perhaps a little holiday before he took her, Betsy, to Cheshire. She fell to pondering which of her three elegant gowns she would wear to meet Lady . . . *Lady* Lovell, her face tranquil and dreaming, for it seemed the lessons Tom's mother had so savagely taught her had not been learned at all!

Tom stood beside the narrow bed, Albert's bed, and watched Ally Pearce's eyes droop and finally close. Her dark lashes, which he noticed for the first time were tipped with gold, lay on her pale cheek and he smoothed back her hair, tangled and uncombed, since he and Aggie had barely been able to restrain her let alone wash her and brush her hair before getting her, at last, deeply drugged, into bed.

They had all four of them been totally taken aback to say the least by the ferocity of her reaction. There was none for the first few seconds as she looked from face to face as though in blank misunderstanding. Albert's was young and confused, Ma's painfully weeping, Aggie's tight-lipped but concerned and angry, and Tom's frowning, doing his best to hide his own devastation. Then she lifted her face to the ceiling and began to howl. To howl like a wounded animal whose body had felt the first sting of the arrow, or the bullet. She lifted her hands and began to tear at her own hair, dragging out two handfuls before Tom, horrified, managed to reach her and pinion her and her flailing arms to his strong body.

"Where is she? Where's the bitch? Where's me money? The lazy greedy slut. I'll kill 'er, I swear I'll kill 'er . . . let me go. I'll find 'er an', by God, when I do I'll kill 'er wi' me bare 'ands."

"Ally . . . Ally, lass, don't say such things," her mother moaned, as though she was sure in her mother's heart there must be some innocent reason for all this.

"This is your fault," Ally hissed, turning on her mother, who reared back, struggling to get free of Tom's grasp. "If you an' Pa 'adn't bin so bloody soft wi 'er she'd not 'ave turned out the little sod—"

"Ally, chuck, yer ma's out of 'er mind wi' worry. Can't yer see? First yer pa, then your Betsy goin' off like this. It's killin' 'er." Aggie put out conciliatory hands, needing to do something for this dreadfully wounded young woman who had become so dear to her, but Doctor Tom, surprisingly, was holding her to him in a passion of protectiveness.

"Killin' 'er, *killin'* 'er! 'As she any idea what I've bin doin' ever since Pa's accident? 'As she? 'Ave any of you? Workin' meself to a shadder, me an' our Jack. Twelve, fourteen 'ours every bloody day, 'umpin' coal an' bricks an' every other cargo we could find."

"Ally, we know, we've all been worried about you," Tom murmured into her hair, for he still had her clasped urgently to his chest, her head tucked beneath his chin. She was becoming increasingly difficult to hang on to as she fought like a madwoman to escape. What she would do if he let her go he shuddered to think, for the Ally Pearce they all knew had disappeared, becoming the virago who seemed bent on destruction, on destroying something, *anything* in revenge for what had been hers and was gone.

"'Ave yer? Is that so? Worried about me? Really. While I've bin walkin' 'undreds o' miles a week, leggin' it through dozens o' tunnels, beggin' fer cargoes, bin treated like I were some brainless nit-wit by men 'oo 'aven't sense they were born with; oh, an' don't ferget that . . . that brute 'oo would 've raped me but fer Teddy."

They all became still, Aggie and Ma's faces whitening, Albert gasping, for though he was an innocent, ignorant lad he knew the meaning of the word, and though Tom did not loosen his hold on her his face spasmed as though at some unimaginable horror.

It was at this moment the front door, which had been left on the "snick" for Jack, opened and banged to and Jack burst into the kitchen.

He skidded to a stop, his frantic glance moving from one to the other, his mouth opening and closing on a question he dared not ask. Their Ally clasped tight in Doctor Tom's arms but obviously struggling to get free. His ma moaning and rocking to and fro in the way of women the world over when faced with grief. Aggie like a rock hewn from granite in her dread of what was to happen, even Albert wide-eyed, frightened. Teddy, who was at Jack's heels, took a couple of steps backwards, his tail drooping, his ears down.

"What . . . what's up?" Jack gulped, unable to decide whether to move to his ma or to demand that Doctor Tom unhand his near-demented sister.

"Tell 'em, Jack," she was shrieking, "tell 'em what 'appened ter me. Tell 'em about Magic an' Gentle an' that bugger; tell 'em 'ow I 'ad ter 'it 'im wi' a shovel. Oh, no ladylike tea parties fer me, no pretty dresses fer Ally, but 'ard work an' abuse by that monster. Go on, Jack, an' while yer at it tell 'em 'ow bloody 'ard we work. Mind, Ma ought ter know since she's a boat-woman, an' then reckon up 'ow much that trollop's stole off us, months of 'ard work all gone down bloody drain, an' Ma let 'er, showed 'er where bloody box were, I shouldn't wonder, sayin' there yer are, sweet'eart, 'elp yerself. There's plenty more where that come from, Ally'll get it, she don't mind workin' like a donkey while you sit on yer arse. Dear God . . . Oh, dear sweet Jesus, I can't stand it . . ."

"Will someone tell me what the 'ell's 'appened," Jack whispered. "It's like a bloody mad'ouse."

"That's where I'll fetch up."

"Ally, don't . . ." Tom began again but she managed to get an arm free, hitting out at him, leaning back in the fierce circle of his arms to spit in his face. She was weeping now, tears streaming across her cheeks and dripping on to her bodice. Ally, perhaps for the first time in her life, had lost total control. Her senses were fast reeling away from her in the utter horror and disbelief of what had happened to her. Betsy had stolen more than the money she had earned so painfully since Pa's accident, she had stolen Ally's dream. She had not stolen the man she loved, for Tom had never been hers to lose, but she'd got him just the same. Now, in one single heartless action, she'd taken the very heart from Ally's breast. The hopeful heart that had clutched at this new beginning. She could not see beyond this moment since she was mindless in her rage and pain, and Tom Hartley knew that if he didn't lead her away from it into the healing arms of sleep, into the unconsciousness her wounded mind and heart needed, she'd slip beyond his help into the depression her mother was in, had been in since Fred Pearce died.

"Help me, Aggie . . . Jack . . . hold her."

"Hold me? Get your 'ands off me. I'm goin' out ter find that
. . . that . . . I can't find a word bad enough to call 'er. Oh, Jack
. . . Jack, all our work . . ."

It took the three of them to hold her while Tom poured some
potion down her throat. Ma wailed, and Teddy whined and
crawled beneath the edge of the red plush cloth that covered the
table, and Albert sat down heavily in his ma's chair as his boy's
heart broke at the wickedness of the beautiful woman who had
caused all this.

She woke to warmth and peace and emptiness, nothing in her
now of the savagery of yesterday. Was it yesterday? How long
had she lain here in Albert's narrow bed, in Albert's boy's
room in which books and model ships were scattered over
every surface? There was a fire in the tiny grate, which flickered in pleasing orange and gold about the walls. Walls that
were covered with coloured illustrations of Albert's heroes:
The Last of the Mohicans, Ivanhoe, Westward Ho, and *Moby-
Dick.* There was the gentle sound of rain against the window
and when she turned her head she could see a square of heavy
grey sky and the windowpane down which the rivulets ran,
meeting and parting. The shadow of them was reflected on the
bedroom wall, merging with the dancing shadows of the fire's
flames.

She also saw the sleeping figure of Tom Hartley. It seemed
quite natural for him to be there, to study him, his tired face,
the deep grooves on either side of his mouth, the tousled dis-
order of his dark hair, just as it had seemed natural weeks ago
to sit beside him on the park bench in the Zoological Gardens
and discuss her problems. He was slumped in a chair by the
window, his head to one side and though she did wonder how
much of a fight he had had with Aggie to be here instead of her,
she didn't find it strange. She wondered why.

In her own pain she had given no thought to his. She had lost a sister, a cruel, self-absorbed, greedy child, whom she could not say she had ever really loved, or even liked. She had, temporarily, she realised that now, lost her reason, and her reason for living. Ma had lost a spoiled daughter who had given her nothing and taken her all, but Tom had lost the woman he loved, the woman he was to marry and what could be worse than that? She, Ally, when she regained her strength and her resolute will, would rise up again, start again, for she had her two canal boats, her loyal crew, her horses. Ma had Aggie, her home with her; she had Ally and Jack who both loved her. But what was left for the man who slept restlessly, exhaustedly in the chair by the window?

She watched him as he opened his eyes, his long lashes lifting, drooping, then lifting again until they focused on her and came alive and concerned.

She smiled. "I'm that sorry," she said simply and watched as his face softened. He stood up and stretched and her eyes loved the length of him, the lift of his arms, his mouth opening, his jaw cracking in a wide yawn. Loved the very bones of him, his strong muscled legs in his creased breeches, the graceful way he moved across the small room to crouch at her bedside.

"What for?" He put his hand on her forehead, a medical man tending his patient but his expression was not one of doctor to patient.

"I'm not the only one ter lose summat."

His face clouded momentarily then cleared. The past was gone and only the future remained, his eyes seemed to be telling her, and though she frowned slightly in confusion it seemed it was all right.

"The sleep has done you good," he said. "I thought we might have to tie you down last night."

" 'Ow's Ma? I were . . . dreadful to 'er."

"Sleeping. I gave her the same sleeping draught you had.

There's nothing a good night's sleep won't cure. Within reason, of course." He smiled whimsically.

"Well, 'appen yer right but I've ter get down ter t' docks an' see what cargo there is ter . . ." Struggling to free herself from the blankets Tom and Aggie had fastened about her.

"No you don't, Ally. It's all taken care of." He looked as though he might be about to smooth her cheek, or perhaps brush her tangled hair back from her forehead and she wished he would. His smile was tranquil, which amazed her, but she felt herself becoming even more calm beneath its warmth.

"What d' yer mean? Jack can't tekk care—"

"No, I know, and so does he, but Pat can."

"Pat!" Her mouth fell open in amazement.

"He was here last night. Very late. He and Jack and the lad . . ."

"Davey?"

"Yes, Davey. They've found a cargo and another man to crew and they'll be halfway to . . . where's the first place?"

"Bootle."

"Bootle by now."

"Oh, Tom."

"Oh, Ally." He grinned. He appeared to be – what was it? – almost *light-hearted*, which seemed daft in the circumstances.

"What am I ter do?" she asked him, after a moment of studying his calm features.

"Rest, and when you're rested, you and I have an appointment with Mr Moore."

"Mr . . . Mr Moore?"

"Mmm! At the Royal Union Bank in Castle Street."

"When? What? Oh, Tom."

"Aggie'll be on her way up with something hot and nourishing and you'd better eat it or there'll be trouble for both of us, and then I want you to sleep, and don't say 'Oh, Tom' again.

Ah, here she is," rising to his feet to open the door for Aggie, who carried a tray with a steaming bowl of broth and several slices of freshly baked bread, judging by the lovely aroma that followed her in.

"Right, queen, sit yer up. Look, put that shawl round her, Doctor Tom, then I'll see to her. Yours is downstairs in t' kitchen."

Though she thought the world of Tom Hartley there was still the proprieties to be observed, despite the fact that he was a doctor. Last night had been an exception, what with Ally being in such a state but today she was better. She had been a patient last night. Today she was a young unmarried woman and Aggie's standards maintained that last night's doctor was this morning's unmarried man.

"Come on, lass, get this inside yer," placing the tray across Ally's knees.

"How's Ma, Aggie? Is she . . . does she . . . ?"

"Yer mam'll be fine. She's frettin' fer that little madam but, God forgive me, I 'ope we never see 'er again. Police are lookin' for 'er, Doctor Tom was a big 'elp there, but I'd like ter bet we'll never clap eyes on 'er again. Good riddance ter bad rubbish, I say. Now tuck in while I fetch summat up fer yer mam."

Tom Hartley rode slowly along West Derby Road, turning right into the lane that led to the gates of Rosemont House. Abby's reddish-brown coat was slippery with rain, as smooth as if it had been greased, and from the leaden skies more fell, a cold heavy rain, a winter rain that penetrated Tom's thick cape and gathered in the brim of his "wide-awake" hat. It ran off his cape, down his saturated breeches and into his boots. It swept across the fields to his left and right, lifting and shifting, parting occasionally to reveal dripping hedges and the sodden ditches where dismal plants huddled under the onslaught.

And yet Tom felt a core of peace within himself, wondering

at it, wondering why he felt a great weight had been lifted from his shoulders. The peace was mixed nevertheless with sadness, with pity, pity for the young girl who had deserted him and gone blithely off with a man known for his wildness, his wickedness, his careless indifference towards women, so what was to become of her? He had learned this morning from the police inspector at Dale Street police station that a young woman answering Betsy's description, and could anyone mistake such loveliness, had been seen several days ago boarding a train at Lime Street, a train to London, and with her was a gentleman who, Tom was well aware, could be none other than Sir Robin Lovell. If that was the case Tom knew none of them had any hope of seeing pretty, naïve, foolish Betsy Pearce again. She would enter Robin Lovell's hedonistic world, expecting marriage but ending up only God knew where. London was a big city where countless thousands lost themselves and when Robin Lovell had tired of her and spent her money, she would be one of them. And yet would she? A survivor, was Betsy, so perhaps, doing what many a lovely, desirable woman had done before her, she would find a protector, a man of money to keep her in the luxury she craved. He wished her well.

The long tree-lined drive up to the house was as immaculate as ever. Hearing his mare's hooves on the gravel, an open-mouthed Seth ran round from the stables, so nonplussed at the appearance of the eldest son who, it was rumoured, had been cast out by his parents, and certainly hadn't been since . . . well, for a long time, he barely had time to mumble a greeting.

Sinclair was the same, his usually expressionless face and his eyes, which always gazed over a caller's shoulder, showing for several moments his consternation.

"Good afternoon, Sinclair."

"Good afternoon, sir," Sinclair answered, not at all sure whether he should stand aside for the son of the house, or ask him his business as he would any other caller.

"Are my parents at home, Sinclair?" Tom asked politely, stepping over the threshold, shrugging out of his soaking cape, and handing it and his hat to the butler.

"Well, I'm . . ."

"Never mind, Sinclair, I'll show myself in." And leaving Sinclair holding his dripping garments, Tom moved towards the drawing-room where he was prepared to eat humble pie!

19

Ally and Tom were ushered respectfully into Mr Moore's office, for if the clerk who showed them the way had no idea who *she* was, he recognised the son of one of their wealthiest depositors.

She wore the same tawny dress she had worn in the Zoological Gardens. It was the only one she had, and the same straw bonnet and shawl but this time, to please Aggie who had lent – *lent* her, mind, Ally had insisted – the money, she had on a new pair of brown boots with a two-inch heel and a ribbon rosette on the instep the identical colour to her dress. She looked stylish, though simply dressed, neat but with a certain elegance which suited her, and was not at all out of place beside Tom, in the rather refined environment of the Royal Union Bank in Castle Street. She and Tom, who had called for her at 10 Blackstock Street, had travelled in the same hansom cab that had brought him from Duke Street. It was the first time Ally had ever ridden in one and Aggie and Ma stood at the door waving her off until the cab turned the corner as though she were away to Princes Dock to board a ship to the other side of the Atlantic.

Mr Moore stood up as they entered his office, nodding pleasantly at them both, then when Tom held out his hand, shaking it, wishing him "Good morning", he seemed somewhat surprised when Ally, as Tom had done, held out her hand, but Mr Moore was a businessman and as this young woman was presumably here on business, he took her hand politely. Mr

Moore had other ladies who used his bank for their financial
dealings, not many, true, but the names Hemingway and
O'Malley, shipowners, came to mind.

"Now then, Miss Pearce, may I offer you coffee, or perhaps
you would prefer tea. I know many ladies do. And you, sir,"
turning from her to Tom, "a glass of Madeira?" When they
both refused he sat back, his hands folded across his well-fed
stomach and beamed at them both. He looked like some kindly
old grandfather who was more accustomed to dandling grandchildren on his knee than a banker who successfully invested
his clients' money, his shrewd brain assessing to the last decimal
point what they should be and at what percentage.

Ally would have been grateful for a cup of tea but this
meeting was as alien to her as a trip up the cut on the *Edith*
would be to Mr Moore. The thought of juggling cups and
saucers was too much to manage on top of this already fraught
visit. Tom had promised to speak for her, so all she had to do
was smile, nod and look pretty, he said. She didn't know about
"pretty" but she was aware that she looked her best. She might
be asked to sign something, Tom said, if all went well and she
must be prepared to show Mr Moore the figures they had gone
over together last night. All the scraps of notepaper and the
notebook in which she had kept a record of the dozens of trans-
actions that had taken place during the past eighteen months
were at this moment tucked away in the locker beside the bed-
hole on the *Edith* which was somewhere on the Leeds to
Liverpool Canal. All the records of tolls paid and indeed every
penny that had passed through her hands were out of reach
until the *Edith* came back to Liverpool, so she only had the
figures in her head, those she could remember, and these
she and Tom had made notes of. Surely the fact that, from the
profits, she had bought another boat and a horse to tow it would
prove to Mr Moore that she was doing well!

"Mr Moore will need to see what he calls your 'books' since

you went into business," Tom told her, while Aggie and Ma, having turned out what had been Betsy's room in preparation for Ally, watched fearfully. Ma still wept and leaped up like a jack-in-the-box every time someone knocked on the door, but a week had gone by without the return of her "baby". Tom had deliberated for hours on whether to tell her that it was thought Betsy might have gone off to London with a "gentleman". Would it alleviate her anguish to know that her little girl was not dead, or would it be far worse for her wondering where she'd got to, and, horror upon horror, with whom? He'd spoken privately with Ally and Aggie and in the end the three of them had decided to say that Betsy had gone to London – with Ally's money – but conceal the fact that she was accompanied by a man! At least Ma would know Betsy was alive and had enough to live on.

Ma had been distraught, relieved and incredulous in that order when they told her and could make no sense of it. How could she desert her family without a word and, what's more, why had she discarded a safe, decent life with Doctor Tom to go off alone into the unknown, which London was? It might as well have been the Australias, it was all the same to Ma, but at least she had the hope, indeed, her mother's belief that her lovely girl would get a letter to her. You could pay to have letters written, couldn't you? she asked Doctor Tom tearfully and Albert could read it to her. To have the words her Betsy would write to her, even in a stranger's hand, would give her great comfort.

"Now then, Doctor Hartley," Mr Moore began, "what may I do for you?" But before Tom could answer, continued, "But first, may I ask after the health of your papa and dear mama?" the latter whom he had never met. Mary Hartley was not in the habit of mixing socially with those her husband dealt with commercially.

"Quite well, Mr Moore," Tom said mildly, "but if we may,

Miss Pearce and I would like to get on. We're in rather a hurry, you see, and if you can't help us then we must go elsewhere."

If Mr Moore was horrified at the idea of the son of one of his wealthiest and most influential clients "going elsewhere", he did not show it. He couldn't imagine what the young lady might be to Doctor Hartley but with the sure instinct of a professional man, one who had steadily climbed the ladder of commerce for the past thirty-five years, his acute brain, which though she had said nothing except "no thank you" told him she was not of the same class as Tom Hartley.

"You have not told me what it is you want, Doctor Hartley." He smiled equally mildly.

Before Tom could answer, Ally leaned forward. Her little straw hat dipped slightly over her forehead and a dark and glossy curl sprang out above her ear and for a breathtaking moment Tom felt a desire to lean across and tuck it neatly back into place. He watched her, holding his breath, watched her eyes, which were the same colour as her dress, lighten and glow and a touch of poppy flagged her high cheekbones. Mr Moore had turned an amazed and fascinated gaze on her, quite as fascinated as Tom's as she changed from plain, quiet, submissive, to sparkling comeliness. She knew she and Tom had agreed that Tom would do all the talking but somehow, since it was *her* business, and she was the one who had the experience of the day-to-day running of it, she felt the need to put her own case, so to speak. Tom was a doctor, not a boatman and though he had a way with words he had no conception, or not much, of the life a boatman led: the acquiring of cargoes, the care of the boats and horses, the knowledge and experience of dealing with manufacturers, a hundred details which were stored in *her* head.

"I run me own business, Mr Moore," she said simply, "on t' canal. We're boat people, me brother an' me. So were me ma an' pa until me pa 'ad an accident leggin' it—"

"Leggin' it?" Mr Moore questioned faintly.

"Aye, through Foulridge Tunnel. Well, me an' our Jack, that's me brother, took over an' we did right well. We bought another boat an' 'orse ter pull it, an' took on extra crew. There's brass to be 'ad on t' cut—"

"Cut . . ." Mr Moore quavered.

"Aye, canal, an' me an' Jack made it until . . ." She sat back in her chair and Mr Moore leaned forward in his, as she reverted from sparkling eagerness, which had been bonny to see, to the rather lifeless creature she had been when she came in. Mr Moore had dealt with many men in his capacity as banker and several women, but this one reminded him of the Hemingway girl who had been one of the loveliest creatures he had ever seen. Miss Pearce had shown for several moments the same spirit as Miss Alexandrina Hemingway, but suddenly it drained out of her at the memory of something that appeared to trouble her immensely.

Then he realised it was not her spirit that had gone but something that had *come*. Something that was tearing at her, threatening to engulf her and only her own icy control held it in check.

It was anger! A furious bitter rage that was corroding that very spirit that had first driven her on. He watched in amazement as Tom Hartley leaned across to her and took her hand between both of his. He bent his head and smiled into her face.

"It's all right, Ally. You have nothing of which to be ashamed. *She* is to blame and your anger is understandable." He turned to Mr Moore, still holding her hand which seemed to settle comfortably in his. Mr Moore noticed that Doctor Hartley's thumb gently smoothed the back of it. What the devil was going on here? Edward Hartley's son, a member of what was known as "good" society, associating with a woman who was, by her own admission, from the working classes? And yet she was respectably dressed, smart even, and for those few minutes as she spoke, most attractive. Was she Tom Hartley's mistress, perhaps? But Tom's next words dispelled that thought.

"Mr Moore, Miss Pearce and I are here to obtain a loan. Miss Pearce has a growing business. In less than two years, ever since she took over from her father as she has just told you, she has not only doubled her profits, she has purchased another boat, a canal boat, and a horse to tow it. Besides herself and her brother, she employs two men and but for an unfortunate mishap she would even now be—"

Mr Moore held up his hand. His curiosity was aroused, his interest was aroused, since he was one of those men, opportune in a banker, who can sense a scheme or a gentleman with a scheme that is a money-maker. This quiet young woman, who for some reason was still clinging to Tom Hartley's hand, unaware, it seemed, of anything unusual in it, had from what Doctor Hartley was telling him turned a business venture from a successful but plodding affair into one that was in the ascendancy. That she had accomplished more in – how long did Hartley say? – less than two years than her father had managed in his lifetime. Some men were like that but – this was a woman he reminded himself – her shrewd, far-seeing brain was willing to take a risk and grab with both hands any gain to be had.

"What exactly was the unfortunate mishap, Miss Pearce?" Fixing her with a steady glance as though daring her to try and blind him with some silly tale when she had actually spent the lot on new gowns.

"Mr Moore, perhaps if I was to—" Tom began but again Mr Moore held up his hand. It was not his habit to interrupt his wealthy clients, not even the son of a wealthy client, but this young woman intrigued him and he wanted to hear *her* explanation. He was, in reality, not in favour of young women or indeed of any woman being in the commercial world unless it was perhaps in one of the many dressmaking establishments in Liverpool, many of them a triumph of success. But he was prepared to let her have her say, particularly if she was . . . attached in some way to the son of Edward Hartley.

"Miss Pearce?"

Ally's hand was held fast in Tom's which was a comfort, and though she was somewhat overawed by the luxury of Mr Moore's splendid office, and the dozen portraits round the walls of forbidding gentlemen whose expressions appeared to demand what the devil she was doing here, the residue of her anger put a stiffener in her spine, holding her upright and giving her the words to ignore them and to speak her mind.

"I were a foolish, trustin' idiot, Mr Moore. Aye, yer might well stare but it's truth and, by God, it taught me a lesson. No, Tom, let me speak," as Tom would have interrupted. "I 'ad a sister, yer see, pretty as a picture an' a way wi' 'er, with me ma an' pa . . . an' wi' men."

She could feel Tom stiffen at her side and she thought for a moment he was about to withdraw the lifeline of his warm, strong hand but though she loosened her own hold, he kept her hand firmly clasped in his. She turned to smile at him, her eyes filled with a lovely, soft expression that moved something inside him and caused Mr Moore to look down at his hands. Then he cleared his throat and Ally turned back to him.

"She was . . . she was without morals, Mr Moore, wicked an' cruel an' a thief—"

"She took your savings, Miss Pearce," Mr Moore interrupted gently.

"She did, Mr Moore, stole 'em more like it. I know now I shouldn't 've left the box wi' Ma—".

"The box?"

"Aye, a tin box belongin' ter me ma. Ma were . . . soft wi' 'er. She were that lovely, yer see. Ter look at, an' she could wind Ma round—"

"Yes, yes, Miss Pearce, and where is she now?"

"I don't know. In hell for all I care! That money she pinched was ter buy me a third boat an' a horse, hire more crew. I want a fleet, yer see . . .."

"A fleet."

"Aye, me own fleet but it'll tekk me a long time ter save up enough ter . . . so we thought, Tom said yer lend money."

"What collateral have you, Miss Pearce?"

"Coll . . . I'm not sure." She swung round to Tom but he was looking at Mr Moore.

"She has two boats, Mr Moore, which are, as we speak, carrying cargoes up and down the Leeds and Liverpool Canal, earning money. Besides which, she and I are to go into partnership. Pearce and Hartley, which will, naturally, have the backing of my father. I have a decent allowance but Miss Pearce and I need" – here he named a sum which made Ally gasp, though Mr Moore didn't even flinch, so she supposed, incredulously, that such amounts were commonplace to a man such as he – "either to buy, or have built at least two more boats and to open an office in Liverpool from which to run the business."

"Tom!" Her voice came out as a squeak. Her clear, golden-brown eyes were wide with shocked surprise and her mouth, she found, would keep opening and closing in the most foolish fashion. Partners! What the devil did he mean? There had been no talk of partners when they had sat up half the night discussing what they would say to Mr Moore in the matter of a loan. Records, receipts, bills of sales, contracts, perhaps the need to request references from the many men of business with whom first her father then she herself had traded. But not once had a partnership been mentioned.

Her mouth thinned to a grim white line. She stood up and tore her hand from Tom's grasp while Mr Moore sat back and watched with great interest. It seemed this young woman was not the quiet creature he had at first thought her to be.

"What the devil are yer talkin' about? I said nowt about

tekkin' you on as partner. I've already got one an' 'is name's Jack Pearce! This is a family concern an' if—"

Tom Hartley also stood up, half a head taller than she was, the expression on his face matching hers. He knew he had been . . . well, *remiss* hardly seemed to describe it, but he realised even as they bristled up to one another that this had been brewing in his mind since he had entered his mother's drawing-room. He had gone to Rosemont primarily to make peace with her, for he had known how deeply distressed she had been when he had announced that he intended marrying Betsy Pearce. Now that he was no longer to do so he was aware that he would be welcomed back into the fold, so to speak. His father had wrung his hand, not speaking much, but telling him gruffly that his allowance, the private allowance that gave him the freedom to treat the poor, those who had not the wherewithal to pay for medicine, would be paid once more into his account at the Royal Union Bank, a fact of which Mr Moore would not be unaware! Tom was preoccupied with clean water, drainage channels, in giving his services free to the infirmary, which he could do now that his allowance had been restored, but added to that was his perplexing need to help this defiant young woman rebuild her business. In some strange way he felt he was at fault in this affair. Had he not fallen helplessly under the spell of Betsy Pearce, taken her about, which had encouraged her to squander money on dresses and bonnets, and surely he should have realised, or at least *wondered* where the money came from, this would not have happened. The chance meeting with Robin Lovell was not his fault, but still he had had a hand, through Betsy, in Ally's downfall.

"What's wrong with having another partner, one with money to invest, tell me that? I'm sure Mr Moore would agree."

"Indeed, I would—" Mr Moore began.

"I don't care. This is my business, mine an' Jack's an' we don't need no charity."

Tom clapped his hand to his forehead, spinning on his heel, then back to her. "Charity! I'm not *giving* you anything. It's an investment from which I shall expect a return. Christ, you're willing to borrow money . . ."

"Aye, from a bank. And what's this about an office in Liverpool? 'Oo's goin' ter sit in an office runnin' the business? Me ma, or 'appen Aggie? I've never 'eard owt so daft in me life."

"May I say a word . . ." Mr Moore interjected, but it was several minutes before, their faces nose to nose, the first faint smiles lit the eyes of the protagonists, followed by a twitch of their lips, then grins which were mirrored unknowingly on Mr Moore's well-fed face.

"Shall we sit down and have that cup of tea?"

"What's wrong wi' – what was it? – Madeira?" Ally asked him, her eyes twinkling and Mr Moore wondered why he had ever thought her plain.

The company in the box at the Prince of Wales's Theatre, where a performance of *The Corsican Brothers* was taking place, consisted of four gentlemen and one lady. They were all five dressed in evening clothes, the gentlemen in stark black and white, the uniform of the upper-class man about town: a black evening-dress coat cut away at the front and reaching at the back to the knee, a white silk waistcoat, a high white necktie over a pearl stud, pleated white shirt, tight black dress trousers and black button-hook boots. All but one wore a centre and back parting with their hair brushed out to the side, and a drooping moustache.

The young lady was so lovely she had caused quite a stir as she and the gentlemen had entered the private box. There were dozens of opera glasses trained on her and whispered conversations among the theatregoers as to who she might be. She was not a lady, a real lady, for her face was delicately painted and her eyelids were tinted, which no female of quality would do, but her evening gown was in the very latest fashion and obviously very expensive. It had a separate bodice and skirt, the bodice cut very low off the shoulders to reveal a great deal of her creamy breasts, with a pointed waist at the front, and at the back. The sleeves were short in a single puff. The skirt had a train and was a lovely pale duck-egg blue, an overskirt of tulle looped up at the side and trimmed with white silk roses, over an underskirt of silk in the same shade of blue. Her hair, a tumble of silver-gilt curls, was contrived into an artless but carefully arranged fall about her head and neck twined with white satin ribbon and white roses. Her satin evening slippers were coloured to match her dress.

Sir Robin Lovell watched with cynical amusement as Reggie and Hugh, both sons of peers of the realm but with no title except "The Hon" before their names since neither was the heir, vied with one another for Betsy Pearce's attention, like young puppies fawning and frolicking and swearing to her great delight that they could not live without her and that she must promise never to desert them for another. The third gentleman, an older man, had the rather bored countenance of a man who believes there is nothing in the world he has not sampled; nevertheless he had an acquisitive gleam in his narrowed eyes as he watched their antics and her excited giggles. He was Sir John Newton, a baronet like Robin, with a wife and six children on his estate in Buckinghamshire. He caught Robin's eye and his cruel, thin-lipped mouth moved in what may have been a smile, and he nodded imperceptibly.

At the interval Betsy, with Reggie and Hugh jostling her, took a turn, as they called it, along the velvet-carpeted hallway at the back of the boxes. As they left Robin moved to lounge in the chair beside Sir John.

"Well, Johnny, what do you think?" he asked casually.

"Mm, she's quite a looker all right. But then so are a lot of young women. I'm . . . well, I'm looking for something special, lad."

"Aren't we all, old chap."

"May I ask why you're—"

"Family matter, Johnny. It seems Mama has found me a wife." Robin grimaced ruefully and Sir John Newton nodded understandingly. Old families must have an heir, the line kept up, unbroken, or the country would go to the dogs. But a fellow must be allowed his diversions and the silly, but quite glorious, young creature was certainly one of those.

"Of course, but . . . well, not to put too fine a point on it, Robin, I need more than a pretty face in my bed. I'm easily bored you see, and need . . . entertaining in a particular way."

"Johnny, on my oath, believe me this one would keep even the most" – he almost said perverted – "demanding satisfied. She is young: I don't know, eighteen perhaps, and was a virgin when I . . . took her in. I've taught her a trick or two . . ." They both smiled in perfect accord. "And I was well satisfied. In fact if I could manage it I would keep her, set her up in a house somewhere handy but to tell the truth I'm strapped for cash and unless I toe the line and behave like a good son and husband, at least until an heir is produced I shall remain that way."

"I see! Well, I'm sure we can come to some arrangement agreeable to both. Had you a price in mind?"

They might have been talking of a horse, a mare perhaps with admirable qualities over which, as gentlemen, they were preparing to bargain.

"She's bloody good, Johnny. Would you like me to describe certain . . . specialities she possesses?"

"Do so, old chap."

For several minutes the two gentlemen chatted, their heads close together so that anyone observing them, noticing their smiles and nods, might have been forgiven for thinking they were discussing the present hunting season, the coming racing season, or any of the numerous pastimes with which their privileged class indulged.

"So in view of this I think a thousand guineas might be a reasonable price," Robin finished enthusiastically.

Sir John laughed out loud, which was so unusual several people in adjoining boxes who were acquainted with him turned to stare. But his face was unnaturally flushed and Robin knew that though he might have to haggle, he would get what he wanted. Perhaps not a thousand, but even five hundred would be very acceptable.

"What about the two lordlings? They know the score. Won't they want to be . . . invited?"

"They couldn't afford her, old chap."

"I'd want a . . . sample."

"Of course. Why not tonight?"

"Does she know?"

Robin smiled a wolf smile. "Hardly, so if you take her . . . well, she might struggle the first time but . . ."

"All the more entertaining, old man. I'll send the cash over to your hotel tomorrow."

20

The door burst open so explosively the pen with which she was neatly entering the profits on the last month's business skidded over the page, leaving a deep score across her careful notations. She was writing with the pen Tom had given her on what he had called the "grand opening" of Pearce and Hartley six months ago. It was her prized possession. Not just because it was a gift from Tom which, of course, was the main reason but because it was such a joy to write with, printing clearly the columns of figures with which she dealt. The quill pen, which was all that had been available until recently, was a fine instrument but it needed constant trimming with a penknife in order to write well. Now, with the advent of the steel nib which was attached to a solid holder of mother-of-pearl, especially made for her at Tom's orders, with her initials painted on it in gold, she could get through the accounts in half the time. It had been designed, Tom told her, to hold a supply of ink sufficient to keep going for a while between visits to the inkwell. At the end of her working day she meticulously cleaned the nib and returned the pen to its case, which had her name on it. It was placed reverently in the bag she took everywhere with her – even to bed where she often sat up against the pillows and studied her accounting books – and which contained many of the documents pertaining to her business. The bag was of leather, somewhat in the design of Tom's doctor's bags, with separate compartments so that she might keep her documents and papers, her account books and ledgers apart from one another.

The bag had a top catch opening down the middle so that it could be pulled wide apart. This again had been a gift from Tom, ordered from the leather merchants where fine medical bags such as his own were manufactured.

She turned sharply on the rather ancient swivel chair with its padded leather upholstery, ready to heap imprecations on the head of the intruder but when she saw who it was she could not stop her heart from lifting, her pulse from quickening, nor her mouth from curling at the corners into a smile. Despite this she deliberately injected a curt note into her voice.

"Tom Hartley, do yer have to burst into me office as though the hordes of Mongolia were at yer heels? Look what yer've made me do across me page," turning back to indicate with her pen the damage done to her accounts. "I'd just finished them an' all. I'll have ter cross the line out and do it again. You know how I like things neat an' tidy . . ."

Tom, dressed in what could only be called "country" attire, tight beige doeskin trousers, knee-high riding boots, a tweed jacket and a cap to match with a large covered button on top, strode across the office and took the pen from her hand. He placed it carefully on the pen stand, for he knew how highly she prized it – though not why – took her hands in his and pulled her to her feet.

"Never mind that. I've come to take you out." He smiled down into her astonished face, squeezing her hands as though in a fever of excitement, like a small boy off on some longed-for excursion. "It's too nice to be indoors, so I've given myself a day off and I demand you do the same. It's Midsummer's Day in case you haven't noticed, downhill from now on towards winter so we'd best make the most of it. Look at the sunshine and the blue sky and tell me—"

She snatched her hands away from his as though his touch was offensive to her, which couldn't be further from the truth. The feel of his strong, slender fingers holding hers made her insides lurch alarmingly but she must not let him see it. He was so good, not just to her, but to Ma and Aggie, to Jack and the others on her canal boats and to the scores of struggling men, women and undernourished children in his care. She was used to his easy good humour, the air of quietness about him, that feeling he seemed to evoke of patience and calm and that there was nothing in life that he could not eventually overcome. She had seen the twinkle in the depth of his brilliant blue eyes when he was amused and the slow curling at the corners of his mouth to reveal the even whiteness of his teeth in a brief smile, but this . . . this *exuberance* was something entirely new. It was as though he had at last thrown off the sadness of the past, for it must have been a sadness to lose the woman he loved, and had regained the youthful vitality, the cheerfulness he must have had in his younger days. She had never known it, or him, before that fateful moment he first saw and fell helplessly in love with Betsy, but though she backed away from him in consternation she could only admit that this Tom was much to her liking.

Nevertheless she could not simply down tools, walk away from the office of Pearce and Hartley, lock the door behind her and go gallivanting off on a day's outing with Tom, as he appeared to be suggesting. There were cargoes to be considered, accounts to be seen to, ledgers to be completed, wages to be made up, bills to be paid, a hundred and one jobs to which she, as a partner in the firm, must attend.

Even now, six months since it all began, she could barely believe what had happened in that short space of time. She often paused for a moment in her busy day to sit back in her swivel chair and gaze dreamily round her tiny office, the one she had insisted upon after viewing half a dozen others, ignoring Tom's complaint that it was no bigger than the pantry off his mother's kitchen. She knew nothing about the pantries, nor the kitchens in the houses Tom Hartley was used to, she only knew that the rent for this one was the cheapest and that its position in Walter Street overlooking Stanley Dock could not have been more convenient. From the window on the first floor, the window on which the name Pearce and Hartley was inscribed in gold lettering, she could watch the activity in the dock basin and see her canal boats, four of them now, work their way down the locks to the warehouse she rented where they would unload their cargo. She could watch the sailing ships moving up and down the great River Mersey, those entering bringing the trade goods of the world, those leaving bearing the thousands of tons of manufactured goods this great industrial nation produced. Frigates and schooners and barques, Pat had told her, for the old man had enormous knowledge of boats, any sort of boat from sea-going to canal-sailing stored in his head. She could see the Black Rock Lighthouse, sailing ships hovering round it like butterflies on the blue silvered waters, their sails billowing gracefully; across Nelson Dock where a forest of denuded masts swayed with the slight movement of the water beneath them, across the busy river to the shores where the ferries busily deposited their multitude of passengers from Liverpool at New Brighton, Egremont and Seacombe.

Mr Moore could not have been more helpful in the setting up of the small business, small to him that is, though Ma and Aggie, Pat and Jack and Davey could not have been more impressed or astounded had she told them she was to take over and run the great White Star shipping line.

"Yer leavin' t' canal," Jack gasped, shocked beyond measure, while Ma's hand went to her mouth in dismay. Leaving the canal! But they had always been boat people. Both she and Fred were the children of boat people and though Betsy had always been something of an unknown quantity, neither flesh, fowl nor good red herring with her beauty and beautiful ways and obviously destined for better things, Jack and Ally had promised to keep on the line as she and Fred had done. Dear heaven, she'd already lost one daughter, her baby, her beautiful girl to some unknown world beyond her comprehension with no word as to whether she was dead or alive, and now Ally seemed to be telling them that she was to desert them as well. Aggie put a steady hand comfortingly on her shoulder, comfort which Edie Pearce still needed having lost half her family in two years. The tall men stood awkwardly about the small kitchen, leaning their backs to the wall, Pat and Davey, who had been summoned with Jack, looking somewhat abashed, wondering, no doubt, what *they* were doing here. Albert rested his arms on the back of his mam's chair. He was now fourteen and about to move on to the Mechanics Institute in Mount Street. He watched and listened intently. His mam was determined he should make something of himself, as he was, and when he had finished his education perhaps there would be an opportunity for a bright, ambitious lad like himself in this exciting set-up!

Tom, who was seated opposite Ally at the table, rested his folded arms on its red chenille-covered surface, his eyes on her, letting her do the talking at that moment since she was the *working* partner.

He himself was what Mr Moore called a "sleeping" partner, putting nothing into the new business but his money. The sum Ally was to borrow from the bank gave her an equal share in the firm of Pearce and Hartley, the loan to be paid back from her share of the profits. Tom had wanted to put up all the capital needed, since Edward Hartley had been delighted with what he saw as his son's entry into the commercial world, unaware at that moment that *Pearce* was a woman, and was more than willing to help financially, but Ally wouldn't hear of it. This was to be an equal association she told him, imperious in her determination. Yes, she knew his father was a wealthy man and that meant Tom could afford to invest a greater amount than she could but if he continued to argue he could forget the whole thing. She'd be beholden to no man . . . oh aye, the bank: well, that was different, Mr Moore was making her a loan on which she would pay interest, a business deal between bank and customer and there was the end to it. He could say what he liked, but she wouldn't budge and if he had time to stand arguing she hadn't. If they were to be partners in forming a canal-carrying firm, she must be allowed to share, not only in the profits but the cost. Tom had tried to reason with her that she would be *working* in the company while all he did was put money in, stand back and wait for a return but she refused to budge. She was, in her way, as stubborn as her missing sister!

"I'm not leaving t' canal, Jack", she said patiently, turning to smile reassuringly at Ma who looked as though a pit had opened at her feet into which she was about to fall. The room was so quiet the crackle of the coals in the fire, the small sound as ash dropped into the ash can beneath could distinctly be heard. The clock above the fire, a wedding present given to Aggie and her new husband many years ago, ticked sonorously as though to remind the occupants of the room that time was marching on, and Ally at least responded, for she was to be a partner in a growing concern where time could not afford to be wasted. Without asking permission, so great was his concentration, Pat took his pipe from his pocket, filled it with the vile-smelling tobacco he smoked, tamped it down and lit it, puffing the equally vile-smelling smoke into Aggie's fragrant kitchen. It was a measure of Aggie's absorption that she gave no sign of disapproval.

"Tom an' I 'ave become partners, business partners," Ally went on. "All done legal at bank, an' wi' your 'elp, Jack, since you're good at it, we're ter buy a couple more 'orses an' 'ave two boats built at Arnold Bridges'. I'll come wi' yer a time or two until all four boats 're—"

"*Four boats!* Me an' Pat an' Davey can't run four boats, our Ally." Jack, who had preened at her praise, turned to Pat for confirmation but Pat was watching Ally with the attention of a hawk surveying the land beneath his wings. Jack could see no further than the end of his nose, or at best the prow of the *Edith*, but Pat, though an untutored man who had worked boats of one sort and another since he was a nipper, could see the potential this young woman was offering them.

"Shurrup, Jack," he snapped. "Let Ally 'ave 'er say."

"Thanks, Pat. Now as I were sayin' we're ter borrow money from t' bank—"

"Borrow! Never! Yer pa never owed a penny in 'is life," Ma began, ready to stand up and give the rounds of the kitchen to this headstrong girl of hers who seemed determined to get the lot of them into the Borough Gaol. But Ally was the one to stand; she twitched her full skirt out of the way, revealing her snow-white petticoats which were lavishly trimmed with the crochet lace at which Ma was so clever. Rows of it flowed about her trim ankles and Aggie, distracted for a moment, noticed Tom Hartley eyeing them admiringly. Aggie's heart softened, for what could be more appropriate, what would make her and Edie happier than to see their Ally and Doctor Tom dovetailed in a more intimate partnership than this one. Then Ally began striding up and down the length of the kitchen, round the table once, twice, then over to the window where she lifted the curtain and peered out into the deserted street. Not a soul had ventured out, not even children in play, only a tattered mongrel scampering up the street on what seemed to be important business of its own. It was nearly Christmas and above the rooftops the heavy pewter sky was beginning to empty its burden of snow, a few flakes at first but already thickening. She was conscious of them at her back, all watching her breathlessly, even Teddy who was sprawled on the rug before the pantingly hot fire.

She whirled about to confront them, unaware of the flushed loveliness her enthusiasm had put in her face. She had a fine smooth complexion, tinted to the colour of pale honey in the summer but now excitement had drained it away to ivory except for the full coral pink of her mouth. Her lashes, as dark as her hair, spread a fan almost down to her cheekbone which retained a touch of rose. Her hair, which Ma cut regularly for her, much against her will, lay in a shining cap close to her head, thick and curling, dark as treacle but where the firelight caught it streaked with rich chestnut. It fell across her forehead to her eyebrows, beneath which her eyes were wide and an incredibly golden amber. Tom watched her, wondering dazedly why he had never before noticed what an attractive young woman she had become. He supposed it was because Betsy, who had drawn all eyes to her, completely eclipsed her sister. Now that she was gone, only God knew where, Ally had stepped out from beneath her shadow and shone, not spectacularly, not stunningly, but with a serene loveliness which was as pleasing to the eyes as a pansy is to a full-blown rose.

"Ma, we can't expand wi'out cash, an' the only place to get cash is a bank. Tom an' me 'ave bin—"

"Eh, Doctor Tom," Edie moaned, "yer never encouragin' 'er ter gerrin ter debt. I can't stand it, really I can't. First our Betsy, now this. It's too much, our Ally. Yer pa—"

"I'm sorry, Ma, but I must do it, I want me own fleet. I want ter be one o't big carriers on't canal. Like John Hargreaves, him from Wigan. 'Is family started from nowt generations ago an' over thirty years back 'e were reckoned to own more canal boats an' 'orses than anyone else in t' country. Even when t' railways came he reduced 'is prices – a right old battle there were between railways an' canal companies – ter get trade. Now it's my turn, mine an' Tom's. There's a deal o' competition but wi' right crews, right boats, 'appen a power boat . . ."

Jack slapped his thighs in delight and did a little jig. He had been, in turn, astonished, disbelieving, truculent, apprehensive, but now the wonder of what it might mean scattered those feelings to the wind. A power boat! By God, that'd be summat, his fresh young face told them, but Ma simply threw her apron over her head and wept.

"Nay, I want my Fred," she said piteously.

Jack did his best to look suitably repentant. "Eeeh, Ma, I'm sorry, but I think our Ally's right."

"You would, yer daft lad," Ma moaned from under her pinny. Aggie leaned forward and patted her knee, for she was well aware that Edie was weeping for not only her lost husband but her lost child of whom not one word had been heard.

"We'll rent an office . . ."

"An office, my Fred never needed an office."

"An' I'll run the business from there. It'll be slow at first until new boats 're built an' good men found ter sail 'em. Family men, I reckon, 'oo'll be glad o't work."

Tom sat quietly at the table while Jack and Davey threw a barrage of questions at Ally, but Pat merely puffed on his old pipe, his expression inscrutable, though had anyone looked closer they would have seen the gleam of anticipation that shone in his eyes. He had thought his days of adventuring were over and had been ready to drift along, slowing down as a man of his age inevitably does, moving towards that harbour where men who loved water and the boats that sailed on it finished up. But now this lass, this young woman who had the courage, the confidence, the sheer bloody nerve many a man lacked, was offering him what looked like a new lease of life. What the hell did he want with a safe harbour when there was so much to be done, not only by Alice Pearce but by Pat Maloney?

Ally, if she believed in such nonsense, would have got down on her knees every night and thanked the God so many millions worshipped for sending Pat Maloney to her. He appeared to know every man who worked in the dockland of Liverpool. Those who not only were sea-going sailors, but those who worked the coastal waters and the canals. And what's more he was aware of those who were out of work, decent men with families who would jump at the chance to be crew members on the new and thriving, small, it's true, but growing concern of

Pearce and Hartley. Fred Pearce had been well known in Liverpool and indeed in every town along the canal from there to Leeds. It was a bit of a facer to be told the new crews would be working for a woman but Edward Hartley's son, surprisingly a doctor, was a partner in the firm. Fred Pearce and Edward Hartley would have been startled to know that their names were coupled together as a guarantee of good value, fairness and conscientious service.

It had taken six months to accomplish and had it not been for the goodwill of Arnold Bridges it would have taken longer.

"Nay, I'm swamped wi' work, lass," he had protested when Ally approached him on the matter of building two boats. "I've orders for new boats as long as me arm, not ter mention me repair work. I can only suggest yer ask one o't other shipyards along cut ter—"

"But I want *you* Mr Bridges," Ally had pressed passionately. "You've a reputation for building t' best canal boats in't country, and that's what I'm after. The best! *Harmony*'s bin a grand boat an' I want *Northern Light* and *Merry Dancer* ter be t' same."

"Yer what?" Arnold Bridges stared in astonishment at the bonny – aye, why had he not noticed how bonny she was – boat-woman, for Ally wore her traditional costume on the canal. Her short hair was tucked modestly beneath her bonnet. The bonnet had a plain stiffened brim, the crown gathered into this with the long frill at the back known as a curtain. It had no strings but about the crown and down the curtain were lace-trimmed frills, bows, insets of lace-trimmed muslin, all new and created by Edie, who obviously hoped that its fresh prettiness might entice her daughter back to the life she and her Fred had known.

"That's what I mean ter call 'em, Mr Bridges, *Northern Light* an' *Merry Dancer*. The Northern Lights are the brilliant splendour of the skies, though not much seen in these parts and Merry Dancer is another name fer 'em. What d' yer think?"

Arnold Bridges lifted his cap, on which a film of sawdust rested, holding it by the peak as he scratched his head in amazement. Half the time he could make neither head nor tail of this lass, but she was gradely, make no mistake and he for one was impressed, so perhaps it was this that encouraged him to "get cracking" on the boats for Pearce and Hartley. He was not a man to be much influenced by the lass's connection with the gentry as it appeared she was but, like Pat Maloney, he did like spunk and Ally Pearce certainly had it.

They had all gone to the boatyard at Burnley, even Ma, Aggie and Albert, to watch *Northern Light* and *Merry Dancer* launched. As on many inland navigations, space was a problem so each craft had to be put in the water sideways. *Northern Light* in March and *Merry Dancer* in May. Two horses were purchased in Burscough from the same farm where they had bought Gentle, and from the same chap who remembered them. Jack had proved his mettle, and his knowledge of horse-flesh, probably come from Pa, Ally decided, spending a long time studying every animal on the farm, so much so that the chap had lost patience, stamping off on other business, telling them to fetch out whatever horse they decided on and they'd discuss price. Teeth, ears, legs, every part of horse anatomy was scrutinised by Jack who would not be hurried, even the way each animal moved, until at last he was satisfied. Ally, Pat and Davey stood patiently by, recognising Jack's particular talent. He haggled amicably with the man in charge who, as *two* animals were to be bought, finally agreed a price Jack liked, and Angel and Daisy entered the firm of Pearce and Hartley.

Now it was June and they were already towing *Northern Light* and *Merry Dancer* on the canals, the name of Pearce and Hartley painted on the boats' cabin sides and stern, with the Pearce and Hartley registration number beneath and the town where it was registered. They were dazzling in their new beauty of rich colour with which all canal boats were painted. Done, of course, by men skilled in it employed by Arnold Bridges. Scrolls, bunches of fruit, flowers, castles done in bold colours and, for good measure, a "liver bird", symbol of Liverpool and which was to be the badge on all Pearce and Hartley canal boats.

Northern Light was crewed by a serious chap of about thirty, name of Zacky Turner, his wife Lizzie, and his family of two boys and a girl, all old enough to give a hand at locks and the boys in legging it through the tunnels.

Dougie Lambert, his wife Maisie and their five children, the youngest barely three months old and called Benjie, since Dougie admired Benjamin Disraeli and his leanings towards reform, squashed themselves into *Merry Dancer*. Pat had interviewed them all, even the children, and Ally had laughed over it with Tom, saying that even young Benjie had been inspected for possible defects.

Aye, a tower of strength was Pat Maloney, appearing to grow younger with every passing day in his role of . . . well, you could almost call him "second-in-command" at Pearce and Hartley. At least he did! He was self-made "captain" of *Harmony* with Davey as his crew, while Jack was in charge of *Edith* and a lad not much younger than himself, Dicky O'Hanlon, whom Ally was convinced Pat had employed because of his Irish connections!

And so it had all begun, and progressed and Ally Pearce thought she would burst with happiness on that day when Tom Hartley, her business partner and, dare she say it, *dear friend*, begged her with mischievous humour to play truant like children from school, and escape into the sunshine of Midsummer's Day.

21

He held her hand in his as they ran down the length of Waterloo Road in the direction of Princes Dock while she clung grimly to her hat with her left. She wore what fashion magazines described as a walking dress which was hitched up at the side enabling women who were so inclined to take active outdoor exercise. It was a soft dove-grey barathea, made, of course, by Edie Pearce, cut on simple lines without the current passion for the bustle, but because of its length, it showed the feet and ankles. The colour was somewhat impractical but it was plain and business-like, though Ally did allow herself a bit of frivolity with a froth of cream lace at the neckline. She wore what was called a cream straw round hat. This had a wide flexible brim with a low flat crown. It was shaped like an upside-down mushroom and trimmed with grey velvet ribbon round the crown, the ends of which hung down her back. The hat was tied on beneath the brim with a ribbon, again grey velvet, fastening under the chin.

Because of the length of the skirt a great variety of footwear and coloured stockings had become fashionable but Ally did not care for black and white striped, nor coloured spots on a contrasting background, or even the plaid stockings or the violet cashmere stockings which were on display at Anne Hillyard's millinery shop in Bold Street. She wore grey kid boots with plain cream stockings and each day Aggie and Edie saw her off to her office with a blend of pride and, on Edie's part, sadness at the death of her boatwoman's costume. She was very fashionable, correctly dressed for her role in life as a working woman but Edie, who herself wore the plain black of a decent widow woman, mourned the days of their boat people life. She had taken to making the simple, everyday dresses the women of her own station demanded, measuring them, sewing on her machine the materials they themselves provided from St John's Market and had a steadily growing clientèle among the wives of the men who worked on the docks and in the businesses connected to shipping. Men in decent employment, tally clerks, tradesmen, lock-keepers, shop assistants and their children, particularly their daughters who needed something special for a confirmation or the festivals that took place at Whitsuntide. She and Aggie did the hand-sewing, sitting placidly one on either side of the fire of an evening; they baked and scoured and fettled number 10 Blackstock Street; they shopped together and shared the expenses of the house, for, as Edie said, she was in a fair way of things where cash was concerned now that their Ally's business was doing so well. She kept the money she herself earned in a new tin box, privately weeping over it at the thoughts of their Betsy.

"Where are we going?" gasped Ally, as she raced to keep up with Tom's athletic stride. They were both half laughing, some shared excitement pumping the blood in their veins and Ally supposed it was because normally they were both serious people. Not solemn or cheerless, but with goals in life which did not usually allow for merriment. And yet they were rushing headlong towards some enchantment, at least *she* was enchanted, in a manner most unlike either of them. Their feet pounded the pavement so that folk moving in the same direction as themselves turned in alarm, then stood aside hastily to let them go by.

"Does it matter?" Tom shouted. "Wherever we like. Wherever *you* like, Alice Pearce. Shall we board this beautiful clipper ship and sail away to China to bring back jade and porcelain, silk and tea, or that packet ship bound for New York?"

"Tom, slow down, please, I can 'ardly breathe an' me 'at's comin' off."

"Well, take it off then." But he slowed his pace until they were walking, though he still held her hand in his, smiling down at her.

"Give over, I'm supposed ter be a respectable workin' lass."

"You *are* a respectable working lass, one who hasn't had a day off, never mind a holiday, in the two years we've known one another and it's about time—"

"Neither 'ave you. 'Ad a day off, I mean. Not that I know of, anyroad."

"Well, there you are. We both deserve it and so I propose . . ."

"What?" Her face glowed and her eyes shone a rich tawny amber, warm, glad, and in them was something Tom began to recognise. He had never seen it in any woman's eyes before, for he knew now that Betsy had not loved him. Only what she hoped he could give her. No woman had ever loved him, as far as he was aware, and he had loved no woman. Wanted, oh aye, lusted after, for he was but a mortal man but he had never known *love*. But what was he saying? he asked himself in amazement. That what lay behind Alice Pearce's laughing, rosy expression was something more than the deepening friendship they now shared? That the business-like relationship that had evolved with the formation of Pearce and Hartley was changing to something warmer?

For the space of several moments his heart missed a beat, then, with a shout of laughter, Ally pulled away from him, making for the Marine Parade that edged Trafalgar Dock, Victoria Dock and Waterloo Dock where dozens of sailing ships moved gently at their moorings on the water, their masts swaying, the figureheads at each prow bowing towards the river.

"Well, you do what yer like, Tom Hartley," she shouted over her shoulder, grinning infectiously. "I'm off ter China ter fetch a chest o' tea fer Ma."

He followed her, the strange moment gone and forgotten. He caught her arm and drew her hand through his. "Shall we settle for a ferry ride to Egremont today?" he asked gently. "China can wait."

"Aye, 'appen one day. Egremont it is."

They sauntered in silence along Marine Parade, her arm through his, towards Princes Dock and the landing stage from where the ferries went at regular intervals to New Brighton, Egremont, Seacombe and Woodside, a constant crossing and re-crossing of the river. The dock was crowded, the dock road busy with the continuous motion of horse-drawn vehicles, hansom cabs, carts and team waggons shifting goods to and from the quayside, from warehouse to ship's hold, the ships tied up alongside the scores of low transit sheds and warehouses. Liverpool docks were six and a half miles in length with twenty-seven miles of quays from their beginnings at the wide estuary of Liverpool Bay to their upper reaches at Warrington.

Dock workers, stevedores, tally clerks, porters, casual labourers loaded and discharged ships, all intent on getting in one another's way but somehow avoiding it as they continued with the day's business, which was to earn a day's pay. Passengers, some disembarking dazedly from ships come from Ireland, these stumbling from their old life to a new; from Europe and Scandinavia, bewildered, afraid, old and young, going only God knew where and praying that when they got there He would be with them. There were others of the upper classes, the ladies drawing aside their skirts lest they be contaminated by this human flotsam, the gentlemen barking orders they expected to be obeyed, making for their first-class cabins on the swift packet ships to Boston.

A flurry of activity at Prince's landing stage heralded the

departure of the Isle of Man Company's Royal Mail steam-ship *Tynwald* heading for Douglas, the sea passage, or so the board told intending passengers, expected to take five hours. Her freight, which had been received at the Clarence Basin five days ago, was all safely stowed away in the hold: carriages, horses, cattle, sheep, pigs, the animals voicing their displeasure, while passengers were ensconced in the comfort of a cabin for six shillings, or took their chance in steerage for half the price.

"Egremont in three minutes," a voice bellowed, following the bell which sounded five minutes prior to sailing. Ally and Tom passed through the double wickets at the top of the slipway in the centre of which two collectors sat to receive the tolls. Though there were several would-be passengers on the pier with the obvious intention of boarding the *Queen* beginning to run to catch the ferry, much to the amusement of those already on board, the ferries ran on strictly punctual lines and these were left behind.

The journey over the sun-gilded water did not take long. They did not speak, for it seemed a curious constraint had fallen between them. This was the first time they had been alone together on what Ally considered to be a special occasion, since you could hardly call their first meeting in the Zoological Gardens a rendezvous. They shared discussions at the office, discussions regarding finance, profits and costs but, as Tom said, he really knew nothing about the business, *any* business and was happy to leave the running of it to her. He still visited Aggie and Ma, though neither of them needed his medical help but Ma seemed to find comfort from seeing him, as though he might, from the link he had once had with Betsy, bring her back to where she belonged.

They sat side by side on the slatted bench that encircled the deck, turned towards one another, each with an arm over the wooden rail, their gaze following the paths of the hundreds of ships on the river, turning their faces up to the sky which was high and cloudlessly blue. The wind caught her hat, tugging it from her head, tossing it to the deck where Tom caught it with a cricketer's grace, handing it back to her with a small bow.

"I'd leave it off if I were you," he said seriously, and she wondered, her heart twisting nervously, where the fine, merry moments had gone. Then, her hair blowing madly about her head, he lifted his hand and smoothed it behind her ears as though it were the most natural thing in the world, but saying nothing. He turned hastily away from her, screwing his eyes up against the glare of the sun on the water to watch the seagulls floating on the wind, crying beseechingly, their grace and beauty in the sunlight quite breathtaking. Snowy wings tipped with grey, black heads, bright eyes watching for the smallest titbit. They circled the ferry while others followed a steamship heading for Liverpool Bay. Ally wondered at the strangeness of this day, loving it, dismayed by it, uneasy with it and him, half wishing it was not taking place.

They disembarked with scores of others, all hurrying away along the wooden pier to the ferry buildings of Egremont beside which stood half a dozen hansom cabs.

"Do you want to walk or ride?" he asked her politely, and it was then that Alice Pearce, the woman who ran her own business, who directed men and boats, horses and cargoes, organising them into one smooth-running entity, broke free and spoke her mind.

"What the devil's up wi' yer, Tom Hartley?" she exploded so loudly several people about to climb into hansom cabs turned to stare in consternation. "You come marchin' inter my office, babblin' on about 'olidays an' such, laughin' yer daft 'ead off, draggin' me out when I've a dozen things ter see to. Now yer 'aven't a word fer't cat. Do I want ter walk or ride? Course I don't want ter ride on a glorious day like this, yer daft beggar, an' if all yer've got ter offer is a ride in a cab, which I can do any day o't week in Liverpool, then I'm off ter catch next ferry back."

She stood with her hands on her hips and glared at him. His face was the picture of amazement for the space of ten seconds then he threw back his head in delighted laughter.

"Alice Pearce, you really are priceless. I must admit I had begun to feel that perhaps this impetuous invitation of mine was a mistake since we seemed to be suddenly uneasy with one another. We have known one another for a long time and we get on well, so maybe . . . well, I would . . . no, I'm saying this all wrong. Let me begin again. Dear Alice, I would trust you with my last penny, with my life even. I know you to be strong and stubborn; now you're going to reproach me again but before you do, let's get ourselves some food, a picnic and strike off up some lane, find a field full of wild flowers and lie in the sun. I feel a great need to get some sun on my face. There must be an inn where a bottle of wine can be had. God, here am I babbling on, as you put it, and the day is so lovely. See, take my arm."

She was laughing with him now, for she knew it would be all right.

The innkeeper was most obliging, providing Tom with a bottle of wine he appeared to find palatable, and with a flagon of ale, and the innkeeper's wife, with a look of smiling approval at Ally, who hovered in the sunlit doorway, said that she might be able to lay her hands on some fresh bread, cheese and apples from the orchard at the back, even a basket to pack it all in if the young lady promised to return it on their way back to the ferry. Ally gave her word, ready to blush as Tom winked at her and gave her his sudden charming grin, since it was evident that the innkeeper's wife thought them to be "courting"!

Egremont was no more than a hamlet, a few cottages, the inn, a church, beyond which lay a lane leading to Liscard Hall and on into open countryside. Though it had been dry for a week the grass was the fresh green of early summer. Meadows were knee-high in lush, sweet-smelling grass and golden with butter-cups, starred with vivid scarlet poppies, sea-pinks which are common to the fields near the sea. Sorrel was coming into flower and in the ditches beside the lane were ox-eye daisies, purple clover and there was a smell of thyme in the air. The hedges themselves were massed with dog roses and honey-suckle above which danced butterflies, whose names Tom seemed to know: orange-tip, small heath and meadow brown. There were small birds, linnets and warblers, whinchats in pairs and several tit-larks diving in and out of the hedge, taking flight as Tom and Ally approached.

"As a boy I used to roam the fields about Rosemont with the gardener's lad who knew every flower, every bird and butterfly and I suppose some of it rubbed off on me," Tom explained when she questioned him about his knowledge. "Despite living so close to a great sea-port I'm a country boy at heart." He stopped to point out a herd of cows who were heads down, knee-deep in the grass of the meadow. "Stand still and watch them. They are the most inquisitive creatures in the animal world." Sure enough the herd moved slowly towards them, pressing their heads over and through the hedge, their large, liquid eyes placidly staring.

The lane was dry and soon Ally's rather elegant boots were coated with dust, as was the hem of her skirt. The sun beat down and midges darted about their heads and the peaceful earth seemed to doze, tranquil and without sound except for the sharp song of the meadow pippit as it rose in flight, and the hum of bees bumbling from flower to flower in the hedgerow.

The meadow Tom chose was so beautiful Ally caught her breath, enchanted, speechless with wonder. On the canal the *Edith* had passed by open fields and meadows through Lancashire and Yorkshire. Either side of the canal boat had been scenery of grandeur and simplicity but to see it from a moving vessel stretching away into the vast distance was not at all like being in it! Now, as Tom opened the five-barred gate, holding it wide for her to pass through, she hardly felt she had the right to pass into the almost waist-high rustle of grass and rainbow wild flowers that filled it from hedge to hedge. About its perimeter were oak trees, old and venerable, their wide canopies of massed leaves having sheltered both animals and humans for generations.

"I should have brought a rug," Tom remarked absently as he began to wade through the vegetation as though it were water. As well as buttercups and poppies there was ladies' smock, meadow saxifrage and clover, a brilliant, swaying coverlet whose heady scent filled Ally's head with delight.

"This will do," Tom told her cheerfully, sinking down in the exact centre of the field and totally disappearing from view. "It's quite dry," he added, popping up again to lead her to him. "Take your shoes off and that ridiculous hat and sit on my jacket," and she was so bemused she did as she was told without arguing. Tom had removed his necktie along with his jacket and undone the top buttons of his shirt to reveal his amber throat, strong and muscular, and the fine tufts of dark hair that began below it. He rolled up his sleeves, his arms also proving to be sunburned and Ally, still somewhat stunned, whether from Tom's proximity, the strangeness of the day or the heat of the sun, wondered how he had come to be such an attractive colour. She had no idea what his life was, apart from the medical practice he revealed to them, but he had told her he was a "country boy", so perhaps his spare time was spent in open-air pursuits, the sort the gentry got up to.

They drank wine from the clumsy goblets the innkeeper's wife had loaned them, ate chunks of freshly baked bread with sharp-tasting Lancashire cheese, then crunched on apples. They talked idly about nothing much, content to look about them above the rippling sea of grasses and wild flowers, eyes narrowed against the glare of the sun and it seemed quite natural to lie back and stare up into the vast bowl of the summer blue sky where Tom invited her to search out and locate the skylark whose exquisite song overlaid the droning of the bees. His voice was soft, rapt, as though the image of the day had him in a thrall and when she fell asleep the murmur of his words were sweet in her ear.

When she did not answer a casual question, he could not remember what it was, he turned on his side towards her, tucking his right arm beneath his head, studying her intently, he didn't know why, but what he saw pleased him. She lay on her back, her head pillowed on her own right arm, her left flung out, her fingers still holding a buttercup, her face slightly turned towards him. Her dark hair was tumbled about her head in a glossy mass of short curls. Her face was flushed with the sun, her dark lashes lay in a childlike curve on her cheek and her lips were parted, full, rosy, moist, and most desirable. Her tiny breasts barely lifted the material of her bodice but the nipples were surprisingly full and peaked. She smelled of the wild flowers in which she was sprawled and though she was not the beautiful young woman her sister was she had something about her, a freshness, a sweet comeliness, a goodness, a quality of simple purity which had nothing to do with piety or the sanctimonious mouthings of those who called themselves "Godly". She was loyal and loving and trustworthy and in the last months, in fact ever since Betsy had disappeared, she had blossomed into an attractive young woman. Not the kind who turned heads but pleasing to the eye of the beholder. It was as though the extraordinary beauty of Betsy Pearce had obscured her own modest attractions, had dimmed her as the sun will outshine the simple, unflickering flame of a candle. But now the candle shone, glowed, gave light and hope. She had humour. She often made him laugh. She was good-hearted. She was spirited and yet had not a mean bone in her body which he was now admiring without reservation, amazing himself. At this moment, as her eyelids fluttered and her lashes slowly lifted there was nothing he wanted more than to bend over and kiss her. Actually he realised he *did* want more. He found he had a great desire to lift his hand and cup her cheek, to smooth under her chin and caress the fine skin of her throat. Her eyes, which had opened dreamily, sprang wide as they looked into his and her pupils darkened.

"Alice Pearce," he murmured, "you're a bonny lass," then lowering his head he placed his lips softly on hers. At once, as though they had been waiting for this moment since the beginning of time, they parted, softened, responded to his and were sweet-tasting.

"Alice . . ." He breathed again, his lips still against hers. Her breath was warm, tasting of the wine she had drunk and when he lifted his head her eyes were misted, slightly narrowed, glowing a deep chestnut with some strong emotion inside her. She smiled, waiting, and when he put his hand on her throat, his thumb caressing her jaw, she lifted the hand that held the buttercup and put her arm about his neck, drawing his head down, drawing his lips to hers again. Her breathing quickened, became deeper and he could feel his own body responding to the evident invitation of hers.

As suddenly as it had begun, it ended. With a great cry which lifted a flock of starlings from the trees she flung him off and sprang to her feet. He sprawled on his back in the grass and stared up at her in consternation while she glared down at him. For a moment he felt the furious anger rise in him, the anger a male feels when, rightly or wrongly, he is spurned by a female, made to look foolish, made to feel crass when after all he had meant her no harm. A simple kiss. The touch of his hand on her throat. He had offered her no hurt, no offence, no insult in his gentle kiss and yet she was glowering down at him, as though he had tried to put his hand up her skirt or down her bodice.

He felt a complete fool and no doubt looked it as he fumbled his way to his feet.

"What the bloody hell—" he began, holding out his hand in bewilderment.

"Don't you swear at me, yer bastard," she hissed venomously. She was trembling violently and her face was bone white, only her mouth retaining its poppy-red fullness. She scrabbled at it with the back of her hand as though his touch had tainted it, grimacing her distaste.

"I'm sorry," he said icily, drawing himself up. "I had no idea I was so abhorrent to you."

"Abhorrent! Yer mekk me feel sick."

"I do apologise."

"An' so yer should. It's only a few weeks since yer were kissin' me sister, an' God knows what else yer got up to. Now she's 'opped it yer think yer might as well 'ave a go at me, is that it? Is this what this *day out* is all about? Alice is 'andy so—"

"How dare you! You've a filthy mind, Alice Pearce, and I'm astonished you should think, after all this time, that I'm capable of transferring my affections."

"So, yer still 'ave 'em then? Yer still love our Betsy."

"Of course I don't, you fool. Dear sweet God, you looked so . . . dammit, can't you believe I kissed you because I bloody well wanted to kiss you? Can you not accept how I feel without immediately jumping to the conclusion, the *wrong* conclusion, I might add, that because Betsy has gone, I'm turning to the first available woman who happens . . ." He pushed his own trembling hand through his hair, turning away from her. "Besides, it's been over six months, not a few weeks. Not that that makes any difference. My advances were obviously unwelcome to you so I'll . . . Dammit it to hell, they weren't even advances in the way . . . A kiss, no more. You're an attractive young woman and I gave way to the perfectly natural . . . well, we'll say no more."

"I won't be second best. I can't . . . I can't bear . . ."

He whirled about, his hand still thrust into his thick hair, on his face an expression of complete astonishment. His mouth fell open and his eyes were the wide, vivid blue of the cornflowers at his feet. Ally thought her heart would break out of her breast as it surged with her love for him and the despair which had filled it as she remembered Betsy. But he must never know, never! He had, apparently, given way to an impulsive but momentary masculine desire to kiss her, only God knew why, but for some reason she felt outraged, probably because of his previous relationship with Betsy who had come damn near to ruining her. In view of what had happened how could she possibly believe that his . . . his kisses, his hand on her cheek were anything other than the casual touch of a . . . of a what? *Of a what?* A philanderer? Did she honestly believe that Tom Hartley was capable of the light-hearted dalliance of which she was accusing him? But could she believe in her sorely tried heart that what he had felt for Betsy, *and she had seen it*, had vanished? Could a man who had loved as Tom had, recover from it so swiftly? She knew he held her, Ally, in affection and respect but she wanted more than that. She loved him with all her heart and nothing less would be acceptable from him. Her confusion made her mind jump from one conclusion to another, from some vague and mystifying hope to a scorn which was aimed at herself for cherishing that hope, and was bringing her close to tears, which, naturally, she would not allow him to see.

It was moving towards late afternoon and the cows in the adjoining meadow were ambling placidly towards the gate at the far side of the pasture, ready for milking, she thought with that part of her mind which still functioned on some level of understanding. They lowed plaintively, their voices lifting across the hedgerow but she and Tom continued to stand in their own circle of silence and stillness, neither, it seemed, knowing what to say or do to break the moment of terrible tension.

Finally Tom spoke. His voice was gentle and so was the expression on his face.

"Alice, I'm sorry if I offended you. I didn't mean to. You are very dear to me and I wouldn't hurt you for the world. But please believe me when I say Betsy has gone. Gone from our world and from my affections. I hope you and I will remain friends, for you are . . . well, perhaps we should leave it at that and get you home."

He smiled, the smile closing like a fist about her heart, the infectious grin she loved so well, as she loved everything about him, then she bent down to gather the glasses, packing them neatly into the basket, and across the meadows the cattle continued to low, a sad sound which echoed in her own heart.

22

She could feel the gradual slowing down of the *Harmony* as they approached Church and though Gentle strained valiantly into her harness, Ally knew that if they allowed her to continue they were facing the possibility of the mare's hooves slipping on the icy surface of the towpath.

It was January, one of the worst months of the year for the canal boatman, especially on the Leeds and Liverpool Canal, for here in the foothills of the harsh Pennine chain the weather could be severely treacherous. The world about the canal was absolutely white except for the stark black outline of the trees along the towpath and the ice-coated walls that divided the fields on either side. Ally could barely see more than a few yards from the stern of the boat where she was huddled, for the world was a still and shifting shroud of mist. She could just make out the blurred shape of Gentle with Davey leading her and though it went against all her inclination to push on to Church where her next cargo and her profits lay, she knew she could no longer risk not only her boat but her horse.

The ice on the canal had thickened in the last hour and it was this that was hampering Gentle's progress. The ice-breaker was reported to be at Clayton-le-Moors, or so Dougie Lambert had shouted across to her as *Merry Dancer* moved slowly in the opposite direction towards Blackburn where a cargo of cotton goods was waiting to be picked up and taken to the docks at Liverpool. Already several boatmen, unwilling to risk their horse, or their boats, were moored on the canalside. Heavy

blankets had been thrown over their animals, for there were no
stables on this particular stretch of the water and she knew that
Gentle would have a miserable night of it.

"Unharness her, Davey," she called out. "Get her as close
ter't boat as yer can an' we'll moor here. Ice-breaker'll be along
first thing in't mornin, I shouldn't wonder, then we'll get on."

"Righto, Miss Pearce," Davey shouted back, pulling the tired
animal to a halt and beginning the task of unharnessing the
"gear" from her. Clouds from their combined breath hung
about the heads of man and beast and Ally watched for a
moment before going below into the warmth of the cabin to
prepare a hot meal for herself and Davey.

He always called her Miss Pearce now, for was she not his
employer, but he would not be sorry when Pat had recovered
from the wheezing, phlegmy cough which Doctor Tom had
told him would turn to pneumonia if he didn't take care of
himself, or allow the two women with whom he was staying at
10 Blackstock Street to do it for him! Pat had been mortified,
informing them all in a rasping, painful voice that he'd never
had a day's illness in his life and he wasn't about to start now
but he was putty in the determined hands of Aggie Wainwright,
for whom he had a secret taking. With Doctor Tom's help,
the women of the house had him tucked up and tied down
on the bed in Albert's room, Albert resignedly transferred to the
attic. A good fire, goose grease on his chest, a hot-water bottle
at his feet, and a concoction of honey, glycerine and lemon, a
sovereign cure for a bad chest, poured down his throat at
regular intervals and he'd be as right as rain in a week, Doctor
Tom told him cheerfully. There was a lot of it about, he chided
him, and he should be thankful he had a warm bed and two
nurses to see to his every need, not like some of his patients who
shivered and coughed – and died – in a bit of blanket on a damp
floor in Naylors Yard, Raymond Street and Pope Row. He'd
call again tomorrow to make sure the old rogue was behaving

himself and obeying not only *his* orders but those of Mrs
Wainwright and Mrs Pearce, he added, then turned to Ally who
sat by the fireside, her eyes unfocused, her thoughts evidently
far away. She had just returned from the office in Walter Street
where she had been doing her best to arrange a replacement for
Pat to accompany Davey on the *Harmony*. A cargo of malt was
already aboard the boat, along with cast iron and mine
machinery bound for Church and from Bolton manufactured
cotton goods were ready to be brought back to Liverpool.

"Can you manage without him?" he asked her politely as he
accepted the inevitable cup of tea from Aggie and sat down
opposite her. That was how they were with one another now
since the picnic over the water. Polite! Restrained! Not exactly
ill at ease but no longer sharing the harmony, the quiet laughter,
the peaceful concord they had once known. Their business
partnership went well and realising she was increasingly able to
deal with every aspect of it on the canal and financially with the
help of Mr Moore, he rarely came to the office.

"I'm afraid there's no one ter spare. *Merry Dancer*, *Northern
Light* an' *Edith* are all on't cut with their crews an' not expected
back until the end o't week an' I'm not prepared ter tekk on
some casual boatman I don't know ter crew wi' Davey. He's a
good lad but needs someone ter guide 'im."

"So what will you do? Cancel the trip until Pat's recovered?"
His tone was casual, since it appeared to him that was the only
feasible thing to do.

Her answer astounded him. It astounded them all.

"No, I'll go meself. Davey can do't leggin' through't tunnels
while I—"

She almost dropped her cup of tea when he leaped to his feet,
his own cup spilling over on to Aggie's rug in his agitation. Both
Aggie and Edie, busy by the window where the light was better,
a bit of sewing in their hands, turned startled faces in his direction. Though they were sorry the old chap upstairs was badly,

it had at least brought Doctor Tom back to them, for they had scarcely seen him since Betsy had run away. They remembered sadly the few months when he and Ally had been as thick as thieves over that business they had set up together and both women had harboured great hopes of some romantic result but it had all come to nothing. Now he was towering over their Ally as though for two pins he might clout her one, his usually good-humoured face working in what appeared to be furious temper.

"You'll what?" he thundered. The two women exchanged bemused glances, their busy fingers stilled. Ally reared back, her mouth dropping open, her eyes wide with bewilderment.

"Tom," she managed to gasp, then leaned across to place her cup and saucer carefully on the table to avoid further spillage.

"Don't Tom me, young lady," he said more quietly. "You cannot possibly believe I would allow you to . . . to go traipsing off up the canal with only a boy to protect you when there are—"

"Traipsing? *Traipsing!* Is that how yer describe the work done by me family an' the families 'oo work fer me? Yer mekk it sound like some idle pursuit, or an outing on a sunny afternoon." She stood up so that they were almost nose to nose and would have been but for his extra height. "An' what d'yer mean, *allow*? I don't 'ave ter ask your permission ter go about me business in any way I think fit. Let me tell you, Tom Hartley—"

"No, let me tell *you*, Alice Pearce, I think it to be the most foolhardy action I've heard of in a long time. You haven't worked on the boats for over a year now, and who is to look after the office, may I ask, and the business, and the hundred and one—"

"We managed wi'out an office before Pa died an' anyroad, it'll only be for a week, no more, an' surely a man as bloody smart as you reckon ter be can keep an eye on it—"

"And my patients?" he interrupted icily.

"Dear God, Tom, what's up wi' yer?" She was dumbfounded, overwhelmed by his reaction to what seemed to her to be the only solution to the problem caused by Pat's illness. He appeared unsteady with some emotion and she was at a loss to understand what it might be. As Tom was himself. He only knew he could not bear the thought of her sailing up the canal accompanied by only a callow youth, unprotected and alone, or almost so. Since he had kissed her in the meadow last year, on an impulse, he admitted to himself, he had made sure there could be no opportunity to do it again. She had been so . . . so offended, so enraged, that he himself had taken umbrage and had vowed to keep a good distance between them on all but business matters. He did not ask himself why, an *honest* why. But now, with his guard down, his instinctive reaction had been to stop her going where she might be harmed, or overworked or . . . or in contact with the rough men who worked the canal with no one but a boy to look out for her.

"I'm against it, Alice," he said stiffly, aware that all three women were staring at him in consternation. "Surely one cargo lost can be of little importance?"

"It's not just cargo, Tom, but the goodwill, the trust, the relationship between boatman an' merchant. We can't afford ter gerron wrong side o't men 'oo give us their business."

"Oh come now, Alice," he began, ready to smile, even to reach for her hand, and again Aggie and Edie turned to look at one another, nodding their heads knowingly.

"Give over, Tom. Stop treatin' me like a child, or a *woman*."

"You *are* a woman, which is why I'd rather you didn't—"

"You'd 'ave summat ter say if them profits that go inter yer bank account each month were—"

His face hardened and he turned away abruptly, reaching for his hat and cape, striding towards the door. He clapped his hat on his head.

"It seems I'm wasting my breath so I'll say good-day to you, ladies," he called back to the gape-jawed Aggie and Edie, then a second later banged the front door behind him. They heard the sound of his mare's hooves on the cobbles, then they died away and there was silence.

"Daft beggar," Ally remarked vaguely.

"Hold tha' tongue, lady," Aggie remonstrated sternly.

And so here she was, two days later, caught fast in the ice a few miles from Church, warming up the leftover scouse Aggie had cooked for them on the night before they left, the enormous pan carried carefully through the streets by Davey – since he knew it might have to last for a while – to the *Harmony*. Davey had steadfastly legged it through two tunnels and over twenty-five locks between Liverpool and their present position as she steered the boat and, while Davey was occupied, a handy lad walked Gentle for a penny or two. She had worn for the first time in many months the trousers, the thick flannel shirt, the jacket and over them Pa's gansey, with his old cap jammed down over her curls.

The cold was intense and she had provided Davey with extra blankets, for the cabin in the prow had no heat, but in the bed-hole where she slept the warmth was delicious. In her head and heart and soul were the words Tom had spoken – shouted – at her before she left Blackstock Street and she had meant to go over them again, as she had done so many times since, but her tired body had overwhelmed her busy thoughts and she had fallen almost at once into a deep sleep. She had heard Gentle move on the towpath beside her bed-hole but that was all before she fell into the black hole of exhaustion.

The shadowed hulk of the enormous man, impervious to the cold, it seemed, remained hidden behind the drystone wall, still as the wall itself. He had been there for more than an hour, watching the activities of the lad, his feeding and watering of the horse, his careful covering of the animal with several blankets; listened to his murmuring voice as he stroked her nose and even bloody well kissed her. It had taken all his self-control, of which he had little, not to snort in contempt for the silly young sod. He had seen *her* go down into the cabin where the light shone out from the hatchway, then the lad, with a last fussing over the mare, followed her. Later the lad, carrying blankets and a candle, had made his way to the cabin in the prow, the lights had gone out and all was quiet and dark. The horse fidgeted, probably aware of his own presence, blowing great plumes of breath from her nostrils, restless, pulling on the ropes that tethered her, stamping her hooves on the iron-hard ground, but the occupants of the boat did not stir.

The man straightened up slowly then reached down to touch gently his genitals which had never recovered from the bite the sodding dog had inflicted on him over a year ago. Nearly took his prick off, it did and had it not been for an old woman from the back streets of Church, one who was too old and withered to be afraid of him, and known to be handy with things medical, getting rid of unwanted bastards, sewing up superficial wounds, that sort of thing, he reckoned he would have lost it. The damned thing would have dropped off and he'd have bled to death. It had gone bad on him, festering for weeks and him in such agony he had nearly gone mad with it. Like a wounded beast he had been forced to hide in the old woman's hovel, paying out good money, not only for the bit of blanket she allowed him, but for her evil-smelling potions and ointments. Inside him his hatred for the woman who had caused all his troubles had festered as ferociously as his flesh. He had seen her boats go by but she had never been aboard; now she was here within a few yards of him. For several long moments he dwelled on the past year. He had tried a dozen times to get his prick up and inside some woman, willing or unwilling but surely now with *her*, his need for revenge on her, his hatred for her, his bitter loathing over what she had done to him would give him not only the strength but the potency which before the bloody dog had had him had raced through his body like fire, ending where it should between his legs!

His time had come!

Slowly he climbed the wall, careful not to disturb the icy cam stones on top, edging his way across the towpath until he reached the boat. He gave his crotch another fondle in the hope that his touch would release what was necessary to "give her one", the bitch who was so close to hand, but he felt the despairing rage flood through him when, as usual, nothing happened. He hesitated. What if he should get it out and the sodding thing just hung there, small and foolish, letting her see what she had done to him? He had taken such pride in his manhood, bigger, thicker, longer than any man's he had ever seen, but now it was mangled and even to piss was agony. He supposed he could kill her, beat her to death with his fists, but then it would be over. His hunger for revenge which had kept him alive for all these months would be satisfied but what would he have to live for then? Beating other men to pulp in the wrestling ring, the prize fights, the frightening of women and their children with his fists, but the core of him, the malevolent need for vengeance against this one woman, which had taken the place of his need to abuse and humiliate women and his oppression of the men he worked with, would be finished. He needed her, strangely enough; he needed her alive so that he could terrorise her, haunt her, keep her jumping at every bloody shadow. Fill her dreams with fear and finally, when he was ready, he would kill her. Take her somewhere where they would be alone, and kill her.

He began to smile then. A terrible smile. He felt a great beat of joy thump through him, a great excitement. This could go on for months, years, as long as he wanted it to go on but he must do something tonight. He had worked himself up to do something tonight. He had walked all the way from Church with the sole intention of doing *something* and he couldn't just walk away, find his way back to his room at Ma Jolly's like some gentrified milk-sop. He *must* start here, and then . . . By Christ, he'd follow her wherever she went and make her life a bloody misery as she had made his.

His head, which was not accustomed to thought beyond food and women and ale and where they were all to come from, and certainly not to planning, since his life up to now had been nothing but the slow drifting from one job to another, began to ache with the effort and again he cursed the woman on the boat. But he smiled as he did so. It was worth a sodding headache to have this goal inside him. His thoughts had been confused, unclear as they wandered in and out of his mind, disjointed, for he had not the vocabulary of an educated man but it had all come together at last. As crisp and clear as the ice that froze the world about him. What the future held for him, *and for her*.

Stepping back from the edge of the canal he sidled towards the horse.

Ally was deep in a dream in which she and Tom were walking hand in hand through the knee-deep, flower-starred meadow where they had picnicked and the hand on her shoulder, the voice shouting in her ear, irritated her. She muttered and flinched away, but the hand and the voice would not go away, continuing to plague her.

"Miss Pearce . . . fer God's sake, wake up, please, Miss Pearce. Ally, summats 'appened ter Gentle. Ally . . . oh please, Ally."

He was weeping, Davey was weeping like a child and it was this surprising fact that brought Ally from her lovely dream into the dark confusion of the morning. It was mid-winter and not yet light and she had no idea what time it was. The small glow from the fire cast a shadowed anguish on Davey's young, distressed face and Ally felt her heart double its beat in a sudden spurt of panic.

"What is it? Davey, what's 'appened?" She sat up clutching the blankets about her, for despite the fire it was not warm. Besides, she had on only her shift. Davey was fully dressed.

"Oh, Miss Pearce, Ally, I 'eard cock crow over at farm, yer know, one across fields by't viaduct an' I said ter messen it's time I were outer bed so—"

"Yes, yes, Davey, but what about Gentle?"

"I were tellin' yer."

"Well, gerron wi' it."

"She's not there, Ally . . . Miss Pearce." In his distress he quite forgot the distinction that lay between him and the woman he had known as Ally Pearce and Pat's instructions that she was now to be known as *Miss* Pearce to them all. Except Jack, of course, who was, after all, her brother, and Pat who was her second-in-command.

"Not there! D'yer mean ter tell me yer've not fastened her properly?"

"No, no, Ally." Tears poured down his boy's face, dripping on to his gansey. He was beside himself, not only at the disappearance of the animal he had fed, watered, groomed, fussed over, *loved* ever since he had been taken on by the Pearces, but at the accusation that he, always so careful in his duties, should be blamed for her loss. "I tetherd 'er real firm, like I allus do."

"Yer can't 'ave done, my lad, an' yer'd best get out there an' find 'er."

"In't dark, miss? Oh, miss . . . oh, Ally, I donno where ter start."

"We'll 'ave ter go different ways. You back in't direction o' Blackburn, me towards Clayton. Go on, get goin' while I put summat on."

"Oh, Ally," he moaned. "I tied 'er up right."

"We'll talk about that when we've found 'er," Ally told him coldly. "Now get goin' an' let me get dressed."

It was the men on the ice-breaker who found her. The cold

had been so intense on the canal that night that the water had frozen from Burnley to Blackburn. The ice-breaking boat towed by three strong horses and led by a man was triangular in section and her keel was of fifteen-inch "greenheart", the toughest of wood. The boat was ballasted so that her bow would rise out of the water and break the ice by crashing downwards through it. At first the two men who manned her wondered what it was that was frozen solid in the ice, something that moved reluctantly out of their way, taking shards of ice with it, bobbing in and out of the cleared water, a large object which they could not at first identify. They shouted to the man leading the horses to bring them to a halt which he did, tethering the lead horse to a post set by the canal. The day was as cold and misty as the one before, the sky leaden and threatening above their heads. Snow by the end of the day, they had told one another and perhaps it might get a bit warmer then. It needed to, by gum. Freeze the balls right off you, this lot would. Their breath wreathed about their heads as they peered anxiously across the broken ice and gently lapping water towards the object in the canal.

One spoke hesitantly. "It's a bloody 'orse."

"Jesus . . . poor beast. 'Ow the 'ell . . ."

"Muster fallen in." They were all sorry, for the men who worked the canals, in any capacity, were fond of the horses without which there would be no trade. Motor-run boats were still rare and the loss of a horse could cause, besides sadness, a serious blow to revenue.

"Is it dead?" one asked.

"Course it's bloody dead, yer daft sod. Nowt could live long in watter that cold."

" 'Oo d'yer reckon it belongs to?" But their ruminations were cut short when a half-demented lad came tearing up the tow-path, crying like a babby and but for the quickness of the man on the canalside would have flung himself into the water and, it appeared to them, done his best to drag the dead animal from the canal.

"Gentle . . . Gentle, lass, it's me, Davey," he was yelling. "Come on, my lovely; let me go, yer daft gobshite," he snarled at the man who was holding him, "it's Gentle an' she'll bloody freeze in—"

"She already 'as, lad. Yer can do nowt fer 'er, not now."

"I tied 'er up proper, 'onest. Sweet Christ, what's Ally gonner say? Please, let me go. Let me fetch 'er out. We can't just leave 'er floatin' there like a bit o' rubbish."

"'Appen wi't boat-'ook, Mick?" one of the men on the boat suggested hesitantly, for the lad was half crazy, but how they could lift a dead horse from the water was anybody's guess. Still, they couldn't just leave it there to rot, could they?

They had Gentle half on the bank, hauled out by two of the three towing horses when Ally arrived along with several boat-owners who, stuck fast in the ice and with nowhere to go, had offered their help in the search.

Ally stopped abruptly, her hand to her mouth, her face as white as the hoar frost that stretched across the fields and hills for as far as the eye could see. Her eyes were great golden pools of horror with no tear yet but filmed with moisture. She sank slowly to her knees on the ice-crusted path, for in her heart she knew this was none of Davey's doing. One of the men placed a compassionate hand on her shoulder. Davey turned and stumbled to the drystone wall beside the towpath. He crossed his arms on the cam, bowed his head and sobbed out loud.

"I tied her proper, Miss Pearce," he was mumbling.

One of the men made a sudden exclamation, a sound of disbelief and everyone who hung about, for quite a crowd had gathered, turned to look at him. Ally got to her feet and moved towards him. He was holding the rope that was attached to Gentle's noseband. "This 'as bin cut, missus," he said, wonder in his voice and a murmur rose about him. Cut? Who the hell would cut the harness of a tethered horse? It beggared belief but the boatman, one of those from the frozen canal boats, was holding the bit of rope which was still fastened to Gentle's noseband.

Davey turned slowly, tears and snot clotted on his young face. He wiped at it with the sleeve of his gansey then moved towards the pitiful corpse of the animal, the gentle, patient, hardworking animal they had all loved. Men were shaking their heads and muttering, but one spoke up.

"She must've slipped . . ."

"But that don't tell us 'oo cut rope, yer fool. If she'd slipped rope would 'ave broke an' be frayed. Anyroad, if she were tethered an' fell in there'd be a' lot o' noise an' . . ."

"D'yer mean some bugger cut rope an . . . an' pushed 'er in?"

"Gerroff," another scoffed. "It'd tekk a bloody giant ter push an' 'orse inter t'cut."

"Then you tell me wharr 'appened."

The group of men exchanged wary glances as though the same thought had occurred to each and every one of them at the same time. They most of them knew the young woman who was sagging despairingly against the shoulder of the lad who was a crew member on one of her boats. They had known her pa and a sound chap he'd been too and though it had taken them some time to come round to admiring the way she'd taken over from him *and* made a success of it, they had reluctantly done so. But they also knew of her connection with the bastard who she'd crossed swords with more than once. Taken exception to the way he'd mistreated her horse, she had, probably the poor beast who lay in a pool of frozen water at their feet, and had landed him one with a shovel. And a while back when he'd tried to get at her on her canal boat, her brother's dog had chewed his balls off, so the story went. If his temper had been dangerously unstable then, it was a hundred times worse now. He was not seen often at Church, taking casual labouring jobs up and down the canal whenever he could and with anyone who was fool enough to employ him, and this was surely his handiwork. He was the only man in this part of the world, and in the country, most like, who could shove a bloody horse where it didn't want to go. *In this case the waters of the canal!* His phenomenal strength and his hatred of and need for revenge on this lass would have given him the incentive.

They shifted uneasily, none of them willing to say his name, but as Ally lifted her head, conscious suddenly of the curious silence that had fallen about the men, a vicious face, a grinning, malevolent face, a bull-like neck, a brutish giant of a monster with hands as big as the hooves on a shire horse, swam into her unfocused vision and she felt her senses reel.

Davey felt her sway and his arms rose to hold her or she would have fallen.

"Miss Pearce . . . Ally?"

"It was him, Davey."

He looked down into her spasming face then round the circle of men who were ready to back away as if even the thought of him made them fearful.

"It was him." Ally's voice was no more than a whisper. "Whipper. Whipper Ogden. It was him what pushed Gentle inter t' canal."

23

Pat was up and about and ready, he told his two fussing nurses, to be off up t' cut the minute their lass got back, and when she and Davey walked through the door into the kitchen he sprang eagerly to his feet as though to prove it. One look at her face wiped away all his resolute determination to escape the cosseting he had been forced to put up with, despite what the women said to deter him, to be off down to the docks where he belonged waiting for the *Harmony* to berth, but now he flopped back into his chair by the fire waiting for what he recognised, as the women did, would be bad news.

Ally stood in the doorway and looked round the circle of faces, Aggie, Ma, Albert and Pat, and it was as though, now that she was safe at home, for this *was* home to her finally, she could give way to the misery, the fear, the sorrow of the past week, let it all out in the knowledge that here, where her family were, there was no longer any need to put on a brave face, which was mainly for Davey's benefit, and she could have a bloody good cry, which she began to do. All right, it was only a horse, not a member of her family but the picture of poor Gentle sprawled stiffly in an undignified heap on the towpath, nothing more than a sodden carcase, tore her heart to shreds. She wept like a hurt child at the memory of it, for the act had been so obscene, so evil. They had loved Gentle and the terror the mare must have known, the hurt inflicted upon her by that crazed brute; the image of it would remain in her mind's eye for a long time. Like the men who muttered uneasily in appalled sympathy, who shuffled their feet and did their best not to meet her eye as they quietly agreed among themselves that only a man of maddened strength could have managed it. She knew it must be him. Who else could have done this thing? It had to be Whipper and Davey had sworn in the high-pitched voice of barely controlled hysteria that he would have his revenge if it was the last thing he did. He had been inconsolable and it was perhaps this that had kept her going, kept her own grief contained, kept her mind clear on what should be done, for a boat without a horse to pull it was neither use nor ornament. There was a cargo of malt, cast iron and mine machinery on *Harmony* that must be delivered to Church before the day was out. Another of manufactured goods to be picked up at Bolton and taken to Liverpool and she could not move the canal boat without a horse!

And there was poor Gentle to be disposed of. Had it not been for the fellowship, the community spirit which existed among the boat people, the support of the men and their wives on the boats that were at last able to draw slowly away from their moorings now that the ice-breaker had freed them, she and Davey would have been in a sorry plight. Archie Fellows, who had known and respected her father, offered her a lift on his boat *Little Bear* as far as Church where, he told her gruffly, for he was as badly affected as most of the men at the cruelty shown to a poor, defenceless animal, she could probably hire a horse to get her to Burscough. The horse farm there would provide her with a decent animal and so it had proved. The cotton goods had been unloaded at the dock in Liverpool and side by side she and Davey had walked silently up the brow to Blackstock Street.

"Dear Lord," Ma whispered, putting her hand to her mouth, for she really did not think she could cope with any more bad news. She was still grieving badly for Fred and Betsy and the sight of their Ally in tears told her that something awful had taken place and how was she to manage another tragedy? It could only be their Jack, her anguished heart told her, for who else would Ally, who *never* wept, be so broken-hearted about? Aggie stood up uncertainly and Pat straightened his suddenly weakened frame and prepared himself for the worst.

It was almost a relief when she told them.

"Gentle! Yer mean yer 'orse," Ma said incredulously. "Yer weepin' over a damn 'orse when I never saw yer shed a tear when yer sister vanished off the face of the earth."

"Ma," was all Ally managed to get out, her face still streaming with tears, when Davey began to howl.

"She were pushed inter t' canal, Mrs Pearce. Poor beast were shoved like a bag o' rubbish no one wanted inter't icy watter an' left ter drown an' if I get me 'ands on't bugger what done it—"

Pat stood up suddenly. "That's enough, lad," he said quietly. "Let Ally tell't tale."

"Aye." Aggie came to life and drew Ally to the fire, pushing her down in the chair she herself had been sitting in. "But afore she starts let's gerra cup o' tea inside yer an' you too, Davey."

"I don't want no cupper tea," Davey began.

"Well, yer 'avin' one just same."

Weeping desolately, the cup of tea trembling in her hand, the hand itself guided to her equally trembling lips by Aggie, Ally told the tale of horror, of Gentle's death, of the kindness of the boatmen and the tribulations she and Davey had suffered to get the body of the mare decently disposed of, since Davey would not hear of her being sent to the knacker's yard and there were men who were reluctant to dig a hole – a grave – in which to bury a horse! Of the ancient beast which was the only one they could hire to get their cargoes to their destination and their difficulty in purchasing what they hoped was a decent replacement for Gentle without Jack's expertise to guide them.

"An' what 'appened to the bugger what . . . what shoved 'er in't cut?" Pat asked quietly.

" 'E vanished," Ally sniffed.

" 'E's still on't loose then?"

"Must be."

Pat and Aggie exchanged significant glances. Ma was still brooding over the lack of concern shown by their Ally over her own sister when here she was skriking over a damned animal. Albert, though a nice enough lad and sorry about Gentle, could not really see what all the fuss was about and Davey was deep in his loathing of Whipper Ogden and the red fire of his need for revenge which raced through his veins. In the last week, ever since he had struggled to get to the horse and drag her from the canal, and through the intervening days when he and Ally had barely exchanged more than a dozen words and those only about the job immediately to hand, Davey had changed from a carefree lad with nothing on his mind but a few pints, a good laugh with Jack and a growing awareness of the opposite sex, into a man. A man with a bitter core to him, a man with only one objective in life, a purpose that was to change him and put him for ever out of step with other men. He had abruptly ceased to bawl his sorrow, turning away towards the door, his young face suddenly old, hard, the laughing, carefree lad he had once been gone.

"I'd best be off," he muttered. As he spoke someone knocked at the front door. "I'll answer it," he said, then they heard the familiar voice of Tom Hartley in the narrow passage.

"Davey?" they heard him ask questioningly, then he was there in the doorway of the kitchen, Davey drifting at his back. "I've just dropped in to make sure Pat's not down at the docks waiting for . . ."

His voice tapered off when he saw the drooping figure of Ally in the chair by the fire and the half smile on his face slid slowly away, for it was obvious that something was very badly wrong. Ally, after she heard his voice, the sound of it lifting her head for a moment, resumed her contemplation of the cup of tea in her hand. She had not yet removed her cap, nor her pa's gansey and trousers. Her hands and face were grimy, for in the drama of the past few days she had had no time even to think of getting a wash nor even of taking off her clothes at night before she fell wearily into the bed-hole. The tears she had shed had left tracks down her cheeks and her eyes were still bright with those she was ready to let fall again.

The silence in the room lasted for no more than ten seconds then they all seemed to speak at once, all except Ally.

"What the devil's happened?"

"Now don't fash yersenn, Doctor Tom. Nobody's 'urt."

"*Nobody's 'urt! Wharrabout poor Gentle?*"

"Now then, Davey lad . . . theer's no need ter—"

"I can't believe it, really I can't. Theer's more fuss about 'orse than my poor Betsy."

"Now, Edie, yer know we was all upset about Betsy."

"*Will you all be quiet and tell me what's happened here?*" Tom thundered, and at once they all turned to him, their faces showing varying degrees of surprise, for Doctor Tom was normally such a quiet, patient man. He seemed to tower over them all, which was ridiculous but that was the impression he gave as he strode across the room, pushing Pat quite rudely out of the way which wasn't right, for the old man was only trying to help. But then none of them knew what was in Tom Hartley, not even himself really. He stood over Ally who continued to gaze apathetically down at her own hands twisting round the tea cup and when he took it off her and put it on the table even the bird in the cage by the window ceased to twitter as though the tense atmosphere in the room had reached even his small understanding.

"What is it? What's happened? Tell me."

"Nothing . . . nothing that you need bother about," she began but Davey was having none of that. *Nothing!* She was saying to this man whom he himself hardly knew, that nothing had happened. Dammit to hell, he wasn't having poor Gentle written off as *bloody nothing*.

"'E drowned Gentle, that's wharr 'e did an' yer sayin' it were nuttin," dropping into the sing-song vernacular of his native Liverpool in his anguish.

"What the hell are you talking about?" Tom swept his hand through his hair then turned in bewilderment to the rest of them as though to say would someone with a bit of sense explain to him what the devil Davey was saying.

"I'm talkin' about that sod what's caused trouble."

"Trouble? For whom?"

"Fer Ally, o'course. Just because she 'it 'im wi' a shovel when he lambasted Magic wi' 'is shoulder and then punched Gentle between 'er eyes. Knocked 'im down, she did, an' 'e were after 'er from then on. Gorron boat one time an' if it 'adn't bin fer Teddy . . ."

"Teddy?" Tom questioned dazedly.

"Aye, bit 'im, did Teddy, right in't balls. 'Ung on like a goodun burrit did no good in th' end. Whipper must've come after 'er and t'other night when we was froze up, Gentle was on't towpath an' . . . Oh, Jesus." Davey put his hand to his eyes and bent double, unable to speak further and again there was an appalled silence.

Pat, who had been present on the occasion of Whipper's previous attacks, made his way to the lad who leaned despairingly against the wall and put a sympathetic hand on his shoulder. He knew of Davey's devotion to the animal whose name could not have been more appropriate and though he had nothing to say on the matter, for what was there to say in the face of such devastation, he understood. He himself would never be deliberately cruel to any animal, but a horse was just a horse, a tool really in the trade of the canal boatman.

"Get yerself 'ome, lad. Tha' mam'll be glad ter see yer." For that was what mams were for, to comfort a child and that was what Davey was, or had been, a child who had been badly hurt.

Tom just stood there, staring about him in what seemed to

be a state of total insensibility. As though he couldn't understand what had been said and if he had he didn't believe it.
Whipper! Who had not only threatened Alice Pearce's horses
but had done his best to *get at her* according to Davey. Pushed
the horse into the canal. A man strong enough to push a horse
into a canal and this woman . . . this woman who was so dear
to him. Oh yes, this woman he admitted now who was so dear to
him had calmly gone off on this last bloody trip, knowing this
man was still on the loose, put herself in danger, offered herself
to the abuses . . . it wasn't to be borne, and, by God, he wasn't
going to bear it for another moment.

"I'd like to have all this explained to me, Alice, if you don't
mind," he said mildly. "It seems you have been having many
. . . er, adventures which you have kept to yourself. It also seems
that Pat, Jack and Davey have known of the dangers you have
brought upon yourself and have—"

Ally's head shot up and she stared indignantly into his face.
She scowled, her dirty face twisting in a frown of annoyance.
Her eyes, which up to now had been heavy with sadness, began
to flash.

"Dangers I brought on meself! Was I supposed ter stand by
an' let that bastard bash me horse's face in? Yer should've seen
'is fists."

"I would have liked to do so. I would have shown him mine."

Astonished, she stared at him for a moment, then she began
to laugh.

"Something amuses you."

"Tell him, Davey." For as yet Davey had not taken Pat's
advice to go home to his mother.

"Yes, do tell me, Davey, for I swear if someone does not
advise me on exactly what this woman gets up to on that bloody
canal I shall lift her from her chair and shake her until her bones
rattle. Dear God, I can't take my eyes off her for a moment . . ."

"What!" Ally began to rise from her chair but Tom pushed

her down again, then, as they all watched, fell to his knees before her. The clock that had stood on the mantelpiece since the day Aggie had moved into Blackstock Street as a bride ticked solemnly and the canary in the cage, sensing perhaps that tensions in the room were easing a little, chanced a small trill. The coals in the fire fell and Edie jumped at the sound but she did not take her eyes from the scene in which her daughter and Doctor Tom were the only players.

"You must give it up, Alice." Tom took her hands between his and the occupants of the room, including Ally, held their breath. "How am I to have a moment's peace if you don't?"

"What?" Ally repeated, her eyes fastened like magnets to his, mesmerised by something she saw in them. Her own, which moments ago had been a dazed, tawny brown became the colour of dark chocolate as the pupils widened.

"I don't suppose you know what the devil I'm talking about, do you?" She shook her head wonderingly. "No, I didn't myself until this moment. Oh, I've felt something: a twinge . . . God, I make it sound like indigestion but believe me it isn't that." He laughed somewhat shakily and the company about them, especially Pat, longed to creep out of the room for it felt as if they were prying, spying on what should be a private moment. That is if what they thought was taking place, *was* taking place. Doctor Tom on his knees at their Ally's feet, her hands in his, her dark eyes glowing with something that was not tears this time and his warm and yet fierce, serious and yet gently humorous. He had recognised the truth at last. He had recognised it before she had, or so he thought and he meant her to be aware of it. He loved this woman. Profoundly and deeply, he loved her. What he had been told in the last half-hour had overwhelmed him and he felt unsteady with it, with the thought of what might have happened to her, that he might have lost her. He recognised at last what she meant to him and he felt an agony of remorse that he had allowed her to go gallantly into danger without him to protect her.

"Alice . . ." He cleared his throat, suddenly nervous, not because there were five other people hanging, gape-jawed, on his words, for to tell the truth he was not aware of them, but because she might refuse him. He had thought he loved Betsy and might Alice remember – dammit how could she forget? – but that had been nothing but the admiration of a man for something exquisitely beautiful, and the lust a normal man would feel, the lust to possess. He longed to possess this woman at whose knees he reverently knelt in every sense of the word but with love, with a consuming emotion he had never before known.

He lifted her hand tenderly to his lips with both of his own, then smoothed her cheek with his fingertips, bending his head to look deep into her eyes. "I think I have loved you since that day in the meadow, my dearest girl. That is what you are to me, my dearest girl," he continued, "and if you are amazed by it, though why you should be I can't imagine, then that is my fault for not making my feelings clear. I'm a stubborn beggar, arrogant, I suppose, and when you told me that day in no uncertain terms that I was not attractive to you I took offence and . . . well, you know the rest. All these months when . . . ." His face spasmed and he bent his head, laying her hands back in her lap, then putting gentle lips to her imprisoned hands. It was a humble gesture, almost like that of a knight paying homage to his lady. The quietness of the room was broken for a moment by the small breath which escaped from between Aggie Wainwright's lips.

Then Tom lifted his head and, gazing steadfastly into Ally's face, said simply, "Will you marry me, Alice? I have to keep you safe somehow and this seems to be a sensible way to do it. To keep you at my side, though let me emphasise that is not the only reason I want you with me. I cannot express . . . bloody hell, Alice Pearce, can't you see how much I love you and if you start that damned nonsense you babbled on about last year in the meadow I swear I shall stop your mouth up with kisses, in fact I think I shall anyway." And to the astounded delight of Aggie and Pat, he commenced to do so, holding her by the fore-arms with a grip of steel. She made no attempt to escape him and when he finally pulled away they remained, forehead to forehead, in a daze of wonder.

Ally, who knew her own capacity for love of this man, looked into his face and saw there what she knew to be the truth. She wanted to laugh, not the laughter caused by amusement, a joke shared, but the laughter of happiness, of sheer radiant, uncon-tained happiness. A glorious, startling thing had happened and for that moment she did not know how to respond to it. Her well-shod, capable feet had carried her from the easy-going, carefree girl who had existed before Pa's death to the serious, hardworking, sober, *clever* woman at whose feet Tom Hartley knelt. She was valued, she knew that now, not just as a skilful businesswoman, a resourceful breadwinner, but as a woman, a woman of worth, and the man who thought so, who had just told her so, knelt at her feet. His eyes glowed into hers and Ally felt the impact of them strike her an exquisite blow, making her heart move inside her with joy. There was a hush about them, as though they were in church, as though this thing were divine, which was silly, foolish, for she was not that kind of woman, the kind who believed in miracles. But this *was* a miracle. *Tom Hartley loved her!*

Pat was the first to break the stunned silence.

"Well, now that's settled an' about time too, I'm off ter't docks ter see ter that boat an' look at hanimal. Jack's the expert there but until 'e gets back I reckon I'm next best thing. Come on, lad," taking Davey by the arm and turning him towards the door. "Get yer ter yer mam's. Yer need summat 'ot inside yer an' a good kip."

Aggie, who had been gazing with the greatest satisfaction at the man and woman by the fire who were still in thrall to one another, leaped into life.

"There's no need fer that, Pat Maloney. There's a perfectly good lamb casserole in't th'oven, enough ter feed an army an' Davey—"

"Davey needs ter gerr 'ome, Aggie, an' 'asn't your Albert a job or two what needs doin' in't yard?"

"What?" Albert straightened up, looking indignantly at his mother who herself appeared somewhat surprised, but Pat winked at her, nodding his head in the direction of Ally and Tom. There was one person who had not yet had her say. Though she and Aggie had pondered on the partnership between Ally and Tom over the past few months, the fuss made regarding the death of the horse and Ally's seeming anguish over it, which did not compare favourably with her indifference to her lovely sister's disappearance, had raked up old wounds. It was over a year since Betsy had vanished and with Aggie's help and affection Edie had healed a little but now here was their Ally kissing and being kissed by the very man who once had meant to marry their Betsy. Perhaps if he'd done so and not dragged his feet, which was how she saw it, Betsy would not have run away. Why, Edie might have been a grandmother by now, with her lovely girl living like a queen up at that grand house she'd often talked about.

"Well, if that don't take the biscuit," she exclaimed heatedly. "No sooner 'as 'e jilted our Betsy than 'e's makin' up to 'er sister. Marry! If I 'adn't seen it wi' me own eyes I'd never've believed it. Alice Pearce, yer should be ashamed o' yersenn, mekkin' up ter yer sister's—"

"Ma, don't, it's not like that."

"Then wharris it?" Edie began to weep, holding her hands to her convulsed face, her shoulders shaking. The tears sprang through her fingers and at once Aggie lifted her up and gathered her into her arms.

"Nay, Edie, yer musn't say such things. Ally an' Tom—"

"Ally an' Tom should be ashamed."

"Ma, please . . ."

"Mrs Pearce, believe me, I love Alice. I think I've always loved Alice."

"Wharrabout our Betsy then? Did yer not love 'er?" Edie's voice rose to a wail of grief and Ally felt the lovely, shining moment begin to slip away. Would the ghost of Betsy Pearce forever stand in the way of happiness for her and Tom? *Her and Tom.* She was loved by Tom Hartley and even as she turned to him, her face showing the rising doubt that her mother's words woke in her, he lifted his arms, pulled her into them and folded her against his chest. He held her firmly, his cheek on her grubby cap. She could feel his heart beating under her cheek, strong, fast with emotion and though Ma's voice was still lamenting on the loss of her child, her baby, her lovely girl, she knew that her words were merely the expression, not of her disapproval of Tom and his love for herself, but at the memory of what might have been. Had Betsy been a different nature, a more loving, kindly nature without the greed that had dominated her life, Tom would be married to her. Ally knew that but Ma had been blind to her faults and chose, for the moment, to believe her frail dream. She moaned quietly in Aggie's arms. "I want my Fred," she told them all, "an' where did my lass get to, tell me that. Where is she, my lovely lass?" But she allowed Aggie to lead her from the kitchen, her voice slowly dying away up the stairs.

Albert, risking one more bewildered look at the couple wrapped in one another's arms by the fireside, dived from the room, through the scullery and into the back yard. Pat and

Davey, Pat wrapping himself closely in an old overcoat which had once belonged to Aggie's dead husband, slipped from the room along the passage and out of the front door. He could be heard repeating to Davey that he must get home to his mam and later, if he behaved himself he, Pat, would stand him a pint at the Black Swan in Dublin Street. But he'd to have a good sleep, mind, his voice dying away as Edie's had done.

Tom put Ally gently from him. The firelight played about them, lighting her eyes to gold and painting her hair with streaks of chestnut. The canary was singing cheerfully now and Tom smiled at the sound, for it seemed to him a joyful sound, an omen of good things to come. He looked down into her shyly smiling face.

"Have you any idea how lovely you are," he murmured, putting a finger under her chin. "Even with coal dust or whatever it is on your face." His own face was vulnerable, made defenceless by the deep emotion that filled his heart. Ally was herself vulnerable, for all this had happened so suddenly and she was defenceless against the onslaught of his words, which, an hour ago, she could not have believed possible. She shook her head and her cap fell off. He laced his fingers through her hair, then drew her to him again, kissing her, his lips pressed harshly to hers, moving his head, then soft, caressing, smoothing, enfolding, his tongue touching hers and when he drew away his eyes were glazed and helpless, his limbs were trembling, blending with hers.

"Don't make me wait too long, my love."

And she, dizzy and bemused with love for him, shook her head, reaching again for his lips, bolder now, her own body responding ardently to whatever it was he needed from her. "No . . . oh, no."

24

"Come back to bed," a sleepy voice demanded.

"You're insatiable, Tom Hartley."

"And you aren't?"

"I have ter get ter work. I've two boats waiting in Stanley Dock, all wi' cargoes on board an' unless I'm down there in half an hour I'll 'ave Pat Maloney or our Jack knockin' on our door an' can you imagine what they'll think if Mrs Hodges tells 'em the master an' mistress are still in their bed."

"They'll think what a lucky devil Tom Hartley is to have a fine and feisty woman like *Alice Hartley* at his beck and call. Come back to bed, lovebud. There's a certain part of my wife's anatomy which I swear I missed last night, and I'd hate to think I'd overlooked—"

"Believe me, there was not one part of me yer missed, nor did I neglect one part of you."

"Dear God, I love it when you talk like that. I can feel my—"

"Well, you'll just 'ave ter tell it, whatever it is, to behave. Tonight, I promise."

"Yes, but what will you do to me, you witch? Please, don't keep me in suspense, come back here; put that brush down and come here or I swear I'll drag you by the scruff of your neck and . . ."

"And?" Alice Hartley as she was now turned on the stool that stood before her dressing-table mirror, hairbrush still in her hand. Her springing glossy hair which she had been brushing lay in a swirling cap about her head and her face was split in a mischievous grin. Her teeth were a white slash in her rosy face and her eyes danced with glee, with the happiness, the love, the joy she had known ever since she had become Tom's wife. She had no more than five minutes since slipped from the bed she shared with him, believing him to be still asleep, and was ready to wash and dress, have breakfast and leave for her day's work at the office of Pearce and Hartley in Walter Street. Tom had been called out in the night, as he so frequently was, to one of the poor souls whom he doctored in Naylors Yard or Raymond Street and, as she always did, she had pretended to be asleep, for she knew he worried that he might wake her. She had a job of work, as he did, and needed her sleep, he had told her, and so, on the nights he crept out, the following morning she did her best to let him sleep on.

Sometimes she was unsuccessful, as today.

"Well, come back and kiss me, then. It's not a lot to ask, is it. A kiss from one's wife to start the day."

"I don't trust you, Tom Hartley. Before I was on my knees you'd have me . . . whatever's this thing called?"

"Peignoir, I believe."

"Peignoir off me back and me in bed wi' yer."

"And what's wrong with that? We *are* married, or so I was led to believe by the vicar at St Martin's."

"Oh, Tom, please behave, you know there's nothing I'd like more than ter get back inter—"

"Come here, woman, and at once."

"Tom . . ."

"Be quiet, my darling . . ." Somehow she was in his arms, her peignoir floating like diaphanous peach-coloured mist to the carpet. His mouth was on hers, the spark of desire which they lit in one another, and had done from their first night as man and wife, bursting into flame and consuming them. His lips travelled from her mouth to the curve of her jaw and his hands reached to cup the tight, hard-nippled buds of her small breasts then began their slow, wandering exploration of the fine bones of her shoulders, the long curving column of her spine, the curve of her waist, the roundness of her buttocks. She knelt over him, her knees on either side of his waist, naked and beautiful now in the rich maturity of her loving, her head thrown back, her mouth open on a moan of pleasure and Tom Hartley sighed, his own content, rich and satisfying as he drove himself deep into the core of the woman he loved. His wife. She raised her arms, displaying her rose-tipped breasts and again his hands reached for them.

"I love you, Alice, God, how I love you," rising up to take each nipple one by one into his mouth, fastening his lips tightly on the cushion of satin flesh and when she cried out so did he, their voices echoing round the room and down to the woman in the scullery. She cocked her head, looking towards the ceiling.

"Dear God, they're at it again," she told the dog who lolled at her feet, but it was said indulgently, for Mrs Hodges had a lot of time for the new Mrs Hartley. A good lass, though not, of course, out of the top drawer, but then who cared, for had she, Kate Hodges, ever seen Doctor Tom so happy. Listen to the pair of them laughing. And the best of it was, the new Mrs Hartley didn't give a tinker's toss for what Mrs Hodges did in the house, nor what she put on the table for her and Doctor Tom to eat. Not that she didn't tuck into it each evening, as did Doctor Tom, both of them praising Mrs Hodges' hotpot, or lamb roast, in between kisses and hand-holding which was a bit embarrassing at first.

Mrs Hodges had tried in the beginning, feeling it was only right and proper, to consult the new Mrs Hartley on what she might like for their evening meal or if there should be any sweeping domestic changes she might have in mind.

"None at all, Mrs Hodges. I'm not what yer might call

housewifely. You just carry on as always and I'm sure me an'
. . . an' my husband" – blushing as she spoke which delighted
Mrs Hodges – "will be perfectly satisfied."

"Right, Mrs Hartley. You leave it all to me. I know what the
doctor likes for his dinner but what you must do is make sure
he sits down to eat it. Tell 'im ter let them wait when they come
knocking on his door at dinner-time. That's what he needs.
Someone to make him do as he's told." Which was easier said
than done.

The dog, who had heard the sound from upstairs, padded to
the kitchen door where he waited, his head cocked, turning to
look at Mrs Hodges. He appeared to be grinning, a knowing
look on his handsome face, as he waited for the housekeeper to
open the door.

"Nay, they don't want you, lad," she said, but nevertheless
she let the dog out. He padded along the passageway and settled
himself to wait patiently at the bottom of the stairs.

Ally had loved Tom's house in Duke Street from the moment
he had led her by the hand through the square in which it stood.
It was winter and the railed gardens in the centre of the square
had been bare and bleak, the trees leafless, the grass white with
hoar frost, the shrubs lifeless, the soil barren of the flowers that
graced it in spring and summer. But the Regency houses, tall
and simple, appealed to something in her. She had lived only
on a canal boat and in one of the working-class boxes of
Blackstock Street but the flat, well-painted window frames, the
arched, ornamental doorways, the delicate wrought-iron
balconies on the first floor of each house, the well-scrubbed
steps, the gardens only a step from the front door, the busy
darting of milk drays, the cheerful whistling of a delivery boy as
he ran down the area steps to the basement below street level
delighted her.

Aggie and Ma, who came with her to look it over, agreed with
her that it was very comfortable. She was shown a large parlour

with a red-covered sofa and two deep armchairs round the hearth, a cheerful, rather worn rug, and several plants in pottery bowls. There was a dining-room with a fireplace in which a display of dried flowers was arranged, a round dining table with six dining chairs, none of which matched, and upstairs a bedroom with a large, half-tester bed where she and Tom would make love every night, or so he had whispered in her ear, and would sleep in one another's arms. There were three smaller bedrooms, one of which was Mrs Hodges', a kitchen and scullery which did not particularly interest Ally though Aggie and Ma gave it a careful scrutiny. They approved of Mrs Hodges, who passed both the women's cleanliness test and so, four weeks after he had proposed, she and Tom were married in the presence of Aggie, Edie, Albert, Pat Davey and whichever of the boat families were not at the time on the canal. Jack gave her away and Ma cried, since the wedding took place in the church where Pa was interred. None of Tom's family was present!

He had held her in his arms when he told her that not one of the Hartleys would come to see their son married. He made no further comment knowing she would, unlike Betsy, understand. He did not describe to her what had happened in his mother's drawing-room.

"You seem to have an affinity with the lower classes, Thomas. First you want to doctor them, and now, for the second time, you wish to marry one of them. Will this . . . this woman last as long as the previous one, do you think? Are you to go blindly through life distressing your mother by taking up with first one and then another of these creatures?" His father had kept a cool, supercilious stance as he leaned on the fire-place, longing, Tom knew, to light a cigar but not quite daring to in the ladylike sanctity of his wife's drawing-room, but though his upper-class breeding decreed that he must be self-controlled Tom could see he longed to smash a furious fist into

Tom's face or aim one of his wife's delicate porcelain figurines
into the hearth.

"Why can you not do as other young men of your station do
and – I beg your pardon, my dear," bowing courteously to his
frozen-faced wife, "and take a mistress until a suitable young
woman, a woman of your own class, can be found for you. Your
mother has invited many good families with daughters for you
to—"

"I'm sorry, Father, Mother, but I do believe I am of an age
to choose my own wife and the one I have chosen – Alice – is a
delightful young woman. She is well read and has a good business head on her shoulders."

"Business head?" his father said incredulously.

"Yes. She runs her own business."

"I beg your pardon? Do you mean to tell me you have taken
up with a dressmaker, or perhaps she is a milliner?"

"No, she is called Alice Pearce and is my partner in the—"

"Dear sweet God. I beg your pardon, my dear," again to his
wife but Mary Hartley stood up and, without a word, swept
from the room, unable, it appeared, to listen to her son tell her
for the second time that, against all her wishes, his father's
wishes, he was to marry some common woman who could
never be accepted in her society, in her home, into her family.

From that day onwards Tom had seen neither of his parents
and the allowance from his father had ceased abruptly. He still
had the small income he had inherited from his grandmother
and the canal boat business of Pearce and Hartley was doing
well. They were not rich, nor even moderately so but their
lifestyle was comfortable and they were content. Their love was
deep and satisfying to them both, in and out of bed, and though
now and again there were some uncomfortable moments with
his mother-in-law who could not forget, it seemed, that once he
had been engaged to her beautiful daughter who had vanished

off the face of the earth, they were always made welcome at Blackstock Street.

Davey was Ally's biggest problem. Well, not a problem, for he still worked assiduously in her employ, but the good-natured, easy-going lad of whom they had all been fond had been replaced by a quiet, inward-looking young man whose smiling face had been transformed to that of such seriousness, they were all worried, especially his mam who, though she had often told him to give over playing the fool, did not really mean it. He was not exactly surly but grim with something that had entered his soul on the night Gentle was killed.

"That young man needs to come off the canal," Tom had remarked, almost casually, as they walked briskly back along Old Hall Street towards the Town Hall and then by way of Castle Street to Duke Street. They had eaten one of Aggie's delicious liver and onion hotpots followed by a creamy rice pudding, the lot washed down with hot, strong, sweet tea, and during the meal Davey and Pat had walked in, just back from bringing a cargo of woollen goods from Bradford. Naturally, being Aggie, nothing would do but that Davey and Pat were made to sit down and tuck in, for didn't she always make enough to feed the whole street. Though the conversation consisted of business matters, the state of the canal now that it was no longer frozen, the progress of the new horse named Moonlight because of her silvery coat, Davey barely spoke a word. He had no sooner finished his meal than he was off to his mam's, who, he said, would be waiting for him.

Ally and Tom had decided to walk as the night was fine, bright with starlight and crisp with frost. Because of the cold the streets were almost deserted. A solitary hansom cab plodded slowly up Dale Street, the horse with a blanket thrown over it, the driver so wrapped about with scarves and mufflers and capes he could have been a tortoise with its head protruding from its shell. Those who were about were hurrying but at the same time careful where they placed their feet on the slippery pavement.

Ally, who was clinging to Tom's arm, stopped abruptly and swung round to look up into his face.

"Come off the canal?" she exclaimed in amazement.

"It's my belief he spends all his time looking for that brute who killed the horse. He's obsessed with the need to find him, to punish him and from what you've told me it might be the death of him. If he finds him, I mean."

"But he's said nothing . . ."

"He's changed, Alice. Surely you must have noticed that. He was the merriest fellow, just a boy larking about with Jack, but Jack says that though he goes with him for a mug of ale when they meet he's always on the lookout, wary, not joking the way young men do, but keeping sober, his eyes watchful and I'm sure he's looking for the man in every place they go."

"But I can't just turn him off, Tom."

"I'm not suggesting that you do. But I've an idea in my mind that . . . well, he's a bright lad, young and with a bit of schooling might be an asset in the office, on the docks, dealing with cargoes. In other words off the canal and at home where he can be watched until he gets over this."

"But he can't even read."

"I know, but he can learn."

"I had the idea Albert might come in wi' us when he's finished wi' school."

"The way the business is growing you'll need a good clerk or two."

"Now then, lad, don't let's run before we can walk."

But business was far from their minds on this bright morning when beyond their window and the small wrought-iron balcony on to which it opened, the birds were in the parlance of northeners giving it what for, the shouts of children out early with their nursemaids and the sunshine in which they played announced the coming of spring. The snowdrops were pushing their green spears through the earth in the gardens and the old man who appeared, or so Tom told her, every year at this time was pottering with something under the shyly budding trees. It was the start of the year, the season of hope, the promise of new life and so it was, for during the past few weeks Ally had experienced what she could not yet bring herself to admit might be the symptoms of pregnancy. For the past week or two she had awoken with a slight nausea which she did not reveal to Tom who, she was sure, had he known would have whisked her away from the office in Walter Street and had her sitting in the parlour with her feet on the worn tuffet. She was not ready yet to give up her charge of the business, if she ever would be, and though she wanted a child, Tom's child, she had not thought it might occur so soon.

But her mind was far away as her husband watched her from the bed as she donned what he called one of her business outfits. It was plain in a fabric called *foulard*, a soft, light, twilled silk which Ma had never seen before but from which she had made the dress. It was well cut, in a shade somewhere between burned almond and coffee. The colour suited her. The fullness of the skirt was in the back leaving the front a flat surface, which, she was aware, would soon give away her condition, if she was with child! The bodice was fitted to her breast which she was convinced had increased in size though as yet Tom had not noticed, which was strange considering the attention he gave it! At the neck, round the wrists and the hem the dress was trimmed with a plain contrast in dark coffee and over the dress she wore a three-quarter fitted jacket of the same colour. Her boots were a rich chocolate brown with a two-inch heel and her hat of the same colour was shaped like a saucer tied under her chin with chocolate-brown velvet ribbons. As yet she had not put on the hat and jacket.

"Well, I suppose since there is no chance that my wife might take off that charming outfit and come back to bed with her husband where, I might say, she should be, I might as well get up."

"Tom Hartley . . ."

"I know, my darling, you are about to ask me where I get my considerable sexual stamina from and I can only answer that . . . my love, oh my love . . ." His voice had softened and the bantering tone left it. "You have no idea how much I love you, how happy you have made me; *happy*: the word doesn't begin to describe my feelings. No, no, it's too late now," as she began to approach the bed, her own face melting with the depth of her emotion. "On the other hand . . ." He began to laugh but as he stretched out his hand to her she evaded him.

At the bottom of the stairs Blaze's ears pricked. He rose to his feet and turned round a time or two then settled down again, his muzzle resting on the bottom stair, for even in such a short time he had learned that eventually his master and the other human who was kind to him and whom he had grown to trust, would come down to him, usually hand in hand. They would go into the room where there was always food and the good smell that accompanied it and if he was lucky, and patient, he would be rewarded with a titbit, or maybe two.

The man who squatted on the kerb on the far side of the gardens straightened up slowly when he saw the door open and the woman come out. His small eyes gleamed. It was full daylight, the pale spring daylight which cannot quite make up its mind that though winter is over and summer is to come it was not yet time to go mad with it. Sunshine touched the gardens which were filled with the shadows from the intricate layers of what would soon be the drooping twigs and glossy leaves on the branches of the tall and handsome plane trees. It coloured the trunks with various shades of brown, grey and yellow, and the old man who was digging vigorously beneath them straightened up to light his pipe and shout a warning to an over-enthusiastic child, a boy, who was doing his best to climb one of them.

"I think I might walk," Ally told Tom who had come out to see her off, the dog beside him, his tail pluming in anticipation of a walk. "Pat will 'ave opened up the office. It'll only tekk twenty minutes an' I feel like a breath o' fresh air."

Though neither of them had noticed it, or if Tom had he did not comment on it, during the last few months Ally had begun to lose much of her northern way of speaking. She no longer clipped the end of her words, or very seldom, nor dropped her aitches. She would never totally lose it, for a northener remains for ever a northener but her grammar had improved.

"Well, it's a lovely day for it."

The man across the square watched as the couple on the steps embraced, on his face an unreadable expression but in his eyes something moved, something frightening, like a shark surfing just beneath the surface of the ocean. His hands were thrust deep in the sagging pockets of his trousers and one of them moved busily at his crotch. He was dressed, if the word could describe the way his clothes hung about him, in the tattered remains of what might once have been a jacket beneath which was a shirt open at the neck. Both were indescribably filthy as were his trousers which had stains of some nasty sort in the area where his hand fumbled. His boots were held together with string and the sole of one flapped up and down as he moved slowly in the direction the woman took. What had once been a red neckerchief was tied about his dirty throat, and holding up his trousers was a canal boatman's embroidered belt. He wore no hat.

The route the woman took once she left the quiet square known as Duke Street was busy. Though it was later than usual for her, since her husband had held her up in the bedroom,

nevertheless she felt inclined to dawdle. It really was a lovely
soft spring day and, unusually for her, she felt no great need to
get to her office. Though there were many tasks ahead of her,
for both the *Harmony* and the *Edith* were due in Stanley Dock
today, or even last night, she strolled along among the hurrying
passers-by, those who had employers to whom they must
report. She smiled at the memory of the past hour, swinging her
small reticule, lifting her head to sniff the air of Liverpool, the
familiar smells from the docks and the ships that brought them
from the far corners of the world. Salt, tar, spices, the tantalising aromas come from the holds of ships just berthed and
which permeated the very pavement beneath her feet and the
roofs of the buildings she walked beside.

On a whim she had sauntered back along Hanover Street
which was in the opposite direction to the docks and into Bold
Street. She stopped to admire the rich and elegant furs displayed in the window of H. G. IRELAND; MRS DAWSON'S
French corsets and stays, speculating what it would be like to
wear such garments, the blond lace, nets, ribbons and flowers
sold by ANNE HILLYARD & CO, and particularly the baby
linen displayed in her window though she was well aware that
Ma would fight tooth and nail to make every garment any
grandchild of hers would wear.

The man followed at a safe distance, for as yet he did not
want the bitch to see him. Not here where the multitude of
people, who crowded the street and darted dangerously
beneath the very feet of the horses passing by, might impede
whatever he decided to do. He had his eyes on the swaying
figure of the woman, walking a straight line behind her, totally
unaware of the terrifying picture he presented to those who
came towards him. They scrambled to get out of his way,
knocking those nearest to the kerb into the road, causing such
mayhem that several began to look around for a constable, for
surely he must be deranged, dangerous, perhaps escaped from

the Borough Gaol in Howard Street, or even the lunatic asylum on the outskirts of the city. Who the devil was he and what the devil was he doing, blundering along this respectable street where the gentry would, later, be shopping? Was he drunk, insane? But those who wondered did not take the terrifying liberty of accosting him but hurried by, glad to be out of his way.

At the end of Bold Street Ally turned into Hanover Street and continued to stroll towards the docks, then looking hastily at the small gold watch, a wedding present from her husband pinned to her jacket, and realising the time she began to hurry. The man behind her shuffled more quickly to keep up with her, crossing Lord Street, Dale Street, along Old Hall Street where the neighbourhood began to run down, to look somewhat seedy, working class, where the man, though still brutish and alarming, was not so out of place as he had been in the prestigious eminence of Bold Street.

She had reached the corners where Brook Street and Rigby Street met and ahead of her was the canal basin, the actual canal ending. She had only the length of Howard Street to walk and she would be at Stanley Dock and Walter Street where her office lay.

The hand on her shoulder startled her but she was not unduly alarmed, for she was no more than a stone's throw from the busy dockland, from Stanley Dock, from Pat and Davey, from Jack and Dicky O'Hanlon. She turned, ready to raise imperious eyebrows, to aim a freezing stare and a sharp word at whoever it was but the words dried up in her throat and she stood, paralysed, mindless with terror and with no thought but to get away from the leering, *smiling* face that thrust itself into hers. She could have cried out but was without the saliva to make a sound. She could have struck out at him as she had done on other occasions but she did none of these things. She could feel the blood drain from her face, from her heart, from her very body so that every muscle and sinew and the bones of her were dry and useless. She could not move, even to wipe away the spittle with which he sprayed her face.

"Aye, me lass, 'tis me. Thought yer'd seen the last o' me, didn't yer?" he hissed. "But yer was mistaken, wasn't yer? Yer'll never see the last o' me, bitch, only when I do fer yer an' I'll be't last face yer'll see."

Something within her, something which is in all women who are mothers or who are to bear a child, sprang to life in defence of what was in her womb. This was Tom's child, Tom, who did not even know of his impending fatherhood. Her mind was filled with racing, half-coherent thought but the one that was uppermost was the safety of the life within her.

With a great cry she pushed Whipper Ogden to one side and began to run through the familiar maze of streets that led to Blackstock Street and safety. She did not look back to see if he was after her but ran and ran, holding up her elegant skirts to reveal her petticoats and the slim length of her legs.

As she hammered on the door of number 10 and it opened to admit her she put out both her hands and encountered nothing at all against her fingers.

"Oh, my God . . ." she heard Aggie whisper in horror and as her strong, working woman's hands took hold of her she felt the bleeding and understood she was about to lose her child.

25

She no longer felt any pain, physical pain, that is, but the ache in her heart was heavy and constant. In the depth of her soul a miserable creature wept though her eyes were dry and even when Tom erupted into Ma's room where Aggie had put her, since the bed had been changed only that morning, and took her wordlessly into his arms she did not shed any tears. He did though.

He could not be found when Aggie had rushed the lad from next door with an urgent message to Duke Street and the doctor Mrs Hodges had sent, an old gentleman who did not really approve of Tom Hartley and his radical views on medicine, was brusque. He assured her that nature, which had put her in this predicament in the first place, would now take its course. This happened to women all the time, he told her bluntly. He would make her comfortable and she was to stay in bed and with proper food and rest, looking about him distastefully at what he considered to be poor surroundings, she would soon be up and about.

"Beef tea, herb tea, red wine and raw eggs, anything you like as long as it is nourishing," turning to look sternly at Aggie and Edie who stood at the foot of the bed.

"Food I purron my table is always nourishing," Aggie protested indignantly.

"That's as may be." And he almost added, *my good woman*, but the expression on Aggie's face stopped him. "No reason to make a fuss, Mrs . . . er, Hartley," turning back to his patient who lay quietly where he and Aggie had arranged her after the detritus of the miscarriage had been briskly, briskly on his part, sadly on Aggie's, cleared away. "This happens every day."

"Not to 'er, it don't," Aggie told him sharply, for had she not herself gone through what Ally had suffered several times in the past. She knew the empty feeling, the hollowed-out pain which did not actually hurt but which was suffering at its worst. There were women who carried child after child, and gave birth to them, women who lived in the back streets and courts of Liverpool in the most dire of straits, not wanting them, weighed down by the dozen they had already, those that lived, but here was a young woman with a good husband, a decent life, healthy and strong, and she had lost hers, as Aggie had. Nature was a funny thing, giving to those would could do without and taking from those who were in need, but it had its own way, choose how.

Edie moved round the bed, kneeling down by the side of her daughter, brushing back the sweated curls from the thin, bone-white face. She began to weep, for she had not known that Ally was pregnant and perhaps, if she and Aggie had been aware of it, this could have been prevented but the doctor tutted and lifted her to her feet.

"Now, now, madam, this won't do my patient any good. Let her rest and should her husband need me he knows where to find me."

As if Tom would need *him*, Aggie thought scathingly as she let him out, then was startled when a horse came round the corner as if it were on the racetrack at Aintree and on its back was Tom Hartley, his face twisted into an expression that seemed to say he was looking into the pits of hell. He flung himself off its back, leaving the poor lathered beast to heave its heart up in the street, reins hanging, and pushed aside the doctor who was ready for a reassuring chat, doctor to doctor.

"Where is she?" He began to bound up the stairs two at a

time, then he was there, his arms about her, lifting her against his chest, kissing her eyes and her cheeks, stroking back her hair, soothing, tender, gentle, loving, his face wet with tears, with the tears she herself seemed unable to shed.

"I didn't know . . . I didn't know," he kept repeating, his body trembling, and it was then she realised that it was she who must comfort him. She was weary to her very bones. She wanted to sleep and sleep but this man who loved her, needed her. He would die for her, she knew that, suffer the tortures of the damned, but at this moment when, in the space of a few hours, he had learned she was pregnant with his child but had lost it he was inconsolable. He would recover. He would be strong and supportive when he had recovered from the shock but until then she must protect him. She knew she must never tell him of the encounter with Whipper. If she did he would scour Liverpool to find him. Find him and kill him. Not with his fists, for no man could do that, she knew that, but with the pistol he kept locked up in the house in Duke Street.

"I wasn't sure, my darlin'," she murmured, soothed and comforted by his arms, his love, even his tears, which were those of a man, a strong man, but a man who has lost the child he dearly wanted. She knew that, for though they had not discussed it at length, a word here and there had let her know it was what he hoped for.

Edie and Aggie left them alone though Aggie had the devil's own job keeping Edie from her daughter. Edie felt a certain resentment that she, who would have been the child's grandmother, had not been told and Aggie was aware and was sorry for it, since Edie was basically a good, kind-hearted woman. Ally's mother could never quite forget that once her Betsy had been engaged to the man who was now Ally's husband.

"Don't leave me, Tom. Lie beside me and hold me."

"You need sleep, my dearest love."

"I've got used ter falling asleep in your arms, Tom."

"I wanted to ask . . . ."

"Not now."

"Then sleep, lovebud. I'll not leave you."

He took off his shoes and jacket, then lay down on the bed beside her, pulling her gently into the shelter of his arms and though he still wept for the child they had lost he held her, feeling her exhausted body finally relax against him as she fell into healing sleep. She was young, strong, healthy and it was in his mind, as it had been in Aggie's, to wonder why she should have lost their child when the women he tended in Naylors Yard and Pope Row gave birth as easily as shelling peas.

When Aggie peeped in an hour later Ally was sound asleep though Doctor Tom was awake. He shook his head to indicate that Ally was in the recovering depths of deep sleep and he would remain with her. Aggie tiptoed away, sad but satisfied.

As the healing days went by Aggie stood over her and watched her sternly as she drank the beef tea, the red wine, fetched from the wine merchants on Dale Street by Tom, for such a thing was not readily available in the area around Blackstock Street. She ate raw eggs, egg custards, milk puddings, all daintily set out on a tray, while at the end of the day Tom came and got into the bed where once Edie and Fred had slept and held his wife until she slept.

"I want to go home," she told him at the end of the fourth day.

"Darling, why don't you leave it for another day or two? You know how Aggie and your mother love to fuss over you. And I would feel happier knowing that you're in good hands."

"What's wrong with Mrs Hodges' hands? She'd look after me just as well. Not that I need any looking after. It's time I was getting back ter the office. God knows what state the books are in."

"Bugger the books. I can—"

"No, you can't, Tom. Only me an' Pat know what's going

where an' what's ter be fetched to Liverpool. Cargoes piling up all over the place an' no one ter say which boat's taking what."

She was sitting up in bed, shaking her head in annoyance, her springing hair, which Aggie had washed for her this morning in a basin of warm water brought up from the kitchen, in a tangle of glossy curls. Edie had helped, climbing the stairs with fresh cans of warm water, then they had subjected her to her daily bed-bath and it was high time they let her see to herself, she told them irritably.

"Well, that's easily solved. Pat was here no more than half an hour ago. He'd just come—"

Pushing back the covers she made to spring from the bed, tutting angrily at the daft occupants of this house who had had in the kitchen the very man she needed to see and hadn't even told her. Tom, who had been lounging in the chair before the good fire Aggie kept going night and day, reared up and before she had her foot to the floor, pushed her back into the bed, pulling the blankets up about her neck and tucking her in as if she were child. He kissed her and shushed her, again as though she were a fretful child but Alice Hartley was having none of it.

"Stop that, Tom Hartley. It's time I was out of here and back at Walter Street."

"Walter Street! Have you gone mad? You're not fit to get out of that bed let alone go gallivanting off to Walter Street. You've . . . you've had a . . . you've lost your . . ." His face spasmed in anguish and to his horror Ally threw back her head and began to howl, to tear at her hair and howl like a soul tormented, downstairs both Aggie and Edie sprang to their feet. Edie was making for the door but Aggie grasped her arms and though Edie struggled and begged Aggie to let her go, Aggie held on to her.

"Let them be, lass. Do 'em good ter cry tergether."

It lasted no more than half an hour, that torrent of grief that

bound husband and wife into a tight fist of shared sorrow at the
loss of their child, but when it was done Ally was calm, her
insides, which had been torn from her with her child, put
together again and though not fully healed, able to be borne.
They lay in one another's arms and as darkness fell and the firelight flickered on the faded brown wallpaper of the bedroom
they finally slept, their first unbroken night since she had
stumbled into Aggie's arms with Whipper at her heels. Not that
Whipper had been at her heels had she but known it, for he had
not chased after her as she had thought but had watched with
great delight as she ran like a scared rabbit up towards Leeds
Street. He hadn't enjoyed anything so much since he had had
what he called *his accident*.

Reluctantly Tom allowed Albert to run down to Stanley Dock
with a message for Pat that Ally wanted to see him as soon as
possible.

"I think you should have a few more days without bothering
about the canal, sweetheart," he had argued but even as he
spoke he knew he might as well try and knit fog, a favourite
saying of Aggie's, who for the past few days had done her best
to keep Tom's wife in bed. Stubborn as a mule, was the lass,
determined to be off and about her business before it fell into
rack and ruin as she put it dramatically.

"Don't be daft, Tom, I'm as right as rain an' if you try ter
stop me the minute yer've gone I'll be off down to Stanley Dock
ter find Pat. I *must* speak to him about his next cargo."

"He's already got one," Tom replied triumphantly. "He told
me he's to be off to Bingley with . . . now I forget what he is to
carry but he's arranged—"

"I don't care. I must see him. Don't you see, if I allow—"

"No, Alice, I don't see and I absolutely forbid it. As your
doctor as well as your husband I must insist—"

"*Forbid! Insist!*" They glared at one another for a moment, wills clashing. She looked better. She had some colour in her face and the wan, forlorn sickroom weakness had left her, for she was a healthy woman who had in the past known no illness. When Tom was not with her she slept for hours on end and the nourishing food Aggie pressed on her had soon repaired her damaged body, but she was aware that she must, to a certain extent, bow to Tom's wishes, not just what he said as her doctor, but as her husband and the father who had lost his child. She herself felt her own personal despair, the terrible realisation that what had oozed so painfully out of her had been a human life, an unrepeatable individual who had been deprived of life and the thought was agony. But if she could make Tom feel better, stronger, knowing that she was safely tucked up in bed with Aggie and Ma cossetting her, she would do anything to achieve that, but there was a special reason why she should speak to Pat before he set out on another journey along the canal.

"Tom, my darling, I would dearly like to have your . . . well, not your *permission*, but approval to have Pat here, just for half an hour, no more, but I'll send for him whether or not. Don't upset me, please, by refusing."

Tom began to smile, leaning forward to place a kiss on her lips, effectively silencing her. "You're a witch, Alice Hartley. Do you know how much joy it gives me to call you that – Alice Hartley, I mean, not witch, even though you are." He sighed. "Very well, I'll send Albert to fetch Pat but no more than half an hour and I shall be here to make sure—"

"No, I . . . well, I'd rather speak to him alone." She could hardly talk to Pat about Whipper Ogden with Tom in the room, could she, but fortunately, at least for her, a message came for Tom from Mrs Hodges, grudgingly sent, for Mrs Hodges believed he should be with his wife at a time like this, that a man was on the doorstep in Duke Street and refused to leave until Tom came to see to his wife who had been in labour for thirty-six hours. A decent man, a clerk down at the docks, a *paying* patient and not one who was taking advantage of Doctor Tom's good heart.

"I'll come straight back, Alice, and if I hear that you and that old fox have been discussing business for more than half an hour I shall know the reason why."

Pat sidled into the bedroom with Aggie at his back, Aggie stiff with resentment, her arms folded over her capacious bosom and an expression on her face that promised the rounds of the kitchen to Pat Maloney if he should upset her girl who was, at last, beginning to pick up.

"Thank you, Aggie," Ally said in her best boat-owner's voice, the voice of a number one who was used to giving orders and having them obeyed.

"I'll be up in a minnit wi' a cup o' that there chocolate yer like, so think on," Aggie warned but at last Ally was alone with Pat.

"Sit down, Pat." Ally indicated the low comfortable chair by the fireside where, now that she was perking up, as Aggie put it, Tom allowed her to sit for an hour or so.

Pat eyed the chair doubtfully. It was so obviously a chair designed for a woman.

"I'll stand, ta." He had shaved that morning, and was dressed in his best boatman's clothes, a clean shirt with a knotted kerchief in the neck, an embroidered belt and braces made for him by Edie Pearce, a jacket somewhat the worse for wear and he held his cap in his hand. Ally wondered what he put on his hair, for it was plastered to his head like a coat of paint. Probably lard as he was not the kind of chap to anoint himself with one of the many pomades gentlemen, or those purporting to be gentlemen, used.

"Now yer've not ter worry yersenn, lass," he began. "I've got cargoes sorted out fer th' *Harmony* an' *Edith*. Jack ses 'e'll be up ter see yer afore 'e sets off. Davey sends 'is best, by't way an' Lizzie Turner – Zacky's off ter Blackburn – wants ter know if

there's owt she can do. Oh, an' Maisie Lambert's . . . well . . ."
He shuffled his feet embarrassedly, not moving from his post
by the door, ready for a quick getaway should she show signs
of succumbing to one of those female things that women who
had suffered what she had were, he was told, prone to.

Ally nearly gave way to tears. The good wishes of all the men
and women on her boats was something she had not bargained
for and yet they were all decent, kind-hearted folk, working hard
and conscientiously and she supposed she was a good employer
who was fair and gave value to those who deserved it, which
they did.

She gulped and Pat got ready to open the door and shout for
one of the women but Ally struggled to put out her hand to stop
him. She was wrapped up like one of those Egyptian mummies
Pat had heard tell of, those found in museums – in fact there
was one to be seen at the Free Library and Museum on Shaws
Brow – so that not an inch of her flesh anywhere but her face
could be seen. Pat recognised Aggie's hand in this, which was
only right and proper, for Ally was a woman and women were
not to be seen in the bedroom except by their husband.

"It's not cargoes, Pat, though they're important. I trust yer
ter carry on, yer know I do an' keep everything workin' an' I
promise yer it won't be fer long. But yer know what Tom's
like."

"Aye, lass, it's bin a sad . . . well, I'll say no more, burrif it's
not cargoes an' the like what—?"

"It . . . it were Whipper. Whipper Ogden." The bald statement hung in the air for a few seconds and Pat seemed not to
have heard, or if he had, had not understood. He had leaned his
back against the doorframe, crossing his arms across his skinny
chest, but now he slowly straightened himself and his seamed
face sagged for a moment then it hardened and his eyes
narrowed and became pricks of ice.

"What were?"

"He . . . followed me."

"Followed yer. What d'yer mean?"

"He's in Liverpool. He must 'ave walked from Church, following t'cut. After he did what he did ter Gentle we thought . . . I thought . . . Well, I don't know what I thought, ter be honest but it seems he's still after me. Dear God, Pat, what are we ter do?"

"Tell us wharr 'appened."

"I walked from home – Duke Street – it was such a lovely day. I never saw him, Pat, but he must 've been followin' me, unless he was waiting by the docks. Anyroad I was just crossing Brook Street when – oh, Jesus, help me – someone tapped me on't shoulder and when I turned, it was Whipper." Her voice had sunk to a whisper and Pat, unheeding now of the niceties of behaviour, crossed the room and sank down by her bed, taking her free, wavering hand in his.

"The bastard."

"I ran, Pat. I just ran and . . . oh, Pat, I lost me baby an' it were . . ."

"'Ave yer told police?"

A look of terror spasmed her face and she clutched desperately at his hand. "No, no, Pat, we mustn't go to the police. Tom mustn't know, yer see. If he did he'd forbid me ever to go over the doorstep again. And he'd go looking for him. You've seen Whipper Ogden. D'yer think Tom could deal with him in some way – yer've seen size of him – so that he'd simply go away and not bother us again? Yer know he couldn't. Whipper'd kill him. He's a devil and somehow he believes I'm ter blame for . . . well, whatever happened to him."

"What yer gonner do then? Just lerrim roam about an' then, when yer not expectin' it, drag yer down some back alley an'—"

"Pat, yer must help me: find someone, you know men, down at docks, 'oo'd do owt fer a few bob." In her overwrought terror she had fallen into her old way of speaking. "Chaps what'd find 'im, beat 'im up, frighten the livin' daylights out of 'im."

"Lass, from what I've seen o' that bugger 'e's frightened o' nowt. 'E's got summat wrong in 'is 'ead an' it'd tekk—"

"I don't care what it takes. Or 'ow much. Mekk some enquiries, but don't let our Jack know. Or Davey. Not after what he did ter Gentle. Yer could go in the pubs, or whatever, down at the docks an' see if . . . find someone, some men who'd . . ."

Pat got stiffly to his feet, standing for a moment to look down at her, his face expressionless. He had a great fondness and respect for this young woman who had taken life by the scruff of its neck and was wringing a living out of it, not just for herself and her family but for all the families who were in her employ. When her pa died she had not fallen apart like the other silly bitch had, nor stood around scratching her head on what to do next, like their Jack. She had pulled it all together, worked like a man, *been* a man in all ways but one and made a huge success of it. But what weighed most heavily in her favour as far as he was concerned was that she had given Pat Maloney his life back. He had been a beached sailor, a shipwreck, a bit of flotsam thrown up on the tide that nobody wanted and now would you look at him. He was illiterate, ignorant of anything that was not to do with the world of the sea and the ships that sailed on it, and yet she trusted him to run her business while she was stuck fast in bed, to find cargoes, to direct her employees, to plan the passage of her canal boats. And now she was asking him to protect her. To find some way to make her life safe again. Trusting him again, as he trusted her!

He tugged at his bottom lip with a gnarled hand then reached into his pocket and pulled out his old clay pipe. Walking slowly to the fire, tamping down tobacco into the bowl from the tobacco pouch in his pocket, he lifted a red-hot coal with the fire tongs and went so far as to forget where he was, lighting the pipe, drawing on it, blowing evil-smelling smoke into the rarefied sanctity of Edie Pearce's bedroom while he stared deeply into the heart of the fire.

Ally watched him, her face white and strained, and when Aggie opened the door and entered the room they were so wrapped up in what had been said they both jumped guiltily.

"Dear God, Pat Maloney," Aggie shrieked, "what the devil d'yer think yer doin', smokin' yer damned pipe in 'ere? D'yer want lass ter 'ave a relapse or summat? Just you put it out at once. I'm surprised at yer, both of yer. It's like a bloody public bar in 'ere."

"Aggie, please, me an' Pat were just—"

"I don't care what yer were just doin'."

"I'm sorry, Mrs Wainwright, but me an' Ally was—"

"Now that's enough, the pair o'yer. You put out that pipe an' get yersenn downstairs and leave this lass ter 'ave a nice rest."

"I'm that sorry, Mrs Wainwright." Pat, who would have faced up to an attack by pirates on the high seas, backed away from Aggie Wainwright, doing his best to put out the small fire in the bowl of his pipe, but the explosive movement from the bed turned them both to stone. Ally thrust aside the blankets in which Aggie had so decorously cocooned her and leaped from the bed. Fortunately she still clasped the large shawl that had been draped about her shoulders but even the sight of her bare white feet reduced Pat to stuttering, red-faced embarrassment.

"Ally," Aggie thundered. "Ger back inter that bed at once, an' you, Pat Maloney, down them stairs before yer feel the flat o' me 'and."

"You stay where you are, Pat. You an' I haven't finished yet."

"Oh, yes you 'ave, madam."

"Pat, sit down in that chair and I'd be obliged, Aggie, if you would give us another ten minutes." She drew herself up with the hauteur of a young queen and Pat didn't know which of the two women to obey.

"Ally Pearce – nay, I should say Hartley – 'ave yer not the

sense yer were born with? Yer've just 'ad a miscarriage an'—"

"I'm well aware of what I've just had, Aggie." The tears which she had been determined to control welled up behind her eyelids and at once Aggie backed down.

"Lass, I'm that sorry. Chuck, I'm sorry, yer know I wouldn't 'urt yer fer't world but—"

"Five more minutes, Aggie, I promise, then I'll get back into bed until Tom comes home. Please."

"Gerrin ter bed now an' then yer've five minutes."

Pat and Ally talked quietly during those five minutes and when Aggie started to climb the stairs, he was on his way down.

"All tekken care of, Pat?" she asked.

"Aye, all tekken care of."

26

She first noticed the man several weeks later. Her heart had lurched in her breast, for she thought him to be Whipper. He was a large man, as big as Whipper but neatly dressed, clean and respectable, his bowler hat set squarely on his head, his jacket buttoned over a waistcoat and collarless shirt and about his neck was a handkerchief folded round the neckband. His boots were polished and, incongruously, from his belt hung a windlass. He was so obviously a boatman but what on earth could he be doing in Liverpool so far from the dock area, but she had shrugged, for it was none of her business, was it?

She had bowed to the pleading of Aggie, Ma and Tom, not to mention Mrs Hodges who, though she herself had never borne a child, told her sternly that after what she had suffered she must rest for at least four weeks. She had conceded to *three*! She was inclined to be nervous as she set off at a smart lick in the cab Mrs Hodges had called for her, since Tom insisted that at least on this her first day she did not go on foot. It was fine and warm with a shouted extravaganza of colours in the garden of the square, a credit to the old man who pottered about there. Dahlias, marigolds, Michaelmas daisies, sunflowers and zinnias jostled one another in the crowded beds edging the well-mown grass and the perfectly raked gravel of the paths that dissected the lawns. She and Tom had stood for a moment on the step, their arms about one another, breathing in not only the particular smell of the sea and the docks which always permeated the city but the fragrance of the flowers. The old man touched his cap to them, calling out a greeting and when Tom held her close for a moment, then placed a grave kiss on her lips, he smiled as though the sight of them had brought back some distant memory to his old heart.

The man on the other side of the square, the sort of man who, apart from his size and obvious physical strength and the windlass hanging from his belt, would arouse no curiosity or comment, for he was so respectable-looking, began to walk towards Hanover Street. He did not appear to hurry but when Ally arrived at Walter Street he was already there, mingling with the men, the dockers, boatmen, clerks, labourers who worked in the area, seeming somehow to blend into the busy landscape. He did not loiter in any one place but moved purposefully from corner to corner, from one side of the street to the other, sauntering around the perimeter of Stanley Dock but never moving out of sight of the doorway to the office of Pearce and Hartley for more than a minute at a time.

That night Tom and Ally made love. He was gentle with her, holding her first in loving arms, smoothing her face and neck, whispering of his love and need, treating her as he had on their first night together when he had taken her virginity. His hands were slow and his eyes reverent as they looked deeply into hers.

"I love you, Alice," he murmured, frowning and serious, drawing her more closely into his tender arms. "You're beautiful," and his face worked with emotion.

Tom Hartley often looked back to those few months of madness he had spent lusting, there could be no other word for it, after his beloved wife's sister. She had lit a fire in him, a fierce conflagration that could have destroyed him, and her, if she had not thrown him over for what she had seen, in her greedy, self-centred way, as a better life with Robin Lovell. He had lost his reason, allowed his loins to rule his head, ignored his own level-headed common sense which told him he was out of his mind to contemplate a life with Betsy Pearce. Her beauty had blinded him and for those months when he was in thrall to her he could not see, for how else had he missed the sweetness, the strength, the goodness of the woman in his arms?

He buried his face in her hair, inhaling the fragrance of it, still slow and dreaming in his contemplation of her breasts, her flat belly, the bush of darkness at its base, the long, slim line of her legs, the perfect turn of her ankle and foot, then lifted his head to search her face again for any sign of hesitation in her. He knew her female body was healed, for he was an experienced doctor but was she ready for his maleness, not physically but with the fearless, trusting need of a woman who loves a man. She had known a great sorrow and he had no desire to awaken the hurt if she was not yet ready.

"I love you, my husband," she answered him simply. "I *want* you to love me." Her lips reached for his and her hands found the centre of his masculinity. He gasped and threw back his head but still he moved gently, softly, slowly, entering her, holding her buttocks and moving deeply and yet with care into the waiting moist, sweet centre of her. She whimpered a little and at once he began to withdraw but she gripped him and would not let him go and with scarcely a sound except a whispering expelling of breath, they both climaxed. Even then he did not move quickly but stayed inside her, holding her to him, loving her without words.

"Tom . . . Tom, I love you with all my heart. I love you."

They slept then in the sweet lassitude of after-love, curled together in the deep, candle-glowed bed and the big man across the square shoved his hand down the encrusted filth of his trousers and fondled what hung there limply. He cursed for several minutes, watching the window where he knew she slept with the bloody doctor. A cat, unknowing, rubbed itself against his leg and with a soft curse the man kicked it across the pavement, breaking one of its legs. It howled piteously, waking the occupants of the house in front of which the man stood, but with a stamp of his boots he cut off the sound. The doctor and his wife slept on, their world slowly mending.

It was the next day when she began to realise that she was being watched. She had reached the corner of Duke Street and had crossed Hanover Street into Paradise Street. The weather continued warm and sunny and the soft blue summer sky formed a thin arch between the roofs of the narrow street. Paradise Street was deep in shadow but a penny whistler was hard at it in a doorway and Ally threw a coin into his cap at his feet. It was as she smiled at him, turning for a moment, that she saw the man, and it was then that she felt a shiver of terror ripple her spine.

"You all right, queen?" the penny whistler asked, removing his whistle for a moment from his mouth.

Ally continued to stare back at the man, for she had realised that it was not the one she had thought him to be. She shook her head, giving the penny whistler a smile of such brilliance he blinked in surprise.

"Oh aye, thanks," she told him. "I just thought . . . well, never mind. Lovely day, in't it?"

"It is that."

She was jumping at shadows, she realised that as she hurried on, thinking every man with a bit of weight on him, every man who was above average height was Whipper Ogden. It had taken a few mornings, and evenings on her way home, to make her recognise that Whipper was about no longer, which she supposed was a bit heedless of her but, after all, she couldn't spend the rest of her life peering round every corner. Besides, she was pretty sure that Pat would have put the word round about the man who had killed Gentle. There were some tough men on the docks, men who would be glad to manhandle Whipper into taking his foot in his hand and moving on. There was no male on earth who was as vigorous and deadly in a fight as the Liverpool docker. With the promise of a couple of pints or a few bob in their pockets they would cheerfully knock a man insensible for no reason at all and with the threat of a serious beating, a broken head or leg, Whipper would be far gone by now.

She forgot him and the man whom she had mistaken for him the moment she climbed the stairs to her office. For the next nine hours she was busy at her desk, going over figures in her ledgers, the distribution of cargoes, the destination of *Edith, Northern Light, Harmony* and *Merry Dancer* and was startled when the little clock on her mantelpiece struck five. Tom liked her to be home for five thirty which was when he tried to be back from his rounds to the delicious dinner Mrs Hodges insisted was on the table for six. He often had time to have a bite to eat at Duke Street at lunchtime, as he, and increasingly she called a snack in the middle of the day. Dinner was eaten in the evening and luncheon at around noon, and though she found the ways of the gentry somewhat strange, she was the wife of a gentleman and must get used to them.

There was the sound of heavy boots on the stairs and as her heart missed a beat she chided herself that she really must get over this silly inclination to be nervous at any sudden sound.

"It's only me, lass," a familiar voice shouted and when the door opened and Pat walked in she relaxed, standing up to greet him with an affectionate kiss on the cheek. He shied away, as was his custom, but she knew very well that he was secretly pleased, for he was as fond of her as she was of him.

"Just got down t'lock wi' a cargo o' coal. I meant ter 'ave me wash first burr I wanted ter see if yer was all right."

"I'm fine, Pat. Why shouldn't I be? I meant to get down to the bank today to have a chat with Mr Moore but I've been that busy time just got away from me. The figures are looking grand and at this rate we'll be lookin' fer another boat an' a crew ter go with her. Even without me while I was . . . well, you know, everything seems to have just run as smoothly as if I was here.

I might as well sit at home with a bit of sewing and drink tea all day like the grand ladies of Liverpool."

"Not you, chuck. Yer'd go potty in a week."

She laughed then turned to lean her hands on the windowsill, looking out of the window and across Great Howard Street to where *Harmony* was just leaving the last of the five locks that led into Stanley Dock. Davey was at the tiller. Even from where she stood she could see the frown on his face and Tom's suggestion that she take him off the canal and put him in some other work for her returned. He was a serious young man with a good head on his shoulders. Now whether he would agree to leave the work he had done for three years was another matter and if she did go ahead she would have to be very tactful about it. Tom was right, however, she really did need someone to deal with merchants and warehouse managers and though Jack would seem to be the obvious man for the job, Jack was still a boy, despite his age, with no thought in his head but having a lark, happy to take his orders from her and no desire to give them.

She was just about to turn away from the window, ready to gather up her hat and reticule in preparation for the walk back to Duke Street when the sight of a man standing against the wall of the warehouse beside the dock caught her eye. He was familiar to her and for several moments she frowned in concentration, wondering where she had seen him before. There was a sound of whistling from some chap on the dock and immediately she remembered where it was she had seen him. *Today!* It was in Paradise Street where she had given tuppence to the penny whistler. That was where she had seen him and now here he was again, almost outside her office door, lounging against a wall and . . . and, dear God, was she going mad, imagining every big man who happened to walk by her or who stood on the dockside as this man was doing meant her harm?

"Pat," she began, backing away from the window but keeping the man in sight. "There's a . . ."

"What's up, queen?" Pat moved to stand beside her, peering out of the window.

"That man, that big chap . . ."

"Which one?" Pat would admit it to no one but his elderly eyes did not see quite as well as they once had. It didn't inconvenience him at all, for he could neither read nor write and the distances he had to look to were manageable. He had thought once or twice of getting himself a pair of those eyeglasses but his pride had forbade it, for how would it look for a man like himself to go about wearing those daft things on his face.

"There, leaning against that bollard."

"Wharrabout 'im?"

"That's twice I've seen him today. I was at the corner of Paradise Street and now he's here and—"

"Now, lass, don't start jumpin' at shadders. 'E's probably—"

"No, no, Pat, you an' Davey must go and . . . and . . ."

"What lass, what d'yer want us ter say to 'im?"

"I don't know, Pat. Oh, dear God, what am I to do? That bugger's got me into such a state a man's only to look sideways at me and I'm . . . I can't even tell my own husband for fear he might . . . Pat, I don't want to live like this. What if—"

"Lass, lass, calm down." For by this time Pat's short-sighted eyes had recognised the man. "Lenny's no threat ter yer."

"Lenny?"

"Aye. Just the opposite, in fact. 'E's . . . well, I asked 'im ter watch yer when yer out on yer own. There's lads scourin' the docks an' canals lookin' fer that sod but until they find 'im yer need protection an' if yer won't go ter't police or tell yer 'usband, there's nowt else ter be done. Fact is, Whipper's gone ter ground somewhere. A chap can get lost in Liverpool as easy as wink if 'e wants to but until us is certain 'e's buggered off, given up this bloody nonsense against yer, yer've gorra be careful. An' that's where Lenny comes in. 'E's a prize fighter burr 'e owes me a favour an's prepared fer a few bob ter look after yer. Mind, if 'e's a fight on 'e can't do it, but 'e'll let me know an' we'll make other arrangements."

"Oh, Pat, I can't live like this," Ally wailed.

"Then tell yer 'usband an' go ter't police," Pat answered bluntly.

"How can I tell Tom? I'm afraid for him."

" 'E's yer 'usband. 'E's a right ter know. So, unless yer tell 'im or until we 'ave word that Whipper's gone yer've no choice. Lenny's a good lad. Gentle as a kitting unless summat upsets 'im. Yer'll be safe wi' 'im. As long as yer willin' ter pay 'im 'e'll not let owt 'appen ter yer."

She became used to seeing the distant figure, large, comforting, respectfully smiling if she happened to catch his eye, nodding from the screen of the trees in the square as she passed into the safety of her own home, going off to wherever he went when she was under the protection of her husband. The months went by and she began to wonder if perhaps she and Pat were being over-cautious. That Whipper had finally taken himself off somewhere, back to the canals or some labouring job in the Lancashire hinterland and anyway, with Davey always about, either in the office or with her when she went down to the docks in the business of finding cargoes for her boats, what harm could come to her.

It had taken some persuading on her part to convince Davey that she needed him to leave his job as a canal boatman and transfer to the task of being her second-in-command in the office.

He had been horrified. "Work in th' office! Me?" Forgetting their different places in the business he proceeded to tell her that she must be mad. And besides, what about their Jack? Surely he was the one to help his sister in that part of the family business.

"I can't read nor write nor do sums so what use ter yer would I be? Eeh, no, Ally, there's nowt fer me in Walter Street. I'm used ter't canal, the boats an' that an' anyroad your Jack wouldn't like me tekkin what should be 'is place. T'wouldn't be right nor proper an' Pat an' me do right well tergether an'—"

"*I* want you to come and work for me, Davey. Not just in the office but down among the men in the warehouses. I need a man, a man I can trust, a man with a bit of sense and Jack hasn't the sense he was born with. He knows his own limitations, what he can do and can't do," she explained when Davey looked confused. "Now let me say that this was my husband's idea but I think it's a good one. You're a man now, Davey, and after three years, three years in which you've proved your worth a dozen or more times, I've decided to offer you the job. I know you can't read nor write but I intend sending you to the Mechanics Institute to learn, and other subjects besides. You would be here in the office with me for many months, here and going with me to do business with the merchants, the boat-owners, the bank and firms that deal in exports and imports. I'm sorry, I'm going too fast for you." For Davey was beginning to look terrified, shaking his head and backing away towards the door that led down the stairs to Walter Street.

She made a sudden decision. "And there is another reason why I need a man – you – working in the office with me." She stood up from behind her desk and walked to the window, beckoning Davey to stand beside her. "D'you see that man down there? See, the one by the edge of the dock with the windlass hanging from his belt. The big chap in the bowler."

Davey nodded that he did but there was an expression of incomprehension on his serious young face.

"That man has been guarding me for months now, Davey. You must have heard, perhaps Jack told you, or Pat, that I . . . I lost the child I was carrying several months ago."

Davey nodded and though there was an expression of sympathy on his face he looked somewhat embarrassed.

"The man who caused me to . . . who frightened me was Whipper Ogden."

Davey's head shot up and his expression, a mixture of awkwardness and sadness for her, changed to one of malevolent hatred. His top lip lifted, like that of a wolf, or a dog that is being threatened and he showed his teeth for a moment.

"Aye, I reckon you remember what that man has done to us, Davey. First the animal you and I both loved and then the child my husband and I . . . well, you can see why Pat decided I must have protection. He wants revenge for what he believes I have done to him. You'll remember the times he and I have crossed swords, so to speak. He's about somewhere, Davey, in Liverpool, I mean, though no one has seen him for months. Now if I had a . . . a . . . well, I don't know what your title would be but you would do what I do now on my own. Davey" – Ally ducked her head and blinked back tears, not purposely trying to influence the young man with her woman's weakness but doing so just the same – "we want another child, Tom and me, and if one should come along it would be invaluable to me to know that I had a man I could trust to run the business for me while I was . . . not for good, of course, for I shall always be involved but, please, Davey, help me. Take this job I am offering you. You would earn a good wage. Your mother would be . . . she would not have to work as she does. No, I'm sorry, I must not do this to you, you must make up your own mind. It's a tremendous challenge for you, a young man, to learn the things you would have to but the rewards would . . . No, there I go again. Take the *Harmony* with Pat, talk to him – where is it – yes, to Clitheroe and think about it and let me know. Good lad." She placed her hand on the arm of the dazed lad, then wondered why she kept thinking of him as a lad, for he was a man now. What age would he be? Twenty? Twenty-one? But it was not his age in years but in experience that concerned her. He had grown in stature as well, with big shoulders, strong and well muscled from legging it through tunnels, walking for miles a day, handling a loaded canal boat. He was a good-looking young man, though solemn as a judge, conscientious and would in every aspect of the work she offered him be ideal.

The autumn came on them slowly and Davey had been beside her for four months now, spending his daytime hours learning to do what she did, and going almost every evening to the Mechanics Institute where he was being taught English, writing, arithmetic, mathematics and something he himself had chosen which was navigation. It might come in handy one day, he had told her and she supposed that, being something to do with boats, or ships, it gave him the feeling that he was still in some way connected to the canal. He was quick to learn, bright and inquisitive, which Tom seemed to think would stand him in good stead, for an inquisitive mind was the first step to learning. Ally had taken him to George Henry Lee's on Basnett Street and fitted him out in a decent suit with shirts and ties and good boots, and on this cool October Sunday she and Tom and he were taking a turn round Princes Park.

Davey had called at the house to leave what he called his homework, the simple sums she had set him the day before and the composition, as she called it, that he had written, entitled "A day on the Canal", which she thought might encourage him since the canal was something he knew intimately. He had read several pages of *The Last of the Mohicans*, for though he struggled with many of the words, Tom believed that if he should read a book that would interest a young man, instead of the children's books Ally had first thought of, he would stick to his studies with more enthusiasm. They were both amazed and delighted at the progress he had made and when it was suggested they should leave the parlour and the lounging somnolence of the fire, though Davey had been somewhat hesitant, and take a brisk walk up Princes Road to the park, he had agreed to come with them. Ally was aware that to talk, man to man, as it were, with a gentleman such as Tom could only improve Davey's confidence and not only that but his manners, his way of speaking, which still had the rough edge of Liverpool about it.

The park was glorious, the trees a kaleidoscope of colours ranging from the palest yellow and gold to tawny, russet, bronze, flame, and from the far corner of the park where one of the gardeners was burning leaves, blue smoke drifted across. The hydrangeas were changing colour and across the grass a dry carpet of fallen, crackling leaves attracted hordes of children to leap and jump on their crisp, dying beauty. The sunlight was a pale amber. The air was soft and warm and still, and the three of them walked in companionable silence, smiling a little at the antics of the children. In Tom and Ally there was a small sadness that after five months she had not quickened and God knows they had tried hard enough and often enough, though Tom said it was early days yet. Her body needed to recover completely, not just from the miscarriage, but from the emotional upset which a woman suffers and besides, it was no hardship, was it, he said, smiling and worn out, or so he said, after an hour of glorious lovemaking.

"How about a cup of tea?" he suggested lazily as they sauntered towards the boathouse at the southern end of the lake. "I don't know about anyone else but I'm parched." Besides which he knew Alice wanted Davey to sit down with them both and, from example, learn the ways of those with whom he might one day be asked to take tea. Not the gentry, of course, but in the offices of the merchants, the businessmen, Mr Moore at the bank and those with whom Alice did business.

They had drunk their tea and Davey had eaten every cake on the cake stand, taking his cue from them, eating with the tiny cake fork and sipping slowly and delicately the rather weak tea that was served in places such as this. His mam wouldn't have served tea like this in a fit, for the working classes liked their beverage strong, sweet and hot and preferably out of a mug, but he was learning to do as those with whom Ally did business.

The path towards the gate that led to Princes Road was crossed by another, both of them edged with shrubs and the last blooming of the flowers which had been so glorious in the summer, and still were. Red-hot pokers and lilies stood side by side with white and crimson scabious, and Davey stopped for a moment to admire them, for it was not often those who lived in the back streets of Liverpool, as he did, saw a flower of any kind, let alone these splendid specimens.

Tom halted abruptly. Ally, who had her arm through his, was pulled sharply back and she turned to look at him in wonder, then turned curiously to where he was staring. His face was pale and yet at the same time strangely pleased and his eyes had begun to grow soft. Two young girls were walking towards them, their arms linked, obviously ladies, their heads nodding together as they talked. One of them looked up and caught sight of Ally and Tom, her eyes going from one to the other and she too stopped, dragging at her companion whom she nudged.

For several fraught seconds, though Ally had no idea why they *should* be fraught the five people stood and stared at one another. The two young women were pretty, one more so than the other, and they were beautifully dressed in the manner thought appropriate for their age and class. White muslin dresses with broad sashes, one blue the other pink. Little jackets known as Zouave jackets, short, loose with square-cut fronts and braided to match the sashes on their dresses, with little bonnets tipped over their foreheads. Their kid boots were white and so were their gloves.

"Angelina . . . Catherine," Tom stammered with a catch in his throat.

"Tom . . . oh, Tom," one of them answered, then with a lovely spontaneity threw herself into his arms. Ally was thrust to one side as Tom's arms rose to embrace the pretty young woman.

"Catherine, sweetheart, I've missed you. Dear God, Angelina," putting out his hand to the second young woman, who moved forward to take it but she was more restrained in her manner.

"Give me a kiss. Oh, Lord, what a surprise." He still held the one he had called Catherine to his side, then he turned to Ally, smiling, his eyes a lovely shining blue and for a moment an arrow of jealousy pierced her, then he took her hand and drew her forward with such pride and love she felt a moment's shame.

"This is my wife, Alice. Alice, these are my sisters, Angelina and this is Catherine. Oh, and this is a friend of ours, Davey Mason, who is—"

"David."

"Pardon?"

"Me name's David." And had Catherine Hartley's mother seen the way her daughter and *David* Mason were looking at one another she would have sent the girl away to her sister's manor in Scotland on the next train from Liverpool.

27

There came a time of peace and quiet content, a time that would serve, Ally believed, as a model for the life she would lead with Tom, a deep, slow-moving river with no sudden, unexpected twists and turns, no stagnant, murky pools, no dried-up, stony places, no waterfalls or underwater weeds, just deep, clean, calm water on which to sail safely. There had been no sign of Whipper for many months and Pat had decided to dispense with big Lenny's services. Besides which, she had Davey beside her for most of the day, in the office, or down on the docks and in the warehouses where she did business. He had grown from the gangling, awkward lad he had once been and was a strong, vigorous young man who, when he wasn't working or studying at the Mechanics Institute, used the gymnasium that was attached to it. He did a bit of sparring, wrestling, exercises to build up his already athletic body and had, or so his mam said, proud as a peacock of her fine son and his fine position in life, grown six inches in as many months.

It was a Sunday, the one day that Ally and Tom looked forward to as a day they could spend together, either sprawling in the big easy chairs in the parlour, reading or sometimes Tom would play the piano, a mahogany box affair with tapering, turned and fluted legs which had belonged to his grandmother. He had brought it with him from Rosemont, having taught himself to play by ear. Put a sheet of music in front of him and he was out of his depth but he had only to hear one of the many popular songs of the day and he could repeat it on the instrument. "Are You Going to Scarborough Fair", "Believe Me if All those Endearing Young Charms", "Greensleeves" often rang through the house and in the kitchen Mrs Hodges would nod her head and hum along with the tune.

Today, though, the parlour was quiet as Ally dozed a little in front of the fire which Mrs Hodges had lit since the day had turned cool. Blaze lay at her feet, his muzzle on his crossed paws, his eyebrows twitching, his eyes opening and closing drowsily. Tom had been called out to what he thought might be a botched abortion, though the small boy who had delivered the garbled message was vague as to what the complaint might be. His mam was badly, that's all he had been told to say, but what else could it be in the rabbit-warren of courts and narrow alleys from which he had come? That's all they did there, breed and die in the filth they scarcely noticed and if a woman decided she already had too many children and one more was one too many, there was always an old crone with a handy knitting needle.

When the doorbell rang, both Ally and Blaze woke from their light doze and turned their heads in the direction of the closed parlour door. Blaze stood up and wandered across, pricking his ears and putting his nose to the gap at the bottom of the door. Mrs Hodges could be heard moving reluctantly along the hall and there was the sound of the front door being opened. There was a murmur of voices and Ally was aware that Mrs Hodges would be arguing with the caller, presumably a patient, telling him, or her, that the doctor was already out and that whoever it was should take themselves off and come back later.

She was surprised when there was a light tap at the door and Mrs Hodges bustled in, her face wreathed in smiles, bobbing her head and ready to curtsey it seemed. Ally stared at her in amazement. Mrs Hodges, in all the months since Ally had become Tom's wife and moved into Duke Street, had never once curtseyed to *her*.

"You've a visitor, Mrs Hartley," she told her, smiling, the width of her smile indicating the distinction of the visitor.

"A visitor?" Ally whispered, indicating with facial gestures that she was not at home but Mrs Hodges was having none of that.

"Yes, ma'am!"

Yes, ma'am! Whatever was up with the silly woman?

As Mrs Hodges was not inclined to turn the caller away, it seemed, Ally whispered, "Who is it?"

"Miss Hartley, if you please, Mrs Hartley." Still preening as though she was herself responsible for the pedigree of the lady who stood at her back.

"*Miss* . . ." Ally sat up, putting her hands automatically to her hair as women do, then standing up and smoothing her crumpled skirt. Mrs Hodges stood politely to one side, no doubt in her mind that their visitor would be welcome, for was she not Doctor Tom's sister, family, and a great deal higher in the social register than any of the callers who had so far rung the bell of Doctor and Mrs Hartley's door.

With the same warm spontaneity that she had shown at their previous meeting Miss Catherine Hartley stepped into the room. She was somewhat shy, despite her lovely smile which was so like Tom's. Her blue eyes, again like Tom's, were the colour of forget-me-nots and her hair, which Ally had scarcely had time to notice before, was the same deep, rich brown. She was elegantly dressed as befitted a well-bred lady, in a gown of saxony, a soft wool of merino quality, in a shade somewhere between apple blossom and peach and over it a shawl mantle with two points at the front and one at the back and shaped to the waist. Her Dolly Varden hat, which was tipped saucily over her forehead, had ribbons about the brim and hanging down her back in the exact shade of her gown. She carried a pale grey muslin parasol trimmed in apple blossom, her boots were pale grey kid and so were her gloves.

"I do beg your pardon, Mrs Hartley" – she smiled, as a child might at some slight misdemeanour – "for calling without leaving my card first, but to tell you the truth I have none of my own yet," expecting Tom's wife to recognise the niceties of polite society which said that an unmarried lady must be included on the calling card of her mama. "I do hope this is not an inconvenient time to call," she continued. "Please say if it is but it being Sunday I was hoping that my brother might be at home and we – you and I – could . . . could . . . We are sisters-in-law now and I was hoping . . ."

She continued to play with the dog who, by now, had one end of her parasol in his mouth, beginning to tug and growl, his magnificent tail waving, his paws digging into the rather thread-bare carpet while Ally watched helplessly, wondering if this was the usual way of things in the social class from which Tom and his pretty young sister came. Did they always treat any home, any room they entered as though it were their own, totally relaxed and at ease as they might be with their own family? Of course, she and Catherine were now related by marriage so perhaps that made a difference even though they had met just the once. She was not to know that Catherine Hartley was just as awkward in her presence though her upbringing had taught her how to avoid letting it show.

Mrs Hodges entered the room, without knocking, pushing the door open with her hip and placing the tea tray on the small table beside the chair in which Ally had been sitting.

"Tea, Mrs Hartley." Mrs Hodges smiled, like a grinning Cheshire cat she was, Ally marvelled. "Sit yer down, lass," she said, and both the young women did as they were told, glad of someone to direct them in this strange situation. For a moment Mrs Hodges hovered, knowing that *her* lass was out of her depth. Though Mrs Hodges had only been employed in the homes of the middle classes she was conscious, having read many women's magazines on the subject and the remarkable

Book of Household Management by Mrs Beeton which she had borrowed from the library, that so far Mrs Hartley had not performed her duties as a hostess in the correct manner. She should have shaken the hand of her visitor and, according to the degree of friendship, invited her to remove her shawl and bonnet, and again, depending on how well they were acquainted, asked her caller to take tea. Mind, Mrs Hartley had not been brought up as *Miss* Hartley had, nor had she read Mrs Beeton's wonderful book. She should pour the tea into the cup and before handing the cup and saucer to Miss Hartley, enquire politely if she would like milk or sugar.

Amazingly, this was what she did.

She waited, breathless with some suppressed excitement while both Ally and Mrs Hodges, enchanted with their visitor, waited too, for Ally had not the slightest notion what to do next. Mrs Hodges took matters into her own hands, for what could be more natural to break the ice, so to speak.

"Tea, Mrs Hartley?" she repeated firmly.

"That would be . . . lovely," Ally responded faintly.

It was Blaze who helped matters along and relaxed the tension in the room. His tail plumed and he pushed his nose into the visitor's gloved hand and then, after waiting a moment to see what next – if anything – her hostess might do, Catherine squatted down, her skirt billowing about her and began to pet the dog.

"Lovely boy, there's a good boy. I do love dogs, don't you, Mrs Hartley, but I'm afraid they do not suit Mama."

Catherine Hartley, as the daughter of one of the most prominent families in Liverpool, had been brought up by a personage known as "Nanny", then by a governess, both strict and well versed in the rearing and educating of young ladies. The guidelines for her and her sister's education were very clearly set down. Respect for authority which led, inevitably, to a wide-eyed, unquestioning docility to the husband she would eventually have, found for her by her father, naturally. They were taught to sing and smile, to speak without saying anything of consequence, innocent, incurious, and how to behave in a situation such as this. Small talk, innocuous chatter and it was with this that she began.

"The weather has turned colder, has it not, Mrs Hartley. Do you find the autumn to your taste?"

"I . . . yes, it's better than the winter." She was about to add that the boats were likely to be iced up in winter when the canal froze but what would this beautifully dressed, exquisitely mannered young woman make of that?

"Where is Tom this Sunday afternoon, Mrs Hartley?" Tom's sister went on, smiling as she sipped her tea. "I was hoping to—"

"He was called out to a patient."

"On a Sunday! Papa does not work on a Sunday."

"Patients become ill on every day of the week and at any time of the day. Tom sees to them whenever he's called."

"What a shame. When we met, it was a Sunday. I assumed . . ."

"He's out at night, too."

Ally didn't want to be curt with this young woman, for she really was the most delightful little thing, but it was evident that she knew nothing of the world, of this city and of Tom's part in it. Nor hers. The trouble was Ally herself had no experience of this sort of call. At Blackstock Street you sat down, put your feet up, drank your tea, spoke your mind, had sometimes serious discussions, laughed at what they all considered funny, so what was she to say to this creature who, now she came to think of it, reminded her in a way of Betsy, or at least what Betsy had aspired to be.

Catherine was glancing round her, very obviously racking her brain for some other safe topic of conversation with which to fill the awkward pauses then, something having occurred to her, she turned back brightly to Ally.

"And what do you do with yourself, Mrs Hartley, when Tom's not at home, that is? Do you like to paint? I do water-colours—"

Ally exploded into spontaneous laughter, almost spilling her tea. Catherine reared back, startled, ready, should her hostess explain the joke, to laugh too and Ally shook her head as she placed her cup and saucer on the tray.

"I'm going to call you Catherine, and you must call me Ally." Not Alice, for Tom was the only one to call her that and it was special. "We can't keep up this nonsense of Miss and Mrs Hartley. I'm your brother's wife and if we're to be friends then we must call each other by our Christian names."

"Ally, oh, I would love that. I wasn't sure . . . well, I know Mama and Papa don't approve." She flushed and put her hand to her mouth, like a child who has said something rude. "Oh, I'm sorry but . . . I'm sorry."

"Don't give it another thought, Catherine. I know exactly what your mother and father think of me. I've stolen their son and me the daughter of a canal boatman. I'm sure they had great plans for a society marriage for him, a bride of their own class, and Tom chose me. But he loves me and I love him and we're happy. Besides, I don't think a woman" – she almost said, "like you" – "a woman brought up in his own class would understand the work he does. Tom must be . . . what? Ten years older than you so perhaps you won't know much about him as a youth, but it seems he has always had a . . . a *feeling* for the underclasses, as a medical man, you understand. Some of his views on the exploitation of his fellow man would not be popular among his own. He believes in . . . well, I won't bore nor confuse you with his ideals. Suffice it to say that I know he is the best man I have ever met and the life I live with him is all I shall ever need. I don't care whether he is wealthy or not. I just want his happiness and I think I can say that is what he has. *Happiness*. And as for painting in watercolours . . ." She laughed merrily. "I'm far too busy with my own business. I like to read though and Tom says he will teach me to play the piano when both of us have a moment. I like music, you see. Tom taught me that."

And though she didn't know why, Catherine joined in her laughter. It was very evident that she was fascinated by this wife of Tom's who didn't seem at all wicked to her, as her parents implied. She was of the working classes, true, but she was not how she had been led to believe the working classes were. She was pleasant, nicely, if casually dressed but then she was in her own home. She spoke with what Catherine supposed was a northern accent but she was intelligible, forthright and Catherine liked her. Most of what Ally, as she had been told to call her, said she did not understand but she admired her and it was worth the trouble she had been obliged to take to get out of the house alone.

Girls like Catherine and Angelina Hartley did not go about unaccompanied and had she not been on good terms with the under-gardener's wife she would not have been able to do so today. Jenny Longman, Matt Longman's wife, had a baby every year, squeezing the new arrival somehow or other into one of the four two-bedroomed cottages at the back of the vegetable garden where the gardeners were housed. Matt was a good gardener, well liked and hardworking but he did like to take a pint or two at the Bowling Green Inn on Tunnel Road. Many's the time he drank his wages away, leaving poor Jenny to feed her children on whatever her neighbours could themselves spare. He needed reporting did Matt but then Mr Hartley would fire him and what would happen to Jenny and her brood?

Catherine Hartley, well brought up and allowed only, as a well-brought-up girl, to walk sedately around the cultivated garden, or to ride with a groom in attendance, though she was on the whole obedient, biddable, had one day taken a fancy to see what was on the far side of the vegetable garden and beyond the high hedge that bordered it. She found Jenny Longman suckling her latest, a baby of three months, and though the sight of the bared breast of the gardener's wife shocked her immeasurably how could she walk away from the desolation of the woman who sat on her doorstep weeping tears of anguish.

"I've no milk, miss. 'Ow am I ter feed poor little lad wi' me milk gone, tell me that?"

"I beg your pardon?" Catherine had asked politely, incomprehensibly, but when the whole sorry tale was told and Catherine had been persuaded not to go to her father, for the last thing Jenny Longman wanted was to lose the roof over her children's head, the relationship had been formed. Compassion and generosity on Catherine's part, eternal gratitude on Jenny's. Cook was often to say she could have sworn she had two quarts of milk, or a half a shoulder of ham, and where the potatoes went was a mystery. Them lads, meaning any of the Hartley boys or those who worked in the gardens and stable yard of Rosemont, must have been raiding her larder but then the larders of Rosemont were overflowing with good things, more than twice the household could eat so no fuss was made and the little Longmans thrived, as did Jenny and her latest.

It was Jenny who had run to the corner of Smithdown Lane and called a cab to pick Catherine up by the small side gate and it wasn't the first time, for Catherine, though mim as a mouse with her parents was a rebel at heart, and the small innocent adventures she allowed herself, only to the Art Gallery, or perhaps a stroll on the Marine Parade, satisfied that rebellion, which was perhaps why she was sympathetic to her brother who had married a woman so far beneath him neither she nor Tom could be accepted in polite society. It was not discussed in front of her nor Angelina, for they were supposed to know nothing of life, but this well-mannered, spirited young woman who was Tom's wife was much to her liking.

They began to relax. Ally told Catherine of her days on the

canal, of her family and Aggie Wainwright, of her business, her horses, the men she employed and promised to take her for a trip on the canal while Catherine sat, her mouth open, her face flushed with the fire's warmth, and was taken into a world she had not known existed. And Ally was the same, listening to Catherine describe the life she led, the balls she went to, the *idiotic* young men she met there, the rounds of afternoon calls, the evening soirées, the parties, the embroidery with which she spent her days, the evenings at home playing the piano, and her sister who was concerned with nothing beyond her wedding which was to take place in the spring.

They were so deep in the conversation which absorbed them both they did not hear the front door open and when Tom entered the parlour, demanding to know what the dickens was going on here, they both jumped guiltily apart as though they were up to no good.

"Catherine, sweetheart, how on earth did you get here? Who brought you? I see no carriage at the door." Behind Tom another figure stood and Ally watched and instantly understood when Catherine's face blazed like the fire in the grate.

"No. Well, I didn't come in the carriage, Tom." And while she spoke to Tom, her eyes went over his shoulder to Davey, who lurked in the hall.

Tom believed in equality, even among women, but it did not extend to his sister. He frowned and took what might have been a threatening step into the parlour.

"Then how did you get here?"

"Now, Tom, does it matter?" Ally began, but Tom put out his hand to silence her.

"Does your mother know where you are?"

"Of course not. Whatever's the matter with you, Tom?"

"That's what I'd like to know," Ally interrupted, "and who is that behind you? Davey, is it you? Do come in but first shout up the hall for Mrs Hodges, will you? Tell her to bring more tea and some of those cakes I know she's baking for Catherine. Oh, yes, Catherine, you are our first *proper* caller and I'd like to make a small bet that she is at this moment baking."

"Alice, would you mind—"

"Yes, I would mind, Tom Hartley. This is my home and Catherine is my guest and I'd be obliged if you'd give over questioning her as though she done something criminal."

"Well, she's not supposed to go about on her own and I'm sure—"

"You allow me to go about on my own and have nothing to say on the matter, so why should Catherine's striking out independently be any different? Did you walk here by yourself, lass?"

Catherine blinked, never having been called *lass* before. "Well, no, I came in a hansom. The cabbie was perfectly respectable."

"There you are then, Tom Hartley." Ally grinned triumphantly. She felt as though she had made great strides in the space of one afternoon. Not only had Tom regained his little sister of whom he was inordinately fond, but she had found a friend, a sister-in-law, and if his expression was anything to go by Davey Mason had discovered the end of the rainbow and the pot of gold that was proverbially to be found there.

28

He had to be careful now, for the old chap who buggered about in the garden, doing whatever daft thing he did each day, had begun to notice him. The old man, he supposed he must be the gardener, spent his time planting and trimming, raking leaves and the dead wood which lay across the forlorn winter beds, the paths and the grass where children played. Every now and then he stopped what he was doing to light his pipe and when he did he would peer short-sightedly across the railing to where he himself did his best to insert his bulk behind the trunk of a tree. When this happened he thought he'd best be a bit canny. He didn't want the old sod to get suspicious and perhaps send for a bobby so he would shuffle off and leave the square, making for the foetid cellar which he shared with a dozen others, wondering to himself how he could find some task, perhaps sweeping the gutters. He could soon get hold of a broom which would give him a legitimate reason for hanging about in the square. Not that his befuddled brain thought exactly on these lines, or with these words, for such thoughts were beyond his limited brain power but even he knew that he could not just hang about without a purpose. He laboured spasmodically on the docks, keeping a sharp lookout for the old Irish chap who worked on the bitch's canal boats but it was easy enough to become invisible among the hundreds of other labourers, many as big and unkempt as himself. He made a few bob and when he didn't, when he was too drunk or lazy to work, it was no hardship to batter another man into *loaning* him something until times got better, or so he told the soft bugger with the bloodied face whom he held down while he went through his pockets!

And he had a double reason now for keeping an eye on the house where the bitch lived and that reason was the sweetest morsel of female flesh he had ever come across. Not that he had ever been fussy about such things in the past. Any woman would do for what was in his mind and trousers: to serve his perverse and cruel pleasures. As long as she had everything in the right place she would do him, but this one had something special that he couldn't put into words. Tasty, she was, small, delicate, *innocent* and his brain grew inflamed as he imagined her in his hands and what they might do together when he got her on his own. It was three months now since she had turned up on the doorstep of the bitch's house in a hansom cab, tripping up the steps one Sunday afternoon and since then coming nearly every weekend. Jesus, she was toothsome and he was convinced that if he had *her* to himself for a few days his prick would come alive again as it once had done. Bloody hell, he could feel it stir every time she stepped down from the cab and rang the bell of the house. The thing was, when she went off to wherever she came from the bitch's husband, the bloody doctor, went with her but if he could get her on her own, or better still, *both of them*, bloody hell, what a time he would have. Sometimes of a night, when he lay among the moaning, scratching, snoring mass of humanity among whom he slept, his mind would become so inflamed with his imaginings it was all he could do to stop himself from manhandling the nearest woman into a corner and giving her what for. The only thing that stopped him was the fear of failure, and in front of the face-less, stinking creatures with whom he shared the floor. He knew he wouldn't be able to get it up. Jesus God, he'd tried hard enough, the last time with some scarecrow of a whore behind the Borough Gaol where the drabs hung about after the sailors. Laughed at him, she had, her painted face split in a sneering smile to reveal her broken teeth. Mind you, he'd taught her a lesson she'd not forget, smashing her teeth down her throat and leaving her for dead for all he knew, or cared.

It was almost dawn and he was stiff and cold. The old chap would be here soon. Already the milk float was clattering up the square so he'd best be off. Slipping silently from behind the bench where he'd spent the night, he stood up and stretched, then, while the milkman was down the basement steps of the house, pinched a can of milk off the float and shambled off in the direction of Hanover Street.

The two young women stopped to glance into the window of the Misses Yeoland, milliners and dressmakers, in Bold Street, in which was tastefully displayed a sample of the Misses Yeoland's wares. The window was changed daily, today against the backdrop of dark blue velvet nothing but a cream silk gown with a high-crowned cream straw hat.

"Shall we go in?" Ally questioned. She was taller than Catherine and had to lean forward to peer under the brim of Catherine's bonnet to see her face. But Catherine drew her on somewhat hurriedly, pulling her in the direction of the establishment of Samuel Cutter's and pressing her face to his window.

"What on earth do you want with feather beds, Catherine Hartley?" Ally laughed, then her face became serious, for it was evident that Catherine was not concerned with Mr Cutter's establishment but wished only to draw Ally away from the dressmakers.

"Well, you see . . ."

"Don't try to cod me, Catherine."

"Cod you! What on earth does that mean?"

"It means to fool me and that's what you just did. Probably your mama has her gowns made at the Misses Yeoland's place and you were afraid."

"Can you blame me, Ally?" The tone of Catherine's voice was passionate. "I have never been so happy, with you and Tom and . . . and . . ."

"Davey?"

"What's wrong with it, Ally? He's a good, hardworking man, decent and respectable and *getting on* in life which I know Papa would admire but . . . well, I know how they were with Tom when . . ."

"When he married me, you mean?"

Catherine bowed her head, and her arm, which was through Ally's, tightened its grip as though she were afraid that someone, probably her family, if they found out, would drag her away from this new friend she had found. How she had managed to escape from her mama's notice for all these months was a wonder to her and every time she sauntered up to Jenny's cottage on some pretext or other, she fully expected her mother to question it. Of course, sometimes she slipped away and spent her time in the woods or the gardens about the house, sketching, painting in full view of the outside servants, presenting her mama, who was not particularly concerned, nor interested, with a hastily contrived watercolour. Often she was forced to arrive at Ally and Tom's in what she called her gardening clothes since she could not actually garden – another excuse to disappear for an hour – dressed in the outfit in which she accompanied her mama to town. When she spoke of gardening she did not mean the work of digging the soil, or even planting a seed or two but sauntering about with a basket on her arm, her gloved hand holding a dainty pair of pruning shears which her mama thought perfectly suitable for a young lady. The gardeners smiled tolerantly as she wandered here and there, well accustomed to seeing her come and go and it was this that helped her to play truant so often – which wasn't as often as she would have liked – and for so long. It helped, of course, that Angelina was to be married shortly, for her mother and sister were totally absorbed with orange blossom, wedding journeys, the colour of the gowns the bridesmaids would wear, of which she was to be one, and were hardly aware of her new absorption with the estate workers nor the garden she was tending and her little sketches elicited no more than an indifferent nod.

Sometimes it was two or three weeks before she could escape on a Sunday afternoon when she knew Davey would be at Duke Street and at first Tom, the most cheerful and obliging of fellows, had proved difficult. He was in a most awkward position, she was aware of that, for he himself had married outside his class – she did not like to say *beneath* his class – which he had, of course, though Ally was lovely and but for her northern accent might have passed as one of her mama's friends. She was clever, well read, a lady in all but name and Tom loved her, but it seemed it was hard for him to accept the same situation for his sister. She was nineteen and already she knew her parents were considering some suitable match for her, but if she had to run away, as Tom had, she would have no one but Davey. She had known from the first moment their eyes had met that he was to be someone special to her and though she had told no one, not even Davey, something strong, sure, enduring was growing between them. They would not have it, Mama and Papa, she knew it, so she and Davey, when the time came, would be forced, as Tom had been, to marry against their will. In the meanwhile, at this time of Christmas festivities, she and Ally had ridden in the cab which she herself had taken from the small gate at the side of Rosemont to Duke Street and were window-shopping.

"Mama and Angelina, and myself, have our gowns made by the Misses Yeoland. I know Mama and Angelina are not there this afternoon because they have taken the carriage to Frank's house."

"Frank is the bridegroom, I presume."

"Yes. Frank Cropper. His father is . . ."

"Cropper and Bensons, imports and exports."

Catherine turned to look into Ally's face, her own startled, for she was not aware that her sister-in-law was acquainted with friends of her parents.

"How do you know them?"

"Lass, I don't know *them*. I do business with George Benson."

"Oh," was all Catherine could think of to say, for she had never in her life known a lady who was in business.

Neither of the two young women, as they continued to stroll along Bold Street, stopping now and then to look at the displays in the shop windows, noticed the elderly lady who had just been assisted from her carriage by her solicitous coachman. She was stout, florid-faced, but retained some of the handsome looks of her young womanhood and was extremely well and expensively dressed. She put her hand on the arm of her companion, clutching it so fiercely the younger woman winced.

"Mama, you're hurting."

"Charlotte, did you see who that was? Dear heaven, surely it . . ."

"Who, Mama?"

"There, looking in Cutter's window."

Both ladies stared in amazement, scarcely able to believe their eyes, while the coachman, ready to escort them across the pavement and into the Misses Yeoland's dressmaking establishment, wondered what was the matter.

"It's Catherine Hartley, Charlotte. *Catherine Hartley*. But who is that with her?"

"I don't know, Mama. I don't believe I've ever seen her in my life before."

"Neither have I, Charlotte. And more to the point, neither has Mary Hartley!"

It was the following Sunday when Tom Hartley became aware that his little sister had fallen in love. Davey and Ally had gone through what he called his homework, checking the columns of figures she gave him, those that she herself had calculated during the week, pleased when she discovered that they had arrived at the same figure.

"You'll be doing the accounts by yourself soon, Davey, lad. Now, let's hear you read. Shall we have something we'd all enjoy. Where's yesterday's copy of *The Times*, my darlin'?" she asked Tom who was half asleep in the chair by the fire, and though Davey was self-conscious with Catherine hanging on to his every word, just as though he himself had written the articles and snippets of news written there, he had made a fair fist of it. Catherine's warm, admiring eyes, the melting look of love which she, innocently, levelled in his direction, made him feel ten feet tall and his gratitude to the man and woman who had done this for him, who had presented him to this beautiful young girl and made it possible that some . . . *some day* she would be his, was inestimable.

The day was brilliant with winter sunshine, icy and sparkling, every stalk of grass, every denuded shrub, every tree branch stark with white hoar frost which spread itself across the garden in the square in Duke Street. A fire roared in the grate and for half an hour the four of them sat with their toes to it, Tom doing his best to edge Blaze from his position on the fireside rug where he lay with his nose almost in the flames.

"You'll get your fur singed, daft dog," he told him lazily, taking his wife's hand lovingly in his and bringing it to his lips.

"He needs a walk, I believe, and I think Davey and I should take him for a turn round the gardens. It will do him the world of good, fat, lazy thing."

"He's not fat," Tom protested, not at all sure, even now, that he quite liked the idea of his pretty, ladylike sister *taking a turn* round the garden with Davey Mason. Davey was a grand lad and Ally thought the world of him, and it was he himself who had suggested that Ally bring him on, educate him, turn him into . . . well, not a gentleman, but the nearest thing to it. He was shyly modest, quiet, well mannered, diffident in a way, but climbing in leaps and bounds up the ladder that Ally had presented him with, taking many of the tasks from her that she herself had mastered. He had a quick brain and grasped what he was being taught with amazing clarity. But he was not a gentleman. As your wife is not a lady, his inner voice whispered to him, but somehow that didn't seem to matter. So why did he balk at the idea of his sister becoming entangled with Davey Mason?

He stood up and moved to the window, watching as the man and woman, the excited dog beside them, crossed the road and through the gate into the garden. The young man picked up a stick and threw it and the dog ran after it while the young couple, hand in hand, ran after him. He could hear their young laughter, their high voices as they ran, their hands clasped as Davey pulled Catherine across the slippery grass. When her feet went from under her Davey was appalled, picking her up, brushing her down, cupping her chin as though looking for damage, their faces close and for a moment it looked as though they might kiss. He took her hand and tucked it reverently in the crook of his arm, holding her close as they began to walk sedately along the path while the dog circled them, still looking for fun.

"Dear God," he whispered. "Oh, dear Lord."

"What is it?" Ally looked up from the newspaper which she was still rifling through.

"This is serious."

"What is?"

"Have you seen them?"

"Who?"

"Catherine and Davey, of course. Don't tell me you don't know what I mean."

"Yes, but does it matter? You married beneath you, my love."

"Of course I didn't." Tom's voice was sharp, angry.

"Come now, Tom. Let's be honest at least with one another."

"That's rubbish, and you know it. We *both* know it."

"Of course we do but are you saying it would be different between your sister and a lad, a *good, decent* lad who is going to be a success, as you have been, and well able to look after his wife?"

"God in heaven . . ." Tom swept his hand through his hair, continuing to look distractedly through the window at his sister and the man who loved her. He did not wish to hurt his beloved wife by telling her the truth, which was that the family of a girl of Catherine's station in life would rather see her dead than married to a man in Davey's. His parents had had no choice where he himself was concerned, for he was a man, a man who had already made his way in life, but Catherine was still a child, at least in their eyes, a child who had to be guarded, protected and passed intact and virginal from her father's hands into those of her husband's, a husband who her father would choose for her.

"Davey is a worthwhile young man who—"

"D'you think they give a damn about that?" he said savagely.

"Tom, I'm amazed that you would think—"

"It's not me who has the deciding, Alice. And they wouldn't allow it, you must know that. This is nothing to do with me, or you, but a young girl of a good family who would ruin herself if she were to marry Davey Mason."

"*Tom!*"

"This is not me talking, this is *them*. I can see nothing but trouble ahead for them and if I'd known this was going to happen I wouldn't have encouraged her to come to our home."

"She didn't meet him in our home, Tom Hartley." Ally's

answer was cool. "She met him in Princes Park totally by accident."

"You know what I mean, damn it."

"Yes, I think I do."

The letter came a week later. It was smudged and grubby, as though it had been passed from hand to hand, or perhaps rested in the pocket of a man who worked the land. There was no stamp on it and the postman was highly indignant, and said so to Mrs Hodges, that someone should write a letter to a respectable household such as this and not pay the stamp duty.

"I'll 'ave ter charge yer, Mrs Hodges, I'm sorry but them's the rules an' I should tell 'ooever wrote it ter be more careful next time."

Ally had called in at Blackstock Street on her way home from work, as she did several times a week. From her office window she had seen the *Harmony* make her way down the five locks to Stanley Dock but had been just about to call on Alfred Hodgkin, a timber merchant with a warehouse on the Timber Quay at the back of Huskisson Dock, and couldn't stop to have a word with Jack. She left Davey in the office, stepping smartly out into the winter's afternoon. There was a touch of rain in the air, the cold snap having ended a couple of days ago. She wrapped her warm woollen cape closely about her and made her way along the busy dock road, her business mind engrossed with profits and deliveries and canal boats.

She was with Mr Hodgkin for more than an hour, for he was one of the men who, though admitting she was fair and reliable, hated doing business with a woman. She was forced to bite her tongue, smile, agree with many of his daft ideas, but in the end they struck a bargain regarding the pit props which were destined for the collieries about Wigan. Well satisfied, she left his office which was redolent with the fragrance of the timber that was just being unloaded from the timber boat on to the dockside.

She did not see the big, silently following figure of the man who had been stalking her for so long. Ever since the day he had spotted her on the canal and pushed poor Gentle into the freezing water. He watched her enter her office, noticing the slender line of her ankles as she ran up the stairs, then stepped back into the shadows to wait for her. He had a sack over his shoulder from which came the sound of whimpering.

It was another hour and quite dark when she left and the lad was with her, and though the big man cursed he did not seem to be unduly put out, for the plan he had now in his muddled brain included the other one, the little one, the *child*, for that was what she was to him in the dark, evil recesses of his mind.

As she and the lad turned the corner of Walter Street and into Great Howard Street he casually smashed the sack against the wall. The whimpering stopped.

The sound of raised voices coming from number 10 Blackstock Street could be heard as she and Davey approached the front door. She had a key but in her anxiety her hand shook and she dropped it, hammering instead on the door which was swiftly opened by Albert. She could hear Jack's voice coming from the kitchen and in it was something she had never heard before. Jack had always been a come-day, go-day kind of a young man, enjoying life, enjoying his work which had no responsibilities apart from getting his canal boat, the *Edith*, from one place to another on the Leeds and Liverpool Canal. He had been doing it ever since he was born, or so it seemed, first with his pa beside him and latterly under the direction of his sister who was the brains of the family. Decisions were made by her and should some problem arise he took it to her, or to Pat. She paid him well and he was popular with the lads with whom he drank. He stood his round with the best of them and had a way with the ladies, for he was pleasant-looking, good-humoured and cheerful. He liked a joke, a good laugh and life was sweet. He had a good home to go to when his canal journeying was over, with two motherly souls to fuss him when he was in Liverpool.

As Ally entered the house it seemed he might be about to burst into tears.

"What's up?" Davey crowded behind her. Both of them were damp, for the drizzle had turned to a heavier downpour and Aggie stood up, reaching for Ally's cloak and draping it over the back of one of the chairs at the table. She did the same for Davey, pondering in an abstracted way on the way things had turned out for her niece's son. His cape was as fine as any she had seen, even on Tom Hartley, and the jacket and trousers, his necktie and shirt, his bowler hat gave him the appearance of a gentleman. That's what the couple who had just entered could have been. A lady and gentleman!

"Our Jack's upset, lass," Edie told her daughter, her hand ready to take Jack's if only he would sit down for a minute instead of tramping from here to there and back again. He'd come in drenched to his underwear but would he go and change into something dry? No, he wouldn't, and her mother's heart worried about such things. She'd lost so many of her children over the years, the last their lovely Betsy to a world she could not even imagine and she didn't want to lose her lad.

"What's happened, Jack? Is summat up wi't boat?" Davey asked anxiously.

"No, it's not boat. It's our Teddy. I can't find 'im."

"Teddy?"

Both Ally and Davey were bewildered. They both knew what store Jack placed on his dog and Ally had a lot to thank the animal for, but really, to get in such a state over him! Anyone would think Teddy was a child or at least a member of the family, but then that was what he was to Jack. He'd had Teddy since he'd found him, no more than a few days old, fastened in a sack and floating, breathing his last, in the canal by the aqueduct near Hebden Bridge. He'd hand-fed the bedraggled little thing, cossetted him, slept with him in his bed, carried him tucked in his shirt where it was warm until the pup had finally decided life was worth living and from then on the pair had been inseparable. Teddy went everywhere with him, even into the pubs where he crouched at Jack's knee or, if the place was busy, actually *on* his lap.

"I've looked everywhere, our Ally," Jack cried, pushing his hand through his damp hair. "Up an' down t'lock, back along canal, 'appen 'e fell in, bur 'e's nowhere. I've bin ter't police—"

"*Police!*"

"An' why not? 'E's a valuable animal," which he was to Jack. "I can't bear ter think of 'im left out in't cold an' wet."

"Jack, lad, he'll turn up. I reckon he's smelled some bitch up one of them alleys an'—"

"Ally, please," Ma protested. "We don't want talk like that."

"Ma, Jack knows what I mean. It's only natural for a dog an' a—"

"That's enough, our Ally," Ma said sternly. "Now then, our Jack, let's 'ave them wet things off yer, an' Ally, yer'd best gerron 'ome ter that 'usband o' yours or 'e'll be worritin'. Davey, run an' fetch a cab fer 'er. I don' want 'er walkin' the streets in the dark."

It was perhaps the picture of herself walking home through the dark street and the danger which Ma was implying that brought him to her mind and though no one noticed it, for they were all watching Jack as he turned this way and that, she felt herself go cold, because she knew without a shadow of doubt that Whipper Ogden was behind this.

Whipper was back!

29

Betsy Pearce swept back into their lives with the same disdain with which she had left, the only addition being the child who clung to her fashionable skirt.

"Good afternoon, Albert," she said to the slack-jawed youth who opened the door to her imperious knocking. "Is my mother at home?" Without waiting for an answer she strode across the doorstep dragging the child with her. For all the attention she paid it, it might have been some impurity she had picked up on the pavement.

Albert clung to the door latch as her perfume wafted about him, knocking him for six, making his young heart beat in the way it had always done ever since she had entered his home all those years ago. Albert was sixteen now and very conscious of the opposite sex though to tell the truth he didn't have much, if anything, to do with them, but even at twelve, the age he had been when he first laid reverent eyes on Betsy, she had bewitched him.

She still did. He was incapable of speech but then what could he have said to warn the two women who sat with their knees up to the roaring fire of the shock in store for them? It was February and though here and there in sheltered corners snow-drops were thrusting their shy heads through the cold earth, the weather was raw. Tom Hartley was run off his feet attending to the needs of the clamouring multitude who shivered and sweated in the dank cellars of the stews of Liverpool, coughing their diseased lungs up, choking on their own phlegm, their undernourished bodies unable to fight off the influenza which turned to pneumonia before Tom could help them. Some were lucky, if you called lying sometimes two in a bed in the infirmary, lucky but at least there was someone to feed them a bit of broth and close their eyes when they died, which they did in their hundreds.

Both women turned their heads curiously, for who on earth was calling this late in the afternoon and on a day like this? When they saw who stood haughtily in the kitchen doorway they cried out in unison as though a ghost had appeared, which in a way it had, and Edie Pearce fell back in her chair, every vestige of colour leaving her face. She clutched at her chest and Aggie, not so badly affected, for this young madam was not *her* daughter, thank God, sprang to her feet, ready, should it be needed, to send Albert running for Doctor Tom.

But Edie was not having a heart attack. Her grey-white face became suffused with colour. It lit up as though a candle was set behind her eyes and she held out her trembling arms to her child, the one she had loved above all others.

"Betsy," she croaked. "Oh my Betsy, yer've come 'ome, yer've come 'ome ter yer ma. Thank God. Thank the dear Lord. Where've yer bin child? I've bin outer me mind."

"Now then, Mother, don't fuss."

"*Don't fuss!*" shrieked Aggie, incensed. "Yer've bin gone best part o' – wharris it? two years, or is it three? – an' yer tellin yer ma not ter fuss. Yer just disappear wi' nobody knowin' where y'are then yer walk in 'ere as if it were bloody yesterday an' tell yer ma not ter fuss."

"What has it to do with you, old woman? This is between my mother and myself."

"I see wherever yer bin yer've learned ter speak proper."

"And I see you still don't. Anyway I haven't come here to argue with the likes of you. Perhaps you'd ask . . . Albert, is it?" – turning her brilliant smile on the mesmerised youth who still hovered, tongue-tied, by the open front door – "if he would be good enough to bring in my luggage. Two pieces. Now then, Mother, let me have a good look at you." Which really meant that she wished Edie to get a good look at her. Edie had risen unsteadily from her chair and was doing her best to drag her daughter into her arms, tears of joy running down her face and falling on to the black woollen bodice of her dress. She still wore her widow's mourning but about her neck and at her wrist was an immaculate white muslin frill.

Betsy looked quite magnificent. She was dressed in pale blue silk, a full skirt with flounces edged with cream lace and a bodice which moulded her splendid breast as though it were painted on her. A row of tiny pearl buttons ran down the front. Around her was thrown a superlative grey fur, draped carelessly about her shoulders and reaching almost to the floor. She wore pale blue kid boots and gloves to match. Her bonnet was nothing more than a wisp of pale blue silk and cream lace, tipped over her eyes and tied beneath her chin with blue silk ribbon. Betsy Pearce did not only shop in London but in Paris where fashion led the world. She was breathtaking in her beauty which time had not dimmed. It was perhaps this, the glorious splendour of her and her outfit that took the sight and minds of the two women away from the child who was, because of its fullness, almost hidden in her skirts. A toddler, no more, who should have been carried but who swayed in the folds of Betsy's skirts and made not a sound.

Edie had managed to get hold of her girl for a moment or two, which was all that Betsy would allow, but as Betsy stepped back from the unwelcome attention the child did not and she fell at Edie's feet.

There was, for a full minute, complete stillness and silence. The child sat where she had fallen, staring at the red bobbles on the plush cloth that covered the table then put out a baby finger and gently touched one. It swung a little and at once she left it alone. Both Edie and Aggie stared at her, their eyes huge, their mouths open, on their faces the same expression. Disbelief mixed with hope, joy, wonder, desire, for surely this quite exquisite baby was Edie Pearce's granddaughter? Why else would Betsy cart her around? She was not the kind of woman to mind another woman's child so surely . . . surely it could only be hers. Their combined glance was riveted on the child and the hubbub made by Albert as he carried in two boxes, putting them in the narrow hallway, Betsy's sharp voice telling him to be careful, the complaints of the cab driver who hadn't bargained, he said, for the humping about of two such big boxes and then the loud argument about not only the amount of the fare but who was to pay it, passed unnoticed.

"I've not got that much on me, Betsy," Albert whispered apologetically and with a soft hiss, and without taking her eyes off the child, Aggie threw her purse at her son who paid the cabbie and shut the door.

Betsy threw off her fur and sat down, sighing dramatically. "You have no idea how difficult it is to travel with a child on a journey that takes so long. Two hundred and six miles, hours and hours cooped up in a compartment with an infant, first class, of course, but still it was very trying."

Two hundred and six miles! Edie had travelled up and down the Leeds and Lancashire Canal and must have done more than that in a year but she had been aboard her own home and it didn't seem the same somehow. Aggie had travelled no further than New Brighton once with her Percy but neither woman was concerned with Betsy's aggrieved and complaining voice. They were focused on nothing but the baby who sat, like some little doll, not a sound from her, nor a movement except for the finger which had hesitantly touched the fringed bobble.

"Well, is nobody going to offer me a cup of tea?" Betsy asked, standing up abruptly and both the women could not help but notice the way the baby shrank back. She plugged her thumb in her mouth and looked at Betsy with apprehensive eyes. "When you've finished staring at Amalie – oh, yes, she's mine – I wouldn't mind a cup of tea and then perhaps a bath, if that could be arranged. Albert, would you take my things up . . . where?" She turned sweetly to Aggie. "Where am I to sleep, Mrs Wainwright. If you could . . ."

"*Yours?*" breathed Edie. "This is yer daughter – me grand-daughter?"

"Yes, I suppose she is and if someone could just—"

"Dear sweet Jesus, yours."

"For God's sake, Mother, pull yourself together."

With a great cry which startled the baby, Edie swooped her into her arms and held her tenderly to her breast. She kissed and stroked her rosy cheek, rocked her silently while tears ran down her cheeks and on to the baby's soft golden curls and Aggie, a daft smile on her face, she could feel it settle there, watched, hovering, longing for a hold, while Betsy tutted im-patiently, turning this way and that as though expecting some servant to appear to do her bidding. Albert had lugged one of the boxes up the narrow stairs, leaving it on the equally narrow landing, waiting for his mother's instruction on which bedroom it was to go in, probably his, he thought, for Betsy couldn't be expected to go up into the attic.

It took a great deal of pushing and pulling of the box, the bath and the cans of water, with sharp commands from Betsy to get her settled into, as Albert guessed, his bedroom, though she did think, she said, that it would be a good idea for Amalie to sleep with her grandmother. She was exhausted after her long journey and if Albert would carry up the bath . . . Oh yes, a fire, of course, and perhaps if Mrs Wainwright would see to the bed, she might, after a cup of tea, go straight to her rest. Was a tray out of the question, perhaps with some toast, thinly sliced and buttered, to go with the tea and . . . thank you, that would be lovely.

Aggie and Edie could not wait to get her upstairs and in her bed. They ran about at her bidding, the one running handing the baby to the other, and when, finally, peace reigned, they sat down and considered their Emily. *Yes, theirs!* Two grand-mothers most children had and here they were. Edie Pearce and Aggie Wainwright. They didn't know why Betsy had come home after all this time, nor did they care. Not now with this lovely child to dote on. Was she married? Did she have a husband back there in London? Again they did not care. The child, as amenable as a sleepy kitten, sat first on one lap and then another. They took off her little duds which were, they admitted, remarkably fine, and studied the lovely child from her fluff of thick golden curls to her baby toes, finding nothing they did not at once adore. They rooted about in the box which Betsy had told them contained Emily's clothes and after bathing her in front of the fire, which she seemed to enjoy, patting the water solemnly, they put her in a nightdress which was embroi-dered so finely Edie gasped. To take such trouble with a garment that would never be seen! The child tottered on her bare feet from one lap to the other, then over to the window to stare in wonder at the bird which sang cheerfully in its cage. She turned to the two women then pointed at it, her eyes wide and they exchanged glances which asked had either of them ever seen a child so clever?

But she did not make one sound. She did not indulge in the childish gurgles which pass for conversation in one so young. She did not cry, nor laugh, nor even smile and when, eventu-ally she fell asleep pressed to Aggie's deep bosom, both women wept silently, for they both were aware that there was something very amiss with Betsy Pearce's lovely child.

"We'd best send fer our Ally an' Doctor Tom," Edie said. "Will yer go, lad," turning to Albert.

*

They were just sitting down to their meal which Mrs Hodges had been trying to get on the table for the past hour, when the doorbell rang.

"Now who the dickens is this?" Mrs Hodges grumbled as she went to answer it. And himself not even settled to his meal yet. She'd give whoever it was what for, see if she didn't. The poor lad had barely time to chuck a bit of something down his throat before they were asking for him again and if it was the last thing she did she'd get rid of the caller and Doctor Tom upstairs in his bed, even if it was only for a couple of hours.

The letter had passed backwards and forwards between them.

> *Dear Ally and Tom,*
> *I was seen in town by a friend of Mama's and now I am locked in my room. Jenny will send this to you, I hope, and as soon as I can I will come.*
> *Your loving sister*
> *Catherine*

"I knew this would happen. She should never have gone into town with you. She was bound to be seen by someone and now . . ." Tom was beside himself, taking the blame for not putting a stop to this ridiculous situation before it got out of hand. Which it had. It had been delightful to have his baby sister as a guest in his house but just look where it had got them. He couldn't believe it. The pair of them marching about the streets of Liverpool, meaning his wife, who he had given more credit for a bit of sense, and his naïve sister who knew no better, he supposed.

"But Tom, such a little thing."

"Little to you, my darling, but a crime of immense proportion to my parents. A girl of good family does not go about unaccompanied."

"She was *not* unaccompanied. She was with me."

"As far as they're concerned she was unaccompanied. They won't let her out of their sight from now on, which perhaps might be a good thing in view of—"

"Davey Mason." Ally's tone was bitter and Tom knew at once it had been the wrong thing to say, even if he hadn't actually said it.

"Darling." He reached for her hand and drew her up into his arms. "I'm sorry but I know them. I know how they think and it wouldn't ever have happened. Not for Catherine and Davey."

"They love one another, Tom."

"Rubbish. She's a child, and he's barely out of short pants."

"How dare you say that!"

They might have gone on for the rest of the evening, their meal going cold on the table had not Albert, to their vast consternation, pushed past a highly indignant Mrs Hodges, his face red with exertion, his breathing fast, and stood dramatically in the doorway.

"Oh, God," Ally breathed, rising from her chair where Tom had just seated her and putting her hand to her mouth.

"What is it, lad?"

"She's come 'ome." Albert pointed with a trembling finger in the general direction of Blackstock Street.

"Come home? Who's come home?" Tom frowned as though somewhere in the depth of his mind a bell was ringing, one that boded ill for them all. He couldn't for the life of him think what it might be but some precognition of trouble rippled his already shaking mind.

"Betsy, an' 'er baby. Me mam ses ter come."

Like her mother before her Ally sank back into her chair and felt the blood leave her head. She knew she was going to faint. All her senses were reeling and though she fought it valiantly she could feel herself begin to sway to the side.

"No, you don't, lass," Mrs Hodges shouted as she leaped

across the room and took Ally by the shoulders. She bent her over until her head touched her knees, looking frantically for Doctor Tom, who stood like a frozen bloody statue by the table, his eyes on the lad as though the words he had spoken made no sense. She didn't know what the dickens was going on but she'd not have Mrs Hartley upset like this, not even by Doctor Tom.

"I'm all right, Mrs Hodges," Ally murmured, sitting up and wondering if she was going to be sick. Betsy . . . Betsy had come home and all she could think of was how was this going to affect the happiness she and Tom had found together. Once he had been mad about Betsy, bewitched as all men were with her beauty, her girlish charm, her seeming innocence. He had intended to marry her and only when she went away had he turned to her, Ally, and had she won him on the rebound? She hadn't thought so. They had been married for a year. They had made a child together, and lost it. There were strong bonds holding them together but now his first love was back and bringing a child. *Was that child Tom's?* Dear God, save her . . .

Albert was sent to fetch a cab, Mrs Hodges ran upstairs for Ally's warm cloak and then stood in the doorway watching as the cab drove off along Duke Street, her hand to her mouth, the dog at her side.

"What next?" she asked him plaintively. "Are we to 'ave no peace in this house?"

There was little either Tom or Ally could do, was there, except watch the two women hang over the little bed they had made for Emily, their faces identical with possessive enchantment.

"Look at 'er, Ally. She's the spit of our Betsy at same age. What d'yer reckon she is, Aggie, twelve months, 'appen fifteen? What d'yer think?" She turned to Tom. "Come on, lad, you're t'doctor. 'Ow old?"

"I'm sure her mother will be able to tell you when she wakens." For Edie had been full of the dangerous and wearying journey their Betsy had undertaken to bring her daughter to see them and her consequent need to get to her bed.

"In't she lovely, our Ally. I wonder 'oo 'er pa was?" But Ally had turned away, her eyes brimming with joyful tears, for it was obvious that the child could not have been Tom's. She *was* like Betsy and yet there was something else in her, a look of breeding, which was ridiculous really, for the baby could have been no more than twelve to fourteen months old. It was twenty-seven months exactly since Betsy had gone away and with a few swift calculations it was very evident that this lovely child was some other man's.

"She's quite delightful, Mrs Pearce," Tom said stiffly, "but I'm afraid my wife and I must get home for we are both—"

From the doorway that led into the hall there came the sudden sound of hilarious laughter and when they all turned, reluctantly on the part of the two older women, fearfully on the part of Tom and Ally, Betsy stood leaning in the doorway, arms crossed, in the most scandalous outfit any of them, even Tom and Alice, had ever seen. It was totally transparent, a nightdress of sorts with a negligee over it both the colour of pale duck-egg blue. It was edged in what might have been feathers of the same colour and quite distinctly through it could be seen the outline of her nipples and the dark triangle at the base of her belly.

"*Betsy!*" her mother shrieked, looking hastily away, praying that Doctor Tom and Albert were doing the same. Aggie edged in front of the armchair in which the baby slept as though to shield her from the appalling sight of her mother's shame.

Betsy continued to shriek with laughter. "So, he wed you, did he? Couldn't have me so he made do with you, did he? Well, I'm not surprised. He always was a bit of a doormat without the gumption to say boo to a goose, or rather to his lah-di-dah parents. You'd be handy, wouldn't you, with your milk and water goodness, and just the type to be a bloody doctor's wife."

"You watch yer mouth, yer slut. Yer can't abide ter see anyone 'appy." Aggie was incensed.

"Happy! They don't look very happy to me. Tom looks as though he'd like to clout someone, probably me."

"That 'e would an' I'll 'old yer fer 'im. Yer must be simple or summat."

"Well, I'll say this for you, old woman, you're the only one with a bit of spunk in this house. Look at them all – yes, you as well, our Ally – standing with their mouths open wondering what the devil I'm doing here. And yes, that's my child in the chair, Tom, and no, it's not yours though you know as well as me that it could have been, times we were at it."

Tom gasped and his face turned to the colour of suet and Ally felt something shrivel and die inside her.

"I don't honestly know who the father is," Betsy went on carelessly. "All I can say is thank the Lord you and I didn't slip up, Tom, for I might have been forced to stay in this . . . this" – she glanced round the bright, cosy room disparagingly – "in this hovel or one like it."

Edie Pearce moaned, for she did not know this virago who had come back to them in the guise of her daughter. Oh, aye, Betsy had always been what you might call a handful but such a beautiful baby, young girl and young woman that she and Fred could not help but worship the ground she walked on. She had been self-willed, vain and greedy and they'd spoiled her, she knew that, putting her above their Ally who was such a good girl, but look how it had turned out. There she was, nearly naked, posing in the doorway for Albert and Tom to see and boasting that she didn't know who the father of her *illegitimate* child was, which could only mean she had been with . . . she couldn't bear to think of it and she was only glad her Fred wasn't here to witness the downfall of the daughter of whom he had been so proud.

The baby made a small sound, not loud but the sound a baby

makes as it wakes and at once she turned, thankfully, to her granddaughter. Standing up, she moved to the chair where Aggie was standing guard, picked up the child who blinked at her sleepily, plugged her thumb in her mouth and accepted this new person in her baby life. Edie kissed her rosy, rounded cheek, then sat back in her own chair, the baby on her lap.

"There, sweetheart, come ter Gran'ma. Put yer little 'ead down . . . there, there, that's it." The baby settled amiably enough but Aggie noticed, even in the midst of this chaos that had blown in with Betsy Pearce, that the child cast several apprehensive glances at the exquisite person of her mother.

Tom could feel the thumping begin in his chest and knew that if he didn't get a good hold of himself he would choke. He could feel the bile rising in his throat. He wanted to turn round to the frozen group of people in the room and say, "One time, that was all, only one." But could a man say such a thing, apologising in a way to them all and especially his beloved wife, and still remain a man. She had cut the ground from under his feet, this . . . this harpy, telling them in words that they could not fail to understand – wrongly so – that she and Tom had had an affair, lying, smiling sardonically, intimating that he was the sort of man who took what he could get from a woman and when it was over moved calmly on to the next who happened to be her own sister. She was painting him in the colours of a lecher, probably the sort of men she now consorted with, and he could do nothing to defend himself. With those words she had branded him and he could tell by the absolute silence in the room, for even, now the baby had settled, his own mother-in-law was looking at him sadly, that they believed what Betsy had told them. Strangely, only Aggie viewed him with what might have been compassion.

Ally knew she couldn't stand it. It was too much for her. Too much for her to bear. She was frozen in an ice-cold shaft of painful flesh, even the blood in her veins refusing to flow so that her pulses slowed, her heartbeat slowed and though the room was warm, for didn't Aggie keep in a good fire, the cold encased her in a pain, a constant searing pain that she knew would never leave her. She wanted to creep away like a wounded animal to its lair, lie in the dark and howl. Betsy and Tom. Tom and Betsy. Betsy and Tom, all those months they were *engaged* – Christ, please let this hurt go, let her die – and then he had come to her. Had he ever loved her? A man who could do what he and Betsy . . . and then come to her . . .

Tom turned to her and his hand rose then dropped again to his side since he knew his guilt showed in his face. Such a little thing, that fumbling moment when Betsy had invited him to plunge himself into her and though he was making no excuses, for would not *any* man have done the same in the circumstances, it had happened and he knew his guilt showed in his face.

"Well," Betsy yawned, having just wrecked her sister's marriage, stolen her happiness, flung her into a whirlpool of horror, "I'm for bed. I'll leave Amalie with you, Mother. She seems settled and after that journey I need a good night's sleep."

She drifted out of the room, leaving the five of them in a state of mindless shock. Albert was really only a lad but he had adored the special beauty, the bright and shining loveliness of Betsy Pearce and the idealism that only a young male can feel. To discover that his idol had feet of clay had stunned him, for he was old enough to understand what his goddess had disclosed to them. Aggie, unlike her son, had always felt nothing but contempt for the lazy little madam who had sponged off her mother, but this was different. Betsy had deliberately destroyed something precious in Tom and Ally's marriage and though it might be mended there was always a weakness in a cloth that had been repaired. They were both of them decent people, good, sweet-natured but strong and perhaps with goodwill on both sides they might recover. At this moment they stood, side by side, but so far apart they might have been at opposite ends of the earth. Dear God . . . dear God, help them, give Ally the strength to understand, to forgive.

Edie rocked her granddaughter, perhaps the only one in the room to be unmoved; perhaps not unmoved but already with something to replace what she had once known for her daughter. The baby was soothing her, giving her comfort, allowing to fade away the dreadful things that had been said this night, and the shameful sight she had seen.

"Fetch us a cab, Albert, there's a good lad," Tom said quietly, making no attempt to touch his wife, and when it came, with no more than a brief nod at Aggie, he got into the vehicle, again without touching Ally, and drove off into whatever hell was to follow.

30

Mrs Hodges was considerably surprised the next day to find that Doctor Tom had occupied the spare room the night before. He'd made some effort to make the bed in that hamfisted way men went about anything domesticated, but she could tell that someone had slept there and who else could it be but Doctor Tom? She had heard them come in and the dog had gone bounding out into the hall to greet them but for some reason he'd come back with his tail between his legs and settled down at her feet, his muzzle on his nose, staring in that sad way dogs have into the fire. The sound of voices could be heard faintly through her kitchen door but she made no attempt to eavesdrop. That wasn't her way.

Tom took off his caped overcoat and moved towards Ally with the intention of helping her with her mantle, as he always did but she avoided him. She seemed uncertain as to what to do next and he was saddened to see the lost, white expression that strained her face, but something had to be said. They could not simply go to bed as though nothing had happened. The horror of it was still with him and he felt that if he was careful with his words he might just be able to convince her that her sister had lied. That she had exaggerated what had happened between them. That he was not the seducer of women she had made him out to be.

"Alice, will you look at me, my darling," he asked her gently. "We must talk about this. Get it out of the way. Betsy has lied to us all, you must know that, surely? I have no idea why she has come back to Liverpool and quite honestly I don't care but we cannot—"

"Did you have an affair with her?"

"Of course, I didn't. Do you honestly believe, knowing me now as you do, that I would have a relationship with—"

"So you never made love to her?"

Tom hesitated, his face wretched, but he knew he must tell the truth. "Well, there was just . . ."

"So you did."

"Alice, listen to me. Let me try and explain how it was with Betsy and—"

"You lied to me." It was not a question but a statement and inwardly Tom groaned. He loved this woman, not just with his passionate need of his flesh for hers but with several layers of love that could scarcely be explained. He depended on her goodness, her sweetness, her honesty, her generosity. She was his strength, his rock, his inspiration. She was his dearest friend, companion, helpmeet, confidante. He could not have gone on without her. She made his life rich and satisfying and the set of her blank, white face terrified him. She must be told the truth. She must be made to understand and if he had to spend the rest of his life on his knees to her, pleading with her to forgive his one fall from grace, he would.

"No, no, Alice," he begged passionately. "I never lied—"

"On the day we went to Egremont you told me, implied that you and Betsy had . . . there was nothing physical between you."

He threw back his head, his pain so great had she been turned towards him Ally would have gone to him, but she presented him only with her straight, unbending back.

"Once, only once and then she . . ."

"Forced you?"

"No, not forced but . . ." How could he, a gentleman, describe to his wife what had happened on that day when Betsy had come to Duke Street in a seemingly dazed and crumpled condition with a tale of being set upon. How she had played on his masculinity, his male need to defend, to protect. How could he tell her that here, in Alice's home, he had . . . well, there was only one word to describe what he had done to Betsy Pearce, a coarse word used by men and he would not repeat it to any lady, and this woman, though she had not been born to it, was a lady.

"So you were willing, but only once you say. But if you lied to me then how can I believe you are not lying now? That you will not lie to me in the future? How am I to trust you ever again? It seems that the child she brought back is not yours but somehow that doesn't seem relevant."

"*Not relevant!* You mean you don't care whether the child is mine or not? Are you implying that I have been seeing Betsy since we married?"

"How do I know? My whole world has been turned around tonight and quite honestly I feel incapable of continuing to discuss it."

"But we must, my darling." Tom pushed his hand through his hair in the familiar way he had when he was distressed but his wife was still staring off into the corner and did not see it. "I can't bear us to go to our bed without—"

"Beds."

"I'm sorry?"

"Beds. You will do me the courtesy of occupying the spare room."

"Confound it, you talk like some character out of a melodrama. I am your husband and I will not be . . . oh, Jesus, I'm sorry. My dearest love, I don't know what I'm saying. I love you so much it is tearing me to pieces and if I don't have your forgiveness now . . . I love you so much being without you is an agony I can't bear, even for one night. Please, Alice, please."

"Then I will sleep in the spare room."

Tom turned away from her just as she turned to face him so that neither of them saw the expression on the other's face. Tom rested his arm along the mantelshelf, bending his head to stare sightlessly into the small fire Mrs Hodges had kept in for them.

"No, I shall not disturb you."

In her heart was a great emptiness. A hollow that was not aching or hurting but a dragging down, a sadness, a numbness that could scarcely believe this was happening to them. Her eyes were heavy with a longing to weep and the sight of him drooping painfully by the fire was almost too much for her. But she could stand no more, not now.

"It's too soon, Tom. Too soon to talk . . . later . . ."

He turned eagerly. "Tomorrow then?"

"Later." She closed the door quietly behind her and Mrs Hodges heard her slow footsteps on the stairs. The dog stood up and listened, head cocked to one side, then slipped through the doorway and padded up the hall, pushing his nose against the parlour door. He whined and the door opened, allowing him to enter, then closed again.

They must have had a quarrel, Mrs Hodges decided, feeling sad really, for the pair of them had been like a couple of love-birds ever since he had brought her home last year. Mrs Hodges, adopting the customary title of *Mrs* which most cooks or housekeepers took, had never been married but she was not daft and she had heard somewhere that quarrels between married folk were almost always made up in bed so what had happened to these two, of whom she was secretly very fond?

She continued to worry; in fact her worry increased as the days slipped by and Doctor Tom continued to spend his nights, when he wasn't out tending the sick, in the small spare bedroom. She made the bed up for him properly, not saying anything, of course, for though she was forthright about most of the day-to-day doings in Doctor Tom's life, she felt she could not possibly intrude into the private matter of his marriage. The pair of them somehow managed to eat at different times too, Mrs Hartley demanding her evening meal as soon as she came in without waiting, as she had used to, for her husband to return from his medical duties and, more often than not, when he did get home she would be in *her* bed.

Ally continued with her everyday life, going each morning to her office in Walter Street, moving among the warehouses with Davey, taking him with her when she called on the growing number of men with whom she did business, checking cargoes, making decisions, which boat was to go where, what should be picked up from towns along the canal and brought back to Liverpool. He had become her right-hand man and in this nightmare which had her in its grip she honestly didn't know how she would have managed to continue to run her business without him. She scarcely slept; her face had taken on an ashen hue and her eyes were sunk in plum-coloured circles. She was wasting away, she knew she was, withering inside, slowly dying like a plant that needs rain, life-giving, and sunshine to bloom. She lay alone in her bed, bereft without Tom, unable even to cry, watching the hours tick by, holding herself tightly, her arms locked about her own body lest she run screaming through the streets of Liverpool and in to Blackstock Street where the woman who had done this to her lay in her bed sleeping the sleep of the uncaring, the sleep that comes to those who are indifferent to anyone but themselves. Curiously, Tom's part in this destruction of her life was pushed to the back of her consciousness, there on the periphery, and one day it would need to be thought about, but not yet, not while she was so terribly injured.

As if she hadn't enough to contend with it had been difficult to tell Davey that he must, for now at least, which was how she put it, forget Catherine.

"What d'yer mean?" His young face, which since he had met Catherine had begun to lose that stern, frowning look of premature middle age, turned to look at her suspiciously.

"She was seen with me in town and her parents have confined her to her home."

"Confined 'er to 'er home? What yer talkin' about?"

"She cannot, at the moment, come and visit her brother so—"

"I'm goin' there then." And if Ally hadn't stood up and barred the door to him he would have put on his hat and taken a cab up to Rosemont as once Betsy Pearce had done. And with probably the same result.

"We had a note, Davey. But be patient. These things have a way of working out. Let . . . let Tom see what he can do." Which was absolutely nothing, even if she could have brought herself to ask him. She and Tom were in enough deep trouble themselves without getting involved with Catherine and Davey.

"Them two aren't mendin'," Aggie said to Edie one day, when the little madam who had ruined it all for them had gone out on one of her mysterious jaunts. God alone knew where she went and she certainly didn't take either her ma or Aggie into her confidence. As neither Tom nor Ally had been round to Blackstock Street since Betsy came home, Aggie and Edie, taking Emily along with them for her ma didn't seem to care *who* had her as long as it wasn't Betsy Pearce, had been very daring and taken a hansom cab one Sunday afternoon to Duke Street. The visit had not been a success. Tom had been out on a call and Ally, dressed carefully as she always was, looked like a bloody scarecrow, Aggie thought. She had welcomed them with cups of tea and some of Mrs Hodges' chocolate macaroons but the usual easy conversation was lacking, and had it not been for the little dear, who took a great shine to Blaze who patiently allowed her to climb all over him, it would have been worse.

"Mind you, I'm not surprised after what that 'ussy said about Doctor Tom," Aggie continued, turning the next row of her knitting. She and Edie were always making something for the child and this was to be a little dress, one with a scalloped hemline through which pale pink ribbon would be threaded. White, naturally, for all babies wore white. "Not that I believe her fer a minnit. A grand lad like 'e is takin' advantage. Did yer ever 'ear such rubbish? She were allus peas above sticks, 'er. Now I know yer 'er mam but I reckon she egged 'im on. Ter gerrim ter wed 'er, like. Offered it on a bloody plate an' what red-blooded chap could say no, tell me that."

She knew Edie was really only half listening, for she made no protest at hearing her once loved daughter *called* by Aggie. Once she would have sprung to her defence, protested angrily that her lass was sweet and innocent and incapable of such shabby *whore's* tricks but the sight of her that evening in her shameless *transparent* night attire had done much to claw Edie's concept of her younger daughter into tatters. The baby had taken Betsy's place. Emily Pearce, as she was, for it turned out that Betsy was not married; in fact she had told her mother to "shut your bloody gob" when she had questioned her.

"'Appen yer right, Aggie. Now will yer look at that child, doin' 'er best ter reach that pot dog on't table."

The child, dressed in one of the exquisite little dresses that had been found in what Betsy had called *her* box – give her her due, Betsy had certainly not been stingy with her brass where the baby was concerned – touched the pot dog with a tentative finger then, on turning and seeing the two women watching her, dotingly as it turned out though she was not to know it, sat down and without a sound crawled beneath the red plush tablecloth.

"Nay, whatever's bin done ter't child?" Aggie begged to know. "Yer'd think we was goin' ter give 'er a clout round't lug, way she acts."

The reason, too horrific for either woman to speak about, let alone contemplate, still occurred to them and they almost fought one another to tempt the baby out from beneath the table with a biscuit and then with hugs and kisses which always seemed to amaze the child. She had, as yet, uttered no sound, even when she needed changing.

The note was delivered by the son of the woman who lived next door to Aggie, a boy of about eight or nine who roamed the streets doing odd jobs for anyone who would employ him. Sweeping the roads of the horse manure which piled up by the hour, running errands, tidying up Aggie's back yard or indeed anything that would give his hard-pressed mam a few pence extra. He, his mam and the rest of his ragged brothers and sister could be seen hanging about outside one of the many public houses in the vicinity, hoping that the breadwinner of the family would emerge with just enough left to buy a loaf. His mam would have been in "queer street" without him, she often told Aggie. Most of Aggie's neighbours in Blackstock Street, though they were by no means well off, were decent, hardworking folk like her and Percy, but once a man took to drink it was down-hill for his family. Sometimes Aggie had even to lend George's mam the rent, but give her her due she always paid it back, thanks probably to George.

The note was delivered to Walter Street and simply said Ally was to go home at once. It had been written by Albert before he had set off for the Mechanics Institute. Albert had been promised a job in Ally's thriving business at the end of the term and, as he said to his mam, he couldn't afford to lose a second's schooling and besides George next door would be glad of the few coppers he would earn.

"She's gone," Aggie said abruptly as Ally approached her. She was standing on a stool on the pavement polishing her parlour windows in the pale February sunshine, breathing on the glass then giving it what for with her leather.

For a moment Ally was confused. Who? Gone? Gone where?

"Don't look so soft, our Ally. Yer know 'oo I mean. When we gorrup this mornin' she were gone, bag an' baggage but she left babby, thank God, or yer mam'd 'ave gone out 've 'er mind. Got right fond o' that bairn, she 'as. We both 'ave. An' let's face it, she were a bloody awful mother that . . . that whore. Whore I call 'er an' whore she were, an' little mite's better off wi' us. A blind man on a gallopin' 'orse could see she were terrified of 'er mam. Anyroad what we need's a bit of advice, like, so if you an' Tom could . . ."

Aggie watched as Ally's face closed up. So it was still the same, her sad old heart thought. That little madam had divided them as absolutely as if she had killed one of them, or both come to that, and them with such a good marriage. She prided herself on her own ability to judge character and Tom Hartley was a good, decent chap who wouldn't dream of carrying on as that there slut had said and if Ally couldn't see it she was a fool. She'd always been a *spoiler* had Betsy but she was surprised that Ally had taken it so badly. Anyroad, time was a great healer and Ally was a sensible lass and would come to her senses and realise what a fool she was being.

"What d'you want us to do, Aggie?" Aggie gave the windows another swipe with her leather then climbed down off her stool and picked up her bucket of water which she emptied in the gutter.

"Yer mam wants ter see one o' them lawyer chaps. Make it all legal."

"Make what legal?"

"The bairn."

"The bairn?"

"Oh, fer God's sake stop repeatin' everythin' I say. Come

inside an' 'ave a cuppa. Yer ma's set on 'avin' Emily adopted an' wants you an' Tom ter see to it."

"See to it?"

"There yer go again. You an' Tom. To adopt Emily so that that bitch can't get 'er 'ands on 'er in't future. Say she's not a fit mother or summat."

Ally reeled back against the door through which Aggie was just carrying her bucket and for a moment, as she had done when Betsy had made her obscene revelation, she thought she would faint. *Adopt Emily!* Take into her home the child Betsy had abandoned, or so Aggie was implying. Have a constant reminder of the sister who had ruined her life in her own home. She could feel the weakness attack her just about the level of her knees and she knew that if she didn't get a good hold of herself she would fall to her knees and be sick, like a dog. She began to shake her head slowly from side to side, her face stricken, her mouth open on a wail of outrage as the idea percolated into her paralysed brain.

No! Oh, no . . . No! No! The word kept getting bigger and louder in her head and she swayed a little as though it were top heavy and might drag her down. Aggie dropped her bucket with such a clatter a cat which was strolling across the road gave a wild shriek and shot up a drainpipe, reaching the safety of the tiles from where it hissed its terror.

"Come inside, lass, come on, hold me arm." And like an old woman Ally crept into the kitchen where her mother sat peacefully nursing the sleeping child. Edie smiled and Ally had a moment or two in the tempest that was raging inside her to realise that it was the first time since her pa's accident that her mother had actually looked utterly contented.

She drank tea and listened to the bird-twittering of her ma and Aggie who seemed to think it was all so simple. Of course, *they* would do the minding, for both Tom and Ally had jobs to do but the little girl would, in law, be theirs. What could be simpler and it would mean that the child would be safe, and loved, and who could not help but love her, Ma demanded. When she got home would she ask Tom to send round that lawyer chappie so that he could see for himself what a good home Emily would have.

"What lawyer?" she managed to croak.

"You know, the one what set you an' Tom up in business."

"He was a bank manager, Ma."

"Well, Doctor Tom'll know someone."

They put her in a hansom and waved her off and for the first part of the journey she sat in a state of frozen calm, her mind blank. No thoughts in it just a dreadful empty humming like a hive into which a stick has been thrust. The calm did not last. How was she to carry on her day-to-day life, her business on which so many families now depended, when her own was in such tatters. She had no one to whom she might pour out her heart, not even the sensible, practical Aggie for, like Ma, Aggie was in a daydream over the baby, riding a mad wave of delight in which she and Ma had sole charge of the baby Betsy had dumped on them. Ma didn't see it like that, of course. Ma was beginning to believe that Betsy had done this appalling thing for no other reason than the welfare of her child. Ally had seen it in her mother's eyes, for here she had, as it were, Betsy in her arms again as she had been at the same age and though the logical section of her brain told her the idea was nonsensical, it pleased her to think so.

And how was she to approach Tom? Good Christ, she and Tom had barely exchanged a word since Betsy's revelation. Oh, by the way, Betsy has buggered off again and left her child, and Ma says you and I are to adopt her! Even though our marriage is finished and I shall probably be moving out soon to a place of my own, since I cannot bear to live with you like this, we are to become parents. Parents of the child whose mother has wrecked us.

Hastily she did her best to creep back into that silent, unthinking mindlessness which had gripped her since Aggie and Ma had told her what they naïvely had in mind but it seemed it was impossible, for as she approached the house in Duke Street it was all there waiting for her. The silences, the politeness, the punctilious courtesy with which Tom treated her. He had, after a couple of days of begging for her forgiveness, appeared to have withdrawn into himself and though now, having had time to go over and over in her mind what Betsy had implied, she herself would have been prepared to talk about it, Tom was not. Dear God, so he had made love once to Betsy. He was a man and it was understood that men did not go virgin to their marriage beds as a woman should so could she not look upon Betsy as one of those women who obliged young gentlemen before they took a wife? Her life was in such a muddle, her mind was in such a state of chaos, pain and apprehension for the future, how could she possibly communicate to Tom the lunatic idea that Aggie and Ma had thought up? She couldn't. She wanted peace, time to think, to be on her own and how was she to manage that with the turmoil that had come upon her?

She paid off the cabbie and climbed the steps that Mrs Hodges had obviously just scrubbed and whitened. She put her key in the lock and entered quietly but the dog came paddling up the hall, his tail pluming, his nose pushing into her hand in welcome, then, as though he were performing the duty of host, he led her to the parlour, the door to which was partially ajar. Mrs Hodges came to the kitchen door, wiping her hands on her apron, a worried frown on her face. She just stood there, saying nothing and Ally looked at her enquiringly.

"What is it, Mrs Hodges?" praying there was not more trouble, for she did not think she could manage one more problem, no matter how trivial, but still Mrs Hodges said nothing, just raising her eyebrows and grimacing.

The dog had already pushed open the door and as Ally followed, a slight figure rose from the chair by the fire and smiled hesitantly.

"I've run away," Catherine Hartley said simply.

31

The dog swirled round them as the two women studied one another, Ally with her mouth open in what she knew was a foolish expression, Catherine hopefully, helplessly, ready to broaden her smile if Ally did, but doing her best to look suitably serious.

"Shall I make some more tea, Mrs Hartley?" Mrs Hodges asked from the doorway, indicating with a nod of her head the tray that already stood on the small table to the side of the chair.

"That would be nice, Mrs Hodges." She felt helpless herself. Here was this pretty, innocent child, for she was no more, smiling and ready to do anything, or go anywhere Ally told her except back to her parents from whom she'd run away, presumably to be with Davey Mason, and she could not have chosen a more inopportune time. Tom would be . . . well, she wasn't sure what Tom would make of it, she only knew that if life, her *own* life did not find some understandable shape soon, she'd run mad. She couldn't take much more and she wished, for the first time since Betsy had exploded into the sweetness of their lives, that Tom would come home quickly and make some sense of this madhouse she found herself in.

She had another dilemma that she had to consider, if what she thought had happened could be called a dilemma. She held inside herself where no one could see, a sweetness, a tiny point of light in the dense blackness of her life, but it was a complication she had not foreseen. She was not absolutely sure but what should have happened had not, twice now, and before the disillusion and wretchedness of Betsy's return and her revelation of how it had been between Tom and her would have delighted Ally, and Tom. But now, as she tried to fight her way through the thicket that was her life she must put it to one side. There was no point in gloating over it, which she was inclined to do in the night, not until the complexities of her world were resolved.

"So, what do you intend doing?" she asked Catherine politely as they sipped their tea. "I suppose you left a note for your parents."

"I told them I was to be married."

Ally spilled some tea on the skirt of her gown. "*Married?* Who to, for goodness sake?"

"Why Davey, of course."

"Does he know?"

"Ally, of course he does. He asked me the last time we were together. When that old cat Mrs Maynard saw you and me together and told Mama I decided it was time I admitted to Mama and Papa that . . . well, that Davey and I were engaged. That was when they locked me in my room. Papa intended coming to see Tom. To scold him, I suppose, for allowing me to visit you both here. There was a terrible row. I thought poor Jenny and her husband Longman, he's one of our gardeners, might be fired so I didn't tell them, Mama and Papa, that it was Jenny who had helped me to get out. They were in an absolute fury, Mama and Papa, I mean, and threatened to send me to Mama's cousin in Scotland so I just put on as many clothes as I could and my good cloak" – indicating the luxurious fur-lined velvet cloak which was thrown carelessly on the shabby sofa – "climbed down the tree outside my window, which was a bit hazardous" – laughing at her own adventure – "and walked here. It's a fairly straight route though there were some odd houses and people in doorways who stared at me."

I bet there were, Ally brooded, as she envisaged some of the mean streets through which Catherine must have walked to get into the centre of town. It was a wonder the girl had got here in one piece, or at least still wearing that sumptuous cloak, the cost of which would have fed ten families for a whole year.

"So, if a note could be sent to Davey telling him I am here he will come and fetch me and we can be married at once."

"I see, and where will you live, you and Davey? With his mam?" She deliberately used the last word which was what Liverpool mothers were called.

"Mam?" Catherine quavered uncertainly.

"His mother. Davey lives with his mother, his brother and two sisters in a three-bedroom terrace by the dock."

"What is . . . what is that?"

"A terrace? It's a tiny house joined on to other tiny houses and though I'm sure Mrs Mason will be glad to see her lad settled with a nice lass I can't imagine there is room for you in—"

"But Davey will get us a house of our own." Catherine smiled brilliantly, no doubts in her mind that it would be so.

"Not on the wages I pay him, he won't. Davey has a long way to go before he earns enough to rent a house fit to put you in."

"I don't care. Anything will do just as long as we're together." Probably picturing a little doll's house of a place, a cottage with roses round the door, a maid in a frilly apron, a cook in the kitchen, a parlour with pretty sprigged paper on the wall and herself and Davey sleeping in one another's arms in a big bed with a deep feather mattress.

Ally felt her heart droop for the innocent naïvety of the girl opposite her, so eager to get on with the life she envisaged for herself and the young man whom she loved, and with sorrow for herself since she had been just the same not so very long ago.

"Well, I don't know where Tom is but I suppose I can send Jem, Tom's stable lad and odd-job man, to ask Davey to come round."

Catherine jumped up and ran to the window, peering out into the raw February dampness of the square just as though Davey might be dashing along the pavement this very minute and she couldn't wait to see his face when he spotted her. She was like a small child promised a treat, jumping up and down excitedly, turning to crouch down on the carpet and play with the dog and then running again to the window to watch Tom's stable lad, on Ally's orders, set off towards Hanover Street to fetch Davey.

The man watched the activity, not from the garden in the centre of the square, since it was now, in wintertime, bare of any foliage behind which he might hide, but from a ginnel that divided two of the houses on its other side. It was a dismal, sunless day and the narrow passage was like a long dark tunnel leading to a yard at the rear of the house. Unless you knew he was there it was difficult to pick out the shapeless hulk of the man who lurked just inside its entrance. He had seen the girl, the one he was after, come trotting up Duke Street and had been so flabbergasted she had been up the steps, knocking on the door and was inside the house before he could even draw breath. He might have had her! He might have darted across the gardens, the gate of which was open, clapped a hand round her mouth and dragged her into the ginnel in the time it took to whisper his own name, but the sight of her, who always came in a cab, tripping daintily along the pavement had taken him by surprise and he had been too late. Then, half an hour later, and at least two hours before she normally came home, *she* arrived in a cab and his jubilation had known no bounds. Both of them here in the same house and all he had to do was nip across there, gain entrance and they were his. Two little birds ripe for plucking but now there was all this flurry of the lad who lived at the back above the stables running off down the street and soon after the bloody husband, followed closely on his heels by the other bugger who seemed to come so regularly.

Oh, yes, Whipper knew all the inhabitants of, and the visitors to the doctor's house in Duke Street. He knew the layout of the house though he had never been inside it. He had watched lights going on and off and had even, in the pitch dark of night, been round the back to scout out the yard and the stable where the horse was and where, above it, the stable man, his wife and brats lived. He knew the gates and the doors that squeaked, needing a spot of oil, which he had in his sagging pocket. He knew the cobbles of the yard and the distance between gate and back door. He had even, when she forgot to draw her curtains, watched the old woman in her kitchen and seen the dog which had lifted its head and growled, padding to the back door, causing the old woman to ask what was wrong with it. That would have to be dealt with. All he wanted now was for the two little bitches to be alone in the house, the men gone, and his dream of sweet revenge and his lust assuaged and he didn't give a bugger what happened to him after. He had often mumbled to himself that he would swing for her and he would, gladly. He moved further back into the darkness of the ginnel, crouched down into a corner of the wall, took out a pasty from his pocket and bit into it, devouring it in seconds. A bottle of whisky was next, one he had filched from the terrified barmaid in the public house on the corner of Great George Street. Tipping it to his mouth he drank deeply, settling himself down to wait, impervious to the cold as the whisky warmed his belly and ran like fire in his veins.

Their faces lit up when they looked at one another and for the space of a second, as she and Tom exchanged glances, Ally felt her heart lift.

"Catherine."

"Davey."

As Tom and Ally watched, mesmerised, Davey crossed the room to the chair where Catherine was seated, took her hands in his and lifted her to her feet. He bent his head and, with the gallantry and reverence of a knight greeting his lady, kissed the back of each hand. They regarded one another, locked in the perfect stillness from which the two other occupants of the room were excluded. Ally recognised it. It was soft, dreaming, familiar, a meeting of two spirits, a *melting* of two spirits so that they merged and became one. She felt Tom's eyes on her and when she turned again to look at him knew that he was in the same place that held her. They were different people to Catherine and Davey, earthy, she supposed, practical, but in harmony, not just in their bed where they had shared a wild rapture, but in their daily lives. They were like the two halves of the same coin, which sounded sentimental as she and Tom were not, but what they had, or *had had* – dear sweet Lord, let it not be lost – was a solid happiness that had been precious to them both. Tom's eyes, a deeper blue than his sister's, had darkened and he frowned a little, his eyebrows raised in a question but still Ally hesitated, for the hurt she had known over the last few weeks must be soothed, healed, before . . . before what?

Davey Mason had, during the time he had worked beside Ally, visiting her home where she had picked up the ways of the gentry from her husband, dining with them, put a certain polish on the rough, good-hearted lad he had been. He had copied their way of speaking. He had learned to deal with men of business, how to dress and hail a cab as gentlemen do. He no longer frequented the public houses where once he and Jack had caroused but spent his spare time learning and the hours he had put in at the Mechanics Institute had gradually made him into a young man who was not unworthy, at least in Ally's opinion, of Tom's sister. Of course, at home he took off his jacket and sat down in his shirt sleeves with his siblings and his mam, and they had become used to what they called his *lah-di-dah* ways. He did not attempt to lord it over them, for he was a lad with good sense and a great fondness for his family but there was no doubt he had gone up in the world and, if she would have him, perhaps wait a while until he had proved himself even further with Ally, he would marry Catherine Hartley. But she must be prepared to wait. He was no gentleman and never would be but he was a gentle man with nice feelings.

She smiled at him, his Catherine then, overcome with the most delicious shyness, which delighted him, making him feel strong and powerful, looked down at their clasped hands. He let go of one, raising his own to touch her chin, lifting it gently and Ally and Tom were devastated by the emotions that worked in both their faces.

Tom and Ally were nonplussed, then, with an inclination of his head Tom moved towards the door, opening it for her and leading her out into the hall.

"I don't think they need us, do you?" he asked her whimsically.

"No. Where shall . . . ?"

"Do you think you could bear to . . ." He swallowed but his eyes were a star shining blue in the darkness of the hall. He held out his hand and she took it, feeling as shy as Catherine, then she turned at the bottom of the stairs.

"I'd better . . ." she began but a voice from the kitchen doorway forestalled her.

"I've made bed up in spare room for Miss Catherine," Mrs Hodges said and her own eyes were bright with something that might have been tears.

"Thank you, Mrs Hodges," Tom answered solemnly. "My wife and I will retire now but I'd be obliged if you would see Davey off the premises in ten minutes."

"I will that, sir. Goodnight to you both."

He knew it would come, his time, and as he watched the doctor, summoned by some chap who knocked at his door, ride off into the night, he knew that it was now. He stood up, in no way

affected by the hours he had spent crouched on the cold
cobbles, and began to slip silently, a way he had learned and
perfected in the years he had stalked the bitch, until he reached
the side of the house in which no light shone. Now and again
during the past years he had stopped to wonder what it was that
had started him out on this action he took, this action that was
such a part of his life. It *was* his life and he never gave a thought
to what he would do when it was accomplished. For years now
he had tracked her, hurt her when he could in some way, frightened her and made her life wretched, but this was what he had
waited for, yearned for and now it was here. Patience, that was
what he had shown and not only was she there, tucked up in
her bed alone, but the other one was available as well. The men
gone, both of them, and no one to defend the women. He
breathed deeply then moved down the passage at the side of the
house, a passage just wide enough for a horse and carriage and
from which Tom Hartley had just come.

To be on the safe side, the big man, somewhat stooped now
after his years of wandering, took a can of oil from his pocket
and attended to the hinges, then opened the gate and moved
into the yard. Across the yard and there was the back door, the
door to the moment he had dreamed of, yearned for, toiled after
and all he had to do was get through it.

It was bolted!

Sod the bloody woman to hell and back! He stepped back and
looked about him. He had been this way a dozen times, sniffing
round the place like an old retriever, studying the position of
windows and openings into the house, for having got this far on
his long and arduous journey from Church where it had all
begun, he remembered now, with the bloody horse, he was not
going to be put off by a bolted door. He smiled, a ghastly parody
of a smile as his eyes lit on the coal hole, the chute of which ran
down into the cellar. The coal hole was covered by a round
metal lid, easy enough to prise off and all he had to do was to

get himself through it, down the chute and into the coal cellar.

It was a tight squeeze and years ago, when he had first come across Ally Hartley, he would not have managed it but Whipper Ogden had known hard times since then, eating off scraps and the weight, and the muscle, gained in his prize-fighting days, had gone. He fell on to the tidy heaps of coal which slithered under him and in the kitchen, where he slept on the rug before the fire, the dog lifted his head and gave a warning growl. When Whipper stepped slowly through the doorway at the top of the coal cellar steps and into the kitchen Blaze was waiting for him. Instead of barking, as one would expect a dog guarding his territory and his people to do, the dog waited, his muzzle lifted, his paws splayed, but Whipper Ogden, crafty, cruel, well trained in the surprises of life and how to deal with them, took Blaze by his scruff and flung him down the steps into the cellar, closing the door on him. The dog's front legs were instantly broken and his head, as it hit an overhead beam, was smashed. He whimpered and lay still.

Whipper stood for several minutes in the kitchen. It was warm and there was a good smell, but though he could have eaten the bloody dog he'd just chucked down the cellar steps he didn't stop to investigate. Bedrooms was where they would be. Separate, he supposed, for the bitch shared one with her husband and the other was in the front to the right of it. He knew, for he had watched the candlelight moving about, flickering, then disappearing.

There was a creak on one of the stair treads and he froze but they were all asleep and the dog was dealt with so, after a moment, he moved on up the stairs and along the landing until he came to the door behind which, he was certain, lay the one he wanted. Mind you, he wanted them both but *together*.

Ally was deep in the joy Tom's hands and lips had aroused in her when she first became conscious of the smell.

Their reunion had been glorious, rapturous, each paying

loving attention to every inch of the other's body, for they had both been starved of it. Not just the physical loving they shared but the contact of minds and souls and hearts, the strong emotional, sometimes unspoken bond that is the mark of true love. Betsy had done her best to destroy it but it had been too powerful, even in its weakest moment, to break.

The smell was putrid. It was as if something had died and was rotting away, a stench that was overpowering and into her sleeping mind there came a picture of dirt, filth, festering rubbish, corruption and as she came slowly to the surface of her dream and opened her eyes she looked up into all of these things in the leering face of Whipper Ogden. He let her have a good look, not really caring if she screamed or fought, and when she did neither, for she was paralysed with crushing terror, he put one foul hand across her mouth, another in her hair, pulling it cruelly and dragging her from the bed. She slumped limply at the end of his arm, her arms and legs useless, her brain dead as he hauled her by her hair across the bedroom, through the doorway and along the hall until he came to the door of the spare bedroom. He flung it open and there was the other one, curled up as nice as pie in the bed waiting for him. He could feel himself stiffening and he was elated, for it seemed the fantasy he had had about getting his prick back into working order with the two of them to help him was about to come true. The one in the bed woke, stretching and yawning, turning her head to see who had entered her room but her terror, like Ally's, was so great she made no sound. Just lay there staring with widening, suddenly sightless eyes at the beast that had entered her bedroom dragging the woman who was her sister-in-law by her hair.

Whipper kicked the door to with one foot, flung the first bitch into the corner, hitting her head cruelly on the skirting board where she lay as one dead. He advanced on the bed and, throwing back the covers, reached for Tom Hartley's sister.

*

Jem Fosdyke moved even closer to his Sal and threw his arm about the plump curve of her hip, burrowing further down into the bed. He had been up an hour ago seeing to Doctor Tom's horse and bloody cold it had been too, but Sal kept his place warm for him and when he got back into it he soon fell into the heavy sleep of a hardworking man. And he did work hard. Doctor Tom was a fair employer and he'd never forgotten that he had saved his Dimity's life years ago and was willing to keep an eye on the two other bairns who'd come after her, free of charge. So he was happy to clean windows, boots, cutlery, the yard, the stables, any job that the doctor found for him. And Sal gave Mrs Hodges a hand in the house and what with the snug little home they themselves had over the stables, Jem considered he was well set up.

But he did wish that damned dog would give over his yap. What was up with the bloody thing, howling his head off like that, the daft beast, but then, why should he howl if there was nowt wrong? He wasn't a young dog. He was well out of the puppy stage and sensible. He played with his children in the yard, acting like a puppy sometimes but it was not like him to carry on like this.

"Bloody 'ell," he grumbled to Sal who had leaned over to put a match to the candle. "What's up wi't ruddy thing? It's enough ter waken dead." And sure enough he saw a light being kindled in the old woman's room. Mrs Hodges had a comfortable bedroom at the back of the house, a room she had chosen for herself since it was just above the kitchen and always warm.

"Yer'd best go see, Jem," Sal said uneasily. "What wi't doctor out an' that."

"Aye." Jem slipped into the trousers he had taken off only minutes before, or so it seemed, dragging his braces over his shoulders. "Lock door after me, Sal," he said, uneasy himself. On the way out he stepped into the stable and picked up the heavy fork he used to fetch muck out into the yard.

The back door to the house was locked and bolted, as it usually was but the dog was not behind it, as Jem had expected. He could still hear the thing going mad somewhere in the house but he couldn't make out where it was coming from. He hammered on the back door, incensing the dog to further ferocious barking and then Mrs Hodges was there shouting through the stout wood, wanting to know who was making all this noise in the middle of the night, waking decent folk from their sleep but she opened the door when she heard his voice, stepping back in alarm when she saw the fork.

"What's up?" she quavered. "And where's that damn dog got to?"

"Nay, but 'e's mekkin enough noise ter wake dead."

"Well, he's not far away." Mrs Hodges' voice died to a whisper as both she and Jem looked towards the door that led down the steps to the cellar. Jem stepped warily forward, opening it cautiously and when the maddened animal crawled out, his head matted with blood, dragging himself on his shattered legs they both fell back in consternation.

"Dear Lord," Mrs Hodges whispered, putting out a pitying hand to the wounded animal and it was then, as she and Jem considered the dog who was doing his best to get to the kitchen door, that the screaming started.

"Oh, dear Lord above, Our Father which art in heaven. Save us." But Jem hadn't time to consider the Lord and His mercies. There was murder being done in Doctor Tom's house and though he had no idea by whom or how many even, Jem was through the door and up the hall, leaping over the wounded dog who was still making his determined way to the foot of the stairs.

The screaming came from the room where Jem knew the master's young sister had been put and with Mrs Hodges hard on his heels for which, later, he was to praise her bravery, he threw open the door. He couldn't make out at first who was screaming, or even who was in the room. An enormous shape had begun to shout, a man, he thought and on the man's back was another shape, smaller and it was this thing that was screaming, and screaming and tearing at the man's hair, battering her small fists into the man's face.

On the bed, naked, curled like a child just come from the womb, a fragile foetus with its thumb in its mouth, was the master's sister.

32

The smell of him remained with her for many months, on her clothes, her hands, beneath her fingernails where she had ripped at his face, on her flesh and in her hair, no matter how many times Jem lugged up the tin bath to her bedroom and Aggie and Mrs Hodges filled it with hot water, so hot they were alarmed for her, saying she would scald herself as she climbed into it. She could taste him, for her teeth had found his ear in the enraged madness that had engulfed her when she came to and found him bending over Catherine Hartley. She had never in her life felt such savage, *killing* fury. She realised afterwards that she had lost her mind, her sanity, her reason and the loss of it had given her the power, the almost inhuman strength to spring to her feet and leap on the back of the animal who was attacking Tom's little sister. His hands were all over her, the frozen, sightless, naked child, for that was how she seemed, clutching, biting, scratching, his fingers prying into the most intimate parts of her and moaning some words which sounded like "*Gerrup, yer bugger . . . get yersenn up . . . gerrup . . . gerrup . . . sod it . . . sod it, gerrup.*"

The ferocious roar of outrage, not from the creature on whose back she clung and who was doing his best to scrape her off, but from the doorway, was just one more hideous sound which did its best to menace her but she would not let go. Someone, she didn't recognise who it was, did their utmost to prise her off the monster's back and another figure, weeping broken-heartedly, bent over little Catherine, covering her abused body with a quilt and it was not until a voice shrieked in her ear, so piercingly it was like red-hot wire going through her head, that she loosed her hold.

"Mrs Hartley, move away . . . move away an' let me gerr at 'im. Yer sod, yer filthy swine. Yer bastard, I'll kill yer." Jem's voice was high with pure, white-hot rage and disgust.

But still she wouldn't have it. She needed a weapon, any weapon would do, whatever came to hand, and for a terrible moment she and the groom wrestled for the pitchfork and as they did so, taking advantage of their momentary distraction, Whipper roared his way out of the room and was off down the stairs, tripping over poor Blaze as he went. He tore open the door and Ally screamed her rage, for she wouldn't allow him to escape, even if she was killed in the process. It wasn't to be borne. Catherine had been subjected to the mauling, the slobbering, the vile obscenities that Whipper had meant for her, Ally, for was it not Ally Pearce who had been the one to drive him – easily done, with his temper – to the loathsome act. Catherine, innocent and pure, had suffered it in her place and Ally wasn't to be denied her moment of retribution.

With Jem hot on her heels shouting to her to come back, he would deal with the intruder, *intruder*, did you ever hear such a ridiculous name for the bugger who was Whipper Ogden, she sprinted up Duke Street following the lumbering figure of the man who had haunted her life for nearly two years. He was holding up his unbuttoned trousers with one hand while the other flailed the air in an effort to get up some speed but she was gaining on him.

Had Whipper Ogden turned and stood his ground it was very possible he could have felled both Jem and Ally but the pitchfork was a formidable weapon and his mind was occupied with escape from it. He had nearly had her. His prick had been ready to plunge into her and had it not been for the bitch who had haunted his life as readily as he had haunted hers, though he was not aware of it in those terms, he would have done it. Triumph. His manhood restored, but for now he needed to get away. Not far, for he would be back.

He turned the corner into Hanover Street just as the sun rose over the Pennine chain to the east. Coming down the slight slope of the street, all polished up, for the drayman was proud of his team, and ready for a day's work, was a pair of great shire horses, glossy, handsome, tawny-coloured, mild-mannered but enormous. They weighed a ton each and needed to, for the brewer's dray they pulled was loaded with barrels of beer. They were thrown into total confusion when the big man, without a glance to left or right, ran straight under their enormous hooves. They reared, neighing in alarm, and though their driver, who had also taken a shock at the sight of the fool in his path, did his best to stop them, before he could shout, "Whoa there, Punch. Steady, Judy," they had trampled him into a disgusting bloody mess on the cobbles.

The savagery, the uncontrollable fury drained out of Ally and she felt the cold and numbness creep over her. She stood, still in the nightgown which her husband had taken from her the night before in an act of love, then, when he left her, put back on her sleepy figure, again in an act of love, murmuring that it was a cold night. She was barefooted. All that was in her mind was the thought, *rough and poetic justice.* She was sorry that she could not have driven the pitchfork through his devil's heart but he was gone now and the healing, of herself and of Catherine, must begin.

Jem was aghast, though he knew the bugger had deserved it, but here was Mrs Hartley hanging about in what looked like her nightgown for the early working men to gawp at and he hadn't even a jacket to throw round her.

"Come away, lass," he said gently, trying to draw her back towards her home but she seemed mesmerised and he could hardly lay rough hands on his master's wife, could he? When the master himself came riding along Hanover Street, from whatever call had fetched him from his home in the night, quickening his pace when he saw the accident, Jem breathed a sigh of relief. He could see the amazement on Doctor Tom's face, and could you blame him, finding his wife in her night-gown, bare feet an' all, standing silently on the corner side by side with his own groom, a pitchfork in his hand.

But he was a doctor and with a doctor's instinct he leaped from his mare's back and made to go to the man in the road.

"Don't touch him," his wife said in a calm, flat voice.

"But I might be—"

"Don't touch him. If he's still alive let him suffer." Then she swayed and Jem and Tom, both appalled in this nightmare which had come at them from nowhere, so to speak, moved to catch her, her husband swinging her up into his arms.

"Bring Abby, Jem," he said, and strode off in the direction of his home and the explanation which surely he would find there. "And then fetch Mrs Wainwright and Mrs Hartley's mother." Without a word he took his wife up to their room, poured some concoction down her throat and left her to her sleep, not a peaceful sleep but one in which she mumbled and tossed and fretted. It all came back to slither like some loathsome creeping evil into her sleeping mind. It was all there in its hideous clarity and would, Tom told her later, being truthful, for they had sworn that that was what they would always be with one another, probably never totally leave her. Her dreams, like memories, even good ones, would slowly fade but still they claimed her and she had it in her to wish that, like Catherine had, she could have closed down her mind to the horror of it.

It had been like a madhouse in Duke Street from then on. It always seemed to be full of people. Pat and Jack stony-faced and silent, for they had known of Whipper and his cruel ways. Hadn't he probably killed poor Teddy, not to mention Gentle and though Pat had done his best to protect Ally, who could have guessed that it would be the little lass upstairs who would suffer the torment of the damned. They were men and could scarcely imagine what she must have gone through but the thought of it sickened them. They were, for a while, ashamed of their own masculinity.

Sal Fosdyke was a tower of strength to them all, for she set to in the kitchen telling Mrs Hodges, who remained at her mistress's bedside, she'd manage and besides, her Jem was that upset nothing would suit him but that he had her in his sight in Mrs Hodges' kitchen as though the dead man might come back for more. Their Dimity was a sensible child and would see to the other two and but for the horror of what had happened to the master's little sister whom she had only glimpsed from a distance, pretty little thing, would have quite enjoyed the change!

Davey simply went mad and it took Tom and Jem all their strength to keep him from running screaming round the square, though there was absolutely nothing he could do. He crouched in a chair and wept while Aggie, who had come tearing at top speed in a hansom from Blackstock Street, Edie beside her, held him to her capacious bosom and stroked his hair, for he seemed like a little lad again. If he could have got at Whipper, beaten him to pulp, eased his pain and rage with his fists or indeed anything that was handy he might have coped more easily, but the thing that was scraped up off the cobbles in Hanover Street was beyond any punishment Davey might have offered him.

The words that finally quietened him came from Ally. She woke to the strange sight of Mrs Hodges dozing in a chair by her bed and for the space of several seconds wondered what the devil she was doing there, then it slashed at her, clawed at her and she leaped from her bed, badly startling Mrs Hodges.

"Nay, lass, Doctor Tom said you'd to stay in your bed."

"What time is it?"

Mrs Hodges consulted the small fob watch pinned to her apron bodice which was not quite as immaculate as usual.

"It's just gone eight."

"What day?"

"What *day*?"

"Yes, what day is it?"

" 'Tis Wednesday."

"I've been here for . . . for what?"

"Over twelve hours."

"Then pass me my clothes. There are—"

"Mrs Hartley, please. Mrs Wainwright an' your mam are 'ere."

"Where is my husband?"

"I can't rightly say, lass."

She found Davey half asleep in the chair in the parlour, under the influence of the same draught Tom had given to her. His face was swollen and he could barely open his eyes.

"It was the horses that killed him, Davey," she told him, calm now that she had slept.

Davey turned his head and stared at her wonderingly. "Horses?"

"Yes. He ran under their hooves. It seemed . . . appropriate."

He turned to stare into the distance as though at some memory. "Yes. I'm glad, burrit don't 'elp my poor Catherine, do it?" He turned again to gaze sightlessly into the bitter future that was to be his without her.

Tom had examined the flaccid body of his sister who stared, somewhat in the same manner as Davey, over his shoulder indifferently while Aggie and Edie, the sleeping Emily having been put into the arms of Sal in the kitchen, both weeping silently as they watched, wondering to themselves if it was quite proper for a doctor to examine his own sister so closely but, as he said ferociously, who else was to do it? Did they want a stranger to see what had been done to her and they had agreed that they did not. She had not been . . . been raped so there was no fear of an unwanted pregnancy but she had been savagely handled and from now on one of the women must care for her, night and day.

And so it began, the vigil kept at the bedside of the silently staring girl in the bed. Edie would sit and rock her grand-daughter in the chair, sad for the little lass but glad it had not been their Ally. One daughter lost to her was surely enough. Emily often toddled about, staring into the face of the quiet figure on the bed but being quiet herself disturbing no one. She played with the dolls and the soft toys, lambs and ducks, a clockwork rabbit which popped out of the heart of a lettuce, and pored over rag books just as though she were reading every word. They had spoiled her, Edie and Aggie, buying her things but who could help it, the blessed little thing. Talk of her being adopted by Tom and Ally had been forgotten for the time being!

Tom had disappeared when his examination was over and it was Ally who found him crouched in a corner of the stable, Blaze in his arms, his own tears wetting the dog's coat.

"I can't seem to cope with it, Alice," he told her. "I don't understand. Who was this brute and why should he break into our house and attack . . . attack Catherine in such a ferocious way? God knows if she will ever recover . . . oh, her body, yes, but her mind has gone. Nature has shut it down for the time being in order for it to heal but whether it ever will, whether she will ever be whole again no one knows. The mind is a mystery to us though there are doctors who try to . . ."

He sighed and the dog in his arms, despite his injuries, did his best to lick his face.

Ally crouched down beside him. She put her arms about his shoulders, drawing his head down to her shoulder and accepted the burden that was to be hers for the rest of her days. He did not connect what had happened to his sister with the incident, such an age ago it seemed, when Whipper had threatened Ally. She could, as she and Tom had promised one another, tell him the truth about Whipper but what good would it do? Who would it help? Certainly not Tom, nor Catherine. Pat knew and Davey and Jack were part of it but with Whipper dead and the threat of him gone surely now was the time to put it behind them, to get on with their lives, to do their best to heal the girl upstairs, to help her put her life, and the one she was hopefully to have with Davey, back into some calm and peaceful respite that would lead to happiness.

And so it began. They were all flabbergasted when Ally told them that she proposed to give up her work in the canal boat business though she would still be available to Davey and Albert – yes, Aggie, your Albert is to be taken on under Davey's guidance – for consultation. She would stay at home to care for her sister-in-law. She was to have a baby in July and would need to spend time resting, for she had no intention of losing this one, taking Tom's hand in hers. She and Catherine would rest together, and though she did not say it out loud, she swore that she would restore the silent girl's health if it was the last thing she did. Davey must come every day after his work at the office was ended and sit with his fiancée; oh yes, Catherine was still that, and she was pleased to see the look of frozen apathy on Davey's face slip a little, for she had given him hope. Tom had lied a little and told him that his beloved had not been – gulping a little at the horror on the lad's face – *raped*, that her injuries would heal and no, he could not see her yet but as soon as he thought fit, Tom would allow him to visit her. Davey was forced to accept it.

He threw himself into his work and, taking Aggie's lad in hand, taught him everything he himself had been taught by Ally. Ally still did the banking and sometimes, when a customer wished to discuss something with her which he thought was his due, he came to the house in Duke Street, and her condition becoming increasingly obvious, thought he understood why Mrs Hartley preferred to remain at home. Strangely, it did her business no harm, for these were decent, home-loving men who thought a wife's place was really in the home, as theirs were.

Spring came into the gardens in the square with a shout of daffodils, standing up like golden-headed spears, pushing through the greening grass in clumps among which lily of the valley peeped shyly under the trees. The old gardener, having heard there was a young lady unwell at the doctor's house, though naturally he had no idea of the cause, often pushed a handful into Mrs Hodges' hand, saying they'd cheer her up no end and would Mrs Hodges wish her well from him. Sometimes it was primroses which were placed by Catherine's bed but her eyes continued to look at nothing except the window where the spring breeze often lifted the curtains. Physically she was totally healed, even *down there*, as Aggie mouthed to Edie. The bruises, which had turned her delicate face all the colours of the rainbow where Whipper had struck her, were gone, as were all the other bites and abrasions, and as she lay there, propped on her pillows, she was exactly as she had been before the horror struck. She was like a beautiful clockwork doll who someone had, for the moment, forgotten to wind up. She uttered no sound nor did she appear to hear any voice that spoke to her. Everyone was eager to help, filled with pity for the poor wretched creature who lay like one dead in her bed, but only Davey was allowed to sit beside her in those first weeks. Not to touch her, Tom insisted, for he was not sure how his sister would react to a man's hand on her. It was the women who soothed her battered body with the ointments Tom gave them, who administered the potions, who moved her to the commode, or the chair or to look out of the window. There was always, night and day, someone with her, for she must be fed and bathed and her hair washed and brushed, but as spring took a firm hold and the old man's garden began to bloom in earnest Ally decided it was time Catherine should venture outside. They had walked her round her bedroom, sitting her in a chair while her bed was changed, but outside birds, swallows and house martins were swooping over the rooftops and even a cuckoo had been heard, or so the old man told them as he handed in a great bunch of poppies which, though short-lived, made a lovely splash of colour to catch Catherine's eye. It did no good.

She began to put on a bit of weight, not to make her plump, of course, but filling out the hollows and smoothing her cheeks to roundness and a certain tint of peach. Tom had been to Rosemont to inform his parents that their daughter had been ill and might she be allowed some of her clothes. He had the door slammed in his face so Ally had called on the Misses Yeoland, who had Miss Hartley's measurements, and several pretty gowns were delivered, along with suitable undergarments. One day towards the end of May when the sun shone on the dappled green loveliness of the garden, which, though he was not consciously aware of it, the old man had been preparing for this day, she and Aggie had got her out of the chair where she sat obediently, dressed her in one of her pretty new dresses and led her out of the bedroom where she had been confined for the past three months. Holding her by her hands they led her down the stairs and along the hallway to the front door. A tearful Mrs Hodges, with Sal and Edie beside her holding Emily, watched as the two women opened the door and let the sunshine fall on the exquisite mindless girl. The old gardener stopped what he was doing and lit his clay pipe and the smoke from it, or so he told himself, got in his eyes and made them water. It could not be said that the lass reacted in any way but she allowed herself to be walked across the road and into the garden where, hurrying forward, he personally brushed down one of the benches with his handkerchief.

" 'Ere las, sit thi' down," he told her but Aggie shook her head, indicating that he was to move away, to his astonishment, for he meant no harm. The lass seemed fair discombobulated, as his old mam used to say but then she'd been poorly for a long time so that explained it.

The inhabitants of the square became used to the lovely girl with the blank face and the unseeing eyes wandering hand in hand with the doctor's wife during the lovely summer weather, for the gods looked kindly on the stricken lass and gave her cloudless skies. The old gardener couldn't do enough for her, in the way of flowers, that is, planting and pruning, weeding and watering, cutting the grass and giving what for to any child bold enough to run across it. The colours almost hurt the eye – peonies of pink and red and yellow, a rose bed of floribundas, scarlet and golden, peach and white – and he even tried his hand at climbers, training them up the railings and all for a bower for the lovely, damaged young girl to sit in, for by then they all knew she *was* damaged in some way.

Alice was getting close to her time, increasingly breathless and really not up to trailing round and round the gardens with his sister, Tom said. Let one of the others do it, he said, but strangely, when Aggie or Mrs Hodges took Catherine by the hand and tried to lead her outside she resisted. There was no emotion displayed, just a total refusal to be moved.

"Oh, leave her be, Aggie. For God's sake I'm only walking a few yards and then I'll be sitting down."

"But Doctor Tom said—"

"Never mind what Doctor Tom said. You can see us from the window and besides the old man will come running with a message if I need you."

"But . . ."

She sat beside Catherine for a while wondering why she had felt so unwell for the past hour. The sun was warm and she was comfortably propped on the cushions which Aggie felt necessary when suddenly the sky and the gardens rushed together and between them she was in a momentary blackness. She felt the first pain strike her somewhere in the small of her back, a tiger prowling ready to attack again, or a knife thrust which nearly had her off the bench and on her knees.

"Catherine," she said steadily, as the pain lessened, "I want you to help me to my feet. I cannot make it back to the house on my own so you must help me. Will you do that? Will you help me, please?"

She felt rather than saw the jerky movement of Catherine's head. The old man was busily digging something urgent in the far corner of the garden and could have been shouted for but somehow it seemed important to have Catherine do whatever was necessary. "Take my hand, darling, and lift me to my feet." She was not even surprised when her sister-in-law obeyed her. "We'll walk home slowly; look, it's not far and if you would give me your arm I shall manage the steps. Mrs Hodges will be there so. . ." The pain was so fierce she bent over in agony while something between her legs gave way and she wet her own bloomers. For a moment she was stranded but still she knew she must not call for help.

"What?" Catherine croaked and when Ally straightened up and looked into her face it was creased with concern and her eyes were bright with anxiety.

"It's the baby coming, sweetheart, and you must help me."

"The baby . . ." But she put her arm, strong now, round Ally's shoulders and began to lead her in little shuffling staggers towards the house. It took several attempts to make the steps, for it seemed Ally was one of those women who give birth easily and quickly and the child seemed eager to get into the world. "Lean on me, Ally." Catherine's voice was strong but loving and when she got Ally up the steps and began to call out her voice was confident, sure.

"Quickly, the baby's coming," she yelled and when they streamed out of the kitchen and into the hallway she began to laugh, for their faces were so funny.

She wouldn't stay out of the room, either, when Gregory Frederick Hartley came roaring into the world, saying again and again she had no idea that that was where babies came from, her mama had never told her. She was the first to hold him, for after all she had been there from the beginning, she told them, not seeing the wink Tom gave his wife, though the others did. The room was full of people, laughing, crying, even the old man from the garden doing his best to get up there, bringing flowers for the young lady, *and* for the young gentleman, not an hour old yet.

They were left alone at last, with their son, Catherine having been persuaded that he would not go away, and yes, she certainly could help to look after him and of course, they agreed, he was the most beautiful child in the world, her brother's son, and how strange it would be to be called Aunt.

They could see her from their bed where Ally lay with her head on Tom's shoulder while he cradled the boy in his arms. She was in the garden with Davey, somewhat graver now all the excitement was over, but breaking into sudden shy smiles as she looked up at him and you could see he thought he had died and gone to heaven where his Catherine was one of the angels come to greet him.

"Will she ever remember, my love?"

"She might, one day, who knows, but she is loved, truly loved and there is nothing that love cannot overcome. Nothing."

"You're so sure."

"Oh, yes," looking down into the rosy, creased face of his son, then into Ally's. He kissed her. "Aren't you?"

"Oh, yes, and I'll have another of those."

"What a kiss or a baby?"

"A kiss first and then the baby."